Organize or Die

By Laura McClure

D1521952

ISBN-13: 978-1470175412
ISBN-10: 147017541X (for use only on Amazon.com)

Contact the author by email at: laura@lauramcclure.org
or go to: www.lauramcclure.org

Cover art by Michael Kaufman

For Michael
and organizers everywhere,

and for Kay Keppler,
my great friend and writing companion

CHAPTER 1

James Shawcross, the new president of the state labor federation, gripped the podium with authority. His silver hair glittered under the lights and his expensive suit gave off a subtle navy sheen. He'd been orating for fifteen minutes and was apparently still hours away from his windup.

I made a study of Shawcross's big handsome head. Calculated the angle. From where I stood, I had a perfect shot. The bullet would enter at the left temple at just the spot where his flawless tan met his flawless coiffure. It would exit at the back of the crown, tearing up a lot of brain matter along the way. I leaned back against the wall and smiled for the first time in days.

"I can't think what would make you smile at James Shawcross — unless you're picturing him dead." John Beck's voice in my ear was just above a whisper.

"Jesus, Beck, I didn't see you coming."

Beck grinned. I tried to ignore that little plume of pain that rose in my chest whenever I saw the man. John Beck was a business and labor reporter for the New York City Star, and he was practically my best friend. Unfortunately, I was also in love with him. Even more unfortunately, he was married. We'd had a fling — actually several of them. Each time I'd walked away. But my wretched feelings for him refused to die.

"Really, Ruth. What are you doing here? I know you didn't come for Mr. Shawcross."

"Waiting for Victoria."

Beck nodded, his eyes scanning the crowd. "Me too. Where the hell is she?"

I shrugged and watched as Beck and a youngish woman across the room smiled at each other.

"Better go say hello," Beck said, pushing away from the wall.

"You do that," I said as I watched Beck strut away. He looked hot in his leather jacket. But it was fucking July.

So what the hell *was* I was doing here? For some reason, I had dragged my ass off the couch to come to hear the labor movement's

star organizer, my old colleague Victoria Shales, impress us with
tales from her latest union drive. If she would just show up. I looked
at my watch and sighed.

Victoria – that tall, blonde, blue-eyed, Versace-clad uber-
organizer, was, I'd heard, on the verge of pulling off one of the
biggest organizing victories of the year at a big printing plant in
New Jersey. She looked like a beauty queen and had a closet full of
three-hundred-dollar high heels, but Victoria had what it took to
organize. In the fifteen years since Victoria and I had worked
together, she had gone on to organize six big shops and a lot of little
ones. And me — what did I have to show for all those years of toil?
Fuck-all.

I squinted up again at Shawcross, still droning. As his eyes
made a grand sweep across the room in his best oratorical fashion,
his gaze fell on me and froze. I squinted some more and tried to
think bullets in his direction. Shawcross stumbled on a sentence. I
broke into a smile. Shawcross looked away and soon regained his
composure.

Shawcross was only the latest in a long line of guys in the labor
movement to screw me over. I was used to it. But those twenty-
seven dishwashers sure hadn't seen it coming.

Until three weeks ago, I had been the associate director of the
strategic campaigns department of the New York state labor
federation. I'd spent months of 16-hour days trying to get those
dishwashers back to their crappy jobs at an upscale midtown
Manhattan restaurant. These underpaid immigrant workers had
committed a crime: They had dared to strike. And so they had lost
their livelihoods and, in some cases, their apartments and their
families. The dishwashers and I had spent the dreary winter in puffy
coats and scarves, shuffling back and forth in front of the restaurant.
For sleepless months we had been twisting management's arm and
organizing solidarity actions and trying to sweet-talk politicians into
taking some action.

And at just the moment when we were sure the screws we'd
been tightening so assiduously were about to break the restaurant
owner's will, shit happened — shit in the form of James Shawcross,
who had just been elected the new president of the state labor
federation. Shawcross knew a bunch of loser immigrants when he
saw them. He decided there was no way these guys were going to
win and ordered me off their case. I refused. He fired me. The

workers were screwed, and so was I. I glared at Shawcross again. The bastard!

And screw Victoria too, I thought. What I really needed was a drink. A hefty scotch, with ice. A few of those would erase Shawcross from my mind altogether. That, and my morose, circular thoughts about what the hell I was going to do with my life now that Shawcross had ruined it.

Up at the podium, it seemed that Shawcross was going to get away with claiming personal credit for the slight slowing in the mass exodus from unions in the past year.

Just then, a smartly dressed young woman quickly ascended the dais and handed Shawcross a slip of paper. Shawcross stopped talking abruptly. Finally. A pair of reading glasses suddenly appeared on his nose. The room was strangely still as he studied the note. Then a guttural "oh" escaped his lips. He looked out at the audience.

"I have just learned some very bad news," Shawcross said. "Victoria Shales can't be here with us tonight. She, uh — I am very sorry to report that according to the information I've just received, Victoria was, that is — she's dead."

"If you're going to cry, I'm going home," Beck said. His hand was wrapped around a mug of fashionable beer. I'd opted for a more efficacious drink, a scotch mixed with nothing.

"I'm not crying." I downed the last of the scotch then nodded at the bartender, tilting my head at the empty glass. She came and picked it up. I sincerely hoped she wasn't the type to hold her customers to any kind of quota.

"What's that smeary stuff right there, then," Beck said, touching the tip of his index finger to the corner of my eye.

I pulled my head away. "I'm not the crying type," I said.

"I never thought so."

When the fresh drink arrived I took a sip and said, "I just can't believe it."

"Me neither," said Beck.

After Shawcross's announcement and the audience's collective gasp, the conference had abruptly ended. Beck had grabbed me by the arm and steered me to the nearest bar. From our sleek upholstered booth in the back, he had called his editor, who assigned him Victoria's obit. He had most of tomorrow to write it. In the meantime, he had been annoying the people in surrounding booths by calling a series of contacts in the police department and pumping them about Victoria's death. All we'd learned so far was that her body had been found in her Soho apartment late that afternoon.

"Victoria definitely did not look like she was about to have a heart attack," Beck said, snapping his cell phone shut. "And there's no way she would have killed herself."

"Maybe it was an accident," I said. "Maybe she fell in the shower."

"Highly unlikely."

We sat quietly for a moment. I closed my eyes. Victoria and I had never been close. But we'd gotten our start in the labor movement together, we'd fought our first battles side-by-side. As different as we were, we were bound together. Had been.

"Wasn't your first organizing drive with Victoria?" Beck asked.

I nodded as I pulled a small compact out of my bag. I wiped the mascara from the edge of my eye. My skin was veering toward a funereal pallor, and my hair was a mess, the black curls springing out in all directions. I needed lipstick too. Victoria wouldn't have been caught dead looking like this, I thought, then inhaled. Dead. It was impossible to believe.

I gave up on my face and dropped the compact back in my bag. "Yeah — we were both twenty-three. If you can believe that. Tommy McNamara was our boss — he'd just been promoted to director of organizing."

"McNamara's a good guy," said Beck. "What was the shop?"

"A little insurance company in Brooklyn. She was the organizer, and I got assigned to take this really crappy clerical job at the company. I mean, that was the job from hell."

"You were a salt? I'd forgotten that part," Beck said, grinning. "You lost, right?"

I blew air from my lips. "Of course."

"So what did you think of Queen Victoria back then?"

"Beck!"

"Sorry. Old habits."

I tilted my drink back and forth and stared into it for a minute. "She was so young. She came from this affluent family in Connecticut somewhere. She'd just graduated from Harvard. What the hell did she know? But she just sashayed in there and did what had to be done. It took me a long time to figure out that she'd been winging the whole thing. She acted so confident."

Beck looked at me. "What about you?"

"Oh, I was better off as the salt. I'd already been working at shit jobs for years. It was Victoria who did the strategy. She was — " I struggled for the right word. "She had chutzpah."

"She did," said Beck, turning to face me. "So do you."

"Plus she was so fucking gorgeous."

"Hey. You're gorgeous too. Though I must say, Victoria…"

"Would you shut up, Beck?"

Beck laughed and then traced a finger down the side of my cheek while I looked uneasily down at my scotch.

Beck and I could talk honestly about anything under the sun — except our "relationship." Maybe Beck didn't really know *what* he felt toward me — so what was there to say? Or maybe we were both afraid of where an honest conversation might lead. I had never asked Beck to leave his wife. So the question just hung there between us. Beck had always implied that it was Iris, his now 13-year-old daughter, that had kept him and Beth in their loveless marriage all these years. Maybe. But the situation still left me feeling that I loved Beck more than he loved me. One thing was sure: It was enough to drive a woman to drink.

I clutched the fat tumbler that contained my scotch. The blue-lit midtown bar was still crowded and some kind of high-tech music was playing. I was surprised by how disoriented I felt, as if I'd just been knocked in the head. Only the scotch — and Beck's company — felt familiar.

I eyed the bartender and smiled until she came over and grabbed my glass. "You're already getting ahead of me," Beck said. "Anybody ever tell you that you drink like a fish?"

I looked over at Beck. "Most people are too polite to mention it."

"I shouldn't be encouraging you like this. You know, I've been worried about you. I get the impression you've been sitting at home drinking all day for three weeks."

"So what?" was my clever reply.

The bartender came back with my refilled glass. Beck passed her his mug and then winked at her. No question, Beck was really broken up about Victoria's death. I thought maybe the bartender would scowl at him, but instead she gave him a small ambiguous grin and then whisked over to the other end of the bar.

"You know, some women don't like that sort of behavior," I said.

"I know that. Prudes." Beck smiled sweetly as the bartender set the fresh beer down in front of him. "It's hard to picture you and Victoria working together. You're so – different."

"Different. That's an understatement. We had a fight during that organizing drive over whether to tell the workers how shitty the union's health plan was. Guess who thought what?"

Beck shrugged. "That's easy. Victoria wanted to lie about it so the union wouldn't lose any votes, and you wanted to tell the workers every shred of bad news and go down in flames."

"Exactly. Victoria actually argued that 'the end justifies the means' – quote, unquote. Can you believe that?"

Beck smiled. "Only you would find that statement so outrageous. What did you say?"

"I said that in my opinion the means determines the end." I set down my scotch with a thunk.

"Yeah. You're all into process."

"*Was. Was* into process. Now I'm into scotch." I twisted the tumbler back and forth a couple of times and watched the gold liquid slosh lazily in response.

Beck clapped a hand on my shoulder. "Ruth, if you don't watch out you're going to end up like your father. I don't want you dying of cirrhosis or whatever it was at forty-five."

"Wow," I said, looking at my watch. "That leaves me only eight years to finish stewing my liver. Where'd that bartender go?"

"You know, Shawcross did fuck you over, but that's no reason to give up. Instead of sitting at home feeling sorry for yourself, maybe you should get out there and show him something. In fact," Beck said, slamming down his drink, "you ought to take over that organizing drive Victoria was working on. The election's only a couple weeks away. Those workers are so screwed, losing their organizer right now."

"I told you, I'm done with organizing. And even if I wasn't, I would never touch that one. Follow in Victoria's footsteps? Not a good plan." Those little Manolo Blahniks of hers — no can do.

"I heard they fired the worker who started the drive. Hired a union-busting consultant. The whole thing."

"Oh god," I groaned. The problem with seeking oblivion in scotch was that it took so damn long. Especially for hard-drinking people like me.

Beck's cell rang and he snatched it off the table.

"Beck," he said into the phone. He looked at me, then frowned and looked away. "Yeah?" he said. "Jesus!"

He pulled a notepad out of his jacket pocket and started writing. I craned to see what he'd put down, but it was in Beck's personal shorthand, which I'd never been able to decipher. Beck glanced at me. He had a strange look on his face.

The instant he beeped off, I said, "What?"

"Well, they think it was a burglary."

"And?"

"And Victoria must have interrupted it."

Suddenly I couldn't breathe. "Murdered?"

Beck nodded. "Shot. Right through her brain."

CHAPTER 2

I woke up to the sound of wood shattering. I bolted upright, sending my cat, Franklin, flying off the bed, his claws scrabbling on the floor. Downstairs, a powerful fist was pummeling my front door.

"Ruth! Ruth!"

"Shit," I mumbled. My mouth was full of cotton. It was my friend and next-door neighbor Sandy LaTour. I had a headache that spanned from my frontal lobe to the nape of my neck.

I dropped back down on the bed and pulled the pillow over my head. This did not succeed in blocking the sound of Sandy's assault on my door.

Suddenly, there was silence, and I dared to hope that Sandy had gone away.

"Okay, I'm using my key now!" Sandy bellowed from the front stoop.

I sat up again. Across from me, Franklin stared wide-eyed at the stairs, expecting the evil giant to arrive momentarily.

"Ruth!" Sandy was charging up the stairs.

It was a testament to Sandy's fitness level that when she appeared in my bedroom she wasn't remotely out of breath. She brought with her a little scented breeze, a spicy and probably expensive cologne.

"Jesus, were you trying to break my door down or what?"

"Aren't you walking with me this morning? Where were you last night?" Sandy knitted her perfect brows at me and put one hand on her hip. The other hand was clutching a bottle of gourmet mineral water.

"No, and none of your business," I replied, flinging myself back down on the bed. For years, Sandy and I had taken brisk early morning walks together. Ever since I'd been sacked by James Shawcross, brisk walks had lost all appeal.

Sandy came around to the side of the bed and squatted so she could maintain her accusatory stare. Sandy was good at squats. In fact, she was a fitness trainer on the side. Her main job was as an administrative assistant in a university admissions office.

"I called you five times last night. I just kept getting your stupid machine, and then this morning, there was no answer. And of course calling you on your cell phone is pointless." Sandy glared at me. Despite myself, I smiled. Sandy was fierce in her guardianship of both me and our corpulent cat Franklin, whom we held in joint custody.

"Oh. Maybe I turned off the ringer." I paused. "Yeah, I think I did."

Sandy rolled her eyes.

I looked blearily out the window. It was a gorgeous July day. I wasn't in the mood for it.

"Ruth, it's been weeks. You have got to pull yourself together. Now come downstairs with me and I'll make you some tea."

"As you know, I don't drink tea. If you're going to make something, make coffee. Strong."

"Caffeine is not what your body needs."

"How do you know?" I said.

A few minutes later, I dragged my body into the kitchen. Sandy had the tea all ready. I went to the refrigerator, pulled out my tin of ground coffee and sniffed it. Coffee was a very big deal to me, since I drank gallons a day. Of course I felt compelled to buy PC coffee, the shade-grown variety that screwed the workers and farmers less than the other stuff did.

"So what's so fucking urgent?" I called to Sandy, my voice reverberating like a foghorn in my head.

"A message," Sandy shouted back from the front room. "A blast from the past."

The coffee machine was gurgling spasmodically as I shuffled into the bathroom. I splashed some cold water on my face. I made the mistake of glancing at myself in the mirror. My eyes were bloodshot, puffy, and bruised looking, like I'd been in a fistfight with an allergen. But Sandy would know exactly what I'd been up to.

I moved stiffly to the front room. Sandy was sitting primly on one end of my couch, a comfy overstuffed number that now needed recovering in a big way. I never had time to deal with household essentials. I collapsed onto the couch and closed my eyes.

"What blast from the past?"

"Tommy McNamara," said Sandy.

I sat up a little. Franklin saw his opening and jumped, with some difficulty, onto the couch between Sandy and me. Sandy scratched his ear delicately with her perfectly manicured index finger.

"Really," I said. Sandy knew McNamara because I'd been working for him twelve years before when I had tried to organize the university where Sandy worked. The employer had trounced us, despite the best efforts of Sandy and the other fearless secretaries. The drive had been a disaster, but at least I'd gotten Sandy out of the deal. A year later, I'd talked her into moving to Brooklyn, into the modest brick-front next door. I'd been very happy with the arrangement until now. It turned out that having a tireless health fanatic and scold as your best girl and next-door neighbor wasn't so good when your greatest desire was to dive headlong into alcoholic oblivion.

"Must. Get. Coffee," I said, forcing myself to rise again from the couch. I came back bearing a mug of the stuff, which I had robbed prematurely from the still snorting coffeemaker.

I took a big sip, groaned with relief, and took my seat on the couch again. I turned toward Sandy, partly to avoid looking at my desk across the room, which was piled high with papers and files from my work with the dishwashers. Unfortunately, my living room was actually an office; the sofa was the only concession to homey comfort. This would have to change, I decided. I wanted a living room given over to creature comforts. Maybe one of those spas right there in the floor. Of course, with no job this would be difficult to afford. I sighed.

Sandy was squinting at me. "I know you were out drinking. You look like shit."

"Thanks, sweetie," I said.

"Were you out with John Beck?"

I glared at Sandy over my mug, refusing to reply.

Sandy sniffed. "Oh, I can tell. You even smell like you were out with Beck last night."

I shrugged.

"Ruth!" Sandy slammed her water bottle down on the end table next to her, startling Franklin, who had been sprawling shamelessly on his back. "I just don't want you to get hurt again!"

I took a sip of coffee. "You gonna tell me about McNamara?" I asked. In fact I already had an idea what McNamara wanted, and I wasn't interested.

Sandy sighed. "He didn't say. But he tried to reach you all last night and then he remembered that I lived next door."

She passed the paper to me and I pretended to look at it, then dropped it onto the couch.

Sandy gave me a dirty look. She had refused to accept my resignation from the cause of union organizing. "So you don't know why he's calling either?"

I sighed. "I think he wants me to help him with an organizing drive at a printing plant in Jersey."

Sandy perked up. "Really? That sounds like just the thing. Force you out of your slump."

"This is no mere slump," I said indignantly. "And I do not want that job."

Sandy narrowed her eyes at me. "Why not?"

"'Cause the last person who had that job was murdered."

"What? Who?"

"Victoria Shales."

"Oh my god." Sandy leaned back against the couch.

"You knew her?"

"You told me about her."

I took another sip of coffee. "Yeah, well, she's dead."

"Oh my god!" Sandy said again. "Was it related to the organizing drive?"

I shrugged. "We don't know. The police say some of her jewelry was stolen. So maybe it was just a random burglary gone wrong."

Sandy sat there, stunned.

"Anyway – do you still want me to take that job?"

Sandy slowly shook her head. "Not if it's going to get you killed."

"There you go," I said.

I got to stare at the floor for a minute before Sandy started in again. "But you've got to take *some* job, Ruth. You can't just lie here drinking all day."

"Can I ask you something?" I said.

"What?"

"Were you afraid you'd get dehydrated going next door for fifteen minutes?"

Sandy looked at the bottle on the table as if she'd forgotten she'd brought it. "It keeps my skin moisturized."

"Huh," I said. "Well, I can't deny the flawless state of your skin."

Sandy gave me a full smile and blinked at me flirtatiously. Her brilliant white teeth only underscored the perfection of her dark and dewy complexion. I rolled my eyes.

I was peacefully snoozing in my bed again when the phone rang. It was mystifying, since I had turned the ringer off the night before. But as the fog in my head thinned, I realized that Sandy must have turned it back on while I was making coffee. She was sneaky that way.

I waited for the answering machine to kick in, but it didn't. Then I waited for whoever was calling to give up. But they didn't. The ringing went on and on, until I couldn't stand it anymore and picked up.

"Yeah?" I said hoarsely.

"Ruthie!" It was the mellifluous voice of my former boss, and Victoria's, Tommy McNamara.

"Tommy," I said in tones that I hoped conveyed my lack of enthusiasm.

"Are you sick?"

"Yeah," I answered.

"Oh. That's not good."

"No," I said.

"By the way, I heard all about what Shawcross did to you back there with the dishwashers. That guy's a first-class bastard. Always was."

I sighed. I did like Tommy. "I heard about Victoria. I'm really sorry, Tommy."

There was a pause on the phone that was very uncharacteristic of Tommy.

"Tommy?"

Tommy cleared his throat. "I can't believe it, Ruthie. I can't believe our gal is gone."

I closed my eyes. It *was* hard to believe.

Tommy cleared his throat. "And actually, that's why I'm calling. You heard about that campaign Victoria was working on out in Jersey?"

"Yup," I said. Here it was. I sat up some more and rubbed my eyes.

"Well, we could really use your help with that thing, Ruthie. In fact we're in a bind. A really bad bind. We got eighteen days. That's nothing."

"Tommy — "

"And you're a damn good organizer, and you know how Victoria works. I just couldn't think of anybody else who could go in there and figure it out and maybe pull this whole thing off. "

Shameless flattery. Disingenuous comparisons to Victoria. It had always worked for Tommy in the past.

"You know we can't leave those workers hanging, Ruthie."

The coup de grace – a brazen grab at my squishy heart. I did detect a little squeezing sensation inside my ribcage. But it was nothing I couldn't resist, nothing a few scotches couldn't wipe away.

"Tommy," I said. "You know I'd help if I could. But I'm sick. And I'm – I'm not in good shape right now. I'm just not the gal for the job, okay?"

I allowed a moment to pass.

"I know what's going on with you, Ruthie." Tommy said quietly.

"No you don't, Tommy."

"Yes I do."

"No you don't."

"Yes, Ruthie, I do. Shawcross screwed you, he broke your heart, and now you're trying to drink away the pain."

I was dumbfounded. Tommy *did* know what was going on.

"Ruthie, we've all had our disappointments in the labor movement — "

"Oh please. Don't tell me about disappointments. I mean, talk about sprinting to stay in place. We've got — what — eleven percent of the workforce organized? Pathetic! But that's not even it, Tommy. It's not the employers who are killing me. It's having to fight with my own side. I'm sick of it! I've had the rug pulled out from under me one too many times. It's not going to happen to me again," I finished, virtually panting.

"Oh, Ruthie, I know," Tommy said with unbearable empathy. "You set your sights so high, and then you get so –"

"Flattened. Like road kill. Look, Tommy, I'm sorry. I really can't do this thing in Jersey. And you wouldn't want me to anyway, not in the state I'm in, believe me. Listen, I've got to go. I got a hangover to sleep off here."

The thing was, the conversation left me feeling so guilty, I couldn't sleep anymore. After awhile I got up and plodded slowly down the stairs. Years ago, in the course of some ambitious home beautification campaign that I found unimaginable at the moment, I had covered the wall next to the stairs with photos. At the top were the really old ones. I passed by the one of my big brother David and me swimming in the water-filled old mine near our house in McCracken, West Virginia. And on to the one of my dad. It was the last photo we had of him. His eyes already had that sunken look.

Some unhealthy impulse caused me to lift the photo off the nail and take it with me downstairs. I flopped down on the couch and stared at it. My dad had been a skinny dark-haired guy with the angular chin and jutting adam's apple you see in so many Appalachians. He was smiling the only way he ever did in pictures, with his mouth closed. My dad had rotten teeth. I wasn't sure why he'd never fixed them. He'd started out poor, but by the time I was born, he'd just about made it into the middle class. He could have afforded to fix his teeth.

I leaned back further on the couch and held the photo up in front of my face. My dad had started out as a coal miner. Thanks to the union, which he'd worshipped, he'd eventually made a pretty good income. And with the money, my dad had gone to night school at a state college and gotten his teaching degree.

After that came about eight good years, during which my dad taught his own rabble-rousing brand of social studies to awed teenagers at McCracken public high school. He also led a successful drive to organize the teachers. The man was dangerous, and I now understood that it had only been a matter of time before the shit hit the fan. There was only so long you could rabble-rouse in McCracken and get away with it.

The first blow was when the school district decided my dad was subverting the youth and trying to instill godless communism into their young brains. My dad was suspended, then fired. The second blow — and this was the killer — was when the union he had organized left him to swing in the breeze.

Of course it wasn't till my late twenties that I appreciated what had happened to my dad. During my dad's last awful years, when

I'd been in high school, I'd only added to his suffering with my resentment and my renunciation of everything he stood for. I'd left home swearing up and down that I would never, never be anything like him. It took all of three years for it to become obvious that I was his clone. And by then, he was dead.

I put the picture down and turned my face into the couch. Before I drifted off to sleep, I had a fleeting moment of alarm — had I drunk up all the scotch last night?

Unbelievably, the phone was ringing again. Would it ever stop? Why the hell hadn't I turned off that damn ringer? And what was I doing sleeping on the couch in the middle of the day?

And the phone rang on. If it wasn't Sandy, it was Tommy again. If it wasn't them, it was John Beck. And I didn't feel like talking to him either.

I seized the receiver impatiently. "Look. Leave me alone!" I yelled into it.

"Ms. Reid?" said a timid female voice.

Crap, I thought, sitting up. "Yeah, that's me. Sorry about that. Who's this?"

The woman cleared her throat. "My name is Silvia Rodriguez, and I work at Pantheon Printing."

Oh hell. Tommy had hauled out the heavy artillery.

"Oh, hi," I said. "I — listen, my heart goes out to you guys. I can't believe what happened to Victoria — " God, I was such an ass.

"Actually, that's what I wanted to talk to you about," Silvia began.

"Look, uh, Ms. Rodriguez. I'm really sorry about your situation. But like I told Tommy, I just can't help you at the moment."

"Tommy said you'd say that, but I just wanted to make sure you understood. There's only eighteen days till the election. And Tommy says you're the only one who can help us now. Victoria — she ran the whole campaign. She had all these plans — and we don't know what they were. We don't know what to do next."

Silvia's plaintive voice was killing me. I couldn't even summon up any words in response. Horribly, she went on.

"The company hired this consultant named F.H. Toro, and he's scaring everybody away from the union. We've put so much into this, Ms. Reid, and now it looks like we might lose everything. And Tommy told us — "

"Wait, wait," I interjected. "Look, Ms. Rodriguez — "

"Silvia."

"Silvia, I really do want to help, but I'm not – I don't think I'd do you much good, even if I said yes — "

"Oh my god, if you would say yes, I *know* we could make it!"

That joyful exclamation sliced my heart in two. A few seconds passed. I sensed a sweaty panic overtaking me.

"I — look, I'll think about it," I said finally. "I'll talk to Tommy. And I'll let you know by the end of the day. Okay?"

After we'd said our goodbyes and I'd hung up the phone, I sat and looked at it for a minute. What in the hell had I been thinking? Silvia and the other workers at Pantheon Printing had no way of knowing what a mess I was in, how unprepared I was to help them. If I said yes, they'd be replacing Victoria Shales, the labor movement's fearless star organizer, with a bitter, disillusioned boozer. A boozer who, I noticed after I'd hung up the phone, really needed a shower.

CHAPTER 3

Tommy McNamara's office was in a handsome prewar building in midtown Manhattan. The lobby had been restored to all its original art deco glory. The walls featured bronze cutwork figures of Egyptians wearing togas, and a glorious starburst chandelier hung from the twenty-foot ceiling. But once you got to the twenty-seventh floor where the Industrial Workers Union had their office, the grandeur was gone. The ceilings were low, the floors were grimy, and the walls were cracked and needed paint.

The union, despite its name, didn't just represent blue-collar workers – over the years, they'd picked up office workers of all kinds, taxi drivers, deli workers, even some exotic dancers. It was a messy business, organizing, and the IWU's office reflected this perfectly. It was virtually impossible to navigate the warren of tiny offices that had been packed onto the twenty-seventh floor.

Back when I'd worked for the union, I could have walked the narrow hallways with my eyes closed. Now I wandered disorientedly down the corridor, looking for Room 2718. Still, everything about this place, especially its smell of old wood and dusty paper, reminded me powerfully of Victoria and of the thrill we'd both felt here in those early years. Our organizing drive was the beginning of something big for both of us, and we'd both known it. Now Victoria was dead. And I was only half-alive.

"Ruthie!"

I backed up and looked into the office I'd just passed. And there was McNamara, all three hundred pounds of him, beaming at me, his arms already open for an embrace.

"Tommy." I gave myself over to a smothering hug from my old boss.

I pulled away and looked at him. I hadn't seen Tommy in over a year. In that period, he'd aged at least five. The beard that he kept clipped neatly around the edge of his jaw was all white now, and the creases in his face had deepened. His blue eyes were watery. He still had the same blustery complexion, accentuated by the broken blood vessels that alcohol produced. I wondered if he saw signs of dissipation in my face. At least I hadn't gotten to the broken blood vessel stage yet.

"Is this your office?" I asked, with Tommy's arm still squeezing my shoulder. I guessed it was. I recognized the towering piles of books and files and the display of little mementos and toys that helped put the nervous visitor at ease.

Tommy swept the room theatrically with an outstretched arm. "Lovely, isn't it?"

"We ought to do a grievance over your ergonomics here. They stink." I sat down in the chair next to Tommy's desk.

"Tell me about it," said Tommy as he dropped into his chair. It was then I noticed the sad cast of Tommy's eyes.

"I'm really sorry about Victoria, Tommy."

Tommy shook his head gently and then looked down at the stained and rippled carpet.

"Thank god we still got you," Tommy said, looking back up at me with a small smile.

I smiled back. Tommy and his union didn't have me. Even *I* didn't have me at the moment.

"You never should have left the union. You'd have been so good here, Ruthie."

"Well, you should've gone for the presidency when you had a chance," I retorted. I'd quit the Industrial Workers because I thought Tommy's boss was an ass.

"If you'd stayed, we would've had two big organizing stars," said Tommy.

"Oh, come on. I never would have been as good as Victoria." Or as cute. Or as anything else.

Tommy looked at me. "Not true, Ruthie. You got the touch too."

I laughed. "Yeah. The touch of death. Just look at the win rate. Mine was less than fifty percent and Victoria's was what? Eighty?"

"That's apples and oranges. You do a different kind of thing. You're the one who goes in at the last minute to pull victory from the jaws of defeat."

I smiled. "Uh-huh."

"Which – uh — brings me to this Pantheon business — "

"Look, Tommy. I told Silvia I'd consider this thing. But I really don't think you understand my situation. You don't know how burned out I am. I'm — "

"You know what?" Tommy interrupted. "That's bullshit, Ruthie. You're telling me you're going to let these workers down? That's not like you. And letting a schmuck like Shawcross be the one to take you out of action? That's not like you either."

My face was suddenly very warm. I didn't know if it was rage or shame or just plain upsetness. They all made me turn a horrifying shade of pink. It was the curse of the Scotch-Irish hillbillies.

"Tommy. That's not the point," I said. My voice sounded strangled and unfamiliar to my own ears. "This is not a fight you can afford to lose, right? Because that's what's going to happen if you hire me to do it."

Tommy just looked at me. "You going to let me tell you about this job or not?"

I pressed my lips together tightly and nodded. My cheeks were still burning.

"Here's the deal, Ruthie," Tommy said, rolling his chair close to mine. "We got eighteen days till the election. And it's a fuckin' mess out there. This place — Pantheon Printing — it's owned by these two brothers, the Maloneys. Built it into one of the biggest printing facilities in the northeast – almost eight hundred employees. They do some big-name magazines, very big deal." He tapped my knee with his meaty index finger for emphasis.

"So the business is going pretty much okay till about a year ago. Suddenly, the company starts laying people off and getting very hard ass."

"What happened? They run into a financial problem?" I asked.

Tommy shook his head. "I don't know. Victoria was trying to figure that out."

"Getting hard ass how?"

"They hire this guy F.H. Toro to increase what they like to call efficiency, right?"

I nodded.

"He gets the supervisors to clock people's bathroom breaks, dock pay for lateness. They speed up the line and people start getting injured. All the sudden this is a really shitty place to work. So people decide they got to organize. This pressman actually calls the union out of the blue – Al Zielinski."

"Al Zielinski," I repeated.

"Right. Bit of a blowhard, but he's hot for the union. Zielinski builds up the campaign, we send Victoria in. She goes in there, starts signing people up like crazy."

"For an NLRB election?"

Tommy nodded.

"How come?"

Tommy shrugged. "That's what Yankel wanted."

I sighed. A lot of unions bypass National Labor Relations Board elections because employers are so good at subverting them. But Yankel, the president of Tommy's union, was from the old school.

"How many signed up?" To get an NLRB election, the union had to have at least thirty percent of workers signing authorization cards in support. But Victoria wouldn't have attempted an election without signing up many more than that.

"Seventy-four percent," said Tommy.

"Pretty good."

"Yeah, but this Toro turns out to be a major union-buster. He brings in a crew of guys and they start doing the usual stuff — closed-door meetings with workers, harassing the union activists, the whole thing."

"You ever heard of this Toro guy before?"

Tommy shook his. "Nope. But he's no slouch. First thing he does is get Zielinski fired."

"Oh, shit."

"Right. Now people get really intimidated. Now they know for sure they'll get fired if they go with the union. Union starts losing support–who would've guessed, right?"

"Any other angles you guys were working on?" I asked. "Do we have any leverage on this company?"

"Honestly, Ruthie? I don't know. I know Victoria was sniffing around, but I don't know if she found anything."

I released a lungful of air I didn't know I had been holding. "Tommy, can I ask you something? You think Victoria's murder had anything to do with this organizing drive?"

Tommy gave me a worried look I didn't like at all. "The cops are still saying they don't think it was about anything but taking Victoria's jewelry. She did have a lot of it."

I nodded. Victoria had a thing for shiny gewgaws, something I'd found incongruous and even a little disturbing in someone whose life was devoted to fighting for the underdog.

"But Tommy. Knowing Victoria — you think maybe she did something that got somebody mad? Or pushed them into a corner?"

Tommy looked down at his puffy red hands. "I just don't know, Ruthie. You know what a loner Victoria was. She never told me she was in any kind of danger. But then, she probably wouldn't have told me even if she was."

I looked at Tommy and he looked at me.

"I wouldn't send you out there if it wasn't safe," said Tommy.

I smiled. "Yeah. Unless the fate of those workers hung in the balance. Which it does."

Tommy smiled back at me, not denying it.

I inhaled deeply, as if oxygen could save me from this job, and sat back in my chair. "So who else you got assigned out there?"

Tommy just looked at me, sad-faced.

"I mean, you had other staff working with Victoria on this, right?"

Tommy sighed. "Yeah. Well, that's the thing. At first I had a couple guys out there, but then they got called back."

I got up from my chair, stepped over to Tommy's door, and closed it.

"Okay, Tommy," I said, turning to face him. "That's crazy. You've got eight hundred workers and one organizer? What's going on?"

Tommy cocked his head. "Right. Well, you heard about this merger thing?"

"Yeah," I said cautiously. "It's going through?"

Tommy scratched his knee. "Looks like it."

I sat down in the chair again. This was depressing news. Over the past decade, the Industrial Workers Union had been losing members in droves, mostly because a lot of blue-collar jobs were now being done by computers. A huge transfer of union funds to the organizing department and Victoria's wins hadn't been enough to stanch the flow. And so, like almost every other labor organization, the IWU now hoped to stay alive by gobbling up another union – or being gobbled up itself. Unfortunately, it looked like the IWU was going to be eaten by the stodgy and bloated Office and Allied Employees Union. Although both unions were calling it a "merger," I feared the IWU's better-than-average union culture would disappear in the process, along with its name.

"So what's the merger got to do with the Pantheon drive?" I asked.

"You wouldn't believe how much staff time the merger is taking. We basically got half our people reassigned to the thing."

"But Tommy. You're telling me there's not a single in-house organizer you can assign to Pantheon? That's nuts."

Tommy shook his head. "People are telling me I got to send Frank DePietro out there. Remember him?"

I stared at Tommy. Oh yeah, I remembered DePietro. The good thing about DePietro was that he'd come up from the shop floor. The bad thing about DePietro was that as far as I could tell nothing excited him more than the shiny new car the union got for him every two years. The car, the suit, all the trappings of being a "player" – that's what DePietro really loved about the job.

"You're telling me you got eight hundred people at Pantheon, and they're talking about DePietro?"

Tommy's bloodshot eyes drifted over to the window, with its view of a dirty brick wall and a rusted fire escape. "Look, the merger's a big energy drain. And I think with Victoria — uh, gone..." Tommy's voice drifted off.

"Oh. I get it now. They think Pantheon's a loser. They're blowing it off."

Tommy said nothing, confirming my theory. I shifted around in my seat. So they wanted to kill off the drive by sending in DePietro. But what about Silvia Rodriguez? Didn't she count for anything? This was exactly the kind of thing that made me want to quit the labor movement. So how come I was sitting here in this depressing office?

"And the really crappy thing is that if we lose Pantheon, it won't be looking too good for me either," said Tommy.

"What do you mean?"

Tommy leaned back in his chair. "See, if this merger happens, there's going to be only four senior slots in the organizing department. As the plan is now, IWU people are filling three of them – including me, this fat old bastard pushing retirement. And there's already plenty of people around here who don't like me all that much."

I nodded. Tommy was a boat-rocker, and that had won him some fierce opposition in the union. "And if you lose Pantheon — " I prompted.

Tommy shrugged. "Well, you know, they'll use it to pressure me into quitting — let one of their guys have the slot. A younger guy, that is."

I sat there in my chair, feeling overheated. Here was a man who had spent his life fighting for workers. Organizing was everything to Tommy. He'd never sold out. And he was going to be consigned to the garbage heap because he was fifty-seven?

My eyes met Tommy's. Suddenly it was all clear. Of course Tommy wanted the Pantheon workers to have a union. But he also wanted to keep his job. Tommy was in a bad place at a bad moment. And he had picked me, of all people, to get him out of it.

"You know I have a lot of faith in you, Ruthie. I always did," said Tommy, just to add to the pressure.

For one desperate moment, I tried to think of some way out of the trap I was about to walk into. But perversely, my mind refused to cooperate. Instead, I thought of Silvia Rodriguez and the way her voice had turned up when she thought I was about to say I would take the campaign. With a sinking feeling, I realized that I was going to be spending the next eighteen days out in the swamps of New Jersey. I was sure the workers at Pantheon Printing did not deserve to be saddled with a loser like me.

I gave Tommy a wan smile.

"I knew you'd come through for us, " Tommy said, getting up from his chair.

I thought maybe I should find the bathroom before I threw up all over his ratty carpet.

Tommy grabbed my hand and gave it a vigorous shake. Tommy's hand was warm, dry, and calloused. Mine was cold and sweaty.

On the subway back to Brooklyn, there were people snoozing, their mouths agape, people playing games on their smartphones, people yawning, people sitting contentedly amid their red plastic bags of produce from Chinatown, and then there was me, in a dead panic. I tried a visualization I usually found supremely comforting, picturing in minute detail the squat glass of scotch I was going to have as soon as I got home. But even this thought brought anxiety: I was going to have to cut way back on booze now. I'd have to start getting up in the morning again. I'd even have to try to act cheerful. I tried to swallow, but my mouth was too dry.

I sped-walked the few blocks from the subway to my house, trying not to think. My little two-story brick rowhouse was cute on the outside, but when I shoved open the door, I was reminded that inside, it was a mess — cluttered, dusty, stale-smelling. I'd never been great at cleaning, but in the past couple of weeks I had reached new lows.

I threw my keys on the little table by the door where I would be sure to not find them later and raced through my office to the kitchen where the scotch bottle was located. As I skimmed by the answering machine, I noticed the red light was blinking.

"Oh shut up," I told the machine. But then I stopped. Damn it, I was going to have to start listening to my messages again instead of deleting them unheard. I pushed the play button.

"Ruth, has anyone told you that your message is hard to hear? I think you need to rerecord it. This is Thomas."

"No kidding," I said to the machine. Of course it was my brother. Who else could it be with that telltale offering of unwanted advice? I plopped down in my desk chair, working my jaw in anticipation.

"So Ruth, I'm calling about Elizabeth," said Thomas. "She's still refusing to go back to school. She's been hanging around here for two months, and she keeps saying she wants to stay with you for awhile. And, uh, I just wanted you to know that we think that might be a pretty good idea, actually. So I just wanted to give you a heads up on that. So let's talk soon, okay?"

The machine clicked off.

"No way, no way, no way," I chanted as I picked up the phone and punched in Thomas's home number.

"Thomas," I told my brother's voicemail. "Look, this is not a good time for Liz to visit. I'm just starting a big campaign and things are very stressful and –" I heard a beep signaling that my thirty seconds were up. Thomas was an important man. He didn't have time to sit around listening to rambling messages from people like me. I slammed down the phone and looked at Franklin, who was blinking at me from his sprawling position on the couch.

"Kitty, what do you think about having my errant niece coming to live with us for an undetermined period of time? Pot smoke, late nights, weird music, that sort of thing?"

Franklin just stared at me as if I were a lunatic who needed to be watched constantly.

"I agree," I said. "We love our niece, but that doesn't mean we want her to live with us, does it? Especially not now."

Franklin rolled over onto his back and yawned, reaching his paws toward me beguilingly.

"Yes, you are a sinful hedonist, but I don't have time for that now," I said as I walked past the couch. "I have an important business date with a bottle in the kitchen."

CHAPTER 4

"Jesus, slow down," I said. Beside me, Sandy was taking yard-long strides along the edge of the cargo terminal, half a block from the Brooklyn shore. A brisk wind from the west whipped up small frothy whitecaps on New York Harbor. The Manhattan skyline looked like the Emerald City, glistening across the harbor in the early morning sun.

"We always walk at this pace," Sandy replied. If anything, she was speeding up.

I took a few galloping steps forward to catch up with her. "But I'm not used to it," I panted. "It's been a long time."

"Well, that's your own fault. Now you can start getting back in shape."

"Aren't you sweet," I huffed. I looked at my watch. It was seven-twenty on a Sunday morning. I hadn't been up at this hour in weeks. But now, because of my stupidity in accepting the Pantheon job, I had work to do. Later that day, I had an appointment in Bloomson, New Jersey, with a few of the drive's most active workers. I was dreading it.

Given the hour, there was no traffic here amid the cobblestone streets of the cargo terminal — only the wind blowing between the buildings, each one a block wide and eight stories high. This giant facility, a few blocks down the slope from where we lived, had once been the heart of the biggest port on the eastern seaboard. Now the buildings brimmed with small garment shops and food processing companies, employing an army of underpaid Latinas and Chinese women.

"I'm just glad you're finally pulling yourself together instead of lying around and drinking," said Sandy.

"Hey. I appreciate the support." I pulled a tissue out of the pocket of my windbreaker. The wind was making my eyes tear.

"I can't believe you're not going to let Liz stay with you for awhile," Sandy said. "Don't you have any feelings of family obligation?"

"Not really."

"I thought you liked Liz."

"I do. But that doesn't mean I want her living in my house. You know how she is. Would you want her in your house?"

"No. But she's not my niece." Sandy looked straight ahead as she spoke, swinging her arms high in front of her with each step. Probably toning her biceps or something. I'd never bothered with that part. I wasn't going to pump my arms if I didn't have to. Besides, it looked silly.

"Look," I said. "I've got damn good reasons for not wanting her to come."

"What?"

"I'm starting a campaign. I won't be around at all."

"That's simple — don't take the job. I don't want you to anyway. It's dangerous."

"I already committed to it."

Sandy looked over at me, trying to decide whether to press her case further. "Well, Liz is nineteen," she said finally. "She can take care of herself."

I laughed. "Like last time, when I had to carry her out of that club and spend the night with her in the bathroom while she puked?"

"Well, she was eighteen then. Maybe she's matured."

I snorted. Liz had been a hellion since birth, which had invited the family to make many comparisons with me. Liz's method of rebelling against her high-achieving parents was to refuse to "apply herself," as Thomas would say. My brother had been fleeing the family tradition of poverty and doomed idealism since kindergarten. He'd become a fancy defense attorney, married another fancy defense attorney, and raised two pampered children in a shockingly affluent suburb of Washington, D.C.: the mutinous elder Elizabeth (as her parents insisted on calling her) and the straight-laced David, now fifteen.

"Besides," I said, "what kind of a role model am I for some wayward kid? I mean, unless we want her to turn into a hard-drinking, sour hussy."

"Now *that's* a good point," said Sandy.

We edged around a building, bringing us to the harbor's edge. Waves lapped on the berm of brown rock slabs that climbed up from the water. We stepped between the tracks of the rail cars that still ferried stuff around on the waterfront. Sandy was taller than me, five-nine to my five-six. Still, in the past our strides had been in sync. Now I felt like a badly conditioned hamster next to my lithe friend. If I didn't watch out, I'd revert to the sad condition I'd been in as a teenager back in McCracken, when my favorite pastime had been eating potato chips on the couch and watching Bewitched reruns.

"On the other hand," said Sandy, "maybe taking care of Liz will distract you from that man you're always waiting around for."

"I'm not waiting for John Beck. What would I be waiting for?"

Sandy rolled her eyes. "Waiting for him to leave his wife."

"Sandy. We broke up, remember? Months ago."

"Uh-huh," said Sandy, looking straight ahead.

We spent the rest of the walk in silence, Sandy gliding ahead, her nose high in the air, and me loping along after her, panting.

When we got back to Sandy's front stoop, Sandy suddenly stopped, turned, grabbed my shoulders, and looked into my face, her dark brown eyes drilling into mine. "I have a bad feeling about that organizing drive, Ruth. I mean it. I want you to tell Tommy no."

"Sandy, I already said yes."

Sandy released me and stomped her foot on the sidewalk. It was a comical sight, and I was almost tempted to laugh.

"How come you always do this? You have a Don Quixote complex!"

"You are very observant," I said. "And highly literate too."

"And besides, there's no way you can win that organizing drive!"

As soon as the words escaped her lips, Sandy's eyes widened and she clapped her hand over her mouth. "I didn't mean it that way. I just mean, *nobody* could win it now — not after what happened to Victoria."

I nodded. Sandy was right. I knew I couldn't win. I already knew I'd made a bad mistake to say I'd try. If I was on the path to oblivion now, imagine how I'd feel once I had firmly established that I couldn't organize worth a damn compared to Victoria Shales? After James Shawcross spread this information all over town? After I'd let down Tommy McNamara and, even worse, Silvia Rodriguez and every other worker at Pantheon Printing?

As I entered my musty-smelling house, it occurred to me that it would be nice to have a mimosa with my morning cereal. I fought off the temptation. Arriving drunk at my first meeting with the Pantheon workers would not inspire confidence. Besides, I didn't have any champagne.

After a vigorous shower I went and stood, nude, in front of my closet, trying to ignore my reflection in the full-length mirror. I'd never been an athlete like Sandy, but I'd always been in pretty good shape — well muscled, slim. How much damage could three profligate weeks do? I did not want to look in the mirror and find out.

And did I have any presentable clothes? If so, where the hell were they? I scooted the hangers back and forth on the rod and hyperventilated. No, I did not have any presentable clothes. Unlike certain other organizers I could name. Everything I had was too big, too small, too dowdy, or irreparably wrinkled. Or stained. And then there was the basket of clothes that needed dry-cleaning — I was pretty sure that dated back to the previous century. It was clear that if, against all expectation, I did not descend into a life of dissipation after this was all over, I would have to invest everything I earned on this job in renovating my wardrobe.

Finally I extracted a pair of slightly stretchy black pants — I needed the give — and a deep blue tailored blouse made of some glossy synthetic material — making it the only shirt I had that wasn't badly wrinkled. Although it did have a little spot on the shoulder. It took me another few minutes to unearth some only slightly scuffed mid-heeled sandals from the dusty depths of the closet.

After some sloppy work with a mascara wand, I finally stepped outside. Clouds were beginning to dominate the sky, but they were still high and white. The birds were happy, or probably just horny, twittering their heads off among the sycamore branches. Whatever it was they were feeling, I couldn't relate.

I made my way to the garage around the corner where Sandy and I paid a mint to park our lime green Dodge Neon. We didn't use the car often, since, like all sensible New Yorkers, we greatly preferred the subway. The last time had been in the spring, when Sandy had decreed that my bedroom was an embarrassment and we'd driven to a furniture superstore in Jersey, where we'd bought a new pine platform bed, a dresser and a wardrobe, cleaning out my checking account.

The car was feeling its age. Or maybe the battery was low. It took a few whining tries to start up, and when it finally did, it coughed and belched. Well, this was fine. At my first meeting with the Pantheon workers, I was going to make it abundantly clear that I was not Victoria Shales. I was not well dressed. My makeup was not flawless. And I did not drive a gleaming silver Volvo. I drove a rusty lime green Dodge Neon that farted whenever it moved. Could it even get me to the damn meeting?

And then, when I'd finally nudged the car onto the street, my cell phone, which was tucked deep inside my backpack, rang.

"Fuck you," I said when I heard the first trill. But what if it was a Pantheon worker calling to tell me the meeting was canceled? Damn! I looked at my bag, still trilling away. I pulled over and put the car in park, fumbled around with my bag till I found the phone.

"Hello!" I bellowed.

"Jesus. You don't have to chop my head off just for calling."

I exhaled. It was John Beck. But I was still in a bad mood.

"I'm in the car. I was just going to New Jersey," I yelled.

"Would you stop yelling? What's in Jersey?"

I could barely hear what Beck was saying. "Pantheon," I yelled. I turned off the engine and looked at my watch. I could talk to Beck for a couple of minutes and still make it to Al Zielinski's house on time. If the car didn't break down.

"Oh, so they *did* offer you the job," said Beck.

"Yep."

"And you took it."

"Uh huh," I said. There was something weird about this call. It was Sunday. Beck never called me on Sundays. He always spent that day with Iris and Beth.

"Beck?"

"Yeah?"

"Where are you?"

"I'm at the paper."

"What are you doing at work on a Sunday? At the break of dawn?"

"The break of dawn was three hours ago."

I rolled my eyes. "But what about Iris?"

"Look. We've been really busy at the paper, okay?" Beck said testily.

"Okay fine. So why are you calling?" I snapped.

"I wanted to see if you were going to take the job. Why else?"

"Why do you care if I take the job?"

"Jesus, Reid. Because you're my friend. And also – I don't know. It's just an interesting situation."

"Oh. I get it. You want to do a story about the drive, right? Big drama. Famous organizer murdered. Will the new girl be able to pull it off? Stay tuned! Is that the plan?"

There was a short pause. "It *would* be a pretty good story."

Well, yeah, I thought. Definitely. People liked train wrecks. Natural disasters. Watch Ruth Reid jump off a cliff, pulling eight hundred workers down with her.

"Yeah, it is a pretty good story," I said. "But I can't talk to you about it right now. I'm on my way to Jersey, like I said." Heading off the cliff as we speak.

"Did you see my Victoria obit?"

"Oh yeah. Some photo." Victoria's head had been tilted flirtatiously, her lips curved in a seductive smile. She wore pearls draped over a satiny blouse. Our salt-of-the-earth organizer must have paid a fortune to get a glamour shot like that.

"Yeah," said Beck. "Rita Hayworth, only blonde."

"Good obit, too," I allowed. That was all the gushing Beck was going to get from me this morning.

"So who's in charge?" Beck asked.

"Me."

"Hey, great. Who else they got?"

"Nobody."

"Really? Shouldn't they be assigning two or three people at least?"

"McNamara says the union's short-staffed."

"Christ, I'll say. That doesn't sound too good. I mean, I hope they're not sticking you with a loser."

I gripped the phone tighter. What was it with these people, my so-called friends? "You're the second person today who's told me I'm incapable of winning this organizing drive," I yelled into the phone.

"Jeez, that's not what I said! I just mean — after everything that's happened, with just a couple weeks to go till the election —"

"Anyway," I said morosely, "I said yes."

"Okay, well, great. I've been doing some research — I've got stuff on the history of the place, the Maloneys, a little on the finances — I'll give you what I got."

This was the upside of Beck's rubbernecking on my Pantheon fiasco. I was going to get research help. "Nice, Beck. Want to meet at the bar tomorrow night and go over it?"

There was a moment of silence on the line. "Uh, maybe — but it would have to be kind of late. There's this new reporter I'm supposed to break in and it's really slowing me down."

"Who?"

"Her name is Yvette Ramirez. She's good, she's smart, and I like her and everything, but she doesn't know what the hell she's doing, you know?"

"Uh huh." Oh yeah, I knew. I could just picture young Yvette. I bet Beck liked her plenty.

"Anyway, meanwhile, I'll just flip the stuff over to you," said Beck.

"Cool," I said. Yvette, I thought.

CHAPTER 5

I took the turnoff to the Verrazzano Bridge, which connects Brooklyn to Staten Island, and rose up over the outer harbor. From the top of the bridge's arch, you could see the crowded old-timey streets of Brooklyn on one side, the desolate oil storage fields along the Jersey shore in the distance, and straight ahead, the gentle tree-studded slope of Staten Island rising from the harbor. I stewed for a moment about Yvette and then chided myself. Beck and I hadn't slept together in months. What did I care if he had a minor fling with some young reporter? And what made me think he was even having a fling?

"Yeah, right," I said out loud. Sandy was right: I needed to get over the guy. I needed somebody to sweep me off my feet — somebody other than John Beck. My last serious relationship had been two years ago, during another Beck sabbatical. Things had just kind of petered out with Gary, a union staffer I'd met on a campaign. In fact, maybe "serious" was too big a word for it, since I'd been more committed to my houseplants than I'd been to Gary. And even my houseplants were wilting.

I turned my mind to the meeting at hand. I'd asked Al Zielinski to invite Silvia Rodriguez and two other workers McNamara had told me about: Nita Montero, who was Silvia's sister and, like her, worked in the plant's bindery division, and Joe Dysart, a second pressman. I hoped to god these people got along. We just had to have a talented and cohesive organizing committee if we were going to win. Of course, you could have the committee of your dreams and still lose big-time, as I'd demonstrated more than once.

My hands gripped the steering wheel tightly as I rocked over the potholes on a beat-up two-lane that took me past every gas station, shoe outlet store, and fast food restaurant imaginable. The sky had turned a uniform dull white, and somehow it made the parade of suburban businesses seem especially shabby. A couple of turns took me to a very new subdivision of this old suburb, a collection of just-constructed and, to my eye, rather large houses

perched on the edge of New Jersey's great swamp. Zielinski's street
was only six houses long, and all the houses on his side backed onto
a vast expanse of grassy wetland.

Zielinski lived in a two-story Tudor-style house that took up
almost every inch of its small lot. It was spanking new. The
pavement that led to his two-car garage still had the chalky look of
just-poured concrete. I pulled up next to the black Ford Explorer
parked there. I stepped out of my car and smelled the air. A slightly
swampy odor, but not unpleasant.

I circled around to the front door, past waist-high trees that
were staked against the wind, went up the steps and rang the bell.

The man who opened the door was tall and big bellied, maybe
in his mid-forties. His tiny hazel eyes were set deep in a puffy, pale
face. His thinning brown hair hung shaggily into his eyes. He wore a
red sweatsuit with white stripes at the sides, his wide middle pulling
the suit taut at the waist.

"Hey! You must be Ruth! I'm Al," he said, thrusting his hand
toward me. He gave my hand a vigorous but clammy shake and
tugged me inside.

I stepped onto a pale blue carpet that looked and smelled like it
had just been installed. The carpet covered the stairs in front of me
and spread to my left, into a spacious living room. The walls were a
stark white. In fact everything about the place seemed sterile. It was
hard to believe a big sloppy guy like Al lived here.

Al led me into the living room. The walls were bare save for a
set of triangular frosted glass wall sconces that only added to the
room's chill. White gauze curtains covered the front windows. Al
gestured toward the floral couch, brand new and perfectly
coordinated with the carpet.

"Hey, have a seat. You want some coffee?"

I stayed standing. It seemed necessary somehow, with Al still on
his feet, shifting his weight from one leg to another. Like maybe he'd
throw me a frisbee and I had to be ready to catch.

"Sure, if you've got some ready."

"Tina!" Al yelled suddenly.

The small, birdlike woman who entered the living room was
Al's opposite in almost every way: Thin, short, her brown hair cut
into fine perfect layers, her cotton pants creased, her blouse neatly
tucked in at her slender waist. She gave me a tense smile.

"Tina, this is Ruth, the new girl the union sent," said Al. "And she'd like some coffee. Could you get that, hon?"

Tina disappeared quickly from the room. Al sat down heavily in the armchair next to me, and gestured for me to sit on the couch. I did.

Al watched me appraisingly. "So how'd you come to get this job?" he asked. "I heard you're not even on the union staff."

"No, I'm just hired for this drive. But I was a full-time organizer for the IWU years ago."

Al nodded slowly. "Who'd you organize?"

"Well, I worked with Victoria on an unsuccessful drive at an insurance company, and then I was on a team that organized a bunch of workers at a mental health clinic, and my last one was at a university where we were trying to unionize the clerical workers."

"Did you win?"

"Not that one."

Al nodded again. He was getting on my nerves. It occurred to me that I had a rollicking headache. I didn't remember drinking all that much the night before. But then my measuring stick wasn't what it used to be.

"Sorry the other people aren't here yet," Al said. "They're kind of like that."

"What do you mean?"

"You always have to, you know, corral everybody to every meeting. That's the way these people are."

"What people?" Al's phrasing made me uncomfortable, given that the workers I was about to meet were black and Latina.

Al looked slight annoyed at my cluelessness. "I'm just saying some people don't have the best work habits, you know?"

Excellent, I thought. Always good to have a core team riven by racism. I decided to change the subject. "I was really sorry to hear you got fired. How have you been holding up?"

Tina reappeared with a tray containing two coffee mugs, milk and sugar. I thanked her and then she disappeared again. I immediately brought the cup to my lips, hoping the caffeine would knock out the hangover, if that's what it was.

"It's a drag," said Al. "I been working at my brother's construction company. Got to make ends meet, you know? And I got this whole new place to pay off." He gestured to the room around us.

I nodded. "But you want to get back to Pantheon?"

"Are you kidding? That's what I do. I'm a printer. But Victoria told me there was nothing she could do about getting me reinstated till after we won the election. I mean, it's completely illegal, them firing me for trying to organize. I kept asking her about filing a charge with the National Labor Relations Board. But she said it would have to wait. It was total bullshit." Al looked at me as if daring me to argue.

It *was* odd, Victoria choosing not to challenge Al's firing. Couldn't she at least have begun the process?

"Why did Pantheon say they were firing you?" I asked.

"They said I threatened this security guard." Al shrugged his shoulders.

"Did you?"

"Sort of. But he threatened me first. Bernie Schmidt. Guy's a total thug and he hates the union. He ought to be committed. He's a danger to himself and others." Al laughed.

"Do you think Schmidt was told to provoke you so they'd have an excuse to fire you?"

"Of course," said Al. "They were just trying to screw up the organizing drive. And scare people into thinking they'd get fired if they spoke up for the union. It worked, too. And now that Victoria's been killed, you can just guess how the guys at Pantheon are feeling."

I looked at Al. "How?"

"Really scared."

"Do you think what happened to Victoria was related to Pantheon?"

Al shrugged. "But it's fucking scary, isn't it?"

"So — " I said cautiously, "it sounds like you and Victoria didn't always agree on things."

Al laughed unpleasantly. "She was a bitch on wheels. Did you talk to her about this drive before — ?"

"No, unfortunately."

"Too bad," said Al. But he looked relieved.

I tilted my head and waited for elaboration, but for once Al didn't say anything.

"And you're a pressman?" I asked.

"Head pressman on our biggest press, the Heidelberg," said Al, puffing up in his chair. "Twenty-two years on the job. When I started, Pantheon was a little print shop. Now we got over a million square feet. My web press is so big, it would hardly fit on this whole block."

The doorbell rang. Tina answered it and showed Nita Montero, Silvia Rodriguez, and Joe Dysart into the room. Al and I stood up to greet them.

Nita, a youngish woman with red lips and a perfect chignon, took my hand and said, "I heard you used to work with Victoria. I just wanted to say, we thought she was amazing. I still can't believe what happened to her." Nita's hand was delicate and cool and I could feel the hardness of the glittery rings she wore on every finger.

Silvia gave her sister a sharp glance and turned to me. She was studious-looking and perhaps a few years older than her sister. Her small squarish glasses had a faint blue tint, her nicely cut beige jacket went well with her classic brown slacks. "Thank you so much for agreeing to do this," she said as she shook my hand.

"Yeah, you are one brave woman," said Nita. "If I was you I'd run screaming."

"Nita," snapped Silvia.

Joe, standing behind Silvia, listened and said nothing. He was an older man whose short kinky hair was threaded with silver. He smiled mildly as we shook hands.

"Yeah really. Don't want to scare away the organizer," Al chortled. "Have a seat."

Nita and Silvia joined me on the couch while Joe took a straight-backed chair.

Who wants coffee?" said Al. He took the orders and then yelled again for Tina. When she didn't reappear immediately, Al looked perturbed and said, "Be right back."

The instant he was out of the room Nita said, "So you must not have known about Al."

I looked at her, puzzled. "What?"

"Victoria didn't trust him at all. She cut him out of the campaign." Nita snugged her form-fitting red knit top down over her black pants.

"Nita, shut up," said Silvia.

Nita glared at her sister. "Don't you think she needs to know what's going on?"

"Why did Victoria cut him out?" I asked the sisters.

"She said he was divisive — that he didn't get along well with people," said Nita said. "And god knows that's the truth."

"Nita — " Silvia said, shaking her head.

"*What?*" Nita screeched.

"Look, maybe we can discuss this later," I said, glancing at the door that Al would be reentering any minute. "So tell me," I said, turning to Joe, "what's your job at Pantheon?"

Joe smiled sadly, as if he felt very sorry for me. That made two of us. "I'm a second pressman."

"And Nita and I work in the bindery," said Silvia.

"It's a bitch," exclaimed Nita. "It's super repetitive. Like I work on the collator machine. You just do the same motion over and over again. Boring!"

"It was always boring," said Silvia. "But then about a year ago, they laid off about ninety people and sped everything up. And then the job got really hard. We can hardly stand at the end of the day."

"Pantheon really wasn't a bad place to work till then," said Nita. "The Maloney brothers — they didn't bother us all that much. But then there were the layoffs. And they hired this guy Toro. And since then, everything keeps getting worse and worse."

Al returned and handed people their mugs.

"So who got laid off?" I asked.

"It was the new hires," said Al. "Since we moved into the new plant five years ago, we got three new magazine accounts. They kept hiring more and more people. And then all the sudden, they started laying the new people off."

"Did you lose some of those new accounts? Why the sudden cutback?"

"No, we still got the magazines to print, just fewer people to do it," said Al.

"And so you've got a speedup," I said, looking at Silvia.

"Oh, yeah," Al said. "This guy Toro, he got them to set up quotas. They had supervisors going after people for too much sick time, they fired people they said weren't productive enough — "

"They put us on this committee to figure out how to increase efficiency," Nita broke in. "But by the time they did that, we hated them so much the last thing we wanted to do was help them — "

"I know how much a productive pressman can turn out," Al boomed. "If you worked as fast as they told you to, you'd die of a heart attack."

As Al talked, Nita and Silvia looked at him with the same irritated expression on their faces — lips pressed together, brows creased. Joe wasn't exactly smiling either.

"And that's why we started to think about a union," said Nita.

Al shot Nita a look. "I started talking about it right after the layoffs. Victoria didn't come in till about four months ago. In March."

"And then – oh my god!" Nita made a stop signal with her manicured hand. "When we started to get serious about the union, Toro got really scary. And the Maloneys do whatever he says. Now it's almost impossible to talk to people about the union at work."

"Have you been visiting people at home?" I looked straight at Joe, hoping he'd respond.

"Of course!" said Al. "I mean, that's the only way we're going to talk to them. You think we can organize people on the plant floor?"

Silvia shook her head. "Actually we had to cut way back on the house visits. Mainly we do calls now. If we visit somebody, the next day the person gets called into a one-on-one meeting with management."

"So now people just hate seeing us come up to their house," Nita added. "Really makes you feel popular, you know?" She delicately smoothed back her hair.

"The one-on-ones are horrible," said Silvia. "My boss cornered me about two weeks ago and told me that if the union comes in, the plant will close down, and then I'm going to default on my mortgage. I mean, he's telling me I won't be able to afford my son's epilepsy medication. How does he know about that? These Toro people do a lot of research."

"They lean right into your face and talk about being loyal," said Nita. "They say if you have such issues with the job, why work here – you know? It's a threat." Nita made a shuddering motion and her dangly earrings rattled.

"And then when Victoria, uh, died — " Silvia was interrupted by a ringing cell phone in the black canvas bag by her chair. She quickly extracted the tiny phone.

"What is it, Pablo?" she said, turning away from us. "No, I told them they could watch that. What? I told you I'd be home by six."

Nita turned to me and whispered, "Her stupid husband. He can't take care of the kids for five minutes without having some kind of problem."

"Pablo, I said it would be okay! I'll see you at six." Silvia ended the connection with a beep. She looked over at Nita and rolled her eyes. "Sorry," she said, turning to me. "My husband was trying to get the kids to change the channel."

"Silvia's got three kids," said Nita. "Jessica, Eddie, and her husband Pablo."

I smiled and turned to Joe. "How much support do you think the union has at this point?"

Al started to open his mouth, then clapped it shut when I gave him a hard glare.

"Well, we got seventy-four percent of people to sign cards at the beginning," said Joe. "You know, I work the lobster shift – eleven p.m. to seven a.m. – and we used to have at least that much support on my shift. But I'd say we'd be lucky to still have fifty percent." Joe spoke slowly, in a smooth, quiet voice. I wondered if he was from the south. But nowhere near West Virginia, where we had a twang that turned around and slapped you in the face. My accent had been so distracting to people that I'd erased all but traces of it from my speech.

"Are you keeping a tally?"

"Victoria had that," said Al.

"You're saying only Victoria knew what the tally was?" I glanced at Silvia for confirmation.

"Every once in a while she'd give us an update," supplied Silvia.

"She tried to keep us in the dark, is what it was," said Al. Nita and Silvia looked at him with disgust.

I stood up and turned to the four workers. "Look, you guys. What you're telling me about the Maloneys makes me think we should try to get a meeting with them. Maybe we can persuade them to reconsider how they're handling this."

"Yeah, good luck with that," said Al.

"Victoria already tried that," said Silvia. "They wouldn't talk to her."

"The person Victoria always went to was Larry Lemke, the human resources director," said Nita. "They talked all the time."

I looked at Nita. "She met with this guy Lemke by herself? Without any of you present?"

Nita gave me a confused look. "Yeah," she said.

"Well, if we had a meeting with the Maloneys, I'd want you guys to come along. You're the ones who work there. You're the ones who'll lead the union if we win."

Nita looked at Silvia. Then they both looked at Joe, who said nothing.

"That's not the way Victoria did it," said Silvia.

"Yeah, I mean, she's the expert. Was," said Nita. "And you are too," she added quickly, flushing.

"Hey, I'm up for it," said Al.

"Look," said Nita, her eyes narrowing on me, "I don't know if you know this, but Al was fired for threatening a security guard. They hate him. I don't want to go into a face-to-face meeting with the owners and *Al*! I mean, I *need* this job."

Al glowered at Nita.

"Well, maybe Al can't be part of this delegation," I said, ignoring Al's outraged countenance. "Maybe this time it's Nita, Joe, Silvia, and me." I looked around the group. Al was scowling and Silvia and Nita were wringing their hands. Joe didn't exactly look happy.

I took a deep breath. Okay. F.H. Toro had apparently taken control of the plant and was terrorizing workers into submission. Victoria had excised the lead organizer from the campaign and excluded the rest of the committee from meetings with management. The plant's key organizers apparently hated each other. And the union had assigned one lonely organizer to this major campaign, and that organizer was me — a shell of a woman whose own best friends didn't think she was up to the job. In sum, the situation was what we labor movement people sometimes call a fucking disaster.

CHAPTER 6

I did not get run over by a truck on my way back to Brooklyn, but I might as well have. I was hungry, thirsty, I needed a shower, and I was pretty sure that if I didn't have a drink in the next hour I was going to develop a case of the DTs. My eyes were dry and my skin itched. But the worst of it was my brain, which had been busily constructing vivid disaster scenarios ever since I'd left Zielinski's house. I was convinced that this campaign wasn't just going to ruin me, it was going to get me killed. Or, even worse, get someone else killed.

My premonitions of doom weren't helping the campaign. I commanded myself to make my mind go blank. Of course, a blank mind never won a union campaign either. But it was better than a full-scale self-assault.

And so my brain was on autopilot as I steered the Dodge into its small dark hideaway, got out, locked the battered garage door, and headed home.

My house still smelled stale. I dropped my bag on the floor and proceeded immediately to the liquor cabinet. When Franklin, seeking attention, blocked my way to the kitchen, I had to resist the urge to kick him out of the way. "Move, kitty," I muttered as I stepped over him.

One sip of my icy scotch and I returned to my resting state – gloomy but not homicidal. I even petted the cat before collapsing on the couch and pulling out my cell phone.

There were two messages, one from my niece Liz, the other from John Beck. Both instructed me to call them.

As Liz's phone rang, I vowed to maintain a steely will on the question of a visit. If today demonstrated anything, it was that I was in no position to entertain unstable houseguests.

"Hello?" yelled Liz. A steady roar in the background was punctuated by happy screams and laughs. Was my niece at a roller rink?

"Liz, it's Ruth."

"Oh hi!" Liz chirped. "How are you?"

"Fine," I said slowly. "I wanted to talk to you about –"

"Yeah, Dad told me you weren't so hot on a visit," Liz broke in.

"I'm sorry Liz. It's just a really bad time."

"Why?" she asked bluntly.

"Because I'm just starting a big campaign," I said. Plus, I thought, I'm suicidally depressed and may need to be hospitalized soon for alcohol addiction.

"But Aunt Ruth, I'm so *tired* of being here in Yuppieville." She drew out the word "tired" until it sounded like a form of torture.

"Well then get your own place," I said. I took a fat slurp of scotch and petted Franklin again. Hey. I could be firm when I had to be.

"I can't. I'm broke."

I sighed. Maybe Thomas and his wife Deborah had cut off the money supply.

"So then I guess you'll just have to stay there," I said cruelly.

"I can't. They told me I had to get out by the end of last week."

Oh. So they were cutting off the money supply *and* the free rent.

"I guess they want you to get a job," I suggested.

"Yeah. And that's just what I was thinking I could do," said Liz, her voice growing animated.

"Err, okay — "

"I thought maybe I could work for you!" Liz burst out.

I swallowed. "Liz, I love you, but that's not a good idea. Besides, I'm not paid enough to afford an assistant."

"But look. I'll just work for room and board. I always wanted to know more about your work and everything — "

"Liz — "

"Please Aunt Ruth? *Please?* I promise I won't complain at all. I'll just help. Couldn't you use help with this — whatever it was you said you were doing? Campaign?"

What a pushover I was. Within five minutes, it was settled: My niece would be arriving just as soon as she could get her stuff packed. However, her tenure would be brief – she'd stay only for the campaign. Seventeen days. I could manage that. Possibly.

Having screwed up one call, I went on to the next. Beck answered his cell from home. Or at least that's what I assumed when I heard him closing a door after I'd said hello. It must be hard, I thought, keeping up with your girlfriend and your ex while living with your wife. Still. I was grateful to have someone who would listen to my tale of woe.

"So what happened?" Beck asked without preface.

"Disaster," I replied. I gave Beck a quick summary of my meeting with the Pantheon workers. "The thing I can't figure out is why Victoria axed Zielinski," I wound up. "I mean, the guy obviously lacks social skills — "

"Sounds like a real boor," Beck offered.

"Right. But Victoria must've had a better reason for ousting him than that. This is the guy who started the drive. We need him on that organizing committee — him and about ten other people. I mean, we barely even have a quorum. Victoria must have had some other angle, because she sure wasn't pinning her hopes on a rank-and-file committee."

"Like what?"

I shrugged. "I don't know. Some leverage against the company."

"Victoria did have a knack for collecting useful information. Or maybe she'd already gotten something. Maybe it was so good they had to kill her."

"Thanks for that, Beck. Very helpful."

"Well, all the more reason you need to find out what it was."

"Yeah. I know. I'm going to take a look at her files tomorrow."

"Good. Let me know if you see anything I can use."

"You got the go-ahead for a story?"

"Yep. I'm trying for an interview with Sam Maloney tomorrow."

"Tell me how that goes, because we're going to try for a sit-down with the brothers. Maybe get them to ease up a little."

"I'll keep you posted. And by the way, you think you could set me up to interview a couple of the organizing committee members?"

"I'll ask. But you realize they may not be too eager to criticize the company in print. Right now, anyway."

"If you'd give it a try, I'd appreciate it. And, umm, it looks like Yvette's going to be shadowing me on this one, so she'll probably be coming out there with me."

"Oh, okay," I said casually. Sure. I was really looking forward to meeting Yvette.

I went into the kitchen, washed my hands and splashed cold water on my face. Then I poured myself another glass of scotch, which I carried outside. It was just after six p.m. and the evening was balmy.

"Ruth?" I heard Sandy call from her front stoop. "Come on over."

I carried my drink down the sidewalk a few feet. Sandy was sitting on a middle step, smoothing lotion on her calves. Franklin was lying flat on his side at her feet, looking suspiciously contented.

"Did he just eat a bird?" I asked as I sat down on the step next to Sandy.

Sandy looked down at Franklin and wrinkled her nose. "Probably."

I took a sip of my drink while Sandy eyed me disapprovingly. I scanned the area under Sandy's little Japanese maple for a bird carcass.

"Well, I did it," I announced after a moment.

Sandy snapped the lid closed on her lotion and glanced at me with a trace of alarm. "What?"

"I said yes to Liz. She's going to be my so-called assistant on the campaign."

"Ruth!"

"What?"

"You're going to have her work on the organizing drive? It's dangerous!"

"I know. But she talked me into it."

Sandy sighed. "You are incorrigible."

"I thought you'd be happy I invited her to stay with me."

"Where's she going to sleep?"

"Sofabed?" I suggested.

Sandy wagged her index finger. "Bad idea. Remember the last visit?"

"Good point." The year before, Liz had dropped in for a little visit that had turned into two and a half weeks. She'd slept on the sofabed next to my desk. Liz liked to stay out all night partying and return home just when I was ready to start work. Needless to say, the sofabed arrangement had produced much irritation.

"What about that little room you have upstairs?" Sandy asked.

I looked at her. "What room?"

"That little room," Sandy repeated impatiently.

"Are you talking about the closet?"

"Well, you use it for a closet, but it's big enough for a single bed and a dresser."

"You want me to buy a single bed and a dresser so my niece can visit for a couple weeks?"

"I have a little rollaway bed upstairs. You can borrow it."

I sighed and sipped the last of my scotch noncommittally.

"I do think it's good you're letting Liz stay with you." Sandy slipped off her sandal and stroked Franklin with her bare foot. Her toenails were painted the same brilliant red as her fingernails and her feet were smooth in a way mine hadn't been since I was a teenager.

"Can you remind me why you think it's good?"

"Because you need to let someone into your life. You're always holding people at a distance."

I looked at Sandy, annoyed. "That is so untrue. I don't hold you at a distance."

"Okay, but name one other person you let be close to you."

I looked down at my feet. "John Beck?"

Sandy snorted. "A case in point. The one person you want to be close to is a guy who is incapable of being close to anyone."

"Here we go with the pop psychology."

"Well, then name another person."

"Sandy, I let people get close to me all the time. Every time I do a new campaign I make new friends."

Sandy clucked. "And now that you've lost your job, name one person you'll still be in touch with."

"Lots of people!" I exclaimed, although in truth I couldn't think of any.

At three-fifteen the next morning, I woke up with a start, my damp sheets coiled around my legs. A nightmare. The nightmare starred Al Zielinski as a bartender at a dingy New Jersey tavern. I ordered a neat scotch and then watched Zielinski fill half the glass with water. "You just watered down my scotch!" I protested. Zielinski plopped the drink down in front of me and said, "I don't know what you're talking about." Instead of protesting further, I gulped down the drink and requested another. Then I heard a heavy clunk beside me, and turned to see that the woman on the stool next to mine had passed out, her forehead pressed to the bar. It took me a moment to realize that this drooling wino was my niece.

I didn't need a nightmare to tell me that I didn't trust Zielinski and that I was a bad influence on Liz. And that I wanted a drink.

I climbed out of bed and crept down the hall to the room I used as a storage closet. I flipped on the switch. Charming. The room's bare overhead bulb shone a harsh light on a collection of dusty items. These included an ironing board – why, I couldn't say, since I hadn't ironed anything since the 1990s — two leaning towers of books and stacks of winter clothes encased in a half dozen big plastic tubs I'd bought for the purpose about eight years ago. It also featured a chair whose cane seat had split (oh, yes, I would repair that – when hell froze over) and three file boxes containing tax records and warranties. My trusty 1993 Raleigh five-speed bike sat dejected in the corner, its tires long since deflated.

I spent the next two hours sweating and pounding around the house in my underwear. I moved the bike, the ironing board, and the boxes and tubs down to my dank basement. I swept the dust bunnies off the scarred oak plank floor and even dusted the sill of the room's one long narrow window, which looked into my tiny backyard, now faintly lit with dawn's early light.

I surveyed the room. It was at last bare, except for an old toy chest, which I thought Liz could set her suitcase on, and a pudgy little clay lamp I'd found on a shelf downstairs. Nothing adorned the off-white walls. The room looked like a prison cell with a window. Oh well, at least it had a door. In a couple of hours Sandy and I would lug her spare bed into the room.

The whole process left me feeling like I needed a valium. What was I thinking, allowing Liz to visit at a time like this? I was in no condition to entertain, let alone nurture anyone. And why was I rearranging furniture for what was supposed to be a brief visit?

Downstairs, Franklin, Mr. Pathos, was meowing to be let out. I stumbled down the stairs.

"What?" I said to Franklin when I got to the front door. Franklin looked up at me with big round eyes. I opened the door and Franklin sauntered out. I decided to follow him. The stone walk felt icy under my feet, but the air that fluttered through the sycamore trees was deliciously mild. A faint pink light washed the leaves. The nearly full moon hung low and milky in the western sky. For some reason, it made me think of John Beck.

I went back inside, leaving Franklin to pee in the begonias. I switched on my computer and went to my mailbox. I had a message from Beck. "Got interview with Sam Maloney ten a.m.," it said tersely. "Here's stuff on Pantheon." I clicked on the attachments — four articles from New Jersey papers. I sent them to the printer.

While the pages were churning out, I went to the Star's website and to staff bios. There was Beck. I smiled at his photo, like an imbecile. Then, of course, I scrolled down to Yvette Ramirez. I clicked on her name, and up came a photo. Glossy black hair, big dark eyes with long lashes, a brilliant smile. Gorgeous. And about sixteen.

I sighed and went to open the door for Franklin, who trotted in with an air of accomplishment. Well, that made one of us.

CHAPTER 7

Be a freelance labor strategist and see the world. My job had taken me to places I would never have known existed. For instance, here I was, hanging around in a deserted public parking lot in downtown Bloomson, New Jersey, a town carved out of a swamp. Bloomson, New Jersey – who knew?

I pondered these and other existential thoughts as I stood under my umbrella in a gentle drizzle, watching for Joe Dysart's brown Ford Taurus. Joe was going to introduce me to the Pantheon Organizing Committee office, where I hoped to god I'd find some clue about how Victoria had planned to win the election, now just sixteen days away.

I saw Joe's aging Taurus pull slowly into the lot. I waved.

Joe parked at the nearest spot and climbed out of the car. He was wearing a pair of neat but loose-cut chinos, a windbreaker, and a Nets cap.

"Hey, sorry I'm late. I had to drop my wife and my daughter off at the mall. The office is over this way a few blocks." Joe pointed, and we started walking down a busy avenue.

"What's your wife's name?"

"Beany – her real name's Beatrice. And my daughter's name is Alicia. She's grown up — just home for the summer."

"College?"

"Yep. Next year we'll have three college grads in the family — Alicia, Dana, and Vanessa."

"That's impressive, Joe."

"A BA is probably no big deal to you, but in my family it's real important." Joe turned to me. "I bet you have a Ph.D. or something."

I shook my head. "I'm a college dropout."

"Really?"

"Uh huh. In your family, you've got upward mobility. I've got a downward mobility thing going on."

Joe smiled, his face turned toward the sidewalk in front of us. I realized Joe didn't smile often. Usually he seemed enveloped in a quiet sadness.

"Has your family been okay with the organizing drive?" I asked. "Must be hard with all the time you spend on it."

"Oh, yes, Beany is all for it," said Joe. "Through thick and thin."

"It has been on the thick side, hasn't it? Not easy to keep your spirits up."

Joe looked down at his crepe-soled shoes. "Well, I guess I'm hoping for the best but –" his voice drifted off.

"Expecting the worst?"

Joe nodded.

"Well, you never know," I said, which was about as much optimism as I could muster.

A couple minutes later, we stopped abruptly in front of a fried chicken place in a sagging two-story wood frame building. The dull patter of rain on Mr. Chicken's tattered and filthy awning didn't add to its charm.

"Hungry?" I asked.

Joe smiled again. It was funny. Every time Joe smiled, it made me feel better. "Nah, the office is up here." He gestured at an unmarked metal door painted maroon and decorated with silver spray-painted graffiti tags. They signified something to someone, but nothing to me.

Joe and I climbed the high-rising steps, which were slanted with wear and covered with dirty linoleum. At the top were two doors. One said "restroom" and the other had an index card taped on the front that said "POC," for Pantheon Organizing Committee. Joe turned the key in the lock and then gave me a funny look. He turned the key back the other way.

"What?"

"I guess somebody forgot to lock the door last night."

"Does that happen often?"

"First time I've noticed it. And I'm usually the first one here in the morning. I like to stop by after I get done with my shift at seven."

Joe opened the door wide and we stepped into a shabby rectangular room. A pair of windows faced south onto the street. The sloping wide-planked pine floor had seen a lot of abuse. There were six desks, three hugging one wall, and three hugging the other. All six had phones and three had computers. A long narrow conference table occupied the center of the room with a half dozen folding chairs assembled around it.

The room had not a single adornment, only piles of papers and newspapers and folders stacked on desks. It was dim and gray and smelled like frying fat. It was hard to imagine the luxurious Victoria occupying this tatty office, yet I knew that rooms like this had been the center of her world for nearly two decades.

"Good enough," I said. The only problem I had with the room was the absence of people in it. This close to an election, it should have been roaring with life. Also, there was no chugging coffeemaker.

"What's the coffee situation?"

Joe pointed to a coffee machine in the corner. "Want me to make some?"

"No, just show me where the coffee is and I'll do it. Want a cup?"

Joe shook his head. "Beany's making me cut back."

I spotted the mini-fridge and opened it. The only thing inside was a bag of grocery store coffee, a quart of whole milk, and a slice of pizza, congealed. I snagged the coffee. "She worried about your health?"

"Worried about how I can't sleep."

I ducked out and filled the pot with water from the bathroom sink.

"Is it helping – cutting back on coffee?" I asked when I came back into the room.

"No," said Joe.

I smiled as I flipped the switch on the coffeemaker and turned back to Joe. "Where did Victoria sit?"

"Right over there." Joe gestured to a desk by the window. "I went through all her stuff yesterday. She didn't keep a lot of paper, but I found a couple of files that I figured you'd want to look at. They're sitting right on top there."

"Perfect." I went back to the refrigerator, sniffed the carton of milk and decided against it. Then I sneaked a cup of coffee out of the machine. I felt I was doing a pretty good job so far of impersonating a fully functional person. But that didn't mean I could do without major doses of stimulants and depressants to prop me up as needed.

Joe settled himself at a desk across the room.

I sat down in Victoria's rolling desk chair and switched on the crane lamp that hung over the desk, casting a circle of light onto the folders — and something else that made my heart stop. It was a cup. Victoria's favorite cup. I hadn't seen it in fifteen years, but the cup was unforgettable, with its dreamy, pearly outer surface and its midnight blue interior. I gently picked the cup up by its stem-like handle, afraid to even breathe on this fragile jewel-like object that had somehow survived all these years, had survived even Victoria herself. Along the edge of the cup, I saw the imprint of Victoria's delicate, rose-colored lipstick, so intimate and so familiar. I carefully put the cup down in an empty drawer. Was it really possible that my old colleague was dead?

I turned to the folders. The one on top had a tab that said, "House Visits" and a flattened bottom that made me think it had once contained a fat stack of paper. But it looked oddly insubstantial now. I opened it. It was empty. I looked over at Joe, who was bent over his own desk, writing in a notebook.

I picked up the second folder, labeled "Lists." It too, was empty.

The third folder had a number written on its tab: "7-29." When I opened the folder, a thin piece of glossy paper fell out. It looked like a page ripped from a magazine. I picked up the page and flipped it over. It was porn – a photo of a nude woman tied to a chair and blindfolded.

"Joe?" I said.

"Yeah?" Joe looked up at me.

"There's nothing in these files. Except this." I held up the picture.

Joe stared. He crossed the room and sat down in the chair next to me, pulling a pair of reading glasses out of his shirt pocket.

"I don't think Victoria was keeping this here for her own enjoyment," I said as Joe studied the photo.

"No," he said. "Where was it?"

I handed him the folder that said 7-29. "Was this one of the folders you left me?"

Joe looked at the tab. "No, I've never seen that before."

"Do you know what it means? 7-29?"

Joe shook his head.

"Maybe it's a date. That would be two days ago – July 29. That was…" I stopped in mid-sentence.

Joe nodded. "The day Victoria died."

I squinted down at the tab. The number had been written with a blue
fountain pen in a small neat hand, just like on the other folders.
Victoria's favorite kind of pen, Victoria's handwriting. I exhaled and
let my shoulders relax. "You know, this isn't as creepy as it seems.
I'm pretty sure Victoria wrote this. And it's not like she knew she
would be murdered on that date. It's just some file she was
keeping."

Joe thought for a moment. "It's funny, though. Because I'm not
aware that she was planning anything special on that day. Can I see
the other folders?"

I handed them over.

"What happened to the papers? Did they fall out? Are they on
her desk somewhere?"

I shook my head and gestured at the pristine desktop. "Were
those the files you'd set out for me?"

"Yeah," said Joe. "And if we can't find them, we're in trouble.
Those two folders had our most important information in them —
one was Victoria's notes from all our house visits and the other had a
list she'd gotten of Pantheon employees with notes about how we
thought they'd vote."

"Uh oh," I said. "Was it the Excelsior list?" The Excelsior list is
the employee roster a company is required to provide to the union
once an NLRB election is set.

Joe shook his head. "Victoria said she didn't trust the official list.
Somehow she got her hands on this other one that the company
uses."

I nodded. It sounded like Victoria. "Do we still have the official
Excelsior list?"

"I got a copy right here in my bag."

"Well, that's something." I looked down at the empty folders Joe
had put back on the desk.

"I never should have just left those things out here. Especially
after what happened to Victoria — "

I put a hand on Joe's forearm. "Joe, this wasn't your fault. Is it
possible someone on the organizing committee took the stuff home?"

Joe shook his head. "Everybody knew how important those
documents were. They wouldn't just disappear with them."

I nodded. "Plus, the door was unlocked and somebody left that
god-awful picture behind. It seems like this was a break-in."

"I feel terrible about this."

"Hey. You weren't the one who stole the info."

What I didn't say was that if the information in those files was now in the hands of our opposition, which it almost surely was, we really were in trouble. "You think some of this stuff might be backed up on the computer?"

Joe shook his head. "Victoria said it wasn't safe to keep sensitive things on the computer. She said people could hack into it. She didn't even like to write stuff down. Except what was in there." He gestured forlornly toward the empty files.

I sat back in the chair. "Well, we'll just have to reconstruct it, Joe. Most of the information is probably in people's heads."

"Not that list. And she only had one copy. She said she didn't want it to fall into the wrong hands." Joe's hands hung limply between his knees.

"What about the house visit notes? What was in them?"

Joe put an elbow on the desk. "Every time we came back from a house visit, we always talked to Victoria. She called it debriefing. We'd tell her what we'd learned about the person, and she'd write it down. She tried to get us to notice everything. She said you never knew what little piece of information we'd need to turn a person around."

"Like what?"

"Well, mostly it was just about how the person felt about the union. But some of it was real personal. You know, sometimes when you sit down with people and you get talking about why they might want a union or be afraid of it — well, a lot of things come up."

"Like…" I prompted again.

Joe tilted his face upwards and scratched his jaw. "Well, there was a fellow I talked to about a week ago. He's got a custody battle going on over his son. And he was telling me how he couldn't afford to get real active with the union because if he got fired like Al, he'd lose his case."

"And that was in Victoria's file?"

Joe nodded.

Ah. How like Victoria, I thought. Even in her early days, she'd been a big one for collecting personal details. Information was power, after all, and Victoria was always hungry for that.

I looked up from my ruminations to see Joe looking at me. "I guess probably the company has those files now," he said.

"It's possible," I conceded. "Or Toro. But do you think they would've left something like this behind?" I asked, holding up the odious photograph.

"Hard to imagine it," said Joe.

I looked at the photo again, focusing on the face of the woman. I'd never seen her before, but with her wavy blonde hair and fine features, she bore a reasonable resemblance to Victoria.

I spent much of the rest of the day scouring the office for some clue about Victoria's strategy in this organizing campaign. I'd gone through every folder on her computer and every damn drawer in the office. But the only sign I'd found of her, besides the cup, was a magical scarf she'd left on a hook, a storm of rich colors on silk, with delicately fringed black edges. It carried the scent of Victoria's dusky perfume. The fragrance summoned up Victoria's presence so strongly, I could almost see her sitting across from me, her legs crossed, one heel released from her 3-inch pumps.

I myself was not wearing designer shoes. I had on a pair of clunky sandals whose heels had lost a half-inch of height to the sidewalks of New York. It was two-thirty. Joe had gone home to sleep and the first shift workers didn't get off till three. Not that I had any reason to believe they would come here when they were done. So it was just me and that other very palpable presence in the office, chicken fat. The smell of the chicken bubbling in grease downstairs at Mr. Chicken had caused me to lose my appetite. For food. I had been thinking about booze for over an hour.

I could hardly believe that just days before, I'd been free to drink as much as I wanted, whenever I wanted. I could sleep till noon and be rude and grumpy to everyone. Hadn't I given up on the labor movement? So what was I doing sitting by myself in this sticky office, inhaling chicken grease? Now I had to live through sixteen days of misery, after which I would suffer one of the worst losses of my so-called career.

"Screw it," I declared. I grabbed my bag and ran down the stairs, my sandals clattering. On the street, it was hot and noisy. And the chicken grease smell was, if possible, even stronger. Hadn't I seen a neon sign with the magical word "liquor" on it somewhere on that next block? I hurried down the street, staring down cars that tried to turn into the pedestrian crosswalk and giving the finger to one driver who leered at me from the window of his Chevy

Suburban. I'd been so sweet and upbeat with Joe. Now I was back to being a cranky bitch.

At last, the "liquor" sign came into view. Just seeing the word made me feel better. I opened the door and found myself in an enclosed foyer that couldn't have accommodated more than four people. I was separated from the store by a wall of cloudy plexiglass. I could just make out the rows of bottles arrayed tantalizingly on the other side, safely out of reach from armed robbers. A sliding window in the plexiglass panel allowed for the exchange of bottles and money.

A man approached from inside the store, slid open the panel and asked if he could help me. I certainly hoped so. I asked for a bottle of my favorite brand of scotch and a shot glass.

Within minutes, I was heading back to the office, toting my bottle of relief and the little shot glass with the Puerto Rican flag on it, feeling guilty anticipation. When I got back to the still deserted office, I washed up. Then I sat down at my desk, opened the bottle of scotch and filled the shot glass to the brim. I held up the glass and admired the amber liquid for a minute before I downed half the contents. I moaned with pleasure and set the glass back down on the desk. One section of my brain was registering concern about this behavior – I'd never drunk on the job before, at least not alone and in the middle of the day. But that was just one section. The rest of my brain was starting to feel kind of mellow.

The phone rang. I instinctively shoved the bottle of scotch into the bottom drawer of the desk. I picked up the receiver and said, "Union." Almost every job I ever had, I could safely answer the phone by saying "union."

"Is this the notorious Ruth Reid?" said John Beck.

"Hey," I said, slightly breathless from all the excitement with the scotch bottle. "How'd you get this number?"

Beck laughed. "I'm a reporter. I can be very enterprising."

I leaned back further and put my feet on the desk. I realized I was pathetically grateful to hear Beck's voice. I held up the glass again. One more swallow left. "So did you interview Sam Maloney this morning?"

"Yep."

"And how was it?"

"I kind of liked the guy," said Beck. "One of those tough old coots, a self-made man. He really doesn't want me to write a story about the drive. He seemed almost scared about it. So I took advantage of him."

"What do you mean?"

"I told him the company would look a hell of a lot better in any story if it seemed like it was playing fair, trying to work things out. So I think you should call him — he might just go for that meeting you said you wanted."

I smiled. "Beck, you're an angel."

"I wouldn't go that far."

"Did he say anything about Victoria?"

"No, except that he was shocked and that it had nothing to do with Pantheon."

"Did you get anything out of him on what set off all the layoffs?"

"Nada. He gave me this vague line about competition and financial pressure. And the more I pressed him, the more nervous he got. I mean, he *really* doesn't want to talk about it."

"Damn. Well, thanks for the info."

"That's okay. And in fact, I need something in return."

In the old days, that would've been a suggestive remark. But now that Yvette was in the picture, I knew it wasn't. "What?" I asked.

"You were going to find me a worker to interview, remember?"

"Oh yeah. I'll get right on it." I looked around the vacant office. Probably Beck thought I was surrounded by worker-organizers right now. Little did he know it was just me, the chicken grease, and that seductive little bottle of booze.

After I hung up with Beck, I called Pantheon Printing. Beck must have primed Maloney well, because not only did I get through to him immediately, but he and his brother were indeed prepared to meet with Silvia, Nita, Joe, and me at the plant the next morning. Unfortunately Maloney also insisted that F.H. Toro would attend — as well as Pantheon's director of human resources, Larry Lemke. I had hoped to get the two brothers alone, since I doubted a professional union-buster would be amenable to the workers' arguments. But Maloney made it clear it was a take-it-or-leave-it offer, so I took it.

I hung up the phone feeling a small measure of accomplishment. I wasn't expecting miracles out of the meeting, but it was a step forward.

After that, I left messages for Silvia, Nita, and Joe telling them about the meeting and asking if they would be willing to do an interview with Beck. Then I sat back in my chair and read the articles Beck had sent me about Pantheon.

By evening, my bad humor had returned. Silvia, Nita, Joe and I had arranged by phone to meet in the Pantheon parking lot the next morning. The sisters declined the interview with Beck, fearing repercussions, but Joe had said yes without hesitation. Still, I was disappointed that none of the workers had managed to drag themselves into the office after work. I was considering seeking solace from that particular desk drawer when the phone rang.

"Ruth?"

"Sandy? I didn't know you had this number."

"I got it from Tommy," Sandy said gravely.

"Is something wrong? Is Franklin sick?"

"Franklin's fine. It's your niece I'm calling about."

"Liz? Don't tell me she showed up already."

"She got here about an hour ago. I'm glad she made it here alive. She's higher than a kite."

"Oh, Christ. What's she on?"

"I don't know, but it's making her pretty happy. She's in the other room singing to herself right now."

"You think she should go to the emergency room?"

"No, it's not that bad. I'll just give her some of this special tea I have and see if that doesn't calm her down some."

Special tea? Great. I looked at my watch. It was a little after seven.

"Okay, look — I should be there in an hour and a half."

"Uhh, and Ruth? Would you mind picking some Pepto-Bismol on your way home?"

"Umm, what do we need that for?"

"You'll see," said Sandy ominously.

I double-parked the Dodge in front of the pharmacy around the corner from my house, put the emergency flashers on, and dashed into the store. When I came out, the driver I'd blocked in was on her high horse.

"Is this your car? You're illegally parked!" she shrieked.

"Okay, okay, I'm moving it," I muttered as I climbed into the Dodge and flung the bottle of pink goo onto the passenger seat. As if half the cars in my neighborhood weren't double-parked.

I pulled out onto the street. Wasn't this great? My spoiled junky of a niece had arrived at my doorstep days before one of the toughest elections I'd ever attempted. I parked the car and walked back to the house, clutching a stack of files and the Pepto-Bismol. My porch light was on, and the light in my office too. I grabbed a handful of mail from my mailbox and went inside.

"Sandy? Liz?" I called into the front room. I put the files and the mail down on my desk and the Pepto-Bismol in the bathroom.

Sandy suddenly appeared at the bathroom door. "She's upstairs," she whispered. "She puked her guts out and after that she seemed much more alert."

"I'll bet," I said.

"So we talked for awhile and then I put her to bed."

I smiled at Sandy. "You're a mensch."

Sandy nodded at this obvious truth.

After Sandy went home, I crept up the stairs. The door to the little room I'd set up for Liz was open a crack. I peeked in. A small mountain of worn luggage was piled into a corner of the room. And on the bed, tucked securely under the covers, was my nineteen-year old niece, her mass of red hair streaming out over the pillow, drooling gently onto the sheet. Kind of like in my dream.

CHAPTER 8

The next morning, Liz was still out cold and snoring like a lumberjack. I decided to let her sleep in while I went to Jersey for the big meeting.

But first I'd have to get dressed. A major clothing crisis ensued. I had absolutely nothing to wear to a meeting with the boss. I had possessed an appropriate suit until a few months before, when a gull had pooped on it during picket duty with the dishwashers. Dry cleaning had done little to erase the hideous stain.

After trying on and flinging to the floor every piece of once presentable apparel I owned, I went over to Sandy's. Sandy was taller than me, but about the same width. However, she was a much flashier dresser.

As a result, an hour and a half later as I approached the Pantheon Printing plant, I looked down with trepidation at the fuchsia silk blazer over the low-cut camisole and the matching flippy skirt. I looked like a high-priced escort. Well, at least higher than average.

I was not prepared for the scale of the Pantheon facility. It was a bright blue metal monstrosity that extended for a half mile in all directions, rising above an ocean of acid green swamp grass. You had to wonder about things like flooding and mold. Behind the plant at least a dozen rigs were pulled up to loading bays. The whole area was devoid of people, except the single uniformed guard who sat on a stool in the booth at the entrance to the parking area. He asked for ID, I gave it to him, he checked a list and then directed me to the visitors section of the parking lot.

Silvia and Nita were huddled together a few yards away from the plant entrance. Both were dressed to the nines, Silvia in a conservative cream-colored suit, and Nita in a tight pink number that was almost as shameless as mine. I brushed my hands over my skirt to clear away any crumbs from the scone I'd eaten for breakfast. This had the added benefit of wiping the sweat from my palms. My t-strap heels clacked on the pavement. I was cute enough, but I wasn't as cute as Victoria. And I definitely wasn't as fearless.

"Hi," said Nita. "We're terrified."

I laughed.

"Nervous anyway," said Silvia.

"I'm just glad Bernie Schmidt isn't here," said Nita. "He likes to hang out right over there and scare people." She gestured to the sidewalk that ringed the building.

I looked at my watch and scanned the road for Joe, just as his Taurus rounded the curve. He parked and walked over to us looking distinctly uncomfortable in a brown gabardine suit that I doubted he'd worn more than twice in his life.

The front reception area was clean, modern and blindingly bright, but not in the least glitzy. I walked up to the front desk and told one of the two women stationed there that we had an appointment with Sam Maloney. She made a call, and a man in a blue uniform appeared and motioned us to follow him down the hall that led from the reception area. He looked barely past his teens, and his nametag said "Kelly." I wondered what he got paid. I glanced at my companions, who were all staring grimly at the hallway before them, like prisoners approaching the electric chair.

I walked slowly and peered around. I'd hoped to get a look at the block-long press Al Zielinski had bragged about. Instead, Kelly led us down a bland carpeted hallway with abstract pictures on the wall. As we walked on, the rhythmic thundering I'd detected in the lobby grew louder. I could feel it through my shoes. I looked at Joe. He nodded and said softly, "Presses."

Kelly stopped in front of a polished wood door and rapped on it, then opened the door and gestured us through.

Inside, four men sat at a glossy conference table, each with a brand-new yellow pad and a glass of water before him. Everyone stood up to greet us except one man, a wiry senior citizen, surely one of the Maloney brothers. He looked up at us sourly, then looked back down at his yellow pad.

Another scrawny senior citizen in an inexpensive brown suit was the first to extend his hand. "I'm Sam Maloney, and this is my brother Oscar," he said in a raspy tenor, gesturing to the seated man. Oscar looked up and drew his bushy eyebrows together. Oscar's features were heavier than his brother's, and he looked grumpy. Sam had a small upturned nose and a wide mouth that gave him an impish appearance.

"This," Sam went on, "is Mr. Toro, our management consultant." Toro wore a dark olive shirt and black sport jacket. If there had been one more button open on the shirt, we probably would've seen an impressive display of black hair on that big buff chest of his.

"And this is Larry Lemke from Human Relations," Sam concluded quickly. Lemke smiled at me with perfectly even, white teeth. He looked to be in his early fifties with a neatly clipped mustache and a haircut that would have made a newscaster proud — only the color was an unnaturally flat black. He wore aviator glasses and a black turtleneck sweater under a tweedy jacket, like a seventies swinger. Maybe that was his golden age.

I turned to my three companions, who stood like statues behind me.

"You might know Joe Dysart, Silvia Rodriguez, and Nita Montero? And I'm Ruth Reid."

There were handshakes all around. Toro was one of those men who try to convince you of their power and virility with their bone-crunching grip. I had a big strong pair of hands myself. Even so, it was hard not to wince.

Finally, we all sat down, with the workers and me occupying the chairs closest to the door, as if preparing for a hasty getaway.

Sam cleared his throat. "First off I want to say we were all very sorry to hear the news about Ms. Shales. We may not have liked what she was trying to do here, but we feel terrible about her death."

"Thank you," I said. I narrowed my eyes at Sam, searching for any hint of insincerity on his face. I saw none.

"And I recognize that things have been a little tense here ever since — well, especially since Ms. Shales died," Sam went on. "I thought if we talked face-to-face we might be able to calm things down a little."

Oscar, who had been staring impatiently at his brother, now looked up from his notepad. "So Ms. Reid," he said, "as we told your predecessor, our workers are not interested in joining a union. I understand that your union may be desperately looking for new recruits, but you're not going to find them here."

I glanced at Joe, Silvia and Nita, who all sat paralyzed in their seats.

"Surely you know that seventy-four percent of your employees signed union cards," I said.

"Well, that's — " Larry Lemke began. But Toro cut him off.

"You people misrepresented yourselves," Toro boomed. Lemke watched him with unmistakable loathing. "You told them that the union was going to get everybody a huge pay increase. Whoa, big surprise — they say they want a union."

"That's not a crazy thing to expect. Union workers do have higher wages."

"If you had any idea of Pantheon's financial situation, you'd know that pay increases are not an option," said Toro.

"Are you saying that Pantheon is in some kind of financial crisis?" I looked at Sam.

Sam glanced at his brother before answering. "Well, not exactly. But we've been forced to do some belt tightening lately — "

"If our employees had any idea what your union is really about, they'd chase you off the property," Oscar snapped, his pale face turning pink.

Silvia fidgeted in her chair. I raised my eyebrows at her, encouraging her to speak. Her eyes widened and she took a deep breath, but then Sam spoke.

"See, we've always cared about our workers here." Sam splayed the fingers of both hands and looked down at them. The hands were ropey with age and had a faint tremor, but still looked strong. He had a narrow gold wedding band on his left ring finger. His index finger had an arthritic knob at the middle joint. "We built this place up from a little copy shop, and we couldn't have done it without our employees. Some of them have been here over twenty years. We've always tried to treat people right. I used to be a printer myself. I did the printing, and Oscar here did the business side."

"We all know that, Mr. Maloney," Silvia put in, her voice wobbling. "And it's true that at one time this was a great place to work. But ever since the layoffs — "

"If you think we're going to let a union take over this company after all these years you are very mistaken," Oscar cut in. He looked only at me as he bellowed, "We've earned the right to run this place a thousand times over. Do you realize that when we started out, Sam and I went eleven years without a vacation? We gave our employees health insurance before we even got it for ourselves! Who are you to walk in here and tell us about how our workers feel!"

"Sir, with all respect," said Joe in a measured voice, "it was the workers who started this drive. All we want is fair rules — "

"Oh, yes, we've all heard that before," said Toro. "Do you know what the union really wants, Mr. Dysart? Your money. They've got a huge organization to support, all those union bosses. And the Industrial Workers Union is in financial trouble. They're hoping *you* can help bail them out. Did Ms. Reid here tell you about that?"

I looked at Joe, wishing that I had briefed him about the state of the IWU.

But Joe's eyes were on Toro. "Well, I can't see that you're one to talk. You've got an organization to support too, don't you?" he said.

Toro was caught off guard and sat speechless for a second. I noticed that Larry Lemke was smiling at Toro's discombobulation.

"The point is," Oscar said, "this company can't afford a union. That's what you people need to understand."

"We can negotiate about wages," I said. "But in fact the biggest issue right now is that people are feeling harassed and overworked." I glanced at Nita and nodded slightly.

"Like, uh, the timed bathroom breaks and the machines running too fast — " said Nita.

"Her union is just trying to get more dues-paying members," Toro roared, pointing at me. "The higher the wages, the more dues she'll get! Did you know that Ms. Montero? Mr. Dysart? You are being duped!"

Nita flexed her jaw in fury.

"Now hold on a minute — " Larry Lemke began.

"Be quiet, Larry," snapped Oscar. "Toro's right. They are being duped."

"No sir, I don't believe I am," said Joe.

I looked over at Larry Lemke, who had just had his head chopped off for the second time. Lemke's face was expressionless, as if his soul had gone into hiding.

I cleared my throat. "Mr. Maloney, thousands of companies in this country operate successfully with unions. You seem to have an equation in your mind that a union equals the end of Pantheon Printing — "

"It does!" yelled Oscar.

"I wasn't finished," I said. "A majority of the workers here have expressed their desire for a union, and in this country, it's their legal right to have one if they want it. The tactics you're using here are illegal under the National Labor Relations Act. You don't have a legal right to harass and intimidate workers to keep them from joining a union. And if you don't stop it, you'll be facing a court injunction."

This was mostly bluff. There was a chance that we could get a judge to issue an injunction against the Maloneys for blocking the organizing drive. But it was almost nil.

"What a load of crap!" Toro yelled. "Nobody's harassing and intimidating anyone. This is what they do, these union people. They're always crying foul and trying to turn that into the main issue."

Nita suddenly sprang up from her chair. "You're standing here and telling us there's no harassment and intimidation at Pantheon?" she cried, pointing at Toro. We all turned and stared at this petite woman with a voice that could break glass. "Isn't that what they hired you people for? Isn't that all you've done since you came to Pantheon? Stop lying!" Nita sat back down but continued to fix Toro with a murderous stare.

Nita's fury had blown like a gale through the room, and for a moment, there was silence.

"You've fired a key union organizer," I said. "You must know that's illegal, and it's a red flag for an injunction."

Oscar and Sam glanced at each other, but said nothing. HR director Larry Lemke finally saw his opening.

"Look, Ms. Reid," Lemke said in a reasonable tone. "Of course it's in your interest to defend workers who have been union activists. But for the safety of all the Pantheon workers, we had to dismiss Mr. Zielinski. He threatened one of our security personnel."

Sam turned to me. "We *had* to fire him," he said.

"There's no point to this discussion," Oscar said irritably.

"Look," I said, facing Sam and Oscar. "I understand your concern about the effect a union would have on the company you worked so hard to build. But the path you're taking now is what's going to damage your company, not the union. As you said, you couldn't have built the company without these workers. But now you're alienating them. Listen to Nita."

"That's your fault," snapped Oscar.

"No, it's Mr. Toro and his people who are getting everybody angry and upset, not the union," Silvia said.

"Well, once you started the organizing drive, we had no choice but to bring in some outside experts," said Sam.

I looked at Sam. "You hired them," I said. "You can call them off." I cast a quick glance at Toro and could almost see the steam blowing out his ears. We were really making some friends here this morning.

"We wouldn't know how to deal with this union business without them," Sam said.

"This is preposterous, you trying to tell us how to run our business!" said Oscar.

I ignored Oscar and leaned toward Sam. "Yes, you *do* know how to handle this," I said, while the rest of the table leaned forward, straining to hear me. "This is not a foreign invasion. These are your own employees, and they've said they want a union. We can have an orderly election and people can decide for themselves, union or not. It would be even simpler if you would just recognize the union without an election."

Sam looked at me soberly. "We're under a lot of financial pressure here. We'll go under if this union comes in."

Next to Sam, Oscar was glowering, but said nothing. Maybe he couldn't hear what Sam and I had said – I'd noticed he wore a hearing aid. Then he started scribbling furiously on his yellow pad like an angry little gremlin.

"I think you're making the wrong choice, Mr. Maloney," I said quietly to Sam.

"It's too late to change now," said Sam. "That other girl poisoned the waters. Nothing's ever going to be the way it was before."

"What do you mean, poisoned the waters?"

Sam just looked at me. He was agitated, but at least, unlike his brother, he didn't look like he wanted to strangle me.

"Ms. Shales got into everyone's business, and that was a mistake," Oscar barked, loudly enough for the rest of the table to hear.

"That's a very dangerous thing to do. We don't recommend it," Toro said slowly, looking at me.

I stared at him. "What do you mean by that? Are you threatening me?"

Sam shot me a look of alarm. "No, Ms. Reid. No one's threatening anybody." Sam gave Toro an admonishing look.

I decided to press ahead, as hopeless as it was. "Here's a suggestion. If you're concerned that the union will put too many demands on the company financially, why don't you open your books — let everyone see what the finances are? The union isn't going to demand more money for workers than the company can afford."

"What are you *talking* about!" Oscar yelled, dropping his pen theatrically onto the table. "Our books are none of your business! This is ridiculous!" He rose from his chair to his full height of about five foot-three.

"Oscar — " said Sam. But Oscar was already storming out of the room.

Sam rose from his chair and said, "I think this meeting is over."

Toro sneered in my direction as he strode to the door, followed by Oscar and Larry Lemke. The Pantheon workers stood up, looking stunned.

Then Sam turned to me and tugged my sleeve. He was as short as his brother and weighed about a hundred and thirty pounds. "I just wanted to say that I hope you're careful. I mean, I don't approve of this union business, but if that's what you're going to do, you should stick to that and not go poking into all kinds of other things."

I stared at Sam. "Now it sounds like *you're* threatening me, Mr. Maloney. Why don't you explain what you're talking about?"

Sam shook his head and said, "Ms. Reid. Do I look like the kind of person who would hurt anyone?"

"No, but — "

Sam turned his back to me. So I left him there and followed my colleagues out of the conference room. Silvia, Nita, and Joe were already halfway down the hallway, steaming back to the lobby, in full retreat.

"Ms. Reid? Ruth?" I turned around to stare Larry Lemke in the face.

"Yes?"

"Uh, look, I'm sorry things didn't go better in there. I guess we're all under a lot of pressure, and there are obviously a lot of tensions — "

I nodded at this profound understatement.

"And I wanted to say how sorry I was to hear about Victoria's death," Lemke continued. "She was a remarkable person."

"She was," I said.

"Of course she and I were on opposite sides of the table here, but that didn't keep me from appreciating her talent. In fact, we managed to keep lines of communication open. So I wanted to make sure to get off on the right track with you." He smiled again.

"Always good to have open lines of communication," I said.

"No, I'm very serious," said Lemke, leaning closer to me and speaking more softly. "Believe it or not, until last year, we had pretty good morale around here. I have to say, I take some credit for that. So you can imagine how concerned I am about how things have been going lately."

Lemke was the picture of sincerity, his murky brown eyes even looked a little moist around the edges. I couldn't say I trusted him. But as head of personnel, he would have a great deal of information.

"I'm glad to hear that you're open to dialogue, Mr. Lemke," I said. "In fact, there are a lot of questions I'd love to ask you — "

Lemke chuckled nervously and glanced up the hallway to the conference room. "And I'd be happy to answer your questions, although right now is not a very good time. But feel free to give me a call, anytime." He pulled a business card out of his pocket and pressed it into my palm. "It's a pleasure to meet you, Ms. Reid. Your union certainly does have an attractive staff."

"Uh, thanks," I muttered as Lemke turned and opened the door to his office, directly behind him. As he stepped into the office I saw a pleasant-faced woman at the reception desk, peering out at me curiously. Then Lemke shut the door firmly behind him.

As I continued down the hall, I wondered why Lemke and his conciliatory approach were not in favor with the Maloney brothers. If I were Lemke, I'd have been revising my resume.

I stepped out of the lobby and into the parking lot. Silvia, Joe and Nita were clustered about twenty feet away.

"I couldn't believe you said those things right to Toro's face!" Silvia was saying to her sister.

"I screwed up, didn't I?" Nita asked me.

"Not at all," I said. "Now the Maloneys know how Toro is making people feel. Though you'll probably get some extra abuse from Toro now."

Nita nodded. "But in a way, it was kind of thrilling." She pulled a cigarette out of her purse and thumped the end, ignoring her sister's disapproving glare.

"How long has Lemke been so sidelined?" I asked.

"Ever since they hired Toro," said Silvia.

Joe nodded. "It was almost a year ago."

"But Lemke's been at Pantheon for ever and ever. So it's kind of weird, the way they've thrown him over," said Nita. She cupped her hand over her butane lighter to keep the flame from blowing out.

"And yet they haven't fired him," I said.

"Not yet anyway," said Nita. She gave the cigarette a furious pull.

"Would you put that damn thing out?" Silvia snapped. "I thought you said you quit."

"I absolutely have to smoke this cigarette," said Nita.

"Okay, people, watch out," said Joe suddenly, his eyes on the plant entrance. I turned around and saw a security guard who was definitely not Kelly emerging from the plant.

"That's Bernie Schmidt," Silvia said to me. Schmidt: the guy Al Zielinski had been fired over, the one Al had called "a threat to himself and others."

"I think it would be better if we went back to the office to discuss this," said Silvia. "We don't have to be back here till ten." We all nodded and scurried off to our cars.

For some reason Schmidt singled me out. He followed me to the Dodge and stepped close to me before I'd had a chance to unlock my door. Schmidt had a fleshy, sunburnt face. His short hair had gone gray and his belly bulged slightly beneath his uniform. But he still had the trunk-like neck of a bodybuilder.

"Hi," I said cheerfully.

Schmidt's face was a leathery mask. He stood by as I unlocked my car. Only as I was climbing into the driver's seat did he utter something.

"What did you say?" I asked once I'd sat down.

Schmidt leaned over the open car door and peered down at my body in a way that made me want to put the car in reverse and step on the gas.

"I said, I know who you are, Ruth Reid," Schmidt said, speaking each syllable in a slow, even monotone.

"Oh, and I know who you are. You're Bernie Schmidt," I said with a little wave. "Excuse me." I grabbed the handle and slammed the door. My heart hammered in my chest as I turned the key in the ignition, silently begging the Dodge to cooperate. It did. I put the car in reverse and squealed out of the parking lot.

CHAPTER 9

Sandy and I were in the bar section of La Cantina, our neighborhood's best Mexican restaurant. She looked like a ballerina sitting on the barstool beside me. You could have set a level along her spine and gotten a perfect reading. Her legs were crossed delicately at the ankle. She took tiny sips from her Perrier.

I, on the other hand, was slumped familiarly over my scotch, one thigh over the other, dangling one of the t-strap shoes from my toes. My feet hurt and I needed to drink a lot more than I could possibly imbibe in Sandy's presence. Liz was a half hour late.

"Don't think I don't know why you chose this restaurant," said Sandy.

I looked at her with wide eyes. "Why?"

"The bar. I certainly hope that's your last scotch tonight."

I frowned. "But it's my first one! How about a margarita with dinner?"

Sandy gave me one of her poisonous looks.

"Let me see that thing again," said Sandy. I handed her the page from the porn magazine.

"That's disgusting," she said for the second time. "And it's really scary, Ruth. What if the person who left this photo is the one who murdered Victoria?"

"Believe me, the thought has crossed my mind."

"You should tell the police."

"Probably this is just somebody trying to screw up the organizing drive." Or so I kept telling myself.

"You think this photo is supposed to look like Victoria?"

"Could be."

"Somebody must have really hated her."

"It kind of goes with the territory. I mean, even the guy who started the drive was mad at her."

"Was he mad enough to do something like this?" Sandy held the photo between her thumb and index finger like a dirty tissue.

I looked at the picture again and thought about Al. "I could maybe picture him leaving porn on Victoria's desk, but I can't believe he'd steal files that are critical to the organizing drive."

Suddenly Sandy sat up and wrinkled her nose. "Is someone smoking in here?"

I rolled my eyes and changed the subject. "Did I tell you I think Beck's got a new girlfriend? She's a rookie reporter at the Star. I'm going to meet her tomorrow."

Sandy turned to look at me. "You think he's serious about this one?"

I took a microscopic sip of the scotch. If I was only going to get one, I was prepared to ration. "Something makes me think he is."

"You know what, Ruth?" Sandy said. "Just let it go. You're too good for that man anyway."

I let out an involuntary laugh.

"What's so funny? You know, you ought to stop feeling so sorry for yourself."

I shrugged. I had to admit that it was probably good advice.

"Anyway," Sandy continued, "you just need to move on."

"What exactly does 'move on' mean? You're talking about one of my best friends."

Sandy glared at me.

"Second best," I added hastily.

Sandy sniffed, partly mollified, as she set down her Perrier. "I just think you need to get a little distance from the man."

I heaved a sigh. I didn't want to lose Beck. I didn't want to push him away.

I watched as Sandy reapplied her lipstick with utter precision. When she was done, she pressed her lips together, expertly evening out the color, a wet magenta. Then she saw something behind me and her eyes lit up. I turned around.

Liz had on a brilliant pink sleeveless T-shirt that showed off her heavily freckled arms. Her frizzy hair was like an orange halo around her gorgeous Appalachian face. I even liked the silvery glow-in-the-dark stuff she had on her eyelids. I'd have worn it myself, but unfortunately I was thirty-seven.

I gave Liz a bear hug.

"What's this?" Liz said, snatching the pornographic picture off the bar.

"Uh, nothing," I said.

Liz laughed. "God, Aunt Ruth! Have you got a secret thing for bondage?"

"Why don't we go get a table?" said Sandy as I stuffed the photo back in my bag.

We wound our way adroitly around the tables, which were about eight inches apart. All around us, diners yelled so they could be heard over the blaring Latin brass. The walls were hung with bright Mexican blankets and a giant painting of a guy who'd always looked to me like John Beck on steroids, carrying the limp but voluptuous body of some Mexican maiden. Was she dead or had she just fainted? I apologized to a couple for bumping their table. They smiled up at me, clutching their drinks tightly. I understood the impulse.

"How are you feeling?" I asked Liz once we'd settled ourselves at the table.

"Great, actually. Sandy gave me this really cool tea that just wipes out your, you know, symptoms."

"Just remember to drink a cup tonight and again tomorrow morning," Sandy advised, while I tried not to let the words "snake oil" cross my lips.

"I can't believe you gave me a whole room upstairs," Liz exclaimed. "I didn't even know that even *was* a room."

"Neither did I," I said. "Only Sandy recognized its true potential."

Sandy produced a brilliant smile.

The waitress came up and took drink orders.

"Could I have a margarita?" I asked.

"Me too!" said Liz.

Sandy gave me her nastiest stare yet this evening. It was like having dinner with your parole officer.

Of the two hours we stayed at La Cantina, one was devoted to Liz's encyclopedic review of my brother and sister-in-law's many faults and irritating qualities. I probably should have protested on their behalf. Except I agreed with almost everything Liz said. They *were* pompous and status-conscious. And boring? Completely! At least I was able to keep these opinions to myself. No point widening the family divide. Sandy stayed mostly silent, but I knew she approved of my self-restraint. I even turned down a margarita refill.

As Liz wound down, I examined the remaining veggie burrito on my plate and vowed not to eat it. I daintily wiped the edges of my mouth with my napkin.

After that, I gave Liz an overview of the Pantheon organizing drive. The tale reminded me of how hopeless the campaign was, and by the end of it, I had returned to my resting state of gloom and foreboding. And the rest of the burrito had vanished.

"I don't get it," said Liz. "Don't those bosses feel really bad about treating people like that? They must be awful people."

"They probably think they're doing the workers a favor. They're making some hard decisions, but at least they're keeping the plant open."

"Sounds like a crock to me," said Liz.

"So what's your plan once we've finished the drive?" I asked. "Are you thinking about getting a real job somewhere?"

Liz rolled her eyes. "You sound just like Thomas and Beth." Liz had taken to calling her parents by their first names, the better to patronize them.

I shrugged. "What about money?"

"Well, they're giving me a thousand a month till I figure out what I want to do."

"Oh," I said. "I thought you said you were broke."

"Well — I mean, a thousand a month? You can't live on that!"

Across the table, Sandy was shaking her head and trying to keep from clucking. Sandy believed that idle hands were the devil's workshop. Her father was a Jamaican immigrant who had worked three jobs concurrently and raised four children to adulthood before dying at the age of fifty-six. Her mother, a South Carolina native, had co-raised the family while working full-time as a licensed nurse. Sandy was no slouch herself, with a full-time administrative assistant job and a second job as a fitness trainer. If we'd won that damn union election, she probably would have been a union officer too.

Liz stretched her arms above her head and yawned. "I mean, it's hard to know what to do. Everything seems so boring."

My face suddenly flushed and I could feel a volcanic eruption coming on. "What do you mean, boring?" I burst out. "I mean, how many homeless people did you walk by on the way over here? How many people do you know who don't have health insurance? My *god*–what a luxury to think it's all boring!"

"Ruth," said Sandy.

"It's just — "

"I know," said Sandy, patting my shoulder. "So does Liz. Calm down."

I took a deep breath. Get off your high horse, Ruth, I thought. Who was I to lecture my niece? I was the one who had decided to give up any useful work so I could stay home and marinate my liver.

"I'm sorry, Liz," I said after a moment.

Liz looked back across the table at me and smiled. I did like Liz. I always had. I put my hand on my stomach. Suddenly I felt very full. The only thing I hadn't had more than enough of at this meal was margarita.

"No, no, no, " I said to the computer screen. Franklin looked at me with wide green eyes, then yawned. When I was at the computer he liked to sit on a nearby upholstered chair, depositing masses of gray hair all over it so that no one else ever wanted to sit there.

It was just after six the next morning, and I'd already gone through all of the new material Beck had emailed me on Pantheon Printing. I could detect nothing that would help us in the organizing drive. In the local papers, the Maloney brothers came off like heroes, self-made men who were now "giving back" to the community.

There'd been some controversy about the construction of their big new facility five years ago. Environmentalists had fought the plant, charging that it would damage the water-cleansing marsh. But the brothers had responded cleverly: This, they said, would be the greenest printing plant ever built. It would specialize in using post-consumer waste and would recycle all its own waste paper. It would use only environmentally friendly inks and provide hazardous waste training for all its employees. It would even set aside part of its grounds as a nature preserve.

Since the plant had been built, no one seemed to be complaining. According to a local paper, the Pantheon nature trail was a favorite outing for high school science classes. Pantheon sponsored the local peewee soccer team and gave generously to United Way. Where was the dirt?

I looked at my watch. It was time to go to New Jersey. I doubted that Liz would be accompanying me. I'd never known the woman to rise before ten.

Unbelievably, two hours later when I arrived at the Pantheon office, my niece was by my side.

"Whoa!" Liz exclaimed, after I'd ushered her in. "This place is a dump!"

"It's not that bad," I said reflexively.

"It smells like chicken fat!"

"Not really." Why had I said that? My niece arrived and suddenly I turned into a pollyanna.

I spent the next half hour explaining to Liz how she was going to help us reconstruct our tally of union supporters. She would begin with our Excelsior list, the official list of Pantheon employees eligible to vote in the union election. Then, using notes from Nita and Silvia, Liz would call our best contacts in each department, confirm the list of employees in the department and ask their estimate of who was definitely pro-union, a wobbler or undecided, or anti-union.

"Aunt Ruth, this is *shitwork!*" Liz whined when I'd finished explaining the task.

"Almost all work is shitwork," I snapped. "You think you should be exempted for some reason? Besides, putting that list together is just about the most important job there is to do. If you don't want to help, then I'll do it myself and you can just go home."

Liz looked down at the stack of paper I'd handed her and pantomimed barfing. I ignored her. The next time I looked across the room at her, she was bent over her desk, apparently hard at work. Only later did I notice that the object of her intense concentration was not the list of Pantheon employees but a clothing catalog aimed at young people with trust funds.

I was on the phone trying to sweet-talk a printer's assistant into supporting the union when I heard voices coming up the stairs. I looked at my watch. It was ten, the time when John Beck and Yvette Ramirez were to begin their interview with Joe.

Joe got up from his desk when he saw who it was. Beck, looking adorable in his sport jacket and black jeans, was beaming. And by his side — touching his side, in fact — was Yvette Ramirez. She was a glam queen all right. I'd seen Beck with other women lots of times — and it always caused a stab of jealousy, which I quickly stowed. This time was worse than usual. Beck looked so content. It was killing me.

I wound up my call and got up to greet the reporters. Beck gave me one of those socially acceptable cheek kisses, and said to Yvette, "And this is Ruth Reid, my partner in crime. And one of the best union organizers around."

I clenched my jaw and turned to Yvette. She smiled at me, displaying her brilliant white teeth.

"Hi," she said breathily as we shook hands. "John's told me all about you."

Oh really, I thought. Bet he didn't tell you about that time we got ousted from our booth at that bar in midtown for bad behavior. Or that aerobic hour in the cab coming back from JFK. Did he mention that hot sunny afternoon at the Belmont racetrack? Beck's story on the betting industry certainly was well researched.

Oh well. Just because my heart was breaking didn't mean it was Yvette's fault. And there was no question the woman was stunning, even if she seemed to me to be just this side of adolescence. Her eyes were big, and her long mascara-enhanced eyelashes made them look even bigger. Her mouth was full and lipsticked a shiny peach. Her lustrous black hair was cut to perfection. And she had the complexion of a high school sophomore, minus the pimples.

Beck was watching her every move. At least he wasn't panting.

I introduced Beck and Yvette Ramirez to Joe. And then I turned to Liz. Liz already knew John Beck, to my shame. She had caught us smooching once on my couch, and she'd been a cheerleader for the relationship ever since. When I introduced her to Yvette, Liz didn't bother hiding her lack of enthusiasm. "Hello," she said coolly.

Yvette didn't seem to notice my niece's snub. As Beck set up his tape recorder and arranged chairs around the table, Yvette played like his shadow, never moving more than six inches from his side.

"Umm, excuse me," Yvette said to me after a moment. "Could you get John a glass of water? He likes that when he's doing interviews."

"The water's in the bathroom right out there in the hall," Liz said.

"That's okay," I assured Yvette as I scurried out of the room with a paper cup.

He likes that when he's doing interviews. What crap, I thought as I filled up the cup at the bathroom sink. How many interviews had she seen John do? Two? And how many had I witnessed? Fifty?

When I got back into the office, Liz was looking at Yvette with squinting, accusatory eyes, as if preparing to spring on her. One thing about Liz, she was loyal.

Beck and Yvette were now seated at the table, side by side. If Yvette had her butt any closer to Beck's, she would have been on his lap. It wasn't as if there was a lack of space at the table.

"Oh, and you don't happen to have any coffee ready, do you?" Yvette asked in a saccharine voice as I plunked the cup of water down on the table.

"Why? Does John like coffee with his water when he's doing an interview?" The words were out of my mouth before I could stop them. Beck shot me a look.

"Oh no," Yvette tittered. "That's for me."

"It's over there, in the pot," Liz called out.

"Liz!" I scolded. "You like milk?" I asked sweetly, turning back to Yvette.

"Please," said Yvette. "And a lot of sugar."

Yeah, I bet, I thought as I rummaged around for a clean mug. The pot was almost empty, leaving Yvette with the half-burnt dregs. Too bad.

I handed Yvette the mug and went over to shut the window on the honking cars. When I turned around, I realized that Yvette was watching me surreptitiously. What exactly *had* Beck told Yvette about me? If she really did know our romantic history, then Beck had achieved a level of intimacy heretofore unknown.

Joe got off the call he'd been on and sat down at the table across from the happy couple. I decided I'd observe the interview from my desk. I'd had my fill of the John and Yvette Show. And besides, I didn't want to make Joe feel even more on stage. Not that he seemed particularly nervous.

"So Joe," said Beck. "Before I turn this thing on, I just wanted to be clear — is this on the record?"

"Oh sure," said Joe agreeably.

"Well, I just want to be sure you appreciate that it could put you in a tight spot at Pantheon."

"I know that," said Joe. He smiled softly and tilted his head at Beck, as if to say, "Let's get on with it."

Beck clicked on his tape recorder. He established that Joe was a second pressman who had worked at Pantheon for eighteen years.

When Beck asked him to describe what his job entailed, Joe got as animated as I'd ever seen him.

"So you sound like a guy who's pretty happy about his job," said Beck conversationally. "What made you want to join this campaign to organize Pantheon? Do you have previous experience with unions?"

Joe shook his head. "I hardly knew what a union was. And you're right, I thought I had it pretty good. Here I was, never got past tenth grade — and I had a decent salary, people treated me good. I always liked the lobster shift, so nice and quiet, nobody bossing you around. It was almost peaceful."

Beck leaned forward. "So what happened?"

"Everything changed a year ago."

Beck tilted his head. "Just like that?"

Joe nodded. "They started with a bunch of layoffs, and they hired this fellow Toro to figure out how to make more cuts, and after that things just got real unpleasant."

I could almost feel Beck's curiosity rising. "Any idea why the Maloneys had to cut back? Was there less work?"

Joe shook his head. "No earthly idea. We had lots of work, but they all of a sudden wanted to do it with fewer people. One minute they were happy to leave you alone to do your job, and the next minute, it seemed like they didn't trust you worth a damn."

"Was there a particular incident, something that happened to you that made you become a union supporter?"

Beck was looking for the colorful anecdote. I wasn't sure he was going to get it from Joe, who was the least talkative Pantheon worker I'd met.

Joe sat for a moment as if trying to decide whether to say what he was thinking. We waited.

"Well, I'll tell you," Joe said at last. "I don't mean to boast, but I've always been a good worker. I always came in on time, kept my mind on my work. And I got along with everybody, even management – you know what I'm saying?"

"Uh huh," said Beck, his eyes locked on Joe's.

"And then one day I had a nasty stomach virus. I came in anyway because we were printing this mailer for a real big client. And as we're doing this big run, I have to go to the bathroom about four times to throw up. Man, did I feel awful that day."

"Oh, I had something like that a couple of months ago. Yuck, " said Yvette. Beck glanced at her impatiently.

Joe nodded at Yvette. "I got over the sickness soon enough. But it turned out that was the exact day that fellow Toro was monitoring my job performance. I didn't even know he was there. They like to sneak up on you, you know?"

Beck nodded.

"So two days later, I'm feeling good again, working at my station, and Mr. Toro comes by with the shift foreman. And right in front of everybody, he gives me this lecture about how I'm not attending to my job and the poor quality of the run. And how I've got to shape up or ship out." Joe looked down at his hands.

"What did you do then?" Beck asked.

"Well," Joe said slowly, "I decided that was never going to happen to me again. The next time somebody disrespects me, I'm going to have a union behind me that's going to fight back. You understand what I'm saying?"

"Yes," said Beck.

"So I put my stock in the union. I already made up my mind, and my wife Beany's behind me a hundred percent. If we don't get the union, then I'm quitting Pantheon. And Beany and me'll just have to make do. Our daughters are almost through school, and we'll just make do."

Beck leaned back in his chair. "And that's why you don't mind going on record with this interview."

Joe nodded.

I turned away from the interview. Joe was probably in his early fifties. A black man with no diploma. His chances of ever finding a decent job after Pantheon were remote. If we lost this campaign, which seemed very likely, I'd have to live with that forever. Or at least until I killed enough brain cells to wipe out the memory.

CHAPTER 10

An hour and a half later, Beck and his delightful girlfriend left the office. Their next stop was the New Jersey Trumpet, where they would do some research on the history of Pantheon Printing. I could hear Yvette's peals of laughter as they clattered down the stairs.

"God, what a little princess," hissed Liz before the two had even exited the building.

I waited till I heard the door slam downstairs. "Well, fortunately she's Beck's girlfriend, not yours."

"Well that would make a lot more sense — she's *my* age!"

"Yeah, she does look young, doesn't she?" I said loftily.

"Aunt Ruth! She was like goo, stuck all over him. And she kept bossing you around."

I glanced over at Joe, who was on the phone across the room. "You know Liz, John Beck is married. And I broke up with him months ago."

"So what? What's he doing with *her*?"

"You know what I want to know?"

"What?" Liz leaned toward me conspiratorially.

"How's that list coming along?"

"Oh," said Liz, leaning back again. "It's coming."

"Any departments you've finished that I could take a look at?"

"Not yet."

Why did I bother? My niece was a pro at work avoidance, a master of evading the demands of authority. She'd spent her life with two controlling assholes, and now she was turning me into one.

"Look. Either do the job or give it back to me, okay? We need this thing done."

"Okay, okay, okay," said Liz as she pulled the stack of paper out from the netherworld of her desk.

What this drive needed most, besides a more competent organizer, was an active and enlarged organizing committee. But we had one big fat obstacle in our way. His name was Al Zielinski.

Just before noon, Joe Dysart and I left the office for the Broadway Diner, where we planned to discuss the Zielinski issue with Nita and Silvia. We had exactly fifty minutes, since the sisters were on lunch break.

The Broadway Diner was located beside a strip mall a few blocks from our office. It was a classic roadside eatery, with pale green padded booths along the walls, tables in the middle, a big salad bar, modern chandelier lights, pictures of nothing in particular in soothing pastel shades, and dessert cases containing towers of rotating chiffon pies, chocolate cakes and every other imaginable treat, probably none of them very good.

The menu item that interested me most was the beer, featured prominently in the beverages section. With herculean resolve, I decided on iced tea instead.

"So," I said, after we'd ordered. "I want to talk about two issues – what to do about Al's job and what to do about Al's role in the organizing drive."

Nita, Silvia and Joe all nodded and looked at me expectantly. I had the sudden impulse to stop the pretense of brisk competence and tell them they were going to have to find someone else to lead them to victory.

Instead I took a deep breath and soldiered on. "Al was supposedly fired for threatening the security guard Bernie Schmidt. Did anyone see him do this?"

"I did," said Joe.

"What happened?"

Joe waited while the waitress put our drinks on the table. When she whisked away again, he said, "Well, Al was handing out leaflets about the union. Schmidt told him he had to leave. And when Al didn't leave, Schmidt acted like he was going to hit Al. And then Al acted like he was going to hit back. So a bunch of us went over there and got between them. And then Al threatened Schmidt."

"You remember what he said exactly?"

"He said, 'I'm going to kill you, you Nazi son-of-a-bitch,'" quoted Joe. Several people nearby turned to look at us, even though Joe had spoken quietly – as though their ears were programmed to pick up the word "Nazi."

"And Al was fired after that?"

"Yep, a few days later."

"You know what was strange about that?" said Silvia. "Al had said threatening things to Schmidt before — and so had about fifty other workers. Schmidt taunts people. He eggs them on, and then they respond. But nobody was ever fired for it until Al."

Silvia's observation gave credence to the idea that Al had been fired because of his role in the organizing campaign. But it didn't prove anything. And "everybody else was doing it" was hardly an argument we could mount in Al's defense.

"This leafleting Al was doing — was it in a work area or during work time?"

"No, this was between shifts, outside the door," said Joe.

"Then it was protected activity," I said. "The company had no right to stop Al from leafleting."

I looked around the table. "It sounds to me like Al's rights were violated. I think he was fired for leading an organizing drive. And I think we should get ready to file an NLRB charge against the company to get him reinstated."

Suddenly, Silvia beamed. So did Nita. Even Joe cracked a smile. I smiled too. Here were three people who had been personally insulted by Al, who really didn't like the guy. And yet couldn't help wanting to defend him against an injustice.

"However," I added, "I don't think we should actually file the NLRB charge until after the election. We should just start the process — alert the union attorney and begin taking testimony. If it turns out we can get Al's job back as part of our negotiations for the first contract, we'll drop the charge. But if we can't get him back that way, we'll try the NLRB." I didn't mention that we could also pursue the charge if the union drive failed — the most likely scenario.

"Great!" said Nita. "And what's the NLRB?"

"It's the National Labor Relations Board. Labor 101!" said Silvia.

"How am I supposed to know that?" snapped Nita.

Our meals arrived and for a moment our table was silent except for the clatter of utensils.

"I feel so much better now," announced Nita a few minutes later, as she daintily wiped her manicured hands with a napkin. "After Al got fired Victoria wouldn't lift a finger for him. It felt wrong."

I leaned back in my chair. "I'm still confused about how Al got thrown off the organizing committee. Was it Victoria's decision alone? Didn't she consult with you guys?"

Silvia shook her head. "Nope. One day she came into the office and told us she was taking Al off the committee because she thought he was a — a liability, is the word she used."

"She said he was turning the blacks and Latinos against the union," added Nita.

"Did you agree with her about that?"

Nita thought for a moment. "Pretty much."

"You saw how he was at that meeting," said Silvia. "But I've got to admit that Al has a lot of allies in the plant, even now."

Joe nodded. "I know a lot of white guys who'd be against the union if it weren't for Al. He worked real hard to get some of those printers on our side."

"But you think that other people are against the union because of Al?" I asked.

"Probably," said Silvia.

"Definitely," said Nita. "That's what Victoria thought."

Silvia was leaning back in her chair, her arms crossed over her crisp sleeveless blouse. "Even so, I'm not sure that's the real reason she got rid of Al."

I looked at Silvia. "What do you mean?"

"Well, all this happened about two months into the campaign. Victoria already knew what Al was about. She knew what was good and what was bad about him — "

"And then all of a sudden, boom!" said Nita, snapping her fingers, jangling the stack of silver bangles on her wrist. "He's got to go!"

"What do you think, Joe?" I asked.

"I guess I had the same feeling, that something turned Victoria against Al all of a sudden. But Victoria and Al never exactly saw eye to eye."

"That's an understatement," said Nita. "Victoria knew what she wanted to do with the drive, and Al kept getting in her way."

"Al couldn't stand Victoria either," Silvia put in. "He thought she was bossy, that she just waltzed in and took over the drive he started."

There was almost surely an element of truth in Al's perception. I'd always thought Victoria had a high-handed style. Victoria and Al on the same campaign. I was glad I had missed the drama.

"Al never hinted at some other reason Victoria cut him out?" I asked.

"No," said Silvia. "He's not the kind of guy who tells you everything that's on his mind. Or at least he's not going to tell people like us."

Hmm. Al was secretive, and Victoria was dead. That made it damn hard to figure out what had happened between the two of them.

"Did you agree with Victoria's decision to cut Al from the committee?" I asked, looking at Joe, Nita, and Silvia in turn. I took another bite of my sandwich.

Silvia was the first to begin shaking her head. It was slow and almost imperceptible at first, but it was a shake. Then the other two joined her. They were doing it again — coming to the defense of their co-worker, despite everything.

I put my napkin on my plate. "Do you think there's any chance that Al could change?"

Nita, Silvia and Joe looked at each other, this time with expressions of extreme doubt on their faces.

I laughed. "Well, if we told him that he could only rejoin the committee if he worked on his behavior?"

Now the expression on Nita's face changed from doubt to something resembling nausea. "Who's 'we'?" she asked.

"Me," I replied.

"Oh," said Nita, nodding.

"I'd go for that," said Silvia.

Joe just nodded. He was even smiling faintly.

When I got back to the office, I found Liz playing solitaire on the computer. However, she had slogged through the list of press floor employees. And she'd put in calls to several printers to get their assessment of who was pro-union. "I'm waiting for call-backs!" she'd wailed when I'd asked how the solitaire game was going.

So I left Liz to finish her game and turned to my own tasks. When I first sat down, I was intensely aware of the scotch bottle in the bottom drawer. If I'd been alone in the office, I probably would've taken a hit. But my niece was sitting ten feet away. Liz knew very well that I was no saint. But taking a swig from a scotch bottle in the middle of the work day seemed a bit much.

So I tried to stamp out the vision of a brimming shot glass and went to work. First I called up Al Zielinski and asked if we could meet at his house the following morning. He sounded a little suspicious about this request, but agreed.

Then I started plowing through the list of Pantheon workers that Joe, Nita, and Silvia had given me to call – people they hoped might be willing to join the organizing committee. I invited everyone — mostly by voicemail — to a meeting the following evening at the Pantheon office.

Then I started in on the much longer list of waverers Silvia had given me — Pantheon workers she thought might go either way on the question of union. It was a good task for me at this stage. The small number of workers who were actually home and willing to talk to me gave me an earful about what a union at Pantheon ought to do. They also told me how intimidated they were by management, how confused and fearful they were about the union — and how freaked out they were by Victoria's murder.

At three-thirty, just when that miserable bottle was beginning to call to me again, I heard the unexpected sound of voices in the stairwell. It was Silvia and Nita, coming to volunteer after their exhausting shift in the bindery.

I gave the sisters a progress report and then Nita turned to her list of phone calls and Silvia sat down at the big table to open the mail. The office was hot and noisy and smelled like chicken fat, but there was a comforting, companionable feeling in the room. I sucked in some of the steamy air and looked down at my still lengthy to-call list. Then I picked up the receiver.

"Ruth?" Silvia said suddenly.

Something in her voice made me drop the receiver abruptly. "Yeah?"

"Look at this." Silvia held up a flat yellow mailing envelope. I got up and went to the table to look at it.

The document Silvia had pulled from the envelope was a familiar looking list. On the top was a yellow sticky note in which these words had been neatly printed: "I believe this is yours."

"What is it?" Nita asked, coming over.

"I know what it is," said Liz, peering over Silvia's shoulder. "It's the Excelsior list. The same one I'm working on."

"Liz, why don't you go get your list and we'll compare them," I said.

"Maybe they just lost track and sent us the Excelsior list twice by accident," said Nita.

"I don't think so." Silvia turned the envelope over. "See, there's no return address. It's not in a Pantheon envelope."

"If it were from the Human Resources Department, you'd think there'd be a cover letter," I said.

Liz came back and dropped her list onto the table.

"They look exactly the same," said Nita.

"I have a feeling they're not the same," Silvia said slowly.

I stared at Silvia. "What do you mean?"

"I think it's Victoria's list."

"The one that was stolen from here?" Nita asked.

Silvia nodded. "What else could it be?"

We all looked down again at the list, at that neat little note. *I believe this belongs to you.*

"I don't get it," said Liz. "Who would have sent it back to us?"

"No idea," said Silvia.

"Does anyone know how Victoria's list differed from the official Excelsior list?" I asked.

"I don't know, but Victoria seemed to think hers was the real one," said Silvia, gesturing toward the newly arrived list.

"And we have no idea how Victoria got the list?" I asked.

Nita and Silvia shook their heads.

It was disturbing how much information Victoria had kept from her own organizing committee. I picked up the list and leafed through it.

"She was always talking to Larry Lemke. Maybe she got him to give it to her," said Nita.

The same thought had occurred to me, given Lemke's clash with the Maloneys. But what would Lemke stand to gain by providing Victoria with such a list? It was hard to know — at least not until we learned how this list diverged from the official one.

"I think we should cross-read this list with Liz's," I said. "Read every name out loud and make sure they match. Maybe that will help us figure out who sent it and why."

"I can do that," Nita volunteered.

"Me too," said Liz.

So for the next hour and a half, the steady drone of female voices — Nita, then Liz — was the background for our phone calls.

By six o'clock, my ears were ringing. Liz and Nita had gotten over halfway through the lists before Liz announced that she was "mega-tired" and left to find the train back to New York. So far, we'd found no difference between the two lists. The minor excitement over the list's mysterious arrival hadn't managed to overcome Liz's boredom with her new job. Just as well, I thought. It wasn't like I wanted my niece to follow my lead and become a foot soldier in the perpetually losing war of labor versus management.

On the positive side, there were still a whopping three people in the office besides me – a record so far during my tenure. A printer named Juan Acevedo had arrived in the office an hour before. He told us that after Victoria's death he'd decided he really had to put his ass on the line for the union. The guy was cute as all get-out.

In fact, something about Acevedo made me think again about that damn scotch bottle. As I struggled to maintain discipline, the phone rang. I picked it up before the end of the first ring. "Union."

"Ruth."

It was Beck. Mmm, I thought. Scotch plus Beck. Even better. "What's up?" I asked.

"I think we got some good info today about Pantheon. I'm still in Bloomson. Is there a bar or someplace we could meet?"

"Ah, sure. You, me and Yvette?" Wouldn't that be nice.

"No, she had to go back and work on another story."

"Oh. Okay," I chirped. "Well, there's a place called the Pretty Pony – " I gave Beck directions, almost giddy with anticipation. I felt like a hyperactive terrier who was just about to be let out of the house after a day of confinement. I couldn't wait. How dumb was that? This was a business meeting. And the guy already had a girlfriend — not to mention a wife.

CHAPTER 11

The Pretty Pony was my favorite kind of bar, an unreconstructed working class tavern just blocks away from our office. Its modest brick front gave no indication of its cavernous interior. The lights were dim, the music funky, and the air was smoky and smelled like stale beer. The motif, of course, was horses. Framed pictures of Tennessee Walkers, Lipizzans and Clydesdales hung next to every booth. Amid the booze bottles behind the bar, a two-foot-high model horse reared. I wondered if there was a real horse anywhere within a hundred miles.

The bar was filling up with people, but Beck wasn't one of them. Not surprising, since I'd practically galloped to the bar after hanging up with him. Just as well, I thought. I can get an early start.

I picked out a table in the bar's dark interior and ordered a different brand of scotch than my usual, flinging tradition to the winds. I also ordered a vodka for Beck.

I was still depressed about the state of the organizing drive, but my day's work had made me feel that if I wasn't making progress, I was at least making an effort. And now, I was meeting Beck. Maybe he'd have some useful info for me. Maybe he'd even tell me that the thing with Yvette meant nothing.

I took a sip of scotch. My mind turned to my meeting with Al the next morning. It wasn't something to look forward to, trying to convince a bigot to change his behavior. And then, in the evening, the expanded organizing committee meeting. Scary! I looked at the scotch and realized that I really couldn't afford to get soused tonight. More than three drinks would saddle me with a hangover on a day I could ill afford one.

Beck arrived, putting his hand on my shoulder as he approached. His touch melted me, At that moment, I would have signed my life away for just one deep kiss.

But I stowed my feelings and instead looked up at him perkily and said, "Hi!"

"Hey," said Beck as he dumped about a hundred pounds of bags and equipment into the chair next to me and pulled out another chair for himself. "I am so tired of lugging that shit around. All these stupid gadgets. When I first started out all I had was this long skinny spiral thing in my back pocket."

"I remember those. They said 'Professional Reporters' Notebook' on the cover. I was so impressed."

Beck smiled at me from across the table. "You go back that far with me? Damn — that was a generation ago."

"Sad, isn't it?" I said. "By the way, that reporter friend of yours is awfully cute."

Beck beamed. The corners of his eyes crinkled. God, the guy looked happy. I should've been thrilled for him.

"A little bossy though," I added.

"Hey, is this mine?" Beck asked, spotting the vodka.

"Of course."

"How'd you know I wanted vodka?"

I looked at Beck.

"Oh. Well, I guess you *have* known me awhile. Thanks." Beck downed half the shot then set the glass down on the table with a thunk.

"So — what did you want to tell me?" I asked. I scrunched down a little over the table so I could hear what Beck was saying over Sly and the Family Stone.

"Well, I've got more questions than answers. Yvette and I scanned every story about Pantheon that the Trumpet ran over the past ten years. That huge plant of theirs, which they built five years ago — guess how much it cost?"

I shrugged.

"Over twenty million."

"Jesus Christ."

"Yeah. Because it wasn't just the building. The Trumpet quoted Sam saying they had all this outdated equipment and if they didn't upgrade, they'd go out of business."

"That makes sense," I said.

"Yeah. But this is a company whose annual gross before that was nine million. How do you think they got such a huge loan? Your average bank wouldn't want to take on that much risk."

I leaned back in my chair. "What are you saying?"

"I'm saying, I'm pretty sure there's something funky going on. And then it backfired."

"You think they had some shaky loan that went bad?"

"Seems likely. My theory is, about a year ago the loan was called in or they defaulted — or something like that. So they started cutting and speeding up — trying to squeeze out as much money as they could in a short period of time."

"Who would have made this loan?"

Beck shrugged his shoulders. "That's what I want to find out. I'm going to file a story about the organizing drive tomorrow. But it won't mention this financial stuff — I want to keep digging at that."

"Will the paper let you?"

"I think so," Beck said. "But they pulled Yvette off the story. They just assigned her to do a profile of some Latina businesswoman. They keep pigeon-holing her like that."

Pity. I looked down at my scotch, at the tiny bubbles that formed around the ice cubes. "You really like her, don't you?"

Beck just nodded, as if to say that this was a major understatement.

"I assume you guys are, uh, sleeping together," I ventured. Annoyingly, my heart was pounding hard in my chest.

"Reid!"

"Oh come on, Beck."

"Well, actually we are," he said. I could barely hear him above the rollicking jukebox.

"Oh. That's nice," I said, stung. I'd already known Beck was sleeping with the woman. So why did I feel like I'd just had my face slapped?

Beck leaned forward. "I'll always care about you, you know," Beck said. "And I'll remind you that you're the one who broke it off – twice."

"John, you're married."

Beck pulled his hand away. "I'm aware of that," he said crisply.

By the time I got home that night, it was almost midnight. The lights were on downstairs, and as I drew near I could hear the muted sounds of a reggae album I hadn't played in decades. I sighed. I was in the mood for bed, not an eighties nostalgia party.

I shoved open the front door and stepped into a solid cloud of pungent pot smoke.

"Liz!" I yelled, slamming the door behind me.

"Ruth? I'm in the kitchen."

"Christ," I muttered, dropping my bag on the desk and flipping off my sandals on my way to the kitchen.

"Hi!" Liz chirped as I stood in the doorway. She was sitting at the little formica table where I usually ate breakfast, wearing a red bandanna, a smudged white t-shirt, and a pair of exceedingly baggy shorts patterned in outsized purple lilies. A bucket of dirty water sat on the floor between her bare feet. They were filthy too.

"I've been cleaning," she announced, giving me a winning smile.

"That's not all you've been doing," I said.

"What?" Liz looked genuinely confused.

"Pot, that's what."

"Oh. Want some?"

I coughed. "No, I don't." I'd liked pot back when I had also been a cigarette smoker. But after the torture of weaning myself from tobacco, I was terrified of inhaling anything. I feared that one innocent toke would begin an inevitable slide back to a two-pack-a-day cigarette habit. Just breathing the air in the kitchen was a toke equivalent. I walked to the kitchen window and threw it open.

"Liz, I don't like drugs." I sounded like a nagging parent.

My niece had the nerve to laugh.

"What?"

"Umm, as in scotch?"

"Okay, well I do like that, but I shouldn't."

"But this is just *pot*, Aunt Ruth."

"What? You think pot is legal? If only."

"God. Since when did you become so uptight?"

"I've always been uptight about breaking the law. People like me have to be."

"Why?"

"Because I make trouble for a living, and I don't want to give anyone an excuse to go after me."

I moved into the living room, continuing my window-opening campaign. After that, I went outside and sat on the porch swing, where it smelled only faintly of burning weed. After a minute, Toots and the Maytals went silent and Liz came outside and sat next to me on the swing.

"I'm sorry. I thought you'd be glad I was cleaning the house."

"I am glad you cleaned the house, okay? I appreciate it." I looked straight ahead. I was still too pissed off to look Liz in the face.

"Okay, okay. I'm sorry. I won't do it again." Liz held her pale legs out in front of her and scissored them back and forth, as if treading water. I remembered her making precisely the same motion when she'd sat on my lap back when she was five.

"Really?" I said, turning to face her.

"Yes," said Liz, looking straight at me with eyes whose pupils were, I couldn't help noticing, greatly dilated.

"Good," I said. I put my arm around my niece and pulled her close.

I had time to gulp down over half a pot of coffee the next morning to counteract the fog in my head. Just getting to Al Zielinski's house during rush hour was going to take some mighty clear thinking on my part. I'd barely found it last time.

I spread a county map out on the kitchen table and went over my route as I pushed down my fourth cup. New Jersey was strange, the way each town faded into the next. Where I'd grown up, the villages were in hollows separated by mountains so steep you literally couldn't stand upright on them. It made you appreciate the distinctness of your community. For what that was worth.

By eight I was out of the house, leaving Liz to do her snoring and drooling routine upstairs. She'd said she would meet me at the office later. I wasn't holding my breath.

As I steered the Dodge in what I hoped was the right direction, I reviewed the things I'd heard Al Zielinski say and do, and what people had told me about him, good and bad. Probably I was naïve to give the guy another chance. I already knew he was a clod. I just wished I knew why Victoria had thrown him off the committee.

Well, I had to make my own decisions. Victoria might have had some grand plan for unionizing Pantheon. But all I had was the organizing committee, and its founding member was Al.

It took me forty minutes to get to Al's house. There was no Explorer in the driveway. Al would be at loose ends without Tina there to act as house servant. Maybe she was out bowling with the gals or taking an art history class. I hoped so.

"Hey, chief!" said Al when he opened the door. He clapped me on the shoulder and drew me into the house.

"I'd get you something, but Tina's out running errands and we're, ah, out of coffee. Unless you want a Coke or something?"

"No, I'm fine, thanks," I said. It sounded like the job of coffee-making was reserved for Tina. I couldn't imagine what it would be like to feel helpless in the face of an empty coffeepot.

Al and I each took a seat in the Zielinskis' pristine living room.

"So Al," I began, "I wanted to talk with you about your role in the organizing drive, and — "

"Yeah, let's get this out in the open," said Al. He moved forward in his chair and leaned his elbows on his knees, giving me an eager beaver look.

"I know Victoria had been relying on you less than you wanted —"

"She shut me out. I wasn't even going to committee meetings at the end. She stopped assigning me to house visits. She wanted total control over the organizing drive, like she was queen of the place — "

"I heard," I interrupted. "Why did she do that?"

Al narrowed his eyes at me. "Well, she said it was because I was racist or something."

"Uh huh."

"But that's not really why."

"Oh, no? What was the real reason?"

"Because she was a control freak! She was the big star and she knew how to do everything better than anybody else. And I wouldn't let her just take over, so she blew me off."

"Oh," I said. "But was there any particular incident that made Victoria take you off the committee? Did you guys have a big fight or something?"

Al's eyes went squinty again. "Have you been talking about me behind my back?"

I took in a breath. "Actually, Al, I have. I had to figure out what to do about you and the committee."

"Oh, so it's *your* decision? I'm the one who started this whole fucking thing!"

Al was like a teapot about to boil. I had to turn off the flame. "No, Al, it's *not* just my decision. That's why I had to consult with the other people on the organizing committee. That's why I'm consulting with you now."

"Christ. Okay, what's the verdict then, boss lady?"

"Well, let me just tell you how it looks to me, okay?"

"Whatever," growled Al.

"My impression is that you tend to dominate discussions — "

"What, you want to ice me out of the organizing drive I started just because I'm not scared to take leadership?"

"Look Al, you obviously have a lot of strengths – you're courageous, you've got a lot of drive, and you've got stamina."

Al leaned back in his chair, for once ceding the floor. If I was going to say stuff like that, he was prepared to listen.

"But I think you overdo it. You need to listen to other people's opinions more. We need to make people feel like they're invested in this thing. Because if we can't create a strong organizing committee, then we can't win this drive. And there are a lot of different people we need to bring together here. That takes a special effort, you know?"

"Oh. Okay, I get it. You're going to tow Victoria's line. I'm a big racist."

"Look, at our first meeting, you hardly gave Joe and Nita and Silvia a chance to talk."

Al rolled his eyes toward the ceiling. "Well, even if I do tend to talk a lot, it doesn't mean it's because I'm a racist. I mean, is that what this drive is to you? Some kind of liberal civil rights thing? I started this stupid campaign, and I did it because I wanted a union, not the fucking NAACP."

"Okay, Al, here's what I propose. We'll bring you back into the organizing committee. We'll also get ready to file a complaint with the NLRB. If we can't negotiate your job back after we win the election, then we'll file a charge. But you've got to agree that you'll try to work on these problems — to try and listen to other people on the organizing committee and in the plant."

Al just stared at me. I couldn't gauge his expression.

I took a deep breath and gave it one more shot. "See, I understand you're fighting to win. But look at it this way – you're not going to get there by yourself. You can only get there by relying on everyone else. You've got to fight to get other people power, not just yourself. You know what I mean?"

Al continued to stare at me through his murky hazel eyes. "You know what?" he said finally. "You're almost as bad as Victoria. Fuck you. Fuck you and get the fuck out of my house."

CHAPTER 12

That went well, I thought as I drove back to the office. It was all I could do not to pull over at the Pretty Pony. If I hadn't had the big meeting that evening, I would have.

It was noon by the time I dragged myself up the squeaking stairs to the office, scrabbling around in my bag for the office keys. I figured Joe would've gone home to bed by now, so I'd be back to working alone.

But when I got to the landing, I found the office door had been propped open. Silvia, Juan Acevedo, and Joe were on the phone. And there, unbelievably, was Liz sitting next to Nita at the big table, cross-reading the lists. Wow. Five people at the office in the middle of the day. And one of them was my niece. Actually working.

"Hey!" I announced to the room. Everybody nodded or smiled, except Juan, who winked.

"How's it going?" I asked Liz and Nita as I put my bag down and pulled out my chair.

"We haven't found anything," Liz said irritably.

"And I can only stay another half hour," said Nita.

"How was the meeting with Al?" Silvia asked when she'd gotten off the phone.

"He told me to get the fuck out of his house."

"You're kidding," said Silvia.

"What an ass!" said Nita.

"Does this mean our whole deal with him is off?" asked Silvia.

I shrugged. "As of now it is."

Everyone turned back to their work while I examined the coffee pot. We were down to the dregs again, just like the stuff I'd served Yvette yesterday. I took the coffee pot into the bathroom and refilled it.

When I returned to the office, Liz was talking excitedly. "No. There's no Timothy Beatty on this list!" she was saying.

"Let me see." Nita leaned over Liz's list and ran her index finger down it. "There *isn't*," she said, turning to me.

"Let's keep going through the shipping department," Liz said.

Five minutes later we had learned that there were five shipping department employees whose names appeared on what we now thought of as Victoria's list, but not on the official Excelsior list.

"And look at this!" said Nita pointing at another spot on the list. "They all have the same start date — February 22!"

"Could it possibly be a clerical error?" Juan asked.

"I don't know," I said. "We need to find out if these people really work at Pantheon or not. Do we have any friends in the shipping department we could call? Maybe somebody on the lobster shift who's off work now?" We all looked over at Joe, the only lobster shift worker in the room.

"I could give Ernie Black a call," he said.

Nita gave Joe the names in question and we all watched as Joe picked up the phone.

When Ernie got on the line, Joe explained our finding. Then he read off the names.

"Are you sure?" said Joe. He looked up at us and shook his head. "Could you have missed them? Could they maybe work in some other part of the department?" Joe listened for a while longer, then he thanked Ernie and hung up.

"He doesn't know those guys and he says he's sure he would if they'd worked in his department since February."

"Even if they weren't on the lobster?" I asked.

Joe nodded. "Ernie says they've been checking every new employee to make sure somebody asks them about the union."

"I don't get it," said Liz.

"Me neither," said Nita.

"And there's something else," said Joe. "He said Victoria already asked him about these guys. She called him up a couple weeks ago."

"So it *was* Victoria's list!" said Nita.

"It's like somebody knew it was stolen and wanted to return it to us," said Silvia.

"Victoria should have told us about this," said Nita. "She kept it to herself for two weeks?"

I leaned back against the table. "What was happening at Pantheon back in February when these guys were supposedly hired? Had you guys started organizing?"

"We were just starting to talk about it. We hadn't called the union yet," said Nita. "Why?"

"I'm just wondering if putting those additional payroll was related to the organizing drive. If those people were on the Excelsior list, I'd guess that the company was padding the personnel list with people who would vote no. It's been known to happen."

"Oh," said Silvia, drawing out the syllable. "I think that would've been too early."

"Plus," I said, "they're not on the list of union voters. So what good would that do?"

"But you think it's possible Pantheon was trying to steal the election?" Liz asked. Her face and neck were splotched with pink. That's what happens when we Reids get even a little excited.

"It's possible," I said.

"But – what would that mean for the organizing drive and everything?"

"Well, it's bad. We don't want them to get away with it."

"What can we do about it?" Juan asked.

"We can see what the NRLB folks have to say," I said. "And in the meantime, maybe we can ask Larry Lemke about it."

"You're going to call Lemke?" asked Nita.

"If we all agree that's a good idea," I said. Everyone nodded.

"You think there are more names like this?" Liz asked.

"Maybe," I said.

"Okay, " said Liz. She glanced at Nita, who nodded. Then she hunched down over the list and started reading off names to Nita again with renewed enthusiasm.

I went back to my desk and stared at the papers before me, illuminated by the crane lamp that bent over the desk like a curious bird.

Larry Lemke. Where had I put that business card? I fished around in three compartments of my complicated backpack, finally retrieving the card the personnel director had handed me on the day of our meeting with the Maloneys. I dialed the number. A receptionist answered. Mr. Lemke, I learned, was out for the afternoon.

I hung up the phone and made a note to try Lemke again tomorrow. And that's when I noticed the little notepad sitting next to the phone on my desk — the phone that had been Victoria's until a few days ago. I hadn't touched the pad since I'd started working on the campaign.

I grabbed the thing and examined it closely under the crane lamp, looking for an impression on the top sheet. Nothing. The paper was perfectly smooth. I slapped the pad back down, feeling silly for acting like a TV detective. Then I grabbed the pad again and fanned through the sheets of paper, sending out a puff of air that blew back a few strands of my hair. I did it again, more slowly. Had I seen writing in there? I stopped and held the pad open to a page in the middle. On it, written neatly in the blue ink of a fountain pen, was a phone number. A Manhattan number. There was nothing else on the page. Or on any other page of the pad.

I pulled out the sheet and stared at it. I was almost sure the numbers were in Victoria's hand. Probably the dry cleaners or her favorite Chinese takeout place. Still, I felt a little charged up.

I punched the number into the phone and waited for one ring.

"Dellafield and Yaeger, how may I direct your call?"

"Oh," I stammered, "could you tell me what kind of company Dellafield and Yaeger is?"

There was a brief pause, in which the receptionist was probably considering how to respond to such an imbecilic question. "It's a law firm," he said flatly.

"Oh. What kind of law do you practice?"

"Listen, is there something I can help you with? If you didn't even know we were a law firm, why do you care what kind of law we practice?"

"Well, a friend of mine who died recently had your number on a piece of paper by her phone, and we've just been sorting through her things, and we wanted to make sure we're not missing anything important — "

"Oh," the man said, contrite. "Well, Dellafield and Yaeger specializes in divorce, alimony, child support, and estate law."

"Umm, no labor law?"

The man laughed, as if labor law was some kind of joke. "Nope."

"Is there any chance I could find out what business a woman named Victoria Shales was conducting with you?"

"None," the man said without hesitation.

After a round of unsuccessful wheedling, I hung up. Divorce, alimony, child support, estate law. Victoria had never been married, never had children, and as far I knew, her parents were both alive and well and not passing on any estates at the moment.

I couldn't help thinking the number was somehow related to the campaign. And yet I hadn't encountered any discussion about divorce, alimony, child support, or estate law at Pantheon Printing. I was stumped.

A gentle chicken-scented summer breeze wafted in through the front windows. I scanned the room. The first-shift workers were all here, milling around as if at a cocktail party. A few of the lobster-shift people we'd invited were still missing. I decided to delay the start of the meeting for another five minutes.

I wiped my slightly moist palms on my black knit skirt. If I'd been any more pumped up, I would have been nervous.

And then I heard raised voices in the stairwell. I went to the landing and peered down at two men arguing. Juan Acevedo and Al Zielinski.

"What's going on?" I yelled down.

Both men looked up at me.

"I thought Al was off the committee," Juan said, his face turned up to me questioningly.

"What complete bullshit!" yelled Al.

"Wait a minute." I skittered down the stairs.

"Al," I said, when I'd reached the bottom. "I told you what the committee's position was, and you rejected it."

"I *started* this fucking organizing drive," said Al, poking his thick index finger in my face.

"I know that, Al. That's why we were trying to bring you back in. We need you. But you said no."

"You gave me this little civil rights lecture — you're saying you don't want me to help organize this stupid place?"

"You know what, Al? That wasn't a little civil rights lecture. That was our best offer. Take it or leave it. I am not going to make these workers live with your rude behavior."

I stomped back up the stairs with Juan at my heels.

"Wait a minute, wait a minute," I heard Al whine below.

I stopped and turned around. "What?"

"Could I just think about it for another day?"

"Fine."

"And in the meantime, can I kind of sit in on this meeting? I want to know what's going on. I put a lot into this thing, you know."

Christ. I went upstairs and, ignoring my own best instincts, got the workers' permission for Al to "sit in," whatever that meant.

And so when the meeting began minutes later, there sat Al, a malevolent presence in a chair by the door.

Silvia opened the meeting and asked everyone around the table to introduce themselves. Of the eighteen workers, six were women. I counted six Latinos, eight whites, and four African-Americans. The ages ranged from bundler Malcolm Brown, who looked like a teenager, to the diminutive platemaker Victor Pucciello, who had to be past retirement age. Most were middle-aged, including the only white woman, Debbie Gustafson, a sales representative with poufy hair and large squarish glasses.

Liz had decided to stick around for the meeting, but stayed seated at her desk. When everyone else in the room had been introduced, Silvia smiled and pointed her out. "And this is Liz, Ruth's niece. She's been volunteering to help us here." Silvia's announcement touched off a short burst of applause and made Liz go splotchy again.

"And I think most of you have already met our new organizer, Ruth Reid," Silvia said, nodding to me to take the floor.

I sat up straighter in my chair, glancing around the table at the expectant faces.

"Well," I began, "we have a huge job in front of us. In the thirteen days we have left till the election, we've got to throw everything we have into this thing. But we've got to be smart about it. We've got to use every ounce of intelligence and energy we have if we're going to win. Now, we're going to lay some plans tonight – "

Kevin McGarry raised his hand. McGarry, a newly hired bindery worker recruited by Silvia, looked like he had just graduated from high school. Where surely he had been captain of the football team, with that bristling blond haircut and muscles bursting from his raised arm.

"Yes," I said to McGarry encouragingly.

"Hey. Thanks. Boy, are we glad you're here." McGarry grinned. "Anyway, I thought you could tell us something about your background. Somebody said you knew Victoria, but you don't really work for the union?"

"Right. Thanks for asking that." Then I explained my early work with Victoria, my years as an organizer for the IWU, and my subsequent twelve years in the state labor federation's "special projects" department. I also mentioned that I'd come from a union family in West Virginia. When I'd finished, McGarry acknowledged my reply with a boyish grin.

"But now I need to hear from you," I said. "Let's focus for a minute on the reason we want to organize Pantheon, the reason you and the people we're talking to need a union. In fact, maybe I'll just start a list up here." I went over to the pad of newsprint we'd set up on an easel near the table.

"The layoffs were bad, but ever since they hired Toro I dread going to work in the morning," began Juan Acevedo. I wrote "Toro" in large letters on the sheet of paper with a fat purple marker.

"Yeah, nobody can keep up," said a stocky young black man named Phil. "I'm a flyer – I, you know, unload the sections of the papers from the press and put them on the skids for the forklift drivers. And we're going so fast, it's like an accident waiting to happen. Just yesterday one of the forklift guys was going so fast he didn't get the load on right and he dropped the whole thing about six inches from my head."

I nodded and wrote "speedup creating unsafe conditions" as the other workers nodded at Phil sympathetically.

Silvia said she and three other operators at the perfect bind machine had developed repetitive strain injuries because the machine, which spewed out fat magazines with glued, square backs, was moving at a pace they'd never seen before.

I wrote "repetitive strain" on the paper.

Malcolm Brown told us about the forty-eight-year-old father of three who had developed two herniated disks from trying to keep up with the bundling machine and who was now afraid he'd never hold a job again. Debbie Gustafson's co-worker spent each day's allocation of timed bathroom break sobbing in a stall, afraid she would lose her job if she didn't increase her output. One organizing committee member had quit his job after he'd been bullied at a one-on-one meeting with Toro.

Pay was an issue for the people at the bottom of the scale – if you could call it a scale. As Joe Dysart said, "Once people started to speak up about what they were making, we couldn't find any logic in it." Nita, Silvia, and Joe were convinced that Pantheon's secret and uneven pay structure tended to cluster women, Latinos and blacks at the bottom of the pile.

By the end of an hour, sheets of newsprint full of purple writing covered the wall, and we were ready to pick up pitchforks and march through town.

But when I asked people to tell me the status of the organizing drive, the mood became subdued. The anger that had fueled the first push to unionize had been smothered by fear. People no one recognized loomed over workers' lunch tables and appeared nearby whenever anybody used a cell phone on break. At shift change, Bernie Schmidt created an ominous mood on the sidewalks and parking lot where workers might otherwise congregate and organize. Schmidt also hung out at the Pretty Pony, the workers' favorite bar.

"Bernie Schmidt is a one-man walking unorganizing committee," said Nita. "Every person that guy touches gets the willies about the union."

In short, it seemed there was no safe place to organize. Although the law said workers were free to talk to their co-workers about a union during "non-work hours" and in "non-work areas," Schmidt and Toro had effectively eliminated that right. And since Victoria's death, the anti-union campaign had taken on new power. Now the printing plant was soaked with fear.

"Look," I said. I stood up and clapped my hands together as if to dispel the evil spirits in the room. "We have to beat back the fear in this place. And we should create some joy."

Al, who had been completely silent till now, couldn't resist that one. "*Joy?* Give me a break."

"No, she's right," Nita said, shooting Al an irritated glance. "We've got to change the climate."

"How?" asked Joe.

I put my hands on my hips. "How about a shift change party outside the parking lot, to start with? The weather's nice, we get some food and some music — "

"Salsa!" said Nita.

We laid plans for our first party, then went on to the nuts and bolts: plans for building support in each sector of the plant, schedules for visiting potential supporters.

At about ten-thirty, the lobster shift workers left to go to work, and a half-dozen second shift workers filtered into the office. The rest of us stayed on to meet with this new crew.

By one a.m., my body was a wet dirty rag. My back hurt, my eyes stung, and my skin was clammy. But I felt strangely cheered. We had managed to redirect people's attention away from their fears and toward a positive plan. And it was a relief to concentrate on outward demons instead of my tiresome internal ones. I hadn't thought about booze in hours.

Nita, Silvia, and I collected the half-filled paper coffee cups, empty donut boxes and dirty napkins from the table. Liz was over at her desk talking with the jock Kevin McGarry. I could almost smell the pheromones from across the room.

Al shuffled up to me as I was emptying waste cans into a plastic garbage bag.

"Uh, listen," said Al. "I'm sorry about getting mad at you yesterday."

I nodded.

"And also, I was sort of thinking about what you were proposing there…You were saying you'd get the union to start work on filing a charge?"

"Yep." Nita and Silvia were still clearing the table, pretending not to listen.

"Is that offer still standing?"

"Yes, if you'll work on the stuff we talked about. But remember we won't actually file the charge unless we can't get your job back at the bargaining table. Because you've got a better shot at it that way than through the NLRB."

Al squirmed a little and then scratched his arm. "Okay," he said finally.

"Good, Al," I said, patting his giant fleshy back. "You want to help me bag up this garbage so we can go home?"

Al just barely managed to stifle a snotty retort. He silently took the garbage bag I held out for him while I berated myself for being a soft-hearted ninny.

Al, Juan, and I wrestled the bags down to the basement. When we got back up to the office, Silvia, Nita, and Liz were clustered by the front windows.

"What is it?" I asked.

"Look." Silvia pointed down to the street at a car parked just below the window.

"What?" I said again.

"See that black Jeep? That's Bernie Schmidt."

"I don't get it," I said. "It's one in the morning. What's he doing here? Is somebody paying him to do this?"

"I doubt it," said Nita. "Schmidt lives to make us miserable. It's a personal thing."

"But what's his goal?"

"He hates the whole idea of a union at Pantheon," said Silvia. "He sees it as a personal affront."

"He's just trying to scare us. He enjoys it," Nita added. "He doesn't have a life, so this is what he does for fun."

"Well, I don't like him being here," I said. "There's five of us and one of him. Why don't we tell him to go away?"

"Not a good idea," said Silvia. "The man is armed. Always."

"Where's Al?" Juan asked suddenly. I looked around the room. Al was gone.

Juan dashed out to the stairwell and then ducked back into the room. "He's going after Schmidt."

CHAPTER 13

By the time we had all tumbled down the stairs, Al was already a few yards down the sidewalk, heading away from the Jeep. I stepped over to the vehicle and peered cautiously inside. Schmidt was reclined in his seat, his eyes closed.

Down the sidewalk Al stopped at his Ford Explorer and unlocked the driver's side door. But instead of getting in, he applied another key to the steering wheel lock.

"Shit," said Nita as Al stood back up with the heavy rubber-coated metal club in his hand.

"Stop, Al!" said Juan, blocking Al's path. He grabbed Al's arm, but Al jerked free and half ran to the Jeep. All five of us ran after Al and grabbed him just as he was raising the club over Schmidt's windshield. Juan got Al's arms lowered and the rest of us helped tug him away from Schmidt's car.

When we were a few feet away, Schmidt suddenly climbed out of his Jeep. "What the hell are you people doing?" he yelled. His eyes moved to Al and the club he still held in his hand. Schmidt smirked. "Planning to fuck with me, you fat ass?"

Al tried to shrug off our collective grip, unsuccessfully. "What the hell are you doing parked in front of the union office in the middle of the night?" said Al, punching a stubby finger at Schmidt.

"Oh, so this is where the union office is. Thanks for telling me, man." Schmidt was wearing a black leather jacket with studs. It was almost funny, the way he dressed his part. In the back seat of his car, Schmidt's ratlike dog was yapping and scratching the door, as if he was itching for a fight too.

"Look, Al, let's just go home. Come on," I said.

"You don't scare me, you scumbag," said Al as he grudgingly turned away.

"Just go home, you fat shit," Schmidt threw out as he ducked back into his car. Al turned around and raised a fist at Schmidt, but kept walking away, with Juan still locked firmly onto his arm.

I let out the breath I'd been holding for about an hour. So far, I was really glad I'd welcomed Al back onto the organizing committee.

"That guy Al is a creep," said Liz from the passenger seat of the Dodge Neon.

"Yeah." I glanced into the rearview mirror as I pulled the car into the dark street. I was exhausted and wasn't looking forward to the long drive home.

"But he was the guy who started the organizing drive?"

"Uh huh."

Liz looked out the window at the passing streetlights. "If things are so bad at Pantheon, how come people don't just leave? Get another job somewhere else? That's what I'd do."

"What? At Wal-Mart? This pays a lot better. And a lot of these people like their work."

"Really? Kevin said he hates his job. He works on some machine that ties things up or something. It sounds really boring."

"Didn't he just start working there?"

"Yeah. I was asking him about those extra people we found in the shipping department, but he said he hadn't worked there long enough to know them."

"So you like him?"

Liz smiled. "Don't you think he's hot?"

"Well, he's not really my type."

"Who's your type? John Beck?"

"I guess," I said.

"I know what you're type is," said Liz.

"Who?"

"Guys who aren't available."

"I thought you liked Beck."

"I do. But he has *got* to lose that Yvette person."

"Right. Not to mention the wife."

Liz laughed. "You got to take it one step at a time, Aunt Ruth. But I know he loves you. I can tell."

I smiled. My niece was only nineteen, I told myself. What did she know?

The phone rang, jarring me awake. I squinted at the alarm clock by my bed. It was seven thirty-five. I groaned. I hadn't drunk anything the day before. So how come I had a hangover?

I fumbled with the phone on my bedside table. "Hello?" My voice came out husky and low.

"Did you see the article?"

I sat up and wiped my eyes. "Christ, Beck. Not yet."

"Sorry if I woke you. Usually you're up by now." Beck's voice was brisk, his manner wired. Like he was onto something, some new lead. It was a bit more than I could manage at the moment. My head felt heavy, and the pillow was exerting a magnetic attraction.

I cleared my throat. "We didn't get home till two last night."

"Oh. Sorry. Anyway, are you heading out to Bloomson this morning?"

"Yeah. Why?"

"Any chance you could swing by the paper on your way? I'll buy you breakfast at the coffee shop. I got the go ahead to research Pantheon for another week, and I really want to pick your brain."

Hmm. What I wanted to know was whether Yvette was part of this breakfast plan. "Oh, so the paper's going to spring for you guys to do another one, huh?"

"Not Yvette."

Ah, that was better. "Well, okay. How's nine sound?"

"Great," said Beck.

On my way back from the shower, I poked my head into Liz's room. She was turned away from the door, snoring softly. Franklin, who was sacked out near her feet, looked up at me and blinked contentedly. The room looked different. Posters, I realized. Liz had put up carnival-colored travel posters for the Dominican Republic and Mexico. Now the room really looked like Liz's. I didn't know whether to be pleased or worried.

Downstairs, I left a note telling Liz I'd meet her at the office, then stepped out into my tiny front yard. The sun had already climbed halfway up the eastern horizon, and down the block some kids were playing tag and dodging traffic. An ice cream truck tinkled a silly tune a few blocks away. In our neighborhood, no time was the wrong time for ice cream.

The Donut House was located just north of Canal, one block from the Star building. It was an old standby for Beck and me, and when I stepped into the place, with its cracked red and black linoleum and the clatter of thick white porcelain coffee cups, it summoned up years of memories of John Beck.

And there he was, waving at me from a booth in the middle of the restaurant. With a gorgeous brunette by his side. Son of a bitch!

I clamped my jaw and walked stiffly to the booth. Either Beck was a complete emotional illiterate, or he was trying to hurt my feelings. Not only was Yvette sitting next to him, she was snuggling up against him in the booth. For Christ's sake, I hadn't even had breakfast yet.

"Hi," I barked as I swung into the seat across from the lovebirds.

"Hi!" chirped Yvette. She'd made a major concession in recognition of my arrival — she had stopped nuzzling Beck's neck. But she still had her arm wrapped in his. They must have been cuddling for awhile, since their coffee cups were mostly empty.

"Hey. Thanks for meeting me," said Beck, looking uncomfortable. He untangled his arm from Yvette's and handed me the menu.

I took it and put it down in the center of the table. I'd been coming here for seventeen years, I was pretty sure I knew what was on the menu.

"So — " I said, my voice clipped. "What did you want to pick my brain about?"

"Well, uh — did you see the article?"

"I scanned it," I said. Beck and his girlfriend had a joint byline on a story on page ten headlined, "Union Drive Continues at NJ Printing Plant After Organizer's Death." The story used Victoria's murder as a lead and included one sober sounding quote from me. The best quotes were Joe Dysart's, which I was sure would generate sympathy for our cause. The Maloney brothers also had ample space to make their case.

"Did you like it?" Yvette asked raising her eyebrows in a perky way that reminded me of certain popular, smart, cute high school sophomores I'd known. And hadn't liked much.

"Sure," I said.

Yvette smiled at me, not looking terribly satisfied by my response.

The waitress appeared. It was Letty, who'd been our server since the Clinton administration. "Well hello, hon! Long time no see!" Letty said, putting her hand gently on my shoulder. She glanced at Yvette and then looked back at me with one eyebrow raised.

"I'll get your coffee right away, hon. Want a refill?" she asked Yvette.

"Oh, thanks, but I'm just going," Yvette said. "I've got a hearing at City Hall."

Tragic, I thought, as Yvette slid out of the booth and gave Beck a little wave.

Beck turned to me. "Sorry about that. She asked if we could have a cup of coffee before her hearing, and I couldn't say no."

Of course not.

Letty came by again and we ordered. "She was cute," Letty said to Beck, nodding toward the spot Yvette had occupied. "But Ruth is cuter." Letty winked at me and disappeared from the table.

Beck gave me a quizzical look.

"Solidarity," I said, shrugging.

"Anyway," said Beck, leaning forward on his elbows. "I want to run a theory by you."

"Okay," I said tentatively.

"That labor conference where we learned about Victoria's murder — don't you think it's strange that Victoria was going to throw away a whole afternoon and evening going to a stupid thing like that while she was in the middle of this hot organizing drive?"

"It is a little strange," I said. "Although Victoria was a bit of a self-promoter."

"A *bit*?"

"But I get your point — I mean, how much press was she going to get from being on a panel at some labor conference?"

"Exactly!" said Beck. "And yet, she took the time to call me and ask me to come to that thing."

I stared at Beck. "You didn't tell me that."

"I didn't think anything about it at first. I mean, she *was* a self-promoter. So when she left a message that I should come to this dumb conference because she was going to talk at it — I just thought she was tooting her own horn, as usual."

"What do you think now?" I asked.

We were silent as Letty set our plates down. I looked at my scrambled eggs and toast. My appetite wasn't what it should have been. I blamed Yvette.

Beck picked up his fork and dangled it over his omelet. "I think I want to find out what she was planning to say that evening."

"You have any theories?" I lifted up my toast and then suddenly put it down and stared at Beck.

"What?" he asked sharply. "What is it?"

"7/29," I said. "One of those empty folders we found said '7/29.'"

"What are you saying?"

"Maybe that's where she kept the information — whatever it was she was planning to say that night."

Beck stared at me. "Was that the folder that had the porn shot in it?"

I nodded slowly. We sat silent for a moment.

Beck leaned forward and said, "Ruth, this doesn't look good."

I stiffened. "Do you think Victoria was murdered because of this information, whatever it was?"

"I don't know. But we better find out."

I exhaled and looked down at my plate again.

"And maybe what I learn will help you out on the drive. Because it sounds like you guys are kind of floundering."

I laughed. "Victoria Shales – hot on the trail. Ruth Reid-- floundering."

"Well — " said Beck, his voice trailing off as if to say, If the shoe fits —

"So where are you going to start?" I asked.

Beck took a sip of his coffee and glanced around the room as he set it down. "I want to keep looking into how Pantheon financed that new facility. I'll go through our news services and then I'm going to start calling people up about permits and environmental impact statements and all that. Somebody has to know something. But I'd be happy to look into any other questions that come up for you guys."

I thought for a minute. "Well, here's one. Who is Toro? Where is he from? What's his history? The union's never heard of him."

Beck nodded encouragingly. "Anything else?"

"Obviously we want to know who stole those files. And what's the deal with the human resources director, Larry Lemke? Why does he seem to be on the outs with the Maloneys? And why are there five people listed as working in the shipping department that nobody's ever heard of?" I stopped and inhaled.

"You said you thought the Maloneys were packing the payroll with anti-union voters."

I shrugged. "Maybe they were trying. But these people aren't on the Excelsior list. And they came on five months ago, when the drive had barely started. Doesn't that seem strange?"

Beck frowned at me. "You've never heard anything about the Maloneys and the mob, have you?"

"The *mob*?"

"I mean, as in no-show employees. Featherbedding?"

I quickly swallowed my orange juice before I could choke on it. "Tell me you're not serious."

Beck shook his head. "Just a thought."

"I can't deal with the mob. I can hardly even deal with the employer." In fact, I can barely deal with myself, I thought.

"Never mind," said Beck. "Probably it's just the usual pre-election shenanigans."

I gave Beck an unhappy look. I looked down at my orange juice and closed my eyes, willing it to turn to scotch. But when I opened my eyes, it was just the same damn stuff.

By the time I got to the office, it was past eleven. Joe was at his desk, talking on the phone and taking notes. Liz was on the phone too. Only unlike Joe, she wasn't talking about grievance procedures. It sounded like she was talking about online dating.

I gave Liz a quick wave, sat down at my desk, and looked at my notes from the previous day, trying to ignore Liz's conversation.

"Really? Oh, I did that once!" she tittered. "Are you kidding? It lasted about ten minutes!" Liz glanced at me and then turned away. "Listen. I've got to go. So I'll see you tonight then. Awesome!"

Liz put the phone down and then turned to me. "That was a work-related call, in case you were wondering."

I shrugged. "Hey. Your phone calls are your business." I looked back down at the list I was beginning to construct.

"It really *was* work-related!" Liz cried. "It was Kevin McGarry. I was just asking him about some bindery workers that Nita wasn't sure about."

"Great."

"And — so anyway, we got talking, and so we're going to go out to dinner tonight," Liz finished hastily.

"That's nice." Liz seemed to think I was going to bite her head off any minute. Maybe I really was morphing into a nagging mom. I vowed that this would stop. I was hardly in a position to judge Liz, given that my own flaws were on grand display.

"You don't like him, do you?" Liz asked as I picked up the receiver to make my first call. I put the receiver back down.

"I did say he's not my type, but who cares? I'm not the one dating him."

Liz drew back in her chair. "I'm not *dating* him!"

I made a stop sign with my palm. "Fine. Dinner. It's your business." I started to pick up the phone again.

"Do you like Malcolm Brown better?" Liz asked.

"Malcolm Brown, the printer's assistant?"

Liz nodded. Malcolm Brown was probably twenty-three, a sweet-faced African American guy. I didn't know him very well, but I didn't have anything against him. At least he didn't seem like a high school jock.

"He seems nice," I said. "Why? Did he ask you out on a date too?"

Liz looked at me with wide eyes. "Aunt Ruth! I *said*, it's *not* a date!"

Jeez. My niece was a busy gal. I guess that's the way it was when you were gorgeous and nineteen. Kind of like Yvette, I thought.

This time I found Larry Lemke's business card next to the phone. I picked it up, thinking that maybe Liz's next project could be to start a database of Pantheon union contacts. That would give the nascent union here a running start. Of course it was ridiculously optimistic to hope that we would actually get a local union established at Pantheon. Even if we won the election, we had nearly even odds of never getting a first contract. I tried not to think that far ahead.

The administrative assistant in Lemke's office put me right through.

"Larry Lemke here." There was that oily voice again. The guy hardly had to say a word to rub me the wrong way.

"Hello, Mr. Lemke, it's Ruth Reid, from the union."

There was a second's pause. Then I heard a click.

"Mr. Lemke? Hello?" I put the receiver down and looked over at Joe.

Joe chuckled. "He didn't just hang up on you, did he?"

I looked at the receiver in awe. "I think he did."

"Maybe the phone's not working right."

I picked up the receiver, heard the dial tone, then hung up again. "That guy is really weird, isn't he?"

Joe shrugged. "I don't know him too well. Victoria was the one who talked to him. It seemed like he bent over backwards for her. I can't see why he'd hang up on you."

I shook my head.

"You were calling him about those extra employees?"

I nodded. "And I thought I'd also tell him we're planning to file an Unfair Labor Practices charge over Al's firing. See if that will get Pantheon to take Al back."

"You think it will?"

"No, but we have to try. But if the guy won't even talk to me –"

The phone rang.

"Union," I said into the receiver.

"Ms. Reid?"

"Mr. Lemke?"

"Listen, I'm sorry about that aborted phone call just now." Lemke let out a nervous laugh that had not a shred of humor in it. "But listen, I wanted to talk with you about a couple of things. Can you meet me at the Broadway Diner around twelve-thirty? I thought we could talk over lunch."

"Umm, hold on." I clapped my palm over the receiver and said to Joe, "Any chance you can you go with me to meet Lemke at the Broadway Diner in a half hour?"

Joe looked surprised, but nodded.

"Okay. I'll bring Joe Dysart with me," I said into the phone.

"I don't want to meet with Mr. Dysart. I only want to meet with you."

"Well that won't be possible, Mr. Lemke."

"I met with Victoria alone all the time," said Lemke, his voice rising.

"Well, I'm not Victoria."

"Look, Ms. Reid, these are issues — "

"Is it about the workers at Pantheon? Because if it is, I need to have at least one of them with me," I barked.

"Well, it is, I guess."

"Right. Do you want to meet or not?"

There was a pause. "Okay. See you there in half hour." said Lemke flatly.

When I hung up, Joe said, "You sure he said the Broadway Diner?"

"Yeah. Why?"

"That's where union people go, and everybody knows it. Why would he want to meet you there?"

CHAPTER 14

We walked briskly down Eastern Avenue, past a laundromat with a cracked window, a seedy-looking grocery store, and a boarded up Italian restaurant. It was ugly, but it wasn't really New Jersey's fault. As far as I could tell, retail America was damn unattractive almost everywhere.

The Broadway Diner was one of the few visibly thriving businesses on the avenue. It was only a ten-minute walk from the union office. But that was just one reason it was a union hangout, Joe explained as we strode along. Two wives of pro-union Pantheon employees worked at the diner. Knowing this, union activists used the Broadway as an auxiliary meeting place. Management people gradually got the vibe and stopped frequenting the diner. So why had Lemke proposed it?

The personnel manager was already there when we arrived. He had snagged the most defensive seat in the house, the corner chair of a corner table, where he had a clear view of the entire restaurant. He held his hand up the instant we came in, the salute-like wave some men use to signal the waiter for the check.

We dodged around the tables to reach Lemke's redoubt.

He half stood up to shake my hand. "Ms. Reid, so good to see you. Mr. Dysart," he turned to Joe and shook his hand too.

Joe and I took our seats, and the waitress handed us menus.

"Will you be having lunch?"

"No thank you," said Joe.

"Me neither," I said. "But coffee would be nice."

"Oh, are you sure?" said Lemke, looking disappointed. "Then I guess I'll have a diet Coke."

Once the waitress was gone, Lemke said, "So," and leaned toward me as though we were old friends who had some catching up to do. He flashed his overly white smile at me, completely ignoring Joe's presence. It seemed he was waiting for me to talk.

"*So,*" I ventured after a moment. "I wanted to let you know that we plan to file an Unfair Labor Practice charge over Al Zielinski's firing. We believe the company fired him as a result of his union activity. Which is illegal, as you know."

Lemke showed no reaction.

"We'd much prefer not to file the charge," I went on. "I mean, we'd rather not put you and us through that whole process."

Now Lemke shifted in his seat and adjusted his aviator glasses. "Well, Ruth — may I call you Ruth?"

"Go ahead," I said.

"Well, Ruth, as we discussed before, Mr. Zielinski threatened another employee. That's a very serious issue."

"From what I understand, the person Al is alleged to have threatened was making some threats of his own," I said. "In fact, I've seen myself how threatening Mr. Schmidt can be." The unwelcome image of Al raising a club over Schmidt's windshield came to mind suddenly.

"So have I. Many times," Joe added.

"I'm sorry, but that's not the issue here." Lemke shook his head and looked as if he was very sad to be right. "The issue is whether Mr. Zielinski threatened Mr. Schmidt."

"Look, Larry," I said, toying with my fork in an effort to avoid looking at Lemke. "You guys have been harassing and intimidating workers for months. And now you've fired the very person who initiated the organizing drive. What you're doing is illegal, and you know it." I plunked the fork back down on the table and looked at Lemke.

Lemke smiled maddeningly. "You're quite a firebrand aren't you? I admire that, I really do. And I want to say that if in fact there *is* any harassment or intimidation of Pantheon workers — which I'm not saying there is — I'm very much opposed to it. But unfortunately the evidence against Al Zielinski is very clear."

"In any event," I snapped, "I'd appreciate it if you would notify the Maloneys that we're preparing to file a ULP charge."

"I'll do that, but I if I were you, I wouldn't expect a turnaround from management," said Lemke. "And frankly, Ruth, I think that's unfortunate. As I mentioned before, Pantheon used to pride itself on its healthy employee-management relations."

"So what happened? Why'd it change" I asked.

"Well, the company had a couple of hard years. It was losing revenue, and so management decided to hire this F.H. Toro firm — "

"Why was Pantheon losing revenue?" I interrupted.

Lemke looked irritated. "Businesses have ups and downs. But that's not the point. The point is that the Maloneys hired Toro to implement an efficiency program. And our employees reacted to the situation by starting this union drive — and to be honest, Ruth, this was a possibility I had raised with Oscar and Sam from the outset."

I nodded and took another sip of my coffee.

Lemke suddenly leaned toward me and said, "May I be frank with you, Ruth?"

Had Joe suddenly become invisible? "I don't know," I said. "Joe, can he be frank with us?"

"Sure," said Joe.

Lemke glanced impatiently at Joe. "I argued against hiring Mr. Toro, and I'm not impressed with the way he has conducted himself at Pantheon. In my view, he and his people have been unnecessarily confrontational. They've frittered away a lot of the good will that we had built up over the years."

"This must put you in an awkward spot, as director of human resources," I said.

Lemke raised his eyebrows cryptically.

"Do you think there's any chance Sam and Oscar could be convinced to get rid of Toro?"

Lemke shook his head. "This union drive has them very worried, and they're convinced they've got to have outside expertise to deal with it. They don't understand how Toro is turning the employees against them. Victoria and I discussed this often."

At the mention of Victoria's name, Lemke's face took on a tragic appearance.

"I heard that you and she talked often," I prompted.

Lemke nodded. "Under the circumstances, I tried to do what I could to lessen the animosity. I must tell you, it hasn't been easy. Speaking of which," Lemke added, "it must be extremely difficult for you now, having to pick up where Victoria left off."

I nodded. What was Lemke probing for?

Lemke's eyes bored into mine. "I hope you've been able to pick up the pieces from — from what she left behind — ?"

I shook my head. "I'm sorry, Larry, but I can't share that information with you."

Lemke leaned back into his chair abruptly, as if I'd slapped his cheek. "Of course not," he said, dropping the napkin that had been in his lap onto the table. "By the way," he added, "since you're making such an effort on behalf of Mr. Zielinski, you might be interested to know that I have already given him a second chance."

"What do you mean?"

"I was at Pantheon when Mr. Zielinski was hired many years ago. There was a little misrepresentation on his application form."

"What are you talking about?"

"You won't be surprised to learn that we always inquire whether our applicants have a prison record."

Lemke paused, impelling me to prompt, "Yes?"

Lemke leaned toward me as if sharing a confidence. "Mr. Zielinski served six months for assault."

"Oh." I looked at Joe, who raised his eyebrows, but didn't look particularly surprised.

Now that Lemke's little bombshell had landed, he surveyed the restaurant, caught the waitress's eye, and made a check-signing pantomime.

"Uh, Mr. Lemke — Larry," I blurted. "There was a question I wanted to ask you — "

"Yes?" Lemke's eyes were still on the waitress, who was tallying up our bill over by the cash register.

"We were going over the list of bargaining unit employees the other day, and we saw something strange — a discrepancy between the Excelsior list and the one we believe accurately reflects the payroll."

Lemke snapped to attention. "What do you mean?"

"Well, there are five men on the payroll in the shipping department that no one in that department has ever heard of. All of them were supposedly hired five months ago. And none of them are on the Excelsior list."

For an unguarded instant, a look of pure shock passed over Lemke's face. And then I knew he hadn't leaked us that list. Lemke knew about those five names. But he was very surprised that we knew about them.

"How do you know they're on the payroll? I mean, what list are you using?" he asked sharply.

I shrugged disingenuously. "It's a list we had in the office."

"Why aren't you using the Excelsior list?"

I tilted my head. "As I said, our impression is that this other list is more accurate."

"I have no idea what you're talking about. It's probably some administrative error. I'd appreciate it if you'd let me know which names these are."

"I'll ask the NLRB election officers about it," I said.

That ruffled Lemke's feathers a bit. "I would ask that before you do that, you let me know those names so we can check our records. This may well be a simple error we can correct without involving the entire bureaucracy. All right?"

"We'll think about that," I said. What did we have to gain by telling Lemke and company what we knew?

"Well, Ruth, I've communicated openly with you here — at some risk to myself. It seems to me the least you could do is extend me this small courtesy."

I just shrugged.

"Excuse me," Lemke said suddenly. He stood up and intercepted the waitress as she was carrying the bill to us. He waved it in the air and said, "I've got this, Ruth. But would you and Joe mind very much waiting a few minutes after I've left before leaving the restaurant?"

I looked at Joe, then at Lemke, puzzled. "Okay. If you'll answer one more question."

Lemke nodded.

"Why did you hang up on me earlier?"

Lemke smiled and bent toward me conspiratorially. "It's not exactly safe to have these conversations in the office, Ruth."

"Why did Lemke say that? Was he kidding?" I asked Joe as we walked back to the office. "Why wouldn't it be safe to talk with us from his office? Does he think it's bugged?"

"I have no idea," said Joe.

The day had started out mild enough, but now the sun was merciless. I took off the thin cotton blouse I'd been wearing over my sleeveless T-shirt. I could almost feel the residue of car exhaust settling on my bare, slightly sticky arms.

"I wonder if Toro or the Maloneys would actually do something like that."

"It doesn't seem like Toro stops at much," said Joe.

We stepped around a cluster of down-and-out people loitering outside a dingy storefront that cashed checks for people who didn't have bank accounts.

"You know, Lemke knew something about those ghost employees," I said. "You could tell by the look on his face."

"Yep. But he sure was surprised we had that other list."

"Right," I said. "I don't think he was the one who leaked it to us."

"Me neither."

We walked on, my sandals slapping against the hot sidewalk.

"Lemke's a weird guy, isn't he?" I said.

Joe nodded.

"Do you think he's for real with this critique he's got of the Maloneys?"

"He might be, but I still don't trust him," said Joe.

"Me neither."

"I was going to order lunch, but I just couldn't get myself to eat a meal with that fellow," Joe said.

"Me neither," I said again.

"So you want to stop here and get a slice of pizza?" Joe gestured to Maria's Pizzeria.

"Sure. Anything but fried chicken."

Before I left the office that night, I gave Beck a call. I wanted to ask him how the Pantheon research was going. No answer. I left a message. Driving home across New Jersey — by myself, since Liz was on her non-date with Kevin McGarry — my mind kept pawing over all the bad news. Victoria's stolen files, the disunified organizing committee, Beck's suggestion of mob involvement. And the puny support the campaign was getting from the national union. I hadn't heard from Tommy McNamara since the day he hired me. He was probably too busy flailing around in union merger politics to attend to me and my dog of an organizing drive. Even Beck was unavailable. Probably out having hot fun with Yvette.

And then unwelcome images of John Beck and Yvette Ramirez began invading my mind. Holding hands, nuzzling each other, laughing their way down the stairs. I'd never seen Beck happier, and I knew I should have been pleased for him.

When I got home I made a beeline for the liquor cabinet. Finally, I had a night at home alone where I could just let myself go. "Veg out," we used to call it in high school. It had nothing to do with vegetables. Unless you counted the barley they made the scotch with.

I flopped down on the couch with a big tumbler of the stuff and started going through the day's junk mail. After two drinks, I tried Beck's cell again. Still no answer. I went and got another drink.

Sitting there on the couch, I determined that I was a spineless idiot. I had decided to quit the labor movement, and here I was in the middle of a major organizing drive that was sure to fail. I had decided to leave John Beck, and here I was pining for him. Franklin, perhaps sensing my despair, jumped onto the coffee table in front of me and laid down on the magazine I'd been reading. He looked up at me with expectant eyes. Yes, here we were again. Me and my cat.

Two hours later, Sandy startled me out of my stupor. "Ruth? Are you in here?" she bellowed from the front door.

I cleared my throat. Wow, did I feel bad. I ached all over. I was somewhere on the continuum between drunk and hung over, but I couldn't tell where. "Yeah?" I said weakly, sitting up.

"Ruth!" Sandy charged in. Damn.

"You're *drunk!*" Sandy exclaimed. One hand was on her hip, the other clutched a bottle of food supplements.

"What are you doing here?" I managed to mutter.

"I told Liz I'd bring these by and your lights were on," said Sandy, lifting the bottle. "Where's Liz?"

"Mmm — she's out with this guy from Pantheon. Kevin something." My drinking binge seemed to have caused the lights to go out in a big section of my brain. I felt like I had a mouth full of dust. And my head was killing me.

"Ruth — why are you doing this to yourself?" Sandy whisked the bottle of scotch off the coffee table. "Did you drink this whole thing?"

I shook my head. In truth, I couldn't remember how much I'd drunk. I knew I was sorry to see that the bottle was empty.

I rose from the couch with a groan and eased myself into the kitchen. I filled up a tall glass with tap water and gulped it down all at once. Sandy scooted around me, tossing the scotch bottle into the recycling bin and putting the glass in the sink. She wasn't saying anything, but she didn't have to. Her worry and disapproval were emanating from her like one of those New Age auras she used to talk about.

Just then, Liz crashed through the door. "Hi!" she yelled. It was just possible she was as drunk as me, I thought.

Nope, not drunk, I realized when she appeared in the kitchen. Stoned.

"Oh my god, you two are driving me nuts!" Sandy stomped her foot. I had to laugh. So did Liz. It wasn't very polite.

"Aunt Ruth. You're really drunk!" Liz exclaimed gleefully.

"And you are stoned out of your mind," I replied.

"Why do I even bother?" said Sandy. "I'll make you both some tea, and then I'm going home. You two are peas in a pod."

"Peas in a pod," said Liz.

"Peas in a pod," I repeated. The phrase seemed hilarious. We started giggling, which turned into a period of hysteria that didn't end till long after Sandy had slammed the door behind her, leaving two steaming cups of her wretched tasting tea on the counter.

CHAPTER 15

The next morning, walking, speaking, and thinking of any kind proved to be nearly impossible. Simply staying upright was a challenge. As much as I liked drinking to excess, the agony almost made me consider a temporary halt to alcohol consumption.

"You okay, Ruth? You seem a little woozy this morning," Joe said sweetly. We were heading out to an early morning house visit with a pressman named Alonzo Lopez. I looked over at Joe as he steered his Taurus, his forearm resting lightly on the steering wheel. Joe looked tired. His hours at the office seemed to be getting longer and longer, and the bags under his eyes were growing in tandem.

"I drank too much last night."

"Oh." Joe nodded, keeping his eyes on the road. "I used to do that. But my age caught up with me."

"Yeah. I think I know what you mean. At least today I do." I gripped the armrest and tried to focus on not throwing up. I really didn't want to get barf all over Joe's immaculate twelve-year-old car. The state of Joe's Taurus was impressive, at least to someone who hadn't cleaned her Dodge in eight years. The dash was dust-free, the seats were neatly covered. There was no detritus on the floor. The windows were spotless. It was an old car you could be proud of. Joe steered it smoothly around each pothole. I was grateful.

We were doing about forty-five miles an hour along a patched six-lane highway through an area that was neither the town, the country, or a suburb — just ugly. I watched the gas stations and RV sales lots go by. I had to focus. If we couldn't win over people like Alonzo Lopez, we would surely lose this campaign.

"So tell me about this guy Alonzo," I said.

"Alonzo Lopez." Joe's eyes stayed on the car about fifty feet in front of us. "I've been working on him for a long time. He's on my shift, eleven to seven. He's assistant pressman on our biggest web press, been at Pantheon over ten years."

"What's he think about the union?"

"Well, he started out pretty gung ho, but I think he's gotten cold feet."

I nodded. Obviously, if we had been able to hold onto all the workers who had signed union cards in the first place, we would have had an easy slide to victory. Instead, the company was scaring people into changing their minds. The key was to stop the process and reverse it.

"So he knows we're coming?" I asked.

Joe nodded. "Not too happy about it though. I think he figured it was the only way to keep me from pestering him at the plant."

"You're not the pestering type, Joe."

"I feel like I am these days. Used to be most people seemed to like me pretty well. Now they tend to move away when they see me coming. It's hard to get used to."

We pulled up to a small white ranch house that was barely distinguishable from the other houses on the street. There was a silver maple in the front yard and a swath of multicolored snapdragons along the sidewalk that led to the front steps. A dented blue minivan was parked in the driveway.

A girl of seven or eight responded to our knock, opening the door wide. As she stood staring at us with wide brown eyes, a woman yelled, "Rosa, shut the door!" Then a thick-limbed woman in stretchy slacks and an oversized silky purple shirt came up behind the girl and spotted Joe and me.

"Can I help you?" she asked sharply. She pushed the girl behind her.

"Hi," said Joe. "Gloria, isn't it? I'm Joe Dysart. I work at Pantheon with Alonzo, and we'd arranged that I'd stop by for a visit." Joe gestured to me. "This is my friend Ruth Reid." I smiled.

The woman did not look pleased. "Dios mio," she muttered, and then said, more loudly, "Excuse me." She turned away from the door. In a moment, we could hear the sounds of an argument going on in Spanish somewhere in the house. It ended with an English sentence we could understand quite clearly: "Just get them away from my door!"

A short, powerfully built man in his early thirties stepped out the door, glancing at us apologetically. He wore jeans with black smears on them and a t-shirt with sweat stains at the armpits. He smelled like machine oil.

"Man, I'm really sorry about this. Could we walk around the block or something? It's kind of crazy around here, you know? I just got off a double shift." Lopez looked rapidly up and down the street.

"Sure," said Joe.

As we went down the steps to the sidewalk, Joe said, "This is our new organizer, Ruth Reid."

"Oh, hi," said Lopez, turning to shake my hand. "I'm sorry we couldn't sit down in the house. It's just, my wife's kind of busy — "

"That's okay," I said.

When we got to the sidewalk, Lopez gestured toward the right, and we proceeded down the quiet street.

"I am so wiped," Lopez said, turning to Joe as we walked. "We just had to rerun this whole job. It was a nightmare, man. And you know what the problem was? I'd been working fourteen hours straight. I was screwing up right and left."

"You were on the second shift too?"

Lopez nodded.

"I appreciate your taking the time to meet with us, Alonzo," Joe said. "I know it's gotten hard to talk at work."

"Tell me about it," said Lopez, wiping his hands on his jeans.

"We just wanted to get a sense of how you're doing, answer any questions you might have about the union — " said Joe.

"Yeah." Lopez was looking down at the sidewalk. "That's the thing, Joe. I really want to be for the union. But at this point, I don't know. I mean, it was bad enough with those management guys calling me in and lecturing me. But now they're threatening my family. I can't take that!"

I shot a look at Joe. "What happened?" he asked.

Lopez ran his oil-stained hands quickly through his hair. "There's this guy driving around — I don't know why he's picking on me. Maybe he knows I've been kind of pro-union."

"What do you mean, a guy driving around?" I asked.

"He drives this big white SUV. He stopped me in the parking lot yesterday and told me he knew where I lived and I better not vote for the union. And then he showed up here," Lopez added, glancing down the street.

"Here?"

"Yeah, today. Gloria saw him drive by our house, real slow right before I got home. She told me I'm putting the family in danger. She says she's going to take my daughter with her to her mother's house, at least until this union thing is over."

"That's awful," I said. "What kind of SUV?"

Lopez shrugged. "I don't know. She said it was one of those big ones."

"And she didn't recognize the driver?" asked Joe.

Lopez shook his head. "It's one thing when they're going after me, but they better stay away from my fuckin' family!" he said, his voice rising.

"We can't let them win at this, buddy," said Joe. "We got to keep going."

Lopez looked up. "And there's a whole other thing that's been bugging me, Joe. I mean, it would be great to have a union and everything, but who's going to lead it?"

"What do you mean?" Joe asked.

"The last visit I got was from that guy Al, and I know he's the big organizer and everything, but... Let me tell you, I don't want to see that guy at my door again."

"What was the problem?" asked Joe.

"He thinks he's the only decent pressman in the place. He always finds a way to get a jab in every time I talk to him. Have you heard his riff about how the Mexican guys at the loading dock ought to learn English? Fuck him!"

"I know what you're talking about, Alonzo, but he's just one person. There are other people on the organizing committee," said Joe.

"But he's the big one, right? So I'm thinking – am I going to risk everything, my job, my family — so I can get Zielinski a new job where he can tell me what to do?"

"No one said he'd be union president," I put in. "People would have to elect him. It would be up to you and the other workers at the plant."

Lopez looked at me. "No disrespect to you, Ms. Reid, but what's your stake in this? I heard you're not even from the union."

I shrugged. "You're right. I'm just here to help if I can. And it's Ruth."

Lopez nodded. "I'm sorry, I don't mean to be rude or anything."

"That's okay," I said. "But in addition to who leads the union, what are the big issues for you? I mean, what would you want a union to do, if you had one?"

Lopez glanced up at the sky for a moment. "I just want a decent job again. Lately the press is always running way too fast, and then I screw it up, and someone comes over and yells at me. I'm really scared they're going to fire me. I'm under pressure all the time. And it's affecting my marriage, you know? I can't afford that. And the fucking lobster shift. I can't get a transfer. They keep telling me no, and then I see other guys getting their requests. It really pisses me off."

I nodded. "If you had a union contract, you'd probably pick shifts by seniority."

"Yeah?" said Lopez.

Joe and I nodded.

With the next turn, we were back on Lopez's street. As we approached Lopez's house, a tiny thought fought its way into my sluggish brain.

"Listen, Alonzo," I said. "Would you mind if Joe and I sat here in Joe's car for a while to see if that white SUV goes by? Maybe we'll be able to get the license plate number and trace it."

Lopez brightened. "Yeah, sure. Just don't be too obvious about it. I don't think Gloria wants you guys around."

Then we shook hands and Lopez went inside. Joe and I settled ourselves in the Taurus for a nice ten-minute bake. I struggled to keep my eyes open as we talked about the shift issue. Just as I was about to cave in to sleep, Joe nudged my arm. "Ruth."

"What?" I said, wiping my mouth and trying to get my eyes to focus.

Joe pointed at the street in front of us. "White SUV. You got that notebook ready?"

"Uh huh," I said, watching the vehicle approach. It wasn't going to be hard to get the license plate number. The guy was driving all of four miles per hour.

"No plate on the front," said Joe.

The SUV — a Ford Expedition — was so fat that it had to pass within a foot of us. I squinted, trying to get a look at the driver through the tinted windows. I couldn't see a thing.

I was startled when, as the vehicle pulled by us, the driver's window rolled down, and the man stared out at me. I still didn't see much of his face. His baseball cap was pulled low and he wore big sporty wraparound sunglasses.

"What are you looking at?" the man said.

"We're looking at you," I said. "Why are you harassing this family? You want us to report you to the cops?"

The man laughed unpleasantly. "I'm just driving down the street. You know, you ought to be home in bed. From what I hear, you must have an awful big hangover."

While I sat there in shock, the SUV suddenly pulled forward with a screech.

"Can you see the plate number?" Joe said.

"Oh Jesus. I totally forgot!" I wheeled around in the seat and stared at the now rapidly moving vehicle.

"K59 — " I began.

"4LT," finished Joe as I frantically recorded the number on my notepad. "New York plates," Joe added.

I dropped the pad in my lap. My heart was pounding hard and fast. "Joe, how did he know that?"

"What, about the hangover?"

I nodded.

"Maybe he was following you when you went out drinking last night," said Joe.

"I wasn't out drinking last night," I said. "I was drinking at home."

CHAPTER 16

On the way back to the office, I called Beck. He didn't answer his cell. He wasn't picking up at the newspaper either. On both voicemails I spelled out the license plate number and asked if he could trace it.

"Where the hell are you?" I muttered as I tucked the phone back in my bag.

"You and him are good friends, I guess," said Joe.

"Yeah."

"I guess that other reporter was his girlfriend."

"It seems that way."

Joe gave me a tender look and then turned back to the road.

I couldn't figure out what I was doing that made it so painfully evident to everyone that I was in love with John Beck.

Back in the office, I found Liz sleeping at her desk, her cheek flat against the surface of the employee list, lightly snoring.

It would have been a real cute scene if I'd been in the mood for it.

"Hey," I barked.

"Huh?" Liz scrunched up her face and groaned as she raised her head slowly from the desk. She squinted at me, as if I were the sun. "Oh my god, I am so wasted," she croaked.

"Yeah, but that hasn't kept you from talking," I said. "You told somebody I got drunk last night. Who was it?"

"What?" Liz suddenly looked much more alert.

"I said, who'd you tell about my drinking last night?"

"Why?"

I sighed in exasperation. "Liz, who?"

Liz rubbed her eyes. "Well, I did kind of joke about it this morning a little. I mean, I was mainly talking about myself, but it was so funny with both of us — "

"Were you in the office?"

"Kevin and I went over to the plant so he could drop something off. We were in the break room and we were kind of comparing notes about how stoned we got last night and how wasted we were this morning, and I said it was kind of funny that when I got home you were drunk as a skunk."

"Great," I said. "And who was in the break room?"

Liz shrugged. "There were a bunch of people, but it wasn't like I was talking to them. But I guess they might have overheard me — "

"Liz. you've got to be more careful. We've got an opposition here. They're going to use everything they can against us."

"But what happened? How did you know — "

"Somehow an anti-union thug got hold of it and taunted me with it this morning."

"Jeez! I'm sorry, Aunt Ruth. Word spreads fast around here, doesn't it?"

That afternoon, we had our first shift-change party. Silvia had borrowed her brother-in-law's pickup truck to haul a picnic table to the wide grassy strip along the two-lane public road just outside the Pantheon plant. I'd brought a banner that I'd found tucked in the back of my closet from some long- ago labor struggle, a big blue silky streamer that declared "Union!" to passersby.

Nita had parked her little red hatchback along the road and left the back open, the better to hear the infectious salsa rhythm that emanated from her CD player.

Fifteen minutes later, there were about a dozen cars parked along the road, and Nita was trying very hard to increase the number. "Hey Ricky! Come party with me!" she yelled. A little yellow Beetle suddenly pulled over to the side of the road.

"This is like Nita's dream come true," said Silvia.

"She is good at it, isn't she?" I said.

"You haven't seen her dance yet," said Silvia. "And look at Al." Silvia pointed to a cluster of workers, all white males.

"Is Al in there?"

"Oh, yeah. All the good old boys saying hi to their pal."

Joe was standing on the grass nearby, talking with a young white woman. I came over and listened in on the conversation. The woman, Nancy, had an office job at Pantheon. And as a "professional," she didn't really need a union. Besides, the first thing the union would do was strike — even if the workers didn't want to. And Nancy couldn't afford that!

No, I thought, not on that fancy "professional" salary she was pulling in. But Joe was patient. He responded thoughtfully to every concern as if he'd never heard it before.

I headed for the cooler of drinks in Nita's hatchback. Juan Acevedo was talking intently with two other workers. As I walked by, he touched my arm and smiled. I glanced back at him, wincing silently at his beauty. Was he married? I still didn't know. I wasn't about to ask someone on the committee. And I wasn't about to ask Juan either.

Al, wearing a pair of quite unbecoming bermuda shorts and black sandals with velcro straps and matching black socks, was now sitting in a lawn chair facing the road. He gave the thumbs up signal to a pickup that honked its way past.

I came over and sat down in the empty chair beside him.

"This is pretty good," Al said. He took a sip of Coke and added, "Wish I had a beer, though."

"That would be tempting fate."

"I just got two new volunteers for the organizing committee. And three others who said they'd definitely vote yes."

"That's great, Al."

"See what Victoria was losing by kicking me off the committee?"

I nodded. "I'm not surprised. You're the guy who started this whole thing after all." I popped the top on the seltzer.

"Hey, thanks," said Al. He let off a belch.

"I can't figure out why she did it," I said. "I mean, I know why she *said* she took you off the committee. But is that the real reason?"

Al looked over at me and squinted. "What makes you think it wasn't?"

I shrugged. "It's just a pretty drastic move, to get rid of the very guy who initiated the drive." I took a swig of the seltzer, hoping that my flattery would get Al to talk.

Sure enough, Al cleared his throat and said, "You want to know why she really kicked me off the committee?"

I turned and looked into Al's little green eyes. "Why?"

"Because I was checking out another union."

"You mean after Victoria had already come in?"

Al nodded and grinned, then wiped his forehead with the back of his big plump hand. "I didn't tell her — I didn't want her to know. But she found out. She was really snoopy, you know?"

"Why were you looking into another union?"

Al laughed. "Why do you think? Because Vicky was a power-tripper. She only pretended to consult with people. She was going to do it her way no matter what anyone else said. And that pissed me off."

"Are you still talking with this other union?" I asked.

Al tilted his head and looked at me. "Now? Not really."

I scratched a freshly acquired mosquito bite on my calf. For the first time, Victoria's decision to oust Al made perfect sense. Nothing would have put Victoria on the warpath faster than the discovery that Al had approached another union.

"Err — heads up," Al said suddenly.

I sat up quickly. Al's eyes were on the road, following the progress of a black jeep. It swerved over to the shoulder near us and stopped. Bernie Schmidt swung out of the car practically before the engine died.

I leapt up from my chair and went to stand with the cluster of workers nearest Schmidt. Unfortunately, so did Al.

Schmidt was wearing black pants and a black leather jacket in the ninety-degree heat. Clearly, he was prepared to suffer for fashion. Behind him his little dog followed, picking its way over the gravel in a way that suggested that the stones were on fire.

"What kind of dog is that?" I asked Juan, who was now standing next to me.

"I think it's a Chihuahua. He calls it Kiki."

"Kiki?"

Juan nodded.

"Oh."

"What kind of bullshit is this?" Schmidt yelled about three feet from our ears.

"It's a party, you moron!" said Nita.

"Nita, be careful," said Silvia.

"You can't do this," said Schmidt, punching the air.

"Says who?" roared Al.

I looked at Juan with alarm. Juan put his arm around Al and tried to ease him away from Schmidt.

I turned to Schmidt and said, "It's not up to you. It's a public space."

"You're so full of shit," said Schmidt. He pulled a cell phone out of his jacket pocket, swung it open, and punched in some numbers while Kiki quivered spasmodically at his feet.

"Yeah, this is Schmidt at Pantheon. We got an illegal demonstration goin' on here. Yeah. Right outside the gate. Cool." He flipped the thing shut dramatically.

Schmidt leaned against his jeep and watched us, smirking as we tried to cajole Al away from the road. Five minutes later, we heard police sirens, then we watched as two squad cars pulled up behind Schmidt's jeep.

"Okay, let's break this up," said one of the officers.

"This is a public place," I said.

"That doesn't mean you can set up a table and all this stuff and blast your music. It's a public nuisance."

"We're not bothering anybody. There are no houses in sight," I said. "And besides, we're exercising our first amendment right to free speech."

The cop actually laughed.

"What's so funny?" I said.

"Okay, let's get the picnic table out of here. And turn that music off."

A few feet away, Schmidt was sniggering. I hadn't come that close to hitting someone in years.

I got home around eleven-thirty that night. The walk from the garage back to my house constituted the only exercise I'd gotten that day, and my body felt stiff and slow. If I was lucky, Liz would be snoring up in her little room and I could sneak right into bed.

I rounded the corner. My street was dimly lit by big ugly silver streetlamps. For years the city had been promising to replace them with cute antiquey ones, but we all knew the change would come late to our immigrant neighborhood. Ahead, midway down the block where Sandy and I lived, I noticed that the street was virtually blocked by a gigantic SUV. A gigantic white SUV. I stopped and squinted. Someone, a woman, was standing next to the car, leaning into the passenger side window. A woman with big frizzy hair. Liz.

I broke into a run, my sandals slapping on the sidewalk.

"Liz! Liz!" I screamed, surely waking the entire neighborhood. But Liz continued to lean against the car.

"Liz!" I yelled again.

And then I tripped on a slab of broken sidewalk and went flying. I skidding painfully on my elbow before I landed with a thud flat on my stomach.

For an instant I lay there stunned. Then a streak of panic ran through me and I sprang off the pavement and started running blindly toward the spot where the car had been. But the car was gone. And so was Liz.

CHAPTER 17

"Liz!" I shrieked. But my niece had disappeared. I stood on the spot where the big white car had idled, directly in front of my house, and looked down the empty street. I'd been sprawled on the sidewalk for only a few seconds. The car must have left in a hurry.

Then I noticed there were lights on in my house. Music was playing in there — some moody female vocalist. Maybe Liz had just gone back inside, I thought with a sudden spurt of hope.

I flew across my tiny yard and yanked open the door.

"Liz? Liz?"

"Aunt Ruth?" Liz's voice came from the kitchen.

"Oh my god." I dropped my stuff on the floor and bent over for a minute, panting, feeling suddenly drained. Franklin was staring at me impassively from the couch.

"Aunt Ruth? What's wrong?" Liz came into the front room, a can of beer in her hand. She was wearing a denim miniskirt and her bright pink tee. She looked at me wide-eyed as I huffed and put my hand on my chest.

I flopped down on the couch next to Franklin.

"Liz, who were you talking to just now in that white SUV?"

"Oh. It was this guy from Pantheon who stopped by to see you. I kept asking him his name but he said you'd know, like it was a joke. You do know him, right?"

"Just tell me what he said, okay?"

Liz sat down beside me and tugged on the four thin rubber bands, red, yellow, blue and green, stretched around her pale, freckled wrist.

"Let's see. I was sitting on the porch swing and he drove up, kind of slow," Liz began. "And then he saw me and he's like, 'Hi, is Ruth around?' And so I'm like, 'She's at work.' And then he's like, 'Oh shoot, I was hoping I could stop in and say hi. You must be Liz.' And so I went over to the car."

I sank down a little lower on the couch and clutched my hand to my stomach. "What did he look like? What did he say?"

Liz looked at me. "I'm *telling* you what he said. Are you going to tell me what's wrong? You look like you're about to puke."

"Could you finish the story first?"

"Okay, okay, let's see." Liz looked up at the ceiling, thinking. "I didn't get a great look at him. It was kind of dark in that car. And he had on these sunglasses and a baseball cap. All I know is, he was white and kind of big."

I nodded. It had to be the same guy who had been harassing Alonzo Lopez. "Then what happened?"

"Umm, well, he said to say hi to your friend John and he hoped John's research on Pantheon was going well. And he said he hoped you were feeling better today. And then he asked if I liked working on the organizing drive."

"Oh, Christ. What did you say?"

Liz shrugged. "I said it was going fine. I didn't say a lot — I mean the guy was kind of weird. And that was basically it. He said goodbye and drove off."

"Let me just go get a drink," I said, pulling myself off the couch.

"Wait! You said you'd tell me what's wrong."

"Just a minute," I said as I marched into the kitchen. I searched the cupboard for the scotch. Damn! I'd finished it off on that bender last night. Reluctantly I grabbed a bottle of vodka I kept on hand for Beck.

"I can't believe you don't know that guy," said Liz, who had followed me into the kitchen. "He knows everything about you."

"Exactly," I said as I threw some ice cubes in a glass, covered them with vodka, then poured in a dollop of orange juice. I carried the concoction back into the living room and sat back down on the couch.

"Remember I asked you who you'd told about me being drunk last night — because this thug knew all about it?"

Liz nodded, sitting back down on the couch.

"That was the thug."

"Oh, god."

"You didn't see him in the Pantheon break room this morning, did you?"

"I don't think so." Liz gnawed on an already painfully short fingernail.

"I should have warned you away from white SUVs," I said. "When I saw you leaning into that car I almost had a heart attack. I was running toward you and screaming all the way down the street."

"I didn't hear a thing. He had one of those horrible classic rock stations on kind of loud."

I nodded and sipped the vodka, then shivered at the strange taste on my tongue. "This whole thing is scaring the shit out of me. And pissing me off too. You didn't see his license plate, did you?"

"No. Why would I be looking at that? Who is this guy? What's he trying to do? I don't get it." Liz pulled her hand away from her mouth and examined her fingers, looking for a chewable nail. Seeing none, she wiped her hand on her skirt and started fiddling with the rubber bands on her wrist.

"If the guy you just talked to is the one I think it is, he's trying to scare people into voting against the union — and now I guess he's trying to scare me into quitting the campaign. We got his license plate number this morning, and I asked Beck to trace it."

"But how does he know all that stuff? About John Beck and me and everything?"

I shook my head. "Maybe he's working for F.H. Toro and Toro's really doing his research. But whoever it is, you've got to be more careful, Liz."

Liz snorted. "Don't talk to strangers?"

"Exactly — especially not that stranger."

"You think that guy is going to kidnap me or something?"

I swallowed. "Jesus, he better not."

All of a sudden I realized that my elbow hurt. I looked at it. Blood was running down the back of my arm. And it had left a big fat bloodstain on the sofa's armrest.

Rain was pounding against the windows of the union office. It was only eleven-thirty a.m., and I was already tired. I'd been meeting with groups of workers since eight, and my voice was now a creaky rasp. I was hungry too. One stale doughnut didn't go very far.

John Beck was incommunicado. I wanted to warn him about the guy in the Expedition, I wanted to find out if he'd been able to trace the license plate. I wanted to know if he'd learned anything about F.H. Toro or Pantheon's finances. And, well, I just really wanted to talk to the guy. Maybe what I truly wanted was reassurance that despite Yvette, we were still buddies. What a comedown.

I was standing in front of the little fan with my arms raised when Silvia told me I had a call. I scampered over to my desk, primed for the sound of Beck's voice.

"Ruthie?"

I plunked myself down in my chair. It was Tommy McNamara, the man who had talked me into taking this suicide mission.

"So how's it going, Ruthie?"

I glanced around the room. Two new activists had just returned from house visits and two more were on their way out. Joe Dysart was working the phones. Silvia and Nita were comparing notes on bindery workers they had interviewed.

"It's going okay," I said. "But somebody's playing some serious hardball — I'm guessing it's the F.H. Toro people."

"What are they doing?"

"Trying to intimidate fence-sitters, tracking my every move."

"That's awful, Ruthie," said McNamara, sounding unimpressed. Whenever you had a professional union-buster on the scene, you had to expect some hardball. "What's the tally?"

"We don't have a good hold on that at the moment. But I think we can count on close to fifty percent. We've got another fifteen percent or so who would vote yes if they weren't so scared."

"Fifty percent," repeated Tommy, sounding disappointed.

"Yeah. We've got to beat back the fear. That's what we're working on now. And we're doing lots of house visits to fencesitters and wobblers. You know Tommy, if we had a couple of staff from the union, it would go a lot easier."

"Yeah, I'm sorry about that, Ruthie. We're real stretched around here right now, or else I'd send some people over there this minute. But, uh, it must be pretty tough trying to carry this thing by yourself. I hope you're taking care of yourself, Ruthie. I mean, you must be under a lot of stress."

I cocked my head at that. Stress? Taking care of yourself? These were not usually Tommy's concerns.

"What's up Tommy? You worried about something?"

"Well, I'll tell you Ruthie —" Tommy paused, as if preparing to drop a bomb on me. I mentally cringed. "I hear that you're, uh, hitting the bottle a little hard. Not that I'm one to talk about that!" He guffawed insincerely.

I let the hand holding the receiver drop down to my side. I took in a deep breath and brought the receiver back up to my ear.

"Okay, Tommy. Who's telling you this? And why?"

"Crap. I'm sorry, Ruthie. It's just I been getting some heat."

"What are you talking about, Tommy?" I leaned forward in the desk chair and wound the telephone cord around my finger.

"Well, it's Shawcross," Tommy said finally.

I leapt up, sending my chair rolling backward. "Shawcross? What the hell does the head of the New York labor federation have to do with me drinking during an organizing drive in New Jersey? How the hell does he even know?"

"Ruthie, calm down. I don't know where his information's coming from. I asked him, but of course he's not saying."

"Tommy, this is outrageous! What's his interest in this?"

"Well, officially his interest is that we're an affiliate of the New York fed, and he's just passing on helpful information. Unofficially, he's out to get you. I realize that, Ruthie. The guy's full of shit."

"How's he going to get me?"

"Well, he's trying to pressure me to fire you."

I sighed. "Tommy — explain what leverage Shawcross has over you."

"Actually it was my boss he told about this. It gives my opposition in the union more ammunition, you know? Like, I hired the wrong person for the job, and now they're botching it."

My jaws were clenched so tightly that my teeth were starting to hurt. "What kind of person would listen to rumor-mongering like that?"

"Ruthie. You know what a hothouse this place is — especially now."

"Oh Christ." I sat back down in my chair and rubbed my forehead. "So are you going to fire me?"

"No way. They'd have to fire me first."

I nodded, thinking that firing Tommy first was a pretty likely scenario.

"So, uh, *are* you drinking a lot, Ruthie?"

"God damn it, Tommy, it's none of your business! If you want to find out how I'm doing, why don't you send some staff over here and they can tell you?"

"Aw, Ruthie, come on. You know I'm on your side."

I took in a big breath and forced myself to relax my shoulders. "Look. I know you're under a lot of pressure and everything. I know what Shawcross does isn't your fault."

"Well, I'm sorry to be shifting some of this crap onto you."

"Listen, Tommy, while I've got you on the phone — any progress on getting the union attorney to start working on Al's NLRB charge?"

Silence. "That may take a little while to, you know, get going."

I pressed my lips together till they hurt and then said in a low voice, "Tommy, I promised Al the union would move on this. Okay?"

There was another pause before Tommy said, "Okay, Ruthie, I hear you. I'll do what I can."

"Tommy, you have got to pass this on to the legal department."

Tommy let out a sigh. "Okay, Ruthie."

When I hung up with Tommy, I sat staring into space for a few minutes.

How the hell did Shawcross know about my private drinking binges? It had to go back to that Pantheon break room where Liz had said too much too loudly. Was Toro blabbing to James Shawcross? Toro must have done a lot of research on the history of Ruth Reid to know that Shawcross was a potential ally of theirs.

The news that the president of the state labor federation was collaborating with a union-busting consultant was a lot more explosive than one more union organizer on a bender. But of course this was conjecture. I had no idea how Shawcross knew about my drinking.

"Ruth? John Beck's on line two for you," said Joe.

I picked up the receiver again.

"Beck."

"Reid."

I leaned back in my chair. "You've been hard to reach lately."

"Yeah. It's been crazy," said Beck vaguely.

"How's the research going?"

"Okay — I've got a little news. Can you meet around ten tonight at the Pine Room?"

"Sure!" I said, with more enthusiasm than I had intended. I looked down at the impractical outfit I had donned that morning — a short black knit skirt, lacy rose-colored top, and vampy sandals. It wasn't that I was intending to flirt with anyone. It was that I hadn't done my laundry in weeks and I was scraping the barrel.

"Did you run that license plate number I gave you?" I asked.

"What was that about, anyway?" Beck said, in lieu of a reply.

I told Beck about the Expedition driver's harassment of Alonzo Lopez and his encounter with Liz, including his message to Beck.

"Jeez, what a creepy guy," said Beck. "I'm not surprised he knows that I'm researching Pantheon. But I get the feeling he also knows there's a connection between you and me, and he's using it to try to scare you away. And how would he know about that?"

"Did you find out his name?"

"Yep. Tim Beatty."

My mind raced. I knew that name. From somewhere.

"Wait a second," I said. I clapped the receiver against my chest and called out to the room, "Does anyone recognize the name Tim Beatty?"

"Yeah," Liz called back. "Timothy Beatty. He's one of those extra employees we found on Victoria's list. Remember?"

CHAPTER 18

When I hung up with Beck, I got out of my chair and paced around the office. Inside the office, it was exceedingly hot and humid. Outside, it was hot, humid, and raining cats and dogs. I looked down at my flimsy high-heeled sandals. It was going to be really fun wearing these shoes out there tonight.

I picked up the phone and punched in the number for the regional NLRB office. After a hellish interval of call-waiting, I got through to the agent overseeing the Pantheon election, a guy named Michael Kristoff. He assured me that in the conference between management and the union that had produced the Pantheon Excelsior list, no one had mentioned the names of those five employees. He had no theories about the discrepancy we'd found.

I hung up and leaned back in my chair. I felt assaulted by disturbing bits of information that were connected in ways I couldn't understand. Victoria's files had been stolen. One of the documents in the files had been returned. The returned file had revealed to us the existence of extra employees on the payroll. And they obviously weren't put there to pack the election vote. And we'd learned that a thug I assumed was sent by F.H. Toro was one of those employees. Worst of all, absolutely everyone, from the thugs to the president of the state labor federation, seemed to know that I drank too much, and I had no idea how. If only I could have a drink right now.

Instead, I put my nose to the grindstone — the grindstone being the phone on my desk and my daunting call list. I sighed and picked up the phone again.

A couple hours later, between calls, I heard my niece shriek "Stop it!"

Liz was sitting shoulder-to-shoulder with Kevin McGarry at the conference table. They were giggling and knocking against each other while ostensibly going through employee lists.

"You okay, Ruth?" Liz asked when she noticed my look.

"Yeah. How's it going with the list?"

"We're almost done. I just have one more department contact to call. Kevin's been helping a lot. He was thinking maybe I could go out on a couple of house visits with him later this afternoon."

"Okay," I said. "Just watch out for Mr. Expedition."

"Who sent that guy?" McGarry asked. "Do we know who he is?"

Something made me decide not to blurt out the name Beck had just given me. But Liz had no such reserve.

"Tim Beatty — he's one of those extra employees," she said.

"Oh," said McGarry. "Weird. What's he doing on the payroll?"

"We don't know," I said. "Do you have any ideas?"

McGarry shrugged his linebacker-sized shoulders. "Beats me. But he better stay away from my contacts — and from Liz." McGarry grinned flirtatiously at my niece.

"We thought we'd go out for dinner after the house visits," said Liz. "So I might not be home till late."

I nodded. "Yeah. I'm out with Beck. So I might be late too."

Liz smirked. I rolled my eyes.

That evening, the office was still hot and sticky, and outside it was still hot, sticky and wet. I was a walking bundle of needs. I was starving, I was exhausted, and I needed a drink. After that came, my throat hurt, my back hurt, and my eyes stung. And I hadn't had sex in months. Probably not coincidently, I felt a burning need to see Beck.

Liz and Kevin McGarry had left long ago. For the past three hours, Joe, Juan, and Al had been sitting around the big table trying to figure out how to win over the press operators. They'd been getting rowdier and rowdier, but I'd been too preoccupied with my phone to find out why.

"We have an excellent plan," Al announced to the room at a moment when I was between calls.

"Thank god for that," I said.

"What is it?" Nita asked.

"Let's all go over to the Pony and talk about it there," said Juan.

"I can't. I'm wearing the wrong shoes," I said mournfully.

Nita put her hand on my shoulder and said earnestly, "Don't ever let your shoes stop you from having a good time. I learned that a long time ago."

"God, it feels like years since I've had a scotch," I said.

"How long has it been?" Silvia asked.

I looked at my watch. "Almost twenty-four hours."

Silvia laughed. "I shouldn't go," she said. "My husband will kill me."

"Screw him," said Nita. "This drive is a once in a lifetime thing."

"I already told him that," said Silvia. "But that doesn't mean he'll let me come home drunk at two a.m."

Nita put her hand on her hip and stared at her sister. "What do you mean, 'let you'? Does he own you? I want to hear what Joe and them have to say about the pressmen. I'm going." Nita tossed her hair over her shoulder and picked up her handbag.

Silvia smiled at me. "That's why I'm married and she's not."

"I'm no slave, I'll tell you that," said Nita. "Are you coming or not?"

Silvia grabbed her bag. "Just one drink."

Excellent, I thought. The Pony at seven, the Pine Room at ten. I saw a happy future before me for the first time in days.

The Pony was loud, dark and comforting. We quickly found a booth in the back and wangled some extra chairs so everybody could sit down.

We ordered our drinks and an outrageous number of appetizers. Moments later, I wrapped my fingers around the icy wet glass of scotch, deeply contented. My sandals were soaked, but I didn't care.

I looked up to see Juan's brown eyes on me. I gave him an uncomplicated smile and tried to ignore the little contraction I felt somewhere in my reproductive system.

Al, having taken a monstrous quaff from his mug of beer, clapped it down on the table and wiped his mouth with the back of his sleeve. "The Maloneys'll be on their knees begging for a union when we get done. Right Joe?"

Joe looked at me and winked. "Could be, Al."

"Okay, okay, tell us your battle plan," said Nita. She tilted her head and tugged lightly on a glittery earring, smiling.

"We're going to fuck them up!" Al crowed.

"We're going to fuck them up with their own demands," added Juan.

"They want to speed up the press so bad? We're going to let 'em!" Al chortled.

"I don't get it." Silvia tilted her head in Juan's direction.

Juan leaned forward. His hair shone blue-black under the lights. "See, the press really can't run as fast as they want it to."

"Not safely," said Joe.

"What do you mean 'not safely'?" I said.

"Okay, you know how a web press works, right?" said Al. "The paper is continuous, it's a huge roll — that's why they call it a web."

I nodded.

"If we run it as fast as Toro's telling us, the paper's going to break," finished Juan.

I leaned back and looked at the men. "What's so bad about that?"

Al and Juan laughed. Joe smiled faintly. "It'll be pretty bad – wait and see," said Al.

"You're not talking about people possibly getting hurt, are you?" I said.

"Nah, that doesn't happen," said Al.

As we talked, Nita squinted into the darkness in the back of the bar. Then she pressed a finger gently to my shoulder and spoke into my ear.

"See that?" she said, pointing toward the back of the bar. There I saw a little rat-like dog that was acting like the floor was on fire, lifting first one leg up then the other, as if trying to prevent paw-burn.

"What?" Al asked.

Nita pointed again and whispered loudly. "Kiki."

Everyone at the table leaned over to look at the dog.

Al seemed to puff up to twice his size. "I'm sick of that guy following us everywhere."

Joe shrugged. "Maybe he just likes to have a drink in the Pretty Pony."

"He's following us," said Al.

"Let's just not bother him, okay?" said Silvia.

When our server came by, Al ordered another beer, then said, "By the way, you allow dogs in here?" He gestured toward Kiki.

The waitress, a wiry woman with short graying hair, frowned in the dog's direction. "I know that guy. And there's no way I'm going to get in a fight with him over a dog."

"How do you know him?" I asked.

"His wife Donna used to work here a long time ago. Ex-wife, thank god."

Nita leaned forward. "Are you talking about Bernie Schmidt?"

"Yeah, you know him?"

"We work with him," said Juan.

"I feel sorry for you," said the waitress. "He's a monster — and he's a monster at home too."

"What do you mean?" I asked.

The waitress scratched her head with her pen and leaned closer to the table. "The guy's a wife-beater, okay? And now he's a deadbeat dad." She stood back up and shook her head. "Donna finally moved away – as far from him as she could get. I haven't heard from her since."

When the woman had gone away, I took a sip of the scotch and looked up at the light that hung low and yellow over our heads. I was thinking, divorce, alimony, child support — Dellafield and Yaeger.

Silvia gave me a ride to the Jersey PATH train, and I made a smooth transfer to the subway in Manhattan. I emerged from the station into a drenching downpour. I opened my umbrella and looked down at my ridiculous little high heels. Screw it, I thought. I took off the shoes and ran the three blocks to the bar.

Like the Pony, the Pine Room was warm, dim and comforting. The sight and smell of it summoned up all my memories of Beck, the years we'd spent flirting and dancing around one another, sitting here on barstools and booth benches. The friendship had been rock-solid. The romance had been deeply unsatisfying. And yet I still craved it.

Beck was sitting on the barstool farthest from the door. When he spotted me, he waved. I waved back, then stuck my umbrella in the stand by the door. I bent over to put my shoes back on and shivered. I glanced down at my skirt and top. I looked like I had taken a nice long shower with my clothes on. I was so glad I had dressed up.

"Babe, you're soaking wet," Beck said, offering me the stool he had appropriated for me.

"No wonder you're a reporter. Nothing escapes you."

"What can I say? It's my true calling." Beck had been wearing a sport jacket, but fortunately he'd taken it off. Leaning over the bar, his thick curving shoulder muscles pulled against the fabric of the shirt. He was damn gorgeous. I took a sharp breath and clenched my jaw against temptation.

The bartender came by and I ordered a scotch, neat. I wasn't in the mood for ice.

"This is my second bar tonight," I confessed.

"Is the campaign driving you to drink?"

"Yep," I said. "And I've acquired quite a reputation for it."

"What do you mean?"

"I got a call from Tommy McNamara this afternoon. He told me I drink too much."

"*He* should talk!" said Beck. "But how does he know about you?"

"James Shawcross told him — or actually, Shawcross told Tommy's boss, who told Tommy."

"Christ, you're famous," said Beck. "Why the hell is Shawcross involved?"

I shrugged. "Well, obviously he hates me. And he's trying to force Tommy to fire me. I don't know why he bothers. My reputation's going to be in the toilet soon enough without any help from Shawcross. And Tommy's going to be right behind me."

"Is it that bad? What are your numbers?"

"Fifty-fifty."

"Shit," said Beck. He plucked a red plastic swizzle stick from a ceramic holder and rattled his ice with it. "Here's what I'm not getting. Where did Shawcross get his info?"

I leaned back in my stool and sipped my scotch. It was cool in my mouth and warm going down. Even my toes were starting to feel toasty. I turned back to Beck. "I'm thinking maybe from Tim Beatty, that thug in the SUV."

Beck choked on his drink.

"Hey — you okay? What's the matter?"

"I sure as hell hope you're wrong about that," Beck said after he'd gotten over his coughing fit.

"Why?"

"Beatty's in the mob."

"*What?*"

Beck nodded. "That's what I wanted to tell you. Beatty is a small-time mobster. He was convicted a few years ago for shaking somebody down. The prosecutor said they knew he was connected to this mob family in Queens, the Cappellinis — but they couldn't prove it."

"Wait a minute. I know that name." I stared down into my drink. Cappellini.

Finally, I raised my head. "I remember now. That family had control of a local union in New Jersey for years. And not too long ago the feds busted them and appointed a trustee to run the local. I even know the guy they appointed. We worked on a campaign together once."

Beck looked at me. "This is ringing a bell. Was it Local 557?"

I nodded. "Out of Elizabeth, New Jersey. It had been mob-dominated forever, and the feds finally cleaned it up."

"Who's the trustee?"

"Mmm. Can't remember." I stirred the scotch around with a swizzle stick. "Scheiner. Phil Scheiner," I said finally.

"Maybe I'll stop by Local 557 tomorrow. See if Scheiner can tell me anything about the Cappellinis. Any chance you could go with me? He might be more forthcoming with a friend."

"Maybe. Give me a call when you're ready to go."

Beck caught the bartender's eye and winked. Suave. She came over and wordlessly grabbed his glass and mine.

"So I don't get it," I said once my new scotch had arrived. "Why is Beatty on the payroll at Pantheon? And why is he harassing us? Is the Cappellini family somehow connected to F.H. Toro?"

Beck leaned back. "Could be," he said. "I only found one other union that had experience with the guy. And they told me they had a feeling he was mob-linked."

"But — if that's true, could it be just an accident that the Maloneys hired a mobster thug like Beatty and a mobster consultant like Toro?"

Beck shook his head. "That's what I'm trying to figure out. But consider this: Five years ago the Maloneys got a really big unsecured loan from somebody and now suddenly they have to pay it back. Who do you think that might be?"

"The mob?"

Beck nodded. "So now they're in big financial trouble, they've got to cut back and speed up — "

"And the mob sends in its experts," I said.

"And its enforcers," Beck added.

"You could be right." For the first time since I'd started working on this campaign, I thought I had an inkling about what Victoria Shales had been up to.

"Maybe Victoria thought this mob thing was the key," I said after a moment. "Maybe that's what she was putting all her energy into." I stopped suddenly and swallowed. "In fact, maybe that's why she planned to speak at that conference."

Beck stared at me. "To expose the mob at Pantheon?"

I nodded.

"If we could prove that, it would make Victoria's murder look a lot like a mob hit."

I looked at Beck, letting that awful thought sink in.

"But Victoria was hardly an anti-mob crusader," said Beck. "I never knew her to be interested in anything but winning organizing campaigns."

"Yeah," I said slowly. "On the other hand, seventy-four percent of Pantheon workers wanted a union until these thugs came onto the scene. Maybe she was trying to unmask them so they'd go away and leave the workers to vote in peace."

"Maybe," said Beck.

This was all just too much. I couldn't sort it all out tonight. I took out my lipstick case and did a quick reapplication. In the tiny mirror, my eyes looked weary. When I looked up, the bartender was leaning over behind the bar, offering us a great view of her rhinestone thong, which cut a shallow V into the smooth tan skin above her jeans. Beck watched casually, a faint smile on his face.

"By the way, how's it going with Yvette?" I asked.

Beck's head snapped up in an unguarded second, and then he relaxed again. Or at least he affected a relaxed appearance.

"Well, actually, I wanted to talk to you about that." Beck was looking straight down into his drink, as if he'd never seen a vodka tonic before.

"Okay," I said. I was irritated to realize that my heart had begun to hammer in my chest.

"Here's the thing," said Beck, turning toward me and taking hold of my hand. "You know, you're my best friend, Ruth. And — I just think you should know how I feel about Yvette."

"Okay," I said warily, sliding my hand out of Beck's.

Beck looked at me. "I really care about her, Ruth."

"But — I mean, she's only a kid, Beck," I managed, my heart still hammering.

Beck's brows came together. "Well, she's twenty-eight."

"She is? Oh. But still," I said, trying to keep my voice light.

"Ruth, I really don't want to hurt you."

"Yeah, I know," I said. Though part of me had to wonder.

"And you are the one who broke it off between us, you know."

"Uh huh," I said, peering into my scotch.

"And — well, I don't mean to brag or anything, but Yvette is just crazy about me."

I swallowed. "That's nice."

"And — when I'm with her I just feel — great! I mean, I actually think I'm in love with her."

"Oh!" I said. I felt a sharp stab in my chest, and before I even realized it, I was pressing my hand against my ribcage like a heart attack victim.

"Ruth!" Beck said, alarmed. "Are you okay?"

CHAPTER 19

"Sweetie, you don't look so good," said Nita, putting a hand on my shoulder. She had just arrived at the union office from work, as she did every day now.

I smiled. "Drank too much last night."

"But you only had one drink at the Pony."

"That was just my first stop."

"Oh." Nita laughed. "The wild life."

"I wish," I said. In fact, I was feeling no ill effects from the three scotches. It was Beck's news that had me dragging my ass around all day. His evidence that the mob was intervening in our organizing drive had set me on edge. But it was his declaration of love for Yvette that had caused a night of almost complete insomnia. I couldn't understand why I felt like a jilted lover. After all, I was the one who had jilted him, months ago. Besides, the guy was married.

Fortunately I'd been able to shut thoughts of Beck out of my mind during my meeting that morning with Al and the union attorney, who was finally beginning work on Al's NLRB complaint. Al had managed almost instantly to insult and annoy both the lawyer and me.

The call I'd made to Dellafield and Yaeger hadn't been very rewarding either. I spoke to the same receptionist I'd wrestled with before. He refused to give me any information about their client Donna Schmidt. He wouldn't confirm that Dellafield even had a client named Donna Schmidt. Despite this, I'd left my number and asked the nice man to have Donna Schmidt call me. His response made it sound like this would happen approximately when hell froze over.

So I was surprised when Joe handed the phone to me and said, "It's Donna Palast, formerly Schmidt."

I grabbed the phone and sat down at the desk.

"Hi, this is Ruth Reid," I said into the phone, twisting around to minimize the cacophony coming from the hungry organizers.

"I got a call from Dellafield and Yaeger that you were trying to reach me," said Donna Palast. "So you're with the union?"

"Yes."

"Where's Victoria?"

I wasn't prepared for the question. "Umm, I have some bad news about Victoria. She passed away."

"What?" Donna Palast's voice suddenly went up an octave. "How did she die? She wasn't sick. I talked to her just a few days ago!"

"She was killed. The police think it was a break-in. Some of her things were stolen, and she was shot."

"Oh my god."

"I'm really sorry to have to tell you this," I said.

There was a moment's silence. When she finally spoke, Palast's voice was shaky. "Do they know who did it?"

"Not yet. But it would really help to know why she'd contacted you."

Palast cleared her throat. "She called me up out of the blue a few weeks ago. An old girlfriend of mine in Bloomson had told her about – about why I left Bernie. I mean, he was violent. It took me years." Palast stopped suddenly.

"I'm sorry to put you through this," I offered.

"Thanks, it's okay. Victoria told me about the union and everything, and how Bernie was terrorizing everybody. And I could just picture it, how Bernie would react to a union drive at Pantheon. He'd go ballistic."

"I don't get it. Why does he care so much whether we unionize or not? He's not even in management. If we win, we could bring the wages up for people like him."

Palast laughed weakly. "That's not the way Bernie would look at it. See, he's worked there for eighteen years, and the whole time he's had running fights with certain people."

"Like Al Zielinski?"

"Oh, he hates Zielinski. But there are a dozen other guys he can't stand either. He needles people, and the people who fight back, he goes to war with. And he feels possessive about the whole place, like he owns it. He has to be in control totally, of everything. It was the same way in our family. If you could call it that."

"He sounds very unbalanced."

"He is. But he knows how to act super sane when he needs to. If anybody complained to management about something he did, he could always make it sound like he was just sticking up for the Maloneys. But he'd apologize and act really sincere about it. And then he'd get back at the person in some horrible way. He used to tell me about it after work. I think he did it to scare me."

"And why did Victoria call you?"

"Well, she knew from my friend that Bernie had been violent with me and that he's way behind on child support. She wanted me to take him to court. She said I should charge him with assault and put him in jail. I have partial hearing loss in one ear because of him, and Victoria said I could really get him for a lot, and stop having to even worry about child support."

I shuddered, imagining the kind of beating that would result in a partial hearing loss. "Thank god you got away. That must've taken a lot of courage."

When Palast said nothing, I prompted, "And Victoria put you in touch with Dellafield and Yaeger?"

"Yeah. I talked with them a couple of times. And now — I mean, I moved to the other side of the country, and now I just wish I'd moved further. Are you sure it was really just a burglary?"

I hesitated. "No, I'm not. Are you worried that Bernie found out about Victoria's conversations with you?" I guessed.

Palast inhaled sharply. "Yes. And the thing is, that's just the kind of thing Bernie could kill somebody over."

When I got off the phone with Donna Palast I stared across the room. Now we had two theories about Victoria's murderer. Was it the mob? Or was it Bernie Schmidt? Or maybe the cops were right and it was neither.

My eyes rested on my niece, who was chatting happily on the phone, probably with Kevin McGarry. Why had I brought her into what I knew from the beginning might be a dangerous campaign?

Now she was dug in. Lately she'd been virtually galloping into the office in the morning. I had a feeling it wasn't because of a newfound passion for the labor movement, but a newfound passion for a studly male. Whatever she was getting out of her involvement in the Pantheon drive, it wasn't worth the risk.

Liz was far too engaged in her phone conversation to notice my gaze. Plus, she had her toenails to worry about. She had propped her sandaled feet up on her desk and seemed to be surveying the state of the dayglo pink polish, perhaps trying to decide whether a fresh coat was in order, or maybe even a total toenail makeover. No doubt about it, my niece was in over her head — and I was the one who had put her there.

That afternoon, I ferried Liz and a few other people to the plant for the shift-change party. It was a warm, humid day, with darkening cumulous clouds that threatened to become thunderheads.

The party was considerably toned down from our debut effort. We still had the union banner, but we'd removed the picnic table and turned down the salsa. Still, it looked like a blue-collar cocktail party out there on the grassy strip. Liz and Kevin were playing their part, giggling intimately under the arching branches of an ash tree.

Joe, Nita, Al, and Juan were each talking with co-workers who had pulled over on their way home. It seemed to me that the sight of Juan Acevedo standing there in his jeans would be enough to cause any female — pro-union or not — to come to a screeching halt. Or gay man, for that matter.

Before I'd had a chance to check in with anyone, Silvia came jogging up to me. "Ruth," she said, huffing. "You need to see something. Over in the parking lot." She tugged me toward the plant.

"What is it?" I asked as I trotted beside her along the highway.

"Bernie Schmidt's doing his thing, and I want you to see it. I think we'll be okay if we stay right by my car."

"Shouldn't we try to stop him?"

Silvia turned to look at me with wide eyes. "My god, no! We could get killed!"

"I was wondering why Schmidt hadn't shown up at our party."

"Yeah, he's having too much fun over here." We turned into the parking area and Silvia pointed to her silver Honda in the middle of the lot. We headed toward it.

Schmidt was standing just outside the entrance wearing his blue security uniform unbuttoned to reveal his white tank undershirt and the silver chains that ringed his thick neck. He was too intent on his prey at the door to notice that Silvia and I were now standing about twenty feet away, on the far side of her car.

A clump of laughing workers pushed open the doors.

"Hey, what's so funny?" said Schmidt, poking a finger into the shoulder of a pudgy bald guy. "I saw what you did today."

"What the fuck are you talking about?" said the man, twisting around to thrust his face into Schmidt's.

Schmidt didn't blink. "I'm talking about, I saw you when you handed off the press to your buddy this afternoon."

"So what?" said the man. His co-workers were trying to pull him away from Schmidt.

"You were yapping to people about the union instead of doing your job, that's what, asshole. That can get you fired, you know."

"I was not, you stupid thug," said the worker, as his friends tugged him away. "Fuck you!" he yelled back at Schmidt as he was transported to his car.

"Jesus," I said.

"I know," said Silvia. "This is what he does now almost every shift change."

"How come the Maloneys don't rein him in?"

Silvia shrugged. "Schmidt's always been a creep. But it's only in the last year he's gotten this bad. We figure Toro likes what Schmidt's doing."

"And Toro's now running the show instead of the Maloneys," I said. Which would fit with Beck's scenario of a business held captive by the mob, I thought.

The next victim to come through the door was a white woman in her mid-thirties, carrying a flat square handbag decorated with sequined flowers. She pulled a pair of sunglasses out of her bag, then recoiled when she saw Schmidt standing there.

"What's the matter, nervous?" said Schmidt. He laughed.

"That's Marie Couillard. I've been working on her," Silvia whispered.

"Better take more of those pills you have — anti-anxiety drugs, right?" said Schmidt.

Couillard's eyes widened and she pulled violently away from Schmidt. Then she spotted Silvia and me and strode quickly toward us, her face red with rage.

"Not good," Silvia muttered beside me.

Couillard stepped up to Silvia's face and hissed, "You bitch! Screw you!" Then she whirled around and marched to her car.

"Marie!" called Silvia. But Marie had already slammed her door.

I turned to Schmidt. He was watching the scene with obvious interest.

"Let's go," said Silvia. We climbed into the Honda and Silvia backed out of the space.

"What was going on back there?" I asked.

Silvia did not look at me as she steered us rapidly out of the parking lot. "I think we just learned something," she said.

"What did we learn?"

"Marie was very private about her anxiety problem — I was surprised she even told me about it. It was during a visit I made to her house a few weeks ago. I think the only reason she mentioned it was that she was looking for an excuse to stay neutral about the union — and so she told me how the whole situation had already gotten her so worked up she got this prescription."

"And the only person you mentioned this to was Victoria," I guessed.

"Right," said Silvia.

"Who wrote it down and put it in that file. Which later got stolen."

"And now we know who's got it," said Silvia.

CHAPTER 20

"Your boyfriend's here," Nita breathed into my ear.

I turned away from my conversation and saw John Beck pulling his red Mazda Miata convertible up behind a rusty Dodge pickup. We were an hour-and-a-half into the shift-change party, and there were only a few other cars still parked along the road.

I looked at Nita. "Unfortunately he's someone else's boyfriend."

"Maybe you should fight for him."

"I tried. It's hopeless."

Apparently unconvinced, Nita shoved me gently in the direction of Beck's car.

"Hey!" Beck looked up at me and adjusted his sunglasses. He looked young for his age, but at the moment he gave the impression of an aging guy in denial.

"Hey. I'd forgotten you'd bought this thing. Very flashy."

Beck grinned. "Beth calls it the midlife-crisis mobile."

I smiled wanly.

"I'm just heading over to meet with Phil Scheiner. Can you come with me?"

I turned to Nita. "This thing is winding down, isn't it?"

"Oh yeah. You should definitely go with him." Nita raised her eyebrows at me.

I located Liz, who was still flirting audaciously with Kevin McGarry, and asked her to take my car back to the public lot a few blocks from the union office.

"Don't worry about me tonight," she said. "Kevin'll give me a ride home. Right, Kevin?"

Kevin nodded enthusiastically. Probably looking forward to some time alone in the car with Liz.

Logistics arranged, I hopped into Beck's little car. As we peeled off I gathered my curls tightly behind my head and tried to pull them into a bun. I knew it was futile. Within seconds my hair was whipping furiously around my face. And despite everything that had happened in the past few days, I smiled. The sensation of getting away — with Beck, in a fast car — was delicious.

"So how's it going?" Beck asked a few minutes later. Our moments of glorious speed were over, ended by the press of rush hour traffic. We were now crawling in the direction of Elizabeth, New Jersey. Our speed, or lack of it, gave us lots of time to admire the swamp grass and refineries along the way.

"I keep learning new things, and none of them are good," I said, stretching my arms out to capture the breeze that riffled through the grass.

"Like what?"

I related my conversation with Bernie's Schmidt's ex, including her fear that Schmidt might have gone after Victoria.

"Wow." Beck's eyes stayed on the road, but I could tell his mind was racing. Probably trying to figure out how to find information that could either nail or exonerate Schmidt.

"And just now we learned that Schmidt's the one who stole Victoria's files," I said.

"What?" The Miata veered toward the shoulder as Beck turned to look at me.

I told Beck about Schmidt's encounter with Marie Couillard.

"It's possible Schmidt got the information some other way," said Beck.

I shrugged. "Maybe. But Silvia doesn't think so."

I stared out at the swamp. The drone of a hundred motors idling around us suddenly seemed overpowering.

"You think maybe you should go to the police?" Beck asked. "This may be starting to add up to something."

"You think?"

Beck glanced at me. "I don't want you to be Bernie Schmidt's next victim."

I breathed in the humid, refinery-scented air. The smell wasn't really that bad. It was a hell of lot better than chicken grease. "Last time we talked, we thought it was the mob. I don't think we've exactly got a smoking gun. Besides, I don't plan on being the kind of threat to Schmidt that Victoria was. Or to the mob. My strategy is to build the organizing committee, not hunt down thugs and mobsters."

"Yeah, except here we are driving to the Cappellini family capitol in Elizabeth, New Jersey."

"This is your interview. It's not my focus. You know, even if Victoria's approach worked and the union won the election, there'd be nobody ready to run the local. Because Victoria did squat to build up these organizers — in fact she was demobilizing them."

Beck glanced over at me and smiled faintly.

"And why did she even choose to go with a traditional NLRB election? It's disempowering. And it's so easy to lose." I crossed my arms. I didn't have to explain my point to Beck, who had written a prize-winning series of articles on the failures of the National Labor Relations Board. Bosses had learned how to subvert the NLRB a long time ago. Like Toro, they used firings, threats, harassment, captive meetings — whatever it took to convince workers to vote against the union. And it usually worked.

But in my opinion there was another problem — NLRB elections tended to put the process of organizing into the hands of experts, people who could wend their way around the stuffy world of labor law. Workers were left on the sidelines. As a result, if you were lucky enough to win an NLRB election and even get a first contract, you were often left without the very thing a strong union required: seasoned and motivated rank-and-file fighters.

Victoria had always hated thinking about that very unglamorous question of what happened *after* the union election. By the time workers got around to the gritty slog of building their new union, she was long gone.

Beck looked over at me to see if that was all I was going to say.

"I'll be damned if I'm going to bust my ass just so the union can get a few extra dues dollars out of people like Joe and Silvia," I said, my voice rising to crescendo. "I want these people to win some control over their lives!"

Beck snorted. "There she is again. Lollypop."

I sank down in my seat like a deflated airbag. Lollypop was what Beck called me when my Shirley Temple qualities started to show.

"I thought you'd given up on being a true believer," Beck said. "I thought you were going to be all jaded from now on."

I looked out at the waving grass. "Don't worry. The true believer is dead. That was her last gasp you heard just now."

A few minutes later, we passed a sign announcing our arrival in Elizabeth, New Jersey. Beck glanced at me again. "How long has Scheiner been trustee of Local 557?"

"I think about six months. Everybody knew for years that the Cappellinis controlled that union. They were raiding the pension fund and cutting sweetheart deals with the employers, the whole thing. The feds finally got them on racketeering and mail fraud and a bunch of other stuff."

"What do you think will happen after Scheiner leaves?" Beck asked.

I shrugged. "I don't know. If we're lucky, the workers will finally be able to freely elect their own leaders. Then they can start fighting and losing like the rest of us."

Local 557's office was located upstairs from an old Woolworths that had since been converted into a permanent indoor flea market.

In front was a shabby reception area whose receptionist had apparently left for the day.

"Hello?" I called out. Beck and I proceeded to the door at the back of the reception area, which led to a short hallway, its floor covered with threadbare, stale-smelling olive green carpet.

"Hello?" Phil Scheiner's head poked out of an office a few feet away.

"Phil!" I gave my old colleague a hug and introduced him to Beck. Phil Scheiner was one of those small skinny men who seem to age at an unnaturally slow pace. He looked almost exactly the way he had the last time I'd seen him eight years ago: wispy blondish hair, a round face with little round glasses. On the surface he had a bookish air. But he was much tougher than he looked. As trustee of a formerly mobbed up local, he would have to be.

We followed Scheiner into his small office. He gestured for us to sit in a pair of chairs in front of his desk. Scheiner sat down behind his modest desk. His chair was padded. I could tell, because some of the padding was emerging from a tear in the vinyl surface.

"Nice office," I said.

Scheiner laughed. "You may have heard — we sold the old Local 557 building. The workers called it the fortress. Anyway, we figured the union shouldn't have so much money tied up in real estate."

I nodded.

"Listen, I read about Victoria in the paper, " said Scheiner in his soft tenor. "I couldn't believe it. I'm so sorry."

"Thanks."

"It must be awfully tough trying to pick up where she left off. I bet Tommy really twisted your arm on that one."

"You don't know the half of it," I said. "But that's actually why we wanted to see you."

"I figured," said Scheiner.

I glanced at Beck, who met my gaze and raised his eyebrows questioningly.

"Uh — how so?" I asked Scheiner.

"Oh, well, you know I sent her those books. I just assumed that's why you wanted to meet with me."

I swallowed. "What books?"

Now it was Scheiner's turn to look surprised. "Oh. You mean you didn't know — ?"

Beck and I both shook our heads.

"Oh, gee. Well, Victoria called me a couple weeks ago. She told me she was investigating whether the Cappellinis might have been involved at Pantheon. And she asked if I could let her look at the books from the Local 557 pension fund. From before the trusteeship. It's called the Columbus United Pension Fund."

I glanced at Beck. He was frantically taking notes.

"Did you give them to her?" I asked.

Scheiner nodded. "Sure. It's all public now. When John called and asked for a meeting I just assumed you were following up on that. You must have looked through Victoria's computer files?"

I shook my head. "We scoured all her files. We didn't see anything like that."

Scheiner stared at me. "I wonder where she stored them."

"Did Victoria tell you what she was looking for exactly?"

"No, she just said she wanted the spreadsheets from the year before the local was trusteed. So I emailed them to her."

"Listen, is there any chance you could forward that stuff over again? Or give us a hard copy?"

"Sure. I can print out a copy right now." Scheiner turned to his computer keyboard and made a few rapid keystrokes. Soon the aging laser printer in the corner began noisily churning out sheets.

Scheiner leapt up from his chair and grabbed the sheets. "So —" he said as he handed me the papers. "I don't get it. If you didn't know about this pension fund stuff, what made you call me?"

Beck cleared his throat. "We turned up something else. We found out that a guy who's been harassing union supporters at Pantheon used to work for the Cappellinis."

"But in Queens," I added, watching Scheiner's face.

Scheiner looked intrigued. "Queens? That's a whole other branch of the family."

"But also in the mob," said Beck.

"Oh, absolutely."

Beck looked at me and then back at Scheiner. "How much do you know about the Queens family? What do you mean, a whole other branch?"

"I'm not exactly an expert," Scheiner replied. "But I do know the Queens Cappellinis have had their hands in all kinds of dirty business — drugs, prostitution, all that. But there's been a rift in the family for at least thirty years. I don't know how that got started, but from what I've heard, they compete for dominance and they've been stealing bits of each others' business for years."

Beck scooted forward in his chair. "Who's in the Queens family? What else do you know about them?"

"My understanding is that there were originally five brothers. They're all in their fifties or sixties now. But I think only three of them are still active. One of the brothers is estranged from the family. And another one's serving time. But that's about all I know."

Scheiner looked down at his watch, then quickly leapt to his feet. "Jeez, I hadn't realized the time. I have to pick up my son. But I think I told you just about everything I know. If you have any more questions, feel free to call me."

Beck and I stood up and followed Scheiner to the reception area. "Just one more question," I said. "How long ago was it that you sent that stuff to Victoria?"

"I know exactly when it was," said Scheiner without hesitation. "It was two days before she died."

CHAPTER 21

"Oh, look!"

"What?" Beck's eyes remained focused on the road ahead.

"The Pretty Pony. Let's have a drink. I can't hear a thing you're saying in this car."

"Can't. I told Yvette I'd meet her for dinner."

"Oh." I turned and looked out at a passing car wash.

"Ruth."

"What?" I said, my face still turned away.

"Okay, okay. But just one." Beck put on the brakes. He'd spotted a parking space.

"Oh, goody!"

Beck laughed. "You're incorrigible."

"Uh huh," I nodded as Beck backed into the spot.

"My god, here it is. Look at this." Beck shoved the papers Scheiner had printed out over to me along the bar's edge.

I stared down at the spot just above Beck's index finger. He needn't have bothered--the words "Pantheon Printing" leapt off the page at me. I looked back up at Beck. "Eighty-thousand dollars a month? How could Pantheon possibly swing that?"

"Exactly," said Beck as he leafed through a few more pages. "It looks like the payment s got bigger as the year went on."

I regarded Beck. "So it's just like you thought. The mob *did* give the Maloneys that big unsecured loan."

Beck leaned back and nodded. "Yep. And when the Cappellinis saw the writing on the wall with this trusteeship, they started calling it all in."

"Which put major pressure on the Maloneys – who then put major pressure on the workers to produce."

"Yeah. Now the question is, what's the story with the Queens branch of the family? Are they the ones who sicced Tim Beatty on you? And if so, why?"

I shook my head. It was all too much. Besides, my scotch was icy and the jukebox was pounding infectiously. Part of me wanted to rub my foot against Beck's calf like old times. The other part was mortified by the thought.

"So now we know for sure that we're hot on Victoria's trail," I said.

"I wonder if she got to Scheiner and his books the same way we did," said Beck.

"You mean by tracing Tim Beatty? Maybe. As far as I know, that encounter Beatty had with Alonzo Lopez was the first time we've seen the guy. But Victoria might have tracked down Beatty because he was one of the ghost employees on that list she had."

"I wish I knew where the list came from." Beck was looking down at his martini, which he was rolling around in the glass. As far as I could tell, he hadn't even noticed the bartender, a bony redhead who might have been on summer break from Rutgers. It wasn't like Beck at all.

I sat up straighter on the barstool. "Maybe Victoria got the list from the same person we did — the one who mailed it back the other day," I said.

Beck looked at me. "But you said you thought Bernie Schmidt stole the list from Victoria's desk — along with those other files. So how would this person have even gotten the list back from Schmidt?"

I shook my head, picturing the neatly written message on the post-it note attached to the list: "I think this belongs to you." Whose hand had penned that note?

"Maybe Larry Lemke sent Victoria the list," said Beck. "Then Schmidt stole it from you and returned it to Lemke thinking that's who it belonged to. And then Lemke sent it back to the union again."

I frowned. "Why would Schmidt give Lemke the list? And why would Lemke send it to us? He might have some problems with the Maloneys, but I don't think he's exactly on our side. Besides, Lemke seemed really surprised that we knew about the ghost employees."

"Oh well. You know what I'm happy about?" Beck asked with sudden spirit.

"Umm, what?" I hoped I wouldn't have to listen to Beck declaring love for Yvette again.

"Now that we've got a Queens angle on this story, the Star is going to give me at least a couple of weeks to work on it."

"Oh," I said, relieved. "I hadn't thought of that."

"Yep. I'm all over the Queens Cappellinis now."

"Good. Just watch yourself."

Beck looked at his watch suddenly. "Oh, shit. Umm, you mind if I make a quick call?"

"No, go right ahead," I said. I reached immediately for my glass while Beck turned the other way on his barstool and punched numbers into his cell. Unfortunately, the pounding music and the roar of patrons weren't enough to drown out Beck's conversation.

"Hi, honey? Listen, I'm running a little late," said Beck into the phone. Honey? Beck had never called me honey. I'd scored "babe" a few times.

"No, no, just the fish is fine. You want me to pick up anything else?"

Wait a second, I thought. He must be talking to his wife. But hadn't Beck said he was having dinner with Yvette?

"Love you too, hon," said Beck. He beeped off and tucked his phone into his backpack.

"Okay, doll, let's blow this joint," said Beck, sliding off the stool.

"Was that Beth you were talking to?" I asked as I retrieved my bag.

"Uh, no. That was Yvette."

"Oh. You sounded so domestic. It almost sounded like you're living together or something."

Suddenly Beck stopped and turned to me. "Listen," he said, standing so close I could feel his breath on my face. "I wanted to tell you last night. But I just couldn't. I guess I was trying to kind of bring you down easy."

My breath caught in my throat. "What do you mean? You mean you *are* living with Yvette?"

Beck nodded. "For a little over a week now."

"You left Beth?"

Beck nodded again. "Wasn't it about time, Ruth?"

Oh, yes, I thought. It was about time nine years ago when we first slept together. "Uhh, where does Yvette live?"

"She's got this little place in Cobble Hill. It's kind of cute, but it's a little small for two people." Beck coughed. Apparently this conversation was awkward for him. I knew it was awkward for me.

"Beck, this all seems kind of sudden."

"I know. It sort of took me by surprise. I had no idea it was going to happen like this."

Beck made it sound like he'd been possessed by aliens.

"I guess you're really in love with Yvette, and you just couldn't pretend with Beth anymore," I ventured. I forced myself to say the words, to accept the idea.

Beck hesitated. "Yeah. Yeah," he said, his voice strengthening. "I *am* in love with Yvette. It just brought the whole thing to a head."

Well. My saying it was one thing. But when Beck said it, it still felt like a knife blade in the heart.

Beck was silent for a moment. "Anyway, you can reach me on the cell anytime. I promise I'll call you right back."

"Great," I said. I didn't want to call him at Yvette's house anyway.

"Ruth," Beck said, gripping my shoulders. "I don't want to hurt you. Are you okay?"

I cleared my throat. "Well, you've been unhappy for a long time. And you already told me you're in love. This isn't that big a surprise."

"Are you sure?"

"Oh, absolutely," I said with conviction.

We stepped out onto the sidewalk, which appeared to me to be rolling back and forth. And I'd only had one scotch. Less than one, since Beck had been in such a hurry to leave.

"Are you sure you're okay?"

"Oh, come on, Beck."

"I'll call you later if you want," said Beck.

If you want. How polite.

"Oh shit!" I said, abruptly stopping in the middle of the sidewalk.

"What?"

"I think I left my notebook in the bar. I better go get it."

Beck stepped back and looked at me questioningly. "I don't remember you having a notebook."

"Yes I did. Remember that little blue thing? I just wrote a couple things down while you were on the phone. Listen, you go on and I'll just go get it."

"Well, okay," said Beck. "You sure you're all right?"

"Would you stop it?" I said. I wheeled around and flung open the door to the Pretty Pony. Then I looked back at Beck and shouted, "See you tomorrow. Have a nice dinner!"

I've tried many times to reconstruct exactly what happened that night. That it's so difficult says something about my state when I exited the Pretty Pony after it closed at two a.m. I knew I shouldn't drive myself home. I thought maybe someone at the office would be willing to ferry me to the train station, so I walked there. Mr. Chicken was still open, its garish lights beaming out onto the sidewalk. I climbed slowly up the stairs to the office, gripping the handrail tightly. At the top I found the door locked and the office empty.

I should call a cab, I thought. No, too much money. I should call Silvia or Joe at home. But that would be too intrusive. I went back down the stairs and walked to the lot where I'd asked Liz to leave the Dodge.

I unlocked the car and sat in the driver's seat for a few minutes, trying to collect myself. My walk had sobered me up a bit, but I was still well under the influence. And bone tired. And ridiculously upset. For years, I'd pretended to myself that I didn't need, want or expect Beck to leave his wife for me. But now that he'd actually done it — for someone else — all nine years of rejection were staring me in the face. For a few minutes I let the tears I'd been suppressing in the bar pour down my face. Then I wiped my face clear with my palms, started the car and backed out of the space.

A surprising number of cars were on the road, sailing down the wrecked pavement at sixty miles an hour. Even in the so-called slow lane, anyone who, like me, preferred a sedate fifty got the finger from irate SUV drivers. I sat up straighter in the seat and gripped the steering wheel hard. I was in perfect control of the car — unless something unexpected happened. I wasn't the kind of alcoholic who lied to themselves about their impairment.

It was damn hot. But there was nothing to do about it. My air conditioner had died long ago, and all the windows were already open.

As I merged into the traffic on its way to the Goethals Bridge, a sentimental song came on the radio and my eyes started to water. I slapped the off button. I signaled and moved into the center lane, checking the rearview mirror. Behind me in the center lane was a green Toyota. And behind that was a large white SUV. A cold prickling sensation ran up my spine.

I stared at the road ahead, trying desperately to stay focused. But I couldn't keep from glancing up at the rearview every few seconds at our little parade — me, the green Toyota, and that big white SUV. And not a lot of space between us. I swallowed and wiped away the sweat that was threatening to roll into my eyes. I realized my arms were quaking.

Don't be silly, I told myself. There are millions of white SUVs around here. Jersey has to be the world capital of white SUVs. I looked up at the mirror again, hoping for reassurance. Instead I saw the SUV pulling out from behind the Toyota into the fast lane. The sound of its screeching tires broke through the general roar of traffic.

I fought panic. I tried to think how I could evade this vehicle if it did turn out to be Tim Beatty's. I could call 911 or the cops. Where was my cell phone? It was in my backpack. And where the hell was that? It wasn't in the seat next to me, where I usually put it. Shit! Had I left it in the bar? I snapped my head toward the back seat. There sat the plump black bag, with the cell phone tidily zipped inside. Useless.

What else could I do? I could take an exit and maybe find a gas station and maybe the attendant would come to my rescue – since, thank god, New Jersey gas stations always have attendants. But I didn't know where to find a gas station. I'd never taken any of the exits on this road, and I had no memory of signs indicating one. And in truth, it was all I could do to stay in my lane.

A few seconds later, my periphery vision registered the presence of the white SUV in the lane directly to my left. It seemed to have decelerated to exactly my speed. I may not have been thinking very clearly, but this much I knew: Things were not looking good.

Reflexively, I glanced in the rearview mirror again. The green Toyota wasn't directly behind me any more. It was now much further back, and it switched lanes. It seemed the Toyota driver wanted to stay the hell away from the erratic SUV. Maybe they sensed something bad was about to happen. I know i did.

I clamped my jaw tight and turned my head toward the SUV. It was definitely an Expedition. The windows were closed. I looked back at the road and pressed my foot down on the gas pedal. The Expedition kept pace.

I swallowed and looked over at the vehicle again. The window was rolling open. The driver came into view. A man in a baseball cap, staring right at me. Tim Beatty. I let out a sound, something between a whimper and a scream. I turned my eyes back to the road. What could I do? I was far too panicked to come up with a plan.

Instead, my eyes were drawn over to the Expedition again. What I saw made me recoil. Beatty was pointing something at me. A small dark object. A gun.

I screamed and unthinkingly slammed on the brakes. I was not aware that in reaction to the gun, I also pulled the car away, into the lane to my right. All I knew was that my car veered, and suddenly I was in new territory, with no cars in front of me. And then I heard the deafening blare of a horn followed by the squeal of skidding tires, all in excruciating slow motion. I was in the middle of having an accident. I had time to consider: Was I about to die? Was someone else about to die?

For all the feeling of infinite time, I didn't have time to figure out how to react — speed up? slow down? I just knew something awful was happening, and it was all my fault for driving drunk. The very instant I had this thought, I received confirmation that I was right: I was jolted forward, then jerked back, my head slamming violently against the headrest. And then my mind registered a sickening crunching sound.

CHAPTER 22

"Are you okay? Are you okay?" A heavy-set woman in a shiny pink shirt was knocking on my window, peering in at me, a look of horror on her face.

Everything was whirling around, and I couldn't find the door handle. The woman wrenched open the door.

"Oh my god, are you okay?" she said again, her hand on my shoulder.

"Uh, I think so," I said, as I struggled to get my feet out of the car and onto the ground. "Did I hit anyone? Was – was anyone hurt?"

"Nobody but you. Hey, why don't you just stay still until the ambulance comes? They should be here soon. I called 911 a few minutes ago."

"Ambulance? I don't need an ambulance." I continued my pathetic effort to extract myself from the car. I didn't want to be behind the wheel anymore. In fact I never wanted to drive again in my life.

Finally standing, I could see that my Dodge Neon was toast. The front end was crushed. Parked beside me, motor still running, was the green Toyota.

"You're the Toyota," I said. "I saw you behind me."

The woman nodded.

"Thank god I didn't hit you!" Suddenly my face was wet with tears.

"Oh hon, there was no danger of that. I was way behind you. It was that guy in the white car that was scaring me. I dropped back after I saw him driving like a lunatic. Was he chasing you? What was he doing?"

I just shook my head, which sent unbearable streaks of pain down my spine. I could hear a siren in the distance. A wave of horror passed through me. The cops. Breathalyzer. Jail. I was so, so, screwed – and so, by extension, were my compatriots at Pantheon. And it was all my fault.

Several hours later, I sat slumped in a folding chair along the yellow-tiled wall of a police station somewhere in New Jersey. The place smelled like sweat, burnt coffee, and the ammonia cleanser somebody had just used to mop down the lime green linoleum floor. My head still pounded, and whenever I moved it, my neck flared with pain. For some reason I had refused to be taken away in the ambulance. Maybe I'd thought that by opting to go to jail instead of to the hospital, I was accepting responsibility for what I'd done. I regretted that decision now. I wanted treatment. At least some pumped up version of aspirin that might ease the pain that filled my skull.

I'd blown into the cops' breathalyzer at the scene and failed the test. No surprise there.

I'd told my story several times, including the part about Tim Beatty pulling a gun on me. "You need to go after that guy — he's dangerous. I know who he is. I even have his license plate number," I'd said with all the conviction I could muster. But in my heart I blamed myself. The officer seemed to concur. He took down what I'd said, but he looked skeptical. Probably to him I was just one more worthless DWI telling one more pathetic lie.

Now I sat in this hard cold folding chair against the wall, waiting to be booked. I occupied myself by staring at the floor and thinking about the consequences of what had happened. I knew I was in line for a suspended license, a fine, and a state-sponsored reeducation program for drunk drivers. I also knew I was going to have to spring for a new car and higher insurance. Or go without a car, which was my current preference.

But who cared about all that? What was killing me was the effect my DWI would have on the organizing drive. I stewed about the many ways our opposition was going to use this lovely new development. And James Shawcross would be thrilled.

Sitting in the chairs next to me were three prostitutes. One of them was stoned on something. Another looked, like me, depressed and catatonic. But the woman who sat closest to me was tapping the stiletto heels of her cheap black pumps on the floor, looking like she had places to go and people to see. She had on a tight black skirt and a bright yellow halter top that showed off her smooth dark skin. Her hair was pulled back sleekly against her skull. I figured she must have been around thirty. Her perfume pervaded my senses — it was one of those clean fruity scents preferred by teenagers — incongruous, I thought. What had brought this woman to this unlovely place?

A stout white police officer appeared in front of us. "Okay, you!" he barked, pointing at me. "Over there." He cocked his thumb at a desk on the other side of the room.

I got up and glanced back at my fellow arrestees — a move that caused a rip of pain to run up my spine.

The woman in the yellow halter top didn't seem to notice my wince. She gave me an ironic smile. "Don't worry, honey, we'll keep your seat warm for you," she said, patting the chair I'd just vacated.

The cop took down all my information, for the umpteenth time. However, the fingerprinting and photo-taking part provided some variety. When the camera snapped in my face, the humiliation of the moment overtook me. I was an awful person, an irresponsible alcoholic, a terrible organizer, an unworthy friend, and a rotten role model for my niece. And on top of that, John Beck didn't love me.

After they took the photo, I just stayed there, leaning against the cold wall and wishing that somehow I could evaporate.

Bail was set at $250. I paid it. And then I was told I could call whoever it was I needed to call.

And who in the hell *was* that? I sat at the battered metal desk I'd been directed to, my hand resting on the smudged beige phone. It was just after six a.m. I looked and felt like a complete ass. I was about to wake someone up so they could come and witness my humiliation. Who was that lucky guy or gal?

Back at the scene of the accident, I'd left a message for Liz, telling her vaguely that I wouldn't be home till the morning. I had tried to sound as buoyant as possible, hoping that my niece would conclude I was out on a date. Well, I didn't want to call her again now. Liz was the last person I wanted to see at that moment.

I put my hand against my pounding temple. Someone in Jersey, I thought at first. But when I went through the list of possibilities, each one seemed worse than the last. Nita? No. Silvia? No way. Joe? Forget about it.

I gave up on the Jersey crew and started going through the list of possible New Yorkers. I knew Sandy would be here in a flash. But did I want to live with the years of ragging that would ensue? I thought not. Beck? Not in this lifetime. Who else could I trust?

Suddenly I knew exactly who I had to call. Tommy McNamara. Tommy would take me home, and along the way I would explain to him that I was a liability to the organizing drive — now even more than when I'd started. Not only was I obviously a drunk, I was a dangerously morose drunk. And now, with the DWI arrest, I had made myself and the organizing drive a perfect target for the opposition. They just couldn't afford to keep me on. The only chance we had of winning the drive was to find a competent, sober organizer to take my place right away.

That resolved, I punched in Tommy's home number. Tommy picked up after a couple of rings.

"Tommy, it's Ruth."

"Hey there, Ruthie. What's up? You in jail or something?"

I managed a laugh. "Actually, I am."

"Oh," said Tommy, not sounding particularly surprised. "What is it?"

"DWI. I'm hoping you can come over here to New Jersey and drive me home."

"Oh jeez, Ruthie. You okay?"

I looked up at the ceiling. "Physically I am. Tommy, I'm so sorry. I've just blown this campaign." Before I knew it, I felt something rising up in me. It crested with tears that spilled down my face in a solid cascade. I wiped them away impatiently. Don't waste Tommy's time with your self-pity, I thought.

"Hey. Don't beat up on yourself," said Tommy. But I could hear from the low, uninflected tone of his voice that my news was very disappointing. Well, of course it was. He had pinned his hopes for those workers' lives, and his own career, on me. And now, I had fucked up. In an especially stupid way.

"So we gotta get a lawyer. I'll call our in-house guy," said Tommy.

I let air out of my lungs. "Okay, Tommy. But not right now, okay? I can't tell anybody this story again right now. Can you just come pick me up?"

"Okay, Ruthie. Tell me where you are."

I had no idea. I put the receiver down and went over to ask the policewoman sitting at the big desk by the doors. She wordlessly handed me a sheet with a map and directions.

I related the information to Tommy. When I was done I said, "We need to talk on the way back. We've got to find a new organizer. Right away."

"Don't be ridiculous," said Tommy.

"Tommy, you've got to listen to me on this — "

"Look. We'll talk about it in the car. Okay? I'll see you soon."

Tommy preempted any further discussion by hanging up. I put the receiver down and went back to my folding chair to wait.

The three prostitutes still hadn't been booked. Only the woman in the halter top was still awake. The other two had let their heads loll back uncomfortably against the wall. I wondered if the cops were punishing them by making them sit here for so long.

"How'd it go?" the halter top woman asked after I'd resettled myself next to her.

I looked at her. "Humiliating."

"Uh huh." The woman made a clicking sound indicating her extreme familiarity with the situation.

"You got the time?" she asked me after a minute.

I looked at my watch. It was blurry. In fact everything was blurry. I squinted at the watch and held it toward the light. "Six-twenty," I said finally.

"Shit." The woman went back to tapping her heels on the floor.

I looked down at her shoes and decided I was tired of self-flagellation for the moment. I cleared my throat. "What are you in for?"

The woman smiled. She was very pretty. Her lipstick was a fragile pink. "What do you think?"

"Yeah, I figured. But I thought it would be rude to assume."

"What are you in for?"

"DWI."

"Bad girl."

I nodded. "That's just what I was thinking. I have so fucked everything up."

The woman glanced at me. "How'd it happen? If you don't mind my asking."

I swallowed. And then, for some reason, I told the whole awful story over again.

"Okay, slow down there," the woman said after a minute. "You're saying there was a guy waving a gun at you on the way to Outerbridge?"

I shook my head. "Goethals."

"No. Wait. I'm talking about the guy with the gun here, not the damn bridge. That's what caused your accident right there. Why was he aiming a gun at you?"

"It's a long story."

"Well, are the cops going to go get this guy? Because from what you're telling me, *he's* the one caused that accident." The woman looked at me with complete concentration, waiting for my answer, like it really mattered.

I shrugged. "They sure didn't make any promises." I sat back in my seat. She was right — I should have pushed the cops harder than I had. But I just wasn't up to it. I was too busy doing battle with myself.

The woman was shaking her head. Amazed, I guessed, at my self-destructive passivity.

"Is this your first offense?" she asked after a moment.

"Uh huh. I mean, other than for protests and stuff."

"Well, it won't be that bad then."

"Oh, it's bad."

I let my head rest against the tiled wall and then turned toward the woman again. "How about you? Is it your first offense?"

The woman looked at me with incredulity. "What do you think, honey?"

"Oh. So I guess you've been here before."

The woman let out a snort of a laugh. "Oh, once or twice. It's what we call an occupational hazard."

"I bet. Crappy industry."

"Baby, you have no idea. At least I'm doing it for myself now, not for that man I used to be with."

I nodded. "But still. Don't you wish you had another option?"

"Are you crazy? Of course I do! Tell me where else I can find a job that pays more than minimum wage? With me being a high school dropout with no job experience — supposedly."

"You know, what you guys need is a union," I blurted.

Oh Christ. If I'd had more energy I would've slapped myself on the forehead. I was a fanatic. Trying to organize a prostitute at a Jersey cop shop at six a.m., at what was probably the low point of my entire life.

The woman wheeled around and looked at me. "You're shitting me, right?"

I couldn't believe I was going to pursue this. "Well? Come on —
wages, benefits, working conditions — you'd do a lot better with a
union." The words were out of my mouth before I'd even thought of
them.

"Girl, where are you from? Hooking is illegal. And I've heard
about those unions. I got rid of my pimp once already."

I scooted forward in my seat, pathetically ready to leap to the
defense of unions. "What do you mean — dues? That's bogus. That's
nothing compared to the wage increases you could get."

"I mean I don't need some fat old white guy out there
somewhere telling me what to do."

"Oh," I said, leaning back again. "Good point."

The pause in the conversation allowed a small portion of my
sanity to return. I couldn't organize this prostitute. I couldn't even
organize myself to get down the fucking highway. I crossed my arms
and went back to my own thoughts. I had to make Tommy get
another organizer. I had to tell Liz to move out of my house, because
I was in no position to babysit. I had to find a way to pay for a new
fucking car.

Tommy arrived just after seven. By then the prostitutes had
finally been booked. I had exchanged business cards with the
woman in the halter top. Her name, Beverly Cross, was spelled out
in raised gold cursive on a black card. Beverly was hoping to get into
the call-girl business. Maybe she'd even run her own house. I told
her maybe it would be a union shop. Beverly thought that was pretty
funny.

Once I was belted into Tommy's Ford Mercury, I told him
everything that had happened since I'd left the bar.

"Ruthie!" Tommy exclaimed when I got to the part about Tim
Beatty and the gun. "You didn't tell me that! What's wrong with
you? Okay, so shouldn't have to drive yourself home. But this
bastard was threatening you with a gun!"

"Yeah — " I said weakly.

"Ruthie. Don't be an idiot. Look what this guy did. And if he
did it to you — who's next, right? Is he going to go after that guy
Joe? Or Silvia or somebody?"

Or Liz? I thought. "You're right Tommy. I know you're right."

"You're saying the cops didn't even try to go after him?"

I shook my head. "By the time the cops heard about it, he could've been in Pennsylvania."

Tommy shook his head.

I seized the opportunity to lay out for Tommy the arguments I had been rehearsing in my mind for the past two hours. The one about my incompetence. My alcoholism. My complete inability to pull off the job. The absolute necessity of assigning another organizer.

Tommy listened to it all in silence. When I was done he said quietly, "You know what you should *really* feel guilty about, Ruthie? Quitting. You're telling me you're just going to walk away and let those workers down?"

I swallowed. Tommy had always known exactly how to get to me. "No, that's not it. I'm letting them down by *staying*. Don't you see that?"

Tommy glanced at me. "No I don't, Ruthie. And besides I got no one else to assign to this thing anyway."

I shook my head. "If you had to, you'd find somebody."

"Oh. You think DePietro's going to save the day? We've already been through that. Look. You're in no position to make a decision like this right now. You just had some bastard chasing you down the freeway with a fucking gun. I don't even know what happened in that bar — " he glanced at me and I looked down at my shoes " — that got you so upset in the first place. I know it was something. On top of that, you've probably got whiplash. Plus you haven't slept in the last twenty-four hours. So just give it a rest, okay?"

I looked out on the hills of Staten Island, cluttered with condos. Tommy was getting tired of arguing with me. I couldn't blame him.

I pulled my backpack onto my lap and got out my cell phone. There were two messages. The first was from John Beck. He'd called while I was still at the Pretty Pony. "Where are you?" he'd said. "I hope you're not back in that bar drinking by yourself."

The next message, left just a few minutes before, was from Joe, who had said I should call him at the union office right away.

Can't, I thought. Can't deal with it. Too tired, too sick. And it's not really even my job anymore. For some reason I listened to Joe's message again. To the sound of his voice. The urgency in it.

I punched the union office number into the phone. "Joe?"

"Hey!"

"What's up, Joe?" I croaked.

"Ruth, you don't sound too good."

"I had kind of an accident on the way home. I'm okay now though." I listened to myself with amazement. I wasn't okay. I wasn't remotely okay.

"What happened? Are you sure you're alright?"

"Joe, just tell me what's happening."

"Well, Juan called for you about fifteen minutes ago from the plant. He said there'd been an accident and he asked if you could come down there to meet with management about it."

"What do you mean an accident?" I said, my voice rising. Tommy looked over at me.

"He didn't say. He probably couldn't really talk from where he was calling. I'm figuring maybe our guys followed through on that plan they had."

Right, I thought. The job action.

"But listen, I could just go down there myself — " Joe began.

"Uh, hold on Joe." I held the phone to my chest. I breathed in and out a few times and looked out the window. Finally I turned my body stiffly toward Tommy.

"Tommy," I said, my voice reduced to a rasp. "Turn the car around."

CHAPTER 23

Joe met Tommy and me in the Pantheon Printing reception area. When he saw me, Joe gave me a hug, then stepped back and studied my face.

"Are you sure you're up for this, Ruth?" he asked.

I nodded. "I know I look like hell. But I think I need to be here. I wasn't kidding about the looking like hell part. Tommy and I had stopped at a gas station before we'd arrived. I'd spent five minutes in the women's room trying to fix myself. I still looked battered, red-eyed, and pasty-faced. Tommy and I had pooled our supply of aspirin — all of four tablets — which I'd downed with a bottle of seltzer. So far it had had no effect on my head, which still felt like a watermelon about to explode.

The receptionist glared at us. "Hello, Ms. Reid. They're expecting you," she said sharply. She picked up the phone, said a few words into it, and listened for a moment. Then she turned back to us, her eyes passing over Tommy and Joe. "They only want to see Ms. Reid."

I glanced at Joe, then at Tommy. "Tommy, this could be awhile. I can get someone to drive me home when we're through here."

Joe nodded in agreement.

"That's okay, Ruthie. I'll just wait here."

I shook my head. "Tommy. I've been enough of a pain already. You just go on, okay? I'll be fine."

Finally, with Joe's reassurances, Tommy gave me a goodbye hug and stepped outside. I was grateful to Tommy for coming to my rescue, but I was also glad to see him go. The humiliation had been wearing on me.

"I'm sorry, " I said, turning back to the receptionist. "But I'm not going into that meeting without Joe here. You know Joe Dysart, don't you?"

The receptionist raised an eyebrow at this, but got back on the phone for another murmured conversation.

"Okay," she said as she hung up the phone. "They're in the conference room." She motioned toward the hallway, where our old acquaintance Kelly stood waiting for us.

As we moved down the hall, I sensed something was different. I stopped for a second and listened. Silence. No vibrations. I looked at Joe.

"The Heidelberg is down," he said.

Kelly opened the conference room doors and Joe and I stepped in. Looking up at us were pressman Juan Acevedo, pre-pressman Victor Pucciello, the young bundler Malcolm Brown, and, most unexpectedly, assistant pressman Alonzo Lopez, the wobbler Joe and I had visited a few days before. It was morning, first-shift time, and Lopez worked lobster. He'd probably pulled a double shift again. But why was he here with our union activists? The last time we'd spoken, he'd been down on the union.

At the far end of the room sat Oscar and Sam Maloney and Larry Lemke, looking queasy. Beside Oscar, F.H. Toro stood, squinting at me as if trying to summon up his powers of x-ray vision. I wondered if he personally had sent Tim Beatty out after me with a gun. For the first time since the accident, I felt a surge of anger at someone besides myself.

Toro gestured for Joe and me to sit down.

"We've had a very serious incident here today," Toro began.

"It was an accident," Juan interjected, looking at me.

"It was *not* an accident," boomed Toro. "It was sabotage. We've called you here, Ms. Reid, because we know that the person behind this action is you."

"It was an accident," Juan repeated. "We've told you people for months that this was going to happen, and now you act surprised."

Toro turned to me. "Your strategy worked. These people started a fire and sabotaged the Heidelberg and now Pantheon has lost thousands of dollars."

"We did *not* start a fire!" said Alonzo Lopez. "You think we would put our co-workers at risk like that?" Lopez's eyes were on fire. He looked nothing like the sad-faced man Joe and I had interviewed before.

"Ha!" said an apoplectic Oscar. "Notice he doesn't even mention that they damaged the press! You wrecked the blanket. I wouldn't be surprised if you ruined a cylinder!"

"Mr. Maloney," said Joe, his voice loud and low. Everyone stopped talking and looked at him. "We've been telling you for months now that the pace Toro's people set for the presses is too fast. The fact is, we've been easing down the speed because we knew we'd have a problem if we ran it that fast. Probably today somebody just gave in to the pressure and tried to go as fast as you folks have been telling us to."

"That's exactly what happened," said Juan.

"What were those open buckets of solvent doing near the press, then?" said Sam. "You know very well that's not our policy!"

"That was me," said Malcolm Brown quietly.

Sam glared at him. "You're a bundler. What do you have to do with solvents?"

Malcolm was visibly shaking when he replied, "The pressmen just haven't had time, so I've been stocking."

"You aren't trained to do that!" said Sam, his voice rising. "Don't you know that solvent has to be in sealed containers?"

"Sam, you're getting it all wrong," Oscar snapped at his brother. "It wasn't an accident. They did it on purpose."

"That is not true!" said Juan.

"And then you disabled the electric eye so the press would keep running after the web broke!" Oscar added.

Juan shook his head. "I don't know anything about that."

In the brief pause in the sniper fire, Toro turned to me and said, "We are suspending these gentlemen pending an investigation into this incident. And if the investigation finds any evidence of sabotage, we intend to file suit against you and the Industrial Workers Union."

I felt rage rising up inside my body. I wanted to leap across the table and wring Toro's neck. "You can't just suspend workers arbitrarily in the middle of an organizing campaign — that's illegal!" I roared. "You can't defeat these workers by instilling fear — you're only going to make them more determined!"

"She's right," said Juan.

I turned to Sam. "Is that what you want, Mr. Maloney?"

Sam stared at me as if a slimy alien had just leaped out of my mouth. As I sat huffing, waiting for a response, I realized that my headache had totally disappeared. I didn't even feel any muscles complaining. I was like Popeye after the spinach.

"Can I just say something?" Larry Lemke had sat quietly till now, looking as moist and white as a mushroom. Now he edged forward in his seat and turned toward the Maloney brothers. "I wasn't consulted about this. Suspensions are handled by my office. We have a procedure — "

Toro was watching Lemke with disgust.

"It's my decision, Larry," said Oscar sharply.

"But at the very least I should be consulted," Lemke pleaded. "You're letting these outside consultants run this company into the ground. Look what's been happening here."

Oscar looked like he was going to jump out of his chair and bite Lemke on the nose. "You are *not* to challenge my authority in this plant, do you understand me? You work at our pleasure, and if we decide we need some outside expertise, then we'll hire some."

Lemke shrank down in his chair.

Lemke's protests had given me time to collect myself. My blood pressure had decreased and I had my breath back. I decided to try a softball this time.

"Mr. Maloney," I said, looking at both brothers, "you can't suspend these workers without any evidence of wrongdoing. We'll have to issue a complaint with the NLRB. And it'll only unify the workers against you."

Sam stared down at his hands. Oscar looked like he was trying to formulate a stinging comeback.

"And what about fixing the press?" said Juan. "It's still down. That's where you're losing most of your money — people are just standing around. You could lose an entire shift. Let us back in there and we'll fix it."

Oscar sneered at Juan. "What, and let you get your hands on that press again? No chance! We've got plenty of managers capable of the job."

"Oh yeah?" said Alonzo Lopez. "So how come over an hour later, it's still down? We could've fixed it by now."

"Just what did you expect this would achieve, Miss Reid?" said Sam, almost sadly. "What good does sabotage do to your cause?" As he spoke, Toro whispered something in Oscar's ear and Oscar nodded.

Before I could reply to Sam, Toro stood up and said, "Mr. Kelly will escort you out of the plant."

"Wait a minute!" I said. "You can't just summarily dismiss these people. And what about Victor Pucciello? What does he have to do with any of this?"

Toro looked at Oscar, who said, "He was working on the Heidelberg. They had him flying the press."

"How does that involve him in a web break?" I said.

"He was there," said Oscar.

"Victor was not involved in the accident in any way," said Juan.

But by then, we were being herded from the room by the stonefaced Kelly. In the course of our rapid walk down the hall, I realized that the spurt of vitality I'd had in the meeting was over. I was dizzy. I found myself touching the walls for support as I moved.

When I got to the parking lot, I leaned against a car and waited for the ground to stop moving while Joe and the suspended workers gathered around me.

"You were perfect, man!" Malcolm said to Alonzo Lopez as they did a low-five palm slap. Juan and Alonzo hooted as Malcolm did a little victory dance. Even I, leaning woozily against the car, had to laugh. These men had just been suspended from their jobs, and yet they were ecstatic.

"Okay, you guys," I said when I felt a little steadier. "What the hell happened in there?"

Juan laughed and clapped me on the shoulder. "It's what we told you about the other night, sister. We ran the press too fast — "

"Actually, it was just the speed they've been saying they wanted," blurted Alonzo.

"Yeah, and just like we said, the damn web broke."

"Did it ever!" laughed Malcolm.

"Okay," I said. "But what about the fire?"

Juan shrugged. "That happens sometimes."

"You mean you didn't start it?"

"No," said Juan. "We're printing on that kind of slick magazine paper, right?" I nodded. "They have to bake the ink in a huge oven so it doesn't just sit on the top of the paper and smear."

I nodded again. The other workers listened, watching my reaction with gleeful anticipation.

"So the web breaks, but the presses just keep rolling, and paper gets all wrapped around everything and it jams up," Juan continued. "And sometimes it gets stuck in the oven too long and catches on fire. Usually it just dies out inside the oven, but sometimes a piece gets stuck outside — "

"Yeah, like today," said Malcolm. "And then I had that solvent bucket right there, and it caught fire."

"Why was there a bucket of solvent there? Is that normal?" I asked.

"It was like I said to them," said Malcolm. "I knew it was kind of a shortcut, but the guys always say it's easier to clean off the presses with rags in a bucket than in those containers, and it's been so crazy lately — "

"So you took the fall for that, didn't you?" I said. Malcolm shrugged, smiling.

"Okay," I went on, holding my hand to my head and trying to concentrate. "So there was a fire with the solvent bucket, but it was an accident."

"Oh, yeah," said Juan. "Believe me, we don't want to mess with fire. We don't want anyone hurt."

"All right, what was that about blankets and cylinders?"

"If a break is bad enough, you can sometimes damage the rubber on the rollers in the press," said Joe.

"Is that a major expense?"

"The really big expense is the lost labor time," said Joe. "Everybody standing around waiting for the press to go back on. That's thousands of dollars."

"Yeah, that was weird," said Juan. "I meant what I said in there. We could've had that thing rolling again in less than an hour. Toro — even the Maloneys — they don't know squat about the Heidelberg. They have no idea how to operate it."

I took a deep breath. So far, it really didn't look like sabotage. The workers had only acted on their commands. "And what was that about an electronic eye?" I asked.

"That was me," said Alonzo Lopez. He looked down, as if repentant, but when his face came up again, he couldn't suppress a grin.

"I *thought* that was you!" said Malcolm.

"What does this eye do?"

"It shuts off the press when its sensor notices that there's no paper going through," said Juan.

"And you broke it?" I said, leaning toward Alonzo.

Alonzo just nodded, then gave me a delighted grin. "Otherwise, it might've been no big deal — just a web break."

"I thought you were on lobster," I said.

"Double shift," said Alonzo.

"I thought you were feeling a little iffy about the union."

Alonzo smiled slowly. "This thing happened, and I was just right there. It's like it had been building up all this time. I had to do something. So here I am." He held out his hands, palms up, as if in wonderment.

"And what about you?" I said to Victor Pucciello. "Were you involved at all in this thing? You don't normally even work on the press, do you?"

"No, I do pre-press work. Plate-making," said Victor. "But we've been so understaffed they had me flying the press. I was bundling papers off the Heidelberg last night."

"And what about the action? Were you involved in it?"

Victor shook his head and shrugged.

"Yeah, Vic got a bum rap," said Malcolm.

"I'm a little worried," said Victor in his thin voice. "My wife's got that throat cancer, and I really need the health insurance."

"Jeez, Vic," said Alonzo. Juan and Malcolm stopped grinning.

Victor noticed the changed mood and laid his stringy hand on Juan's. "It's okay. I'm glad we did it," he said.

I gave the group the most confident smile I could muster. I tried to formulate some words that would be both honest and reassuring, but I just couldn't think of them. Then I felt my periphery vision disappearing. I was looking down into a narrow tunnel of light with darkness all around. I felt my knees give way. And then I sank to the pavement.

CHAPTER 24

"Ruth?" Someone was peering down at me. Juan Acevedo. My eyes flew open.

"I'm okay, I'm okay," I said from my position flat on the pavement.

"We need an ambulance," Joe said, stooping over me.

"No." I sat up much more quickly than I should have, and the world went momentarily dark again except for the cascade of little white stars behind my eyelids.

"Ruth, what happened?" said Juan, resting his palm on my shoulder. "Are you sick?"

"She was in an accident last night," said Joe.

"What?" Juan said. "What accident?"

"You guys, come on," I said, trying to climb to my feet. I grabbed onto the hand Juan offered. He pulled me up and then steadied me against his shoulder. Once standing I tried to smile. "I'm okay. I wasn't injured at all, I'm just woozy. And tired."

"Ruth, at least sit down," said Juan, guiding me over to his aging blue Camaro. He opened the passenger door and I collapsed onto the seat with my feet still resting on the pavement. The workers gathered around the open car door.

"Look. I need to tell you guys something," I said, wiping a film of sweat from my forehead. "I made a mistake. I had too much to drink, then I got in my car — "

"Oh — " Malcolm blurted involuntarily.

"Right," I said. "Really bad. They got me on a DWI. This is going to be terrible for the campaign. I am so sorry. I apologize to all of you." I felt tears welling up again. I swallowed and willed the tears not to flow.

"Was anyone else hurt?" asked Joe, resting his hand on my shoulder.

I shook my head.

"Ruth, we're just glad you're okay. If you *are* okay," said Juan, peering into my face.

I was so embarrassed I could barely look at Juan or the others. First I had been stupid enough to commit a DWI. Now I was about to blubber in front of half the organizing committee. I sniffled, wiped away an incipient tear, and took a deep breath.

"So how'd it happen?" Malcolm asked.

"Well, I was trying to get away from Tim Beatty – you know, our thug," I said. "He pulled a gun on me on the way into Staten Island."

"*What?*" said Joe.

"He pulled a gun on you? My god!" said Juan. "Right on the highway?"

I nodded. "If I'd been sober, I probably could have evaded him."

"Look," said Juan. "I think you need to go to the hospital."

I shook my head, causing more stars to appear. "No, please. I just need to go home and sleep for awhile."

Juan looked at me skeptically, but said, "I can drive you to Brooklyn right now."

Ah, I thought. A shower. And then bed. Smooth sheets, fluffy cool pillows. My eyelids got heavy at the very thought. "Really? You wouldn't mind?"

"Hey — I just got fired. I got all the free time in the world." Juan walked over to the driver's side of the Camaro, opened the door and tucked himself into the seat next to me.

"Listen, you guys," I said, still looking up at Joe, Malcolm, Alonzo, and Victor. "You're incredible, what you did today. I'm really sorry to be letting you down like this — "

"Ruth, you stop that," said Joe, leaning down to pat my shoulder. "You just go home and get some sleep. We'll take care of things here today."

"Are you sure you don't need to go to the hospital?" Juan asked again as he shifted the car into reverse.

"No, I'll be fine." I smiled weakly at Juan and leaned back against the headrest.

Juan was a fast and skilled driver. He maneuvered the Camaro through the streets with a minimum of bouncing and a maximum of speed. When he got to a stretch of road that was in decent repair, he glanced over at me.

"Do you mind if I ask you something?" he asked.

"Go ahead."

"You joke a lot about drinking. Do you really have a problem with it? Or was this DWI thing a fluke?"

I inhaled deeply. "I love to drink, and sometimes I drink too much. But I'm not in the habit of driving under the influence."

Juan shot me another quick look then turned back to the road. "What made you do it last night?"

I looked out the window at the swamp grass waving in the breeze. Heat shimmered over the wetlands.

"Never mind, forget I asked," Juan said suddenly. "You should just be resting."

"No, no, that's okay." I cleared my throat. I had no idea what I was going to say. "I guess I was kind of upset last night. And obviously my judgment was terrible."

"Upset about the organizing drive?"

"Oh, no, not really."

"A personal thing?"

I looked over at Juan's profile, his strong, straight nose, his full lips. His black, silver-streaked hair was so thick, it barely riffled in the breeze from his half-open window.

"Yeah, personal," I said finally. "This man I'm friends with — we've been involved on and off, and now it looks like he's finally found the woman of his dreams."

Juan glanced over again and I gave him a small, wry smile. It hadn't been as hard to say as I'd thought.

"Beck?"

I nodded.

"You learned this last night?"

"Uh huh."

"He broke your heart."

I looked down at Juan's hand on the shift. "Yeah, kind of."

"Ruth," said Juan. And then he took his hand off the shift and rested it on my shoulder. I felt like I'd just made contact with an electric fence. Nerves were zinging all through my body.

This is insane, I thought. This was not the way I was supposed to feel about a member of the organizing committee. I stiffened and Juan immediately removed his hand.

"Thanks, Juan. I'll get over it," I said, crisply brushing nonexistent crumbs off my skirt. "I just feel awful about what this is going to do to the drive."

"Ruth, stop worrying about that. It's not that big a deal. I'm just glad you were willing to step in to help us at all." Juan gave me a warm smile. If I hadn't been sitting down, I would have swooned.

"Ruth?" Juan's hand was on my shoulder again, but this time he was patting it gently. Trying to wake me up.

I raised my head and looked out the windshield. "How did you find my house?"

"You gave me directions, remember?"

No, I didn't remember. I rubbed my eyes and opened the car door. It was a hot, humid, classic August day in the city. The air was thick with the smell of flowering trees mixed with the scent of overripe garbage somewhere in the distance.

"Let me walk you inside," Juan said.

As we approached the door, Liz came flying out. She was wearing white cutoffs, a cropped t-shirt and a red bandanna. Her face was flushed.

"Aunt Ruth! I just talked to Joe. Are you okay?" She stopped suddenly. "Oh. Hi, Juan." I saw a tiny smile flicker across her face before she stepped up to me and took the arm Juan wasn't holding.

"You guys, it's not like I broke my leg," I said.

"Uh huh. Joe already told me you fainted in the parking lot," said Liz.

"She refused to go to the hospital," Juan volunteered.

"I just need to get some sleep," I said. Juan and Liz exchanged glances.

An hour later, I was sitting in bed, freshly showered, drinking a tall glass of ice water. I'd shoved off all the covers except the sheets. The ceiling fan whirred a lazy rhythm over my head.

Juan had gone back to New Jersey. And, to my dismay, Sandy had arrived home from work early. She was now sitting on one side of my bed and Liz on the other, both silently studying me as I sipped my water. Perversely, I was now too wired to go back to sleep, and I would have enjoyed the company if they hadn't been perched over me like watchful gargoyles.

"Hey. You guys are making me nervous."

"You're making *us* nervous," said Sandy.

"Fine. But could you stop staring at me?"

"You never listen to me," Sandy said. Maybe this will teach you."

I rolled my eyes. "I feel awful, okay? I'll never drive drunk again in my life, I promise."

Sandy cocked her head as if waiting for a better response. When I said nothing she said, "You are an alcoholic. You should quit drinking."

I shut my eyes. In truth, I couldn't imagine myself without alcohol. Everything about me had been shaped by booze. Jukeboxes, stools, tumblers of amber liquid — that was my world.

"John Beck is treating you like shit," offered Liz.

I shrugged. "He fell in love. Can you blame him?"

Sandy sucked her teeth. "Mmm hmm."

"You know what?" Liz said, suddenly perky. "I think that guy Juan has a crush on you, Aunt Ruth." Liz raised a powerful arm up to her head and pushed the bandanna back, wiping the sweat from her forehead with the back of her hand.

"Anybody ever tell you you look like Rosie the Riveter?" I asked.

"Who's that?"

Sandy and I looked at each other. "You don't know who Rosie the Riveter is?" I said. "What did they teach you in that prep school anyway?"

"Aunt Ruth! That wasn't a prep school."

"Private school, whatever," I said.

I took another sip of water and shut my eyes. When I opened them, Sandy and Liz were still doing their gargoyle thing. "You know, Liz, while I was sitting in that awful cop shop, I got to thinking — "

"What? I feel a lecture coming on," said Liz.

"Well, I love you and everything, but I really think you should go back to D.C. for awhile. This campaign is getting too hot. I'm putting you in harm's way by having you here. I'm scared Tim Beatty's going to go after you next."

Liz sat up straighter and gave me a look of offended pride. "Aunt Ruth. Would you please give me some credit for being a grownup? I know you think I'm a totally spoiled, irresponsible teenager. But I'm not! And I'm not leaving — especially not now. You need people on your side. In case you hadn't noticed."

Sandy finally removed her gaze from me and turned to Liz, smiling faintly. Sandy approved of people with backbone. Even when they were being foolish.

"Sandy. Aren't you going to back me up on this?"

Sandy looked at Liz. "I don't know. Liz is right, she is a grownup. Maybe we should start treating her like one. And as for you," she added, turning back to me, "I wish you would quit this campaign. It's not worth dying over. They've already killed one organizer." Sandy's eyes bored into me.

I looked at Sandy, suddenly realizing that in fact I was *not* going to quit the campaign. I couldn't. And Sandy knew it too. After a moment, she flicked her eyes away.

"Sandy, I can't quit."

"She'll be fine, Sandy. I'll make sure of that," declared Rosie the Riveter from the other side of the bed.

I was lost in sleep when the phone on my nightstand erupted into sound. I bolted upright, then fell back again when I realized that someone had answered it. I glanced at the clock. It was four-fifteen p.m.

"She's sleeping. I don't want to wake her up now," Sandy was saying from downstairs. I propped my head up on my hand so I could hear better.

"I don't care. If you're so worried, why did you treat her that way the other night?"

Oh god. Sandy was yelling at John Beck. Did she really think that admonishing him would make him be any less in love with Yvette? But Sandy wasn't thinking about consequences. She was just lashing out at a man who had hurt me.

"Of course it's your choice," Sandy was saying. "But it wouldn't hurt to consider how your choices affect other people, would it?" Sandy's tone was icy.

"Oh, now I see why you're calling. I should have known. I'm sorry, but I don't think your deadline trumps Ruth's need to rest — "

Okay, that's it, I thought. I rolled over and sat up, an act that produced a wave of nausea. I stood up shakily and took baby steps out to the top of the stairs. Sandy was leaning against the wall in the foyer below me.

"Sandy?" I called down.

Sandy looked up, the phone still pressed to her ear. She gave me a crabby look and waved her arm at me, trying to shoo me back to bed.

"Sandy, let me talk to Beck," I said as firmly as I could.

Sandy clapped the receiver against her chest. "Ruth. You need to rest."

"I'm going to go pick up the extension." I went back to my bedroom and picked up the receiver from the nightstand.

"Beck?"

I heard a clattering sound as Sandy banged down the phone. A moment later I heard the front door slam.

"Ruth. How are you doing? And how come you aren't in the hospital?"

"All I need is sleep. I heard you're trying to make a deadline."

"Look, I'm really sorry about the other night. I had no idea you'd be so upset — "

Oh god. This was exactly the conversation I didn't want to have. "Beck. Just tell me about the story, okay?"

"I'm doing a story on your accident."

"What? Why the hell would you do that? Are you trying to kill the organizing drive?"

"Ruth. Listen to me. It's going to be in the papers no matter what I do. I'm sure the Jersey dailies have a hold of it. And they may not be the only ones — "

"I doubt that. Nobody's called to get a quote."

"You think anybody could get by that gatekeeper of yours?"

"But Beck, how come *you* need to write about this?"

"Wouldn't you like to have at least one story that describes what really happened?"

"What do you mean, 'what really happened'?" What really happened, I thought: Lovesick alcoholic organizer goes berserk on the highway.

"Reid. I'm talking about the fact that the person who caused this accident was a mobster named Tim Beatty. And that the police apparently refused to investigate your charge."

"Oh." I sat up again and leaned against the headboard. "How did you learn all that?"

Beck sighed. "Honey. You *are* tired, aren't you? I called the union office and Nita told me everything. I've already drafted a story, but I can't run it without confirmation from you. And deadline's in an hour and a half."

I swallowed. I was still stuck on the beginning of Beck's spiel, the "honey" part. I wasn't Beck's honey — that was Yvette's job now.

"Ruth, come on. Just give me a run through of last night. Okay?"

So I related every gruesome detail I could remember, from my excess scotch consumption to the accident to the cop shop. I threw in that morning's developments too — the meeting at Pantheon and the suspension of the printers. I could hear Beck tapping on his keyboard in the background as I talked. When I was through, he hurried off the phone to finish the story.

Late that night, the phone startled me awake again. This time, it rang four times before Liz picked it up downstairs.

"Hello? Oh hi! Huh? Oh, she's fine. She's just sleeping it off."

Ah. Another humiliating phone call.

"No, she was totally sober by the time she got home. She was just really upset."

I rolled over on my back. The ailanthus tree in front of the streetlamp outside created a shadow play on my bedroom wall.

"No, see, it's this guy she's been in love with for, like, forever," Liz was saying. "It's that reporter John Beck. And last night at the bar he told her he'd left his wife and moved in with his new girlfriend. Did you meet her? That Yvette reporter?"

Oh, Christ. Liz was telling her new boyfriend all my deepest secrets. I debated whether to stomp downstairs and tell her to hang up. Or maybe pick up the extension and start yelling. But she'd already done the worst — she'd given him Beck's name. How stupid was that? Tomorrow, I was going to have to have a serious talk with my niece.

CHAPTER 25

A strange thing happened when I woke up the next morning. I sat up and looked outside. The day was hazy, soaked in a sweaty brine of heat and moisture. And I was ready for it.

Everything was fucked up, I knew that. We had only seven days till the election. And I had to face not only my DWI arrest and the ensuing publicity, but two vicious thugs, Bernie Schmidt and Tim Beatty, and an employer that would do anything to defeat the union. And on top of that, John Beck had left his wife for someone besides me.

Deal with it, I thought. Act like Victoria. Brazen it out. No more whining. I put my feet on the floor and went to the bathroom to wash up. I was stiff and achy all over, and my neck was killing me. But the dizziness was completely gone and I felt rested for once. And from the way my jeans fit, it seemed I had lost about seven pounds. No doubt mostly in the form of sweat and tears.

Downstairs, another strange thing happened. I found a note from Liz. It said, "Gone to office. Call if you need anything."

Wow. In the old days, you couldn't have gotten Liz out of bed by ten, much less out the door and off to work.

A half hour later, I stepped outside and headed toward the garage. I was halfway there before I realized that I no longer had a car. I stopped, pivoted around and headed for the subway. Mass transit. Get used to it.

It took me over two hours on the subway, a train, and then a bus to finally arrive at the stinky chicken joint we called home. I climbed up the last step, huffing, and steeled myself against what I would encounter inside.

When I walked in the door, everyone looked up. To my immense embarrassment, Joe, Nita, Silvia, Liz, and the four suspended printers all started clapping. Liz got up from the computer and gave me a hug.

"Wait, wait," I said, holding up my palm. "Maybe you guys haven't heard. I just got arrested for drunk driving. I'm a major fuck-up. Not exactly cause for a standing ovation."

"Ruth," said Nita, wrapping her arm around my shoulder. "You're not looking at this the right way. Have a seat and we'll tell you our version." She guided me to a chair at the table.

"Want a cup of coffee?" Joe asked.

"Oh my god, please," I said.

"Okay," said Nita as she sat down next to me and Joe handed me a mug of steaming coffee. "Let me explain what happened the other night." She rested her sparkly fingers on my forearm and smiled. "First, you were in a bar, all tired and — well, sad." Nita looked at Liz and then back at me. How come everybody always seemed to know more about my love life than I did?

"You had too much to drink," Nita continued, "and you made a bad decision to drive yourself home. You should have called one of us."

"I know, I'm sorry," I mumbled.

"But," said Nita, patting my forearm again, "you were just slightly over the legal limit, and you were doing fine on the road. Until this crazy guy in a white Expedition started weaving around, chasing you down the highway with a gun. He pointed it straight at your face, and you veered to avoid him."

"Yeah, but — " I started.

"Any of us probably would have done the same thing if we were cold sober," said Silvia.

"Maybe, but — "

"Let me finish!" Nita exclaimed. "Okay. You had whiplash symptoms, but you refused treatment. You were taken to the police station where, believe it or not, you tried to organize a prostitute."

"How the hell did you learn that?" I asked.

"John Beck interviewed her," said Joe. "It's in his piece this morning."

"Okay," Nita continued. "You finally got Tommy McNamara to drive you home. But before you even got out of Jersey, you got a call from Joe that the workers needed you."

"And you told him to turn the car around," said Juan.

"Then," Nita said, "you went to this horrible meeting. And afterwards you stood there in a hot parking lot trying to sort out what happened. And in the middle of that, you faint."

"Nita — " I began.

"Almost done," Nita said, holding her hand up to stop me. "You finally got home. Slept a total of about — " Nita looked at her watch — "ten hours. And when you woke up, look what you did."

"What?" I said, confused.

"Came straight here to help us with the organizing drive," Silvia said.

"You get what we're telling you?" Nita said, squeezing my shoulder. "You made a mistake. But you did a lot of other things real good, okay? You are busting ass for us. We appreciate it."

"Nita." I got up and gave Nita a tight hug. "You guys," I said finally. "I still want to say that I'm really sorry for what I did. And I'll do everything I can to pull us out of this thing."

"Of course you will," said Silvia.

"But before you start making calls, I think there's something you should see," said Silvia. She picked up a copy of the New York Star from a big stack on the table. "I take it you haven't seen this yet."

I shook my head.

Silvia flipped the paper open to a metro section story whose headline read, "Union organizer goes head-to-head with the mob."

"What?" I said. "Talk about an overstatement!"

"Just read it," said Silvia.

I sat down at the table and read Beck's story. The piece certainly put the best possible light on my actions and the union's cause. "Unions frequently charge that organizing is next to impossible these days," Beck wrote. "But most union campaigns don't have their first organizer murdered and their second pursued by a gun-toting thug." Unfortunately, even in this context my DWI arrest didn't make me look too good. The story went on to point out the unanswered questions about the Cappellini family's role at Pantheon. I could tell Beck was positioning himself for an investigation of the mob family.

"Pretty good, isn't it?" Silvia said when I'd finished. "Unfortunately there are two more."

"Brace yourself," Liz warned from her seat at the computer across the room.

Silvia handed me a copy of the New Jersey Trumpet, folded open to page fifteen. There it was, with its screaming headline, "Union organizer arrested for drunk driving!" The story covered some of the same ground as Beck's, but its main aim seemed to be to portray me as a lowlife — and by association to instill doubt about the morals of union organizers everywhere.

But the Trumpet story was nothing compared to what Renee Natavsky, the famously reactionary gossip columnist for the New York Daily Mail, had to say. My DWI arrest was just the peg for a five-paragraph rant about me and my scandalous personal life. It had one substantiating quote, from none other than James Shawcross. Shawcross said he had fired me because I was an "unreliable loose cannon with bad personal habits. I'm not at all surprised to hear she was arrested for driving drunk." And then the real slammer: "It's widely known in the labor movement that Ruth Reid has a years-long sexual liaison with (married!) New York Star reporter John Beck. Sources say that Reid had a tearful episode with Beck in a New Jersey bar several hours before her arrest."

I slapped the paper down on the table. I couldn't believe it. Where in the hell had Natavsky come up with this? It was awful for me, but much worse for Beck. His wife would see it. So would Yvette. And his editor.

"Incredible, isn't it?" said Silvia.

"It's outrageous. And it's not true, either," I said. "I didn't have a tearful session in a bar with John Beck. I did meet him at the bar, but I certainly wasn't crying there."

Silvia nodded her head slowly. I had a feeling Liz had already confirmed for these workers the substance of Natavsky's report about Beck. Well, I wasn't going to compound my embarrassment by discussing the issue in the office.

"Has Beck called this morning?" I asked.

"Yep. He wanted to set up an interview with the suspended workers," said Joe.

"Oh," I said, fiddling with the newspaper. "What did you say?"

"I told him he should come to the shift change party today and talk to the guys there."

I nodded. I wondered where Beck was right now. Probably in Queens, trying to nail the Cappellinis.

"Take a look at this too, if you can stand it." Silvia passed a single sheet of paper over to me. It was a copy of the Natavsky story, but someone — Toro's people, probably — had topped it with their own intro: "Pantheon Organizer Ruth Reid a Drunk and a Libertine, according to New York Daily Mail." Under that it said. "Reid was arrested yesterday for drunk driving. But that's just the tip of the iceberg. Read on."

I looked at Silvia.

"This thing had totally blanketed the plant by eight this morning. Every worker has at least one copy."

"Shit," I said. I looked at the introductory lines again. A libertine? Who even used words like that anymore? Was I a libertine? I certainly didn't feel like one. I sure wasn't getting any — from John Beck or anybody else.

"We've already started distributing Beck's piece," said Silvia. "Liz pulled the whole thing together first thing this morning — wrote the intro, made the copies. We've handed out a couple hundred so far, and we're planning to do another blitz before the shift change party. People are totally eating up the mob stuff. They can't believe that guy tried to kill you."

I glanced at Liz, hunched over her computer. She looked up and gave me a dazzling smile. I smiled back. Well. I was impressed.

"Now I'm doing a broadcast email to all the workers we have addresses for," said Liz.

"Liz, that's great."

My niece shrugged as if it were all no big deal and went back to her computer.

Beside me at the table, the four printers were assembling sets of leaflets for distribution. I watched them in silence for a moment. I'd had an eventful forty-eight hours, but so had these men. This morning, for the first time in years, they had woken up with no job to go to. Right now, they seemed pretty cheerful. But sooner or later anxiety and depression would probably set in. How long would it be till they began to wish they had never dared to stand up to their employer?

All I knew was that until we got their jobs back, we had to make the best possible use of their now-available labor. Not only to help us win the organizing drive, but to give them structure to their days and meaning to their sacrifice.

Juan looked up and smiled. "Feeling sorry for us?"

I smiled back and shook my head.

"Do you think we'll ever get our jobs back?" Juan asked. Malcolm, Alonzo and Victor didn't look up from their assembly job. But of course they were listening.

"I think we have a shot. Especially if we win the drive. Then we can probably negotiate your jobs back at the bargaining table."

Malcolm looked up. "But what if we don't win?"

"It'll be harder then," I said.

Alonzo swallowed.

"But look at this way," I said. "Now we've got four incredibly talented full-time organizers to make sure we do win." I said the words with gusto. The workers smiled at me, but I could tell they were not greatly reassured.

I refilled my coffee cup and took it over to my desk. I sat there in my chair, inhaling chicken fumes and trying to figure out what the hell I should be doing. Everything that had happened before the accident seemed like ancient history now. I turned on the crane lamp, opened my notebook and tried to reconstruct the events of the past few days. Once I'd finished, my palms started to sweat. We had huge hurdles to clear, and only seven days left till the election.

One: We had enlarged the organizing committee and empowered its members to get creative. The result: a major job action that had resulted in the suspension of some of our best union fighters. I couldn't allow this to happen again. I had to make sure that from now on our job actions were smart and strategic, not suicidal.

Two: For every worker we won over, Bernie Schmidt scared away two. And now we knew his secret weapon: the highly personal information he'd apparently stolen from Victoria's file. Maybe we finally had a way to stop Schmidt: Report him to the police. After all, we now had reason to believe Schmidt had pilfered the files and left behind the gruesome porn shot. And Schmidt's ex, Donna Palast, had been worried about the possibility that Schmidt had killed Victoria. We needed to tell the police our evidence against Schmidt.

Three: In addition to Bernie Schmidt, it now appeared we had the mob on our ass. From Phil Scheiner, we'd learned that there had been a financial relationship between the New Jersey-based Cappellini family and the Maloneys. From Beck, we'd learned that Tim Beatty was also connected to the Queens branch of the Cappellinis. Were the Queens mobsters picking up where the New Jersey clan left off? Maybe Beck would eventually uncover the truth. But in the meantime, Tim Beatty was, like Schmidt, terrorizing us.

I sighed and leaned back in my chair.

Joe looked over at me. "Penny for your thoughts."

I smiled. "Well, one thought is, we should go to the cops with our information about Bernie Schmidt — the stolen files, the porn shot, the info from Donna Palast."

Joe nodded. "I was thinking the same thing."

We looked at each other. The idea of voluntarily returning to a police station was literally nauseating.

"Maybe Silvia and I could do it," said Joe.

"Really?"

"Sure. Why not?"

"Joe, you're a doll. You want the number for the detective investigating Victoria's death?"

"Just hand it over, and Uncle Joe will take care of it." Joe smiled at me.

I found the number in my notebook and jotted it down on a scrap of paper. The paper weighed less than an ounce, but when I handed it to Joe I felt a ton lifted off my shoulders.

Later that day I got a call from Tommy McNamara.

I clamped my jaws together and tried to collect myself. I'd been expecting the call. I knew that the morning papers were sending shockwaves through the New York City labor movement. Unions don't get a lot of press and when they do, they tended to overreact. Any whiff of negativity in a story incited fury and outrage at the reporter, the newspaper, the media in general, and often at whoever was believed to have invited the unwanted attention.

Well, I had generated a whole lot more than a whiff of negative coverage. Tommy himself wasn't the hysterical type. But his boss, Industrial Workers Union president Allen Yankel, was famous for his tantrums.

"Tommy. Let me just guess why you're calling," I said, my hand gripping the handset as if my life depended on it.

"You really scored big this morning, Ruthie." Tommy's voice was hard to gauge. Was he sad, worried, or pissed off?

"Well, Beck's piece wasn't too bad."

"You got a point there," Tommy said diplomatically.

I was already tired of prancing around the issue. "Okay, Tommy, what's the fallout? Are you firing me?"

To my wonder, Tommy laughed. "Ruthie, I got good news for you. I think maybe Shawcross has crossed the line this time."

"Shawcross? What do you mean?"

"Yankel didn't appreciate Shawcross slandering our organizer in the middle of a campaign. He's royally pissed."

"No kidding."

"Well, you know how Yankel is about airing dirty laundry."

I laughed. "So that's all I am to him? Dirty underwear?"

"You could put it that way. Yankel says he wants to lodge a complaint against Shawcross with the state fed exec board."

"Whoa. I never thought I'd see Yankel going to bat for a troublemaker like me."

"Don't hold your breath. Even if he follows through, I doubt Shawcross'll get more than a wrist slap. I just wanted you to know that they're not going to send a posse over to string you up. Not today, anyway."

An hour later, I looked down at the phone. Why hadn't John Beck called me this morning, after all that had happened? I should call him, I thought. But I just couldn't get up the nerve. I rested my hand on the receiver.

Just then, Al Zielinski burst into the room, red-faced and breathless.

"What the fuck's going on here?" he shouted to the room. "How come nobody tells me anything?"

Juan rose from the table, ready to face Al down. "What's up, buddy?" he asked. Malcolm and Alonzo stood too.

Al turned on Juan, his small eyes glittering. "You little spic. Are you the one who fucked up the Heidelberg?"

I stepped up next to Juan. "Wait a second here. What's the problem?" I could smell the alcohol on Al's breath. His face was sweaty, his hair unwashed.

"Oh, fuck you. I can't believe you even have the nerve to show your face after what you've done to this drive. My god, you really know how to make a fucking splash, don't you?" Al turned toward Malcolm and Alonzo. "You realize she's the second whore that union sent over? You got to wonder, right?"

"Shut up, Al," said Juan. "If you got a problem, just tell us what it is." Juan was about three inches shorter than Al and many pounds lighter, but he was in much better shape.

Al rolled his eyes. "You know exactly what it is. You guys sabotage my own press, and I'm the last one to know. And I'm the one who started this fucking drive!"

"Al," said Juan, his voice softer. He rested a hand on Al's shoulder. Al knocked it off. Juan went on anyway. "Al, you helped plan this thing."

"We didn't decide it was happening yesterday and we definitely didn't talk about the Heidelberg!"

"What's the matter with using the Heidelberg?" I asked.

Al glared at me. "You said you were going to fight to get me my job back. You haven't done shit."

"I told you, Al. Our best shot at getting your job back is when we negotiate the contract. And we're moving on the NLRB charge."

"What crap!" Al slapped his palm down hard on the table to punctuate the word. "You're icing me out, just like Victoria."

I shook my head. "No, Al, that's not the plan."

Al stared at me through his watery hazel eyes, then looked around the room, as if searching for a handy item to throw. Finally he pushed Juan back with the flat of his hand, wheeled around and left the room.

As Al thundered down the steps, Juan and I looked at each other.

"He was drunk," I said.

Juan nodded. "What are we going to do with him?"

"What can we do?" I said.

CHAPTER 26

"Uh, could somebody give me a ride?" I asked as we packed up for the shift change party that afternoon. I was beginning to realize how delightful this was going to be, having no car and no license. I felt like a twelve-year-old.

A few minutes later, I was once again in Juan's Camaro. My neck and head screeched with pain every time we hit a bump. I pressed my lips together to keep from whimpering.

As soon as we'd gotten onto the main road that would take us to the plant, I twisted in my seat to face Juan. "Listen, I'm wondering if you could do something for me."

"What's that?" Juan asked, a little grin appearing on his face, as if I were going to ask him to do something naughty.

"Could you let people know we're having an emergency meeting after the party tonight?"

"Sure. What for?"

"I'm worried about job actions. I'm afraid if we don't get more strategic about them, the whole organizing committee will get suspended."

"Good plan." Juan was silent for a moment, his eyes on the road. Then he glanced at me. "Are you doing okay?"

"Yeah. I'm just a little nervous about seeing everybody this afternoon."

Juan looked puzzled. "Why?"

I looked out the window. "Well, you guys were very sweet to give me a standing ovation for my DWI, but I have a feeling the other workers aren't going to see it quite that way."

Juan laughed. "You know, it's not like you stole money from the drive or ratted on somebody. You just made a mistake."

"Yeah, well. And then there's that awful column and the whole John Beck business. Beck will probably be there this afternoon to interview you guys — "

Juan looked over at me. "Is that why you're nervous? Because John Beck will be there?"

I didn't say anything, but it was true. For some reason the idea of seeing Beck made my palms sweat.

"Well, it's none of my business," Juan said, "but I just want to say that I know how complicated relationships can be. And I'm real sorry for your — your heartbreak."

Juan's eyes met mine. And then, almost reflexively, I looked down at Juan's hand on the stick shift. It looked just like it had yesterday: Brown, strong, and capable.

About twenty cars were parked along the side of the road — twice the number we'd drawn before. On the grass, clutches of workers talked excitedly. Liz was handing out copies of Beck's article.

"I hope all this isn't about me and my screwed up personal life," I said as we climbed out of the car.

Juan laughed. "I doubt it. Let's ask Silvia."

Silvia was surrounded by a knot of gabbing bindery workers. When she saw us approaching, her face lit up. She grabbed my hand. "Did you hear what happened?"

"No," I said cautiously.

Silvia beamed. "We stopped the bindery for two hours."

"Almost every single worker supported us, except two," added Nita beside her.

Both sisters were grinning broadly, their eyes flashing.

"How did you do it?"

"She started it." Nita laid a hand on Silvia's shoulder.

Silvia leaned toward Juan and me and whispered, "The bundling machine broke. What could I do?"

I looked at this mild-mannered mother of two in wonderment. "Then what happened?"

"We got really back-logged," said Silvia. "We had pallets waiting in the bindery and the loaders were just standing around."

"Then people at the other binding machines saw what was going on and started going in slow motion. It was hilarious," said Nita.

"The distribution people got mad," said Silvia. "They were two hours behind on their routes. We just said, 'Sorry guys, what can we do?'"

"Did Schmidt or Toro's people come around?" Juan asked.

"Oh, yeah," said Silvia. "Schmidt came over and yelled at us."

"Then he went away and came back with this Toro guy," said Nita.

"What did he say?" I asked.

Silvia frowned. "He said he knew what we were doing and we would all be brought up on charges."

I inhaled sharply. "What happened then?"

Silvia shrugged. "We fixed the machine and we went back to work."

"Could they, like, prosecute us for this?" asked Nita.

"They could try," I said. "But it's more likely they'd just fire you."

Nita looked stricken. "Do you think they will?"

"I hope not," I said. "But I think the organizing committee needs to meet about this tonight. I'm afraid we're making ourselves too vulnerable."

Silvia nodded, her thick silver hoop earrings glistening in the afternoon sun. "It was strange. I kind of knew we should've planned this out, but once it started happening, we couldn't stop."

Debbie Gustafson stepped up to me. "Ruth? I need to talk to you," she said, straightening her big square glasses.

"What's up?" I turned to face Debbie.

"Well, it's about that article in the Trumpet."

I braced myself. "I'm really sorry about that, Debbie."

"Yeah," Debbie said, her voice soft and uneven. "I just don't feel right about it. I'm — well, my nephew was killed by a drunk driver — " Debbie's words came out in a halting stutter.

"Debbie, I'm so sorry for what I did. I hope you don't let my mistake affect your support for the drive."

Debbie was looking down at her feet. "Well, I still support the union. But — I just can't go to meetings anymore. Because what you did, it really upsets me."

"But Debbie — the drive isn't about me — it's about you and Nita and Silvia and Joe. In a few days, I won't even be here. If you think Pantheon workers should have a union, you should come to the meetings."

Debbie made an expression that she might have intended as a smile, but looked more like a grimace. "I don't know. You're so bound up in it all. And then that other article, by that gossip columnist — I don't know if what she says is true. But, well, that's just not the kind of thing I believe in."

"Look, how about this?" I said after a moment. "Could you be a sort of adjunct to the organizing committee? You wouldn't attend meetings, but you'd have a liaison — somebody like Silvia — who would always keep you posted and get your thoughts about things and give you assignments. Would that work?"

Debbie was silent for a moment. "I don't know. Maybe."

"Maybe you can talk to Silvia about it. I'll mention it to her. Okay?"

"I guess so," said Debbie, looking down at her feet again. "Well, anyway, I better get going now."

I watched as Debbie walked slowly back to her car, head down, her shoulders slumped under her LL Bean sweater set.

There were no beers in the big blue cooler Nita had brought to the shift change party. There weren't any in the red cooler either. Now that I thought about it, I remembered we had decided not to bring alcohol to these gatherings. Probably just as well. I was dying for a beer. For any alcoholic drink whatsoever. But if there had been beer, would I really have taken one? I didn't know. I hadn't yet made any decisions about my drinking future.

As I was standing there with my diet soda contemplating my relationship to alcohol, John Beck's Miata came into view down the road. I felt my body tense.

As the car got closer I saw there was a passenger in the seat next to Beck. It was Yvette Ramirez. At that moment I would have preferred an interlude with Bernie Schmidt. I knew I needed to talk to Beck. But I sure as hell didn't want to talk to him while Yvette was nuzzling him.

I postponed the encounter by joining Nita and a few others who were having an excited discussion about future job actions.

But minutes later, Beck appeared by my side. Yvette was about ten feet behind him, looking like she had just been ordered to stay. I caught her looking in our direction. We both quickly averted our eyes.

"Reid." Beck's voice was raspy and his eyes were bloodshot. Like maybe he hadn't slept ever since that wretched gossip column came out.

I turned away from Nita and her group. "Beck, I am so sorry I got us into trouble. I don't know where she got that rumor. But I was a complete idiot to leave myself open to it."

"I'll survive," said Beck. "How much damage can Renee Natavsky do to my reputation at this point? The important thing is, how are you feeling?"

I shrugged. "My neck aches, but I've had worse." I glanced over at Yvette, still eying Beck and me while trying to look like she wasn't. "How did Yvette take the story?"

"Well, she already knew we'd had a fling. But she was still pretty upset. It's like she's been made a fool of, you know?"

"Uh huh," I said, thinking, a *fling*? Is that all the past nine years had been to Beck?

"Anyway, after she saw the Natavsky column my editor decided it wouldn't look good to give me a solo byline on a story about your campaign — so she reassigned Yvette to the story."

"Oh."

"What I can't figure out is how Natavsky knew about us. Is it common knowledge or something?"

"I don't know," I said miserably.

Beck scratched his arm and glanced at Yvette.

"So, uh — were you and Yvette working on the story today?"

"Yeah. We were in Queens, and we learned some stuff about the Cappellinis that you should know."

"Oh yeah? Tell me. Maybe we could just sit here on the grass, so I can take notes," I said, pulling a small spiral notebook out of my bag. I noticed that Yvette had now moved to a spot a few feet away. I mentally pleaded with her to back off, but she wasn't picking up my thought waves.

"Okay," said Beck.

"Mind if I join you?" Yvette's words were polite but her voice had an edge to it. So did the look she gave me.

"Oh sure, hon," Beck said, putting his arm around Yvette's shoulder. "I was just about to tell Ruth what we found out this morning. We thought we'd just sit down here so Ruth could take notes."

Yvette looked down at the grass with dismay. "But I have white pants on."

Well, we don't, I thought.

"Sweetie, I think I see a lawn chair right over there," Beck said, pointing. "Why don't you bring that over?"

Yvette gave Beck a look that seemed to say she had expected him to get the chair, but she dutifully trotted off to get it herself.

Beck gave me an embarrassed smile. I didn't say anything. I just plopped down on the grass. I had a denim skirt on. And it wasn't white.

"So tell me," I said, my pen poised over the notebook. I glanced at Yvette as she put down the lawn chair and sat. Her sandals were now about four feet from my face. They had sexy straps and little pointy heels. They were awfully cute, but not ideal for walking around in damp sod.

"Okay," said Beck briskly as he sat down cross-legged in the grass beside me. "First thing this morning we went out to Astoria and interviewed an assistant district attorney named Tad Cornwall. Cornwall tried to nail the Queens Cappellinis three years ago. He had a lot of background info."

I nodded. "What's the background?"

"The rift between the two parts of the Cappellini family started back in the 1940s. There were two brothers, Leo and Vincent, and they got into a fight over heroin distribution. So Leo moved off to Jersey with his wife and three kids and set up shop over there. That part of the family got very involved in labor racketeering, including that great gig they had with the Columbus United Pension Fund."

Beck paused. I looked up from my notes and saw that he and Yvette were exchanging a look. Maybe Yvette was already getting tired of sitting on her lawn chair and wanted Beck to hurry up.

"What about the Queens branch?" I asked, giving Yvette an insincere smile.

"Okay," said Beck. "The brother who stayed in Queens, Vincent, had five sons, and four of them went into the business with him."

"What about the fifth brother?"

"Cornwall said he was the runt of the Queens litter, and he got dissed a lot by both his dad and his four brothers. Back in the seventies, he declared he was going straight, changed his name, and moved away."

"And since then?"

"Well, the other four brothers have been real busy out in Queens. Busy and wily. Cornwall went on and on about how hard it's been to nail these guys. They've got all kinds of shady businesses, but on the surface they keep it pretty clean."

"Didn't Scheiner say one of them was in jail?"

"Not for long," said Beck. "They only got him for check-bouncing."

"So what did Tim Beatty do for them?"

"According to Cornwall, they periodically send him out to beat someone up."

"That fits. What I don't get is how Vincent's family got involved at Pantheon."

Beck leaned back until he was lying on his side, his head propped on one elbow. I had a sudden flash of a picnic Beck and I had had once in a park in Brooklyn, which had also begun with a long conversation on the grass. About two hours later, after we'd finished a bottle of merlot, a cop came by to tell us to get a room. The memory made me feel both embarrassed and sad, and it was already causing my skin to flush. I glanced at Yvette. She was looking at her fingernails. I looked back at my notes.

"Okay, here's a lead on that," Beck was saying. "We learned that the Queens family's most lucrative business is paper recycling."

"Oh," I said, suddenly looking up.

"Yep," said Beck. "That's what I'm wondering too. I don't know if the New Jersey family had a hand in the recycling business at Pantheon. But I bet the Queens people do."

Yvette shifted in her chair. "But hon, that's where you're losing me," she said. She crossed her legs, bringing one of her sandals that much closer to my face. "I mean, the recycling business is so PC, right? I don't get what the mob is doing with that."

Beck gave me a hapless look.

"The mob's been all over the recycling business," I said. "They do the same thing they do with garbage — force people to pay too much money for the service of disposing of their waste paper. And then they do cheap illegal things with it so they can pocket the difference."

"And that works perfectly for the Queens guys," Beck said, animated. "They're already in the business and if we're right that they assumed that loan, then they've already got leverage over the Maloneys. They're probably charging the Maloneys a fortune to do their recycling."

"So what do we do about all this?" I asked.

"I need to talk to one of your people about recycling at Pantheon." Beck glanced at Yvette, but she was looking out at the road, piqued because I had answered her question instead of her great mentor.

"Ask Juan Acevedo and the other printers you're interviewing today," I suggested.

Beck nodded and sat up.

"One more question," I said. "Did Cornwall say anything else about Tim Beatty?"

"Not really. But he was fascinated when I told him that Beatty has been screwing around with this organizing drive. He thinks Beatty may give him a way to nail down this whole Queens-New Jersey connection."

"How?"

"He wasn't sure. But he said he'd stay in touch. Personally, I'd like to tail Beatty for awhile. Maybe I'll get something on him."

"Beck! You're not a cop. You don't even have a gun. Don't be such a macho idiot!" The words were a little stronger than I'd intended. Yvette stared at me.

But Beck was oblivious. "Oh, sweetie, calm down."

"*Sweetie!*" exclaimed Yvette, suddenly rising from her seat.

"Hon — " Beck pleaded, but Yvette was already stomping away.

I turned to look at Beck and shrugged.

Beck gave me a funny look. "Listen, it would be better if you could, you know, watch how we are around Yvette. Okay?"

Yvette got enough of her cool back to be the note-taker in Beck's interview with the suspended workers. Beck started out by asking the printers about recycling.

"They're into being environmentally cool — or at least they say they are," Malcolm said. "They make a big deal about recycling all the roll ends and set-up copies."

"Has there been any change in who's doing the recycling?" Beck asked.

"Actually, yes," said Juan. "They switched companies about two months ago."

Beck gave me a meaningful look. "You know the name of the new company?"

"I think it's Atlantic Environmental Services," said Alonzo Lopez. "I'm pretty sure I saw that on the side of their truck."

"This is great, guys," Beck said, writing the name in his notebook.

"Ruth — " Silvia was saying in my ear. "Ruth, look."

Silvia was pointing toward the road. Probably another visit from Schmidt. I squinted into the sun and saw a vehicle moving down the road toward us. But it wasn't Schmidt's black jeep. It was a white Expedition.

CHAPTER 27

The dozen workers around me swiveled to watch the approaching SUV.

Beck, who was standing closer to the road than anyone, had to be a hero. Instead of moving away or heading to his car like a sane person, he stood there and stared at the vehicle.

Maybe Beatty would just roll by and shout out some obscenity. But what if he pulled a gun? Surely Beatty wasn't crazy enough to shoot someone with a dozen witnesses.

The SUV came to an abrupt stop right in front of Beck. Beatty flung himself out the door, slamming it behind him. He came loping toward Beck. I clinched my fists and focused my eyes on Beatty's hands. He might have a gun, but at least he wasn't holding one.

Beatty came to a stop in front of Beck. He was almost a half a foot taller than Beck and probably weighed fifty pounds more. Beck continued to be an idiot, standing there facing Beatty.

I started walking toward the pair. Juan, Alonzo, and two other men did the same.

"You son of a bitch!" Beatty gave Beck's shoulder a hard knock with his fist. Beck didn't react.

"Keep your hands off him!" I said.

"Oh that's right. He's your boyfriend, isn't he?" Beatty grinned humorlessly.

"Bastard!" Beck said. Before I knew what was happening, Juan and Alonzo had seized Beck's arm, seconds before his fist made contact with Beatty's stomach.

"You better fucking watch your back, asshole," Beatty said, pointing his finger at Beck. "If you keep poking around, you're going to get yourself killed."

Beck's body was pulled as taut as piano wire. His face jutted, chin forward, into Beatty's space. "And if you keep pulling guns on people, it's going to land you in jail," he growled.

"I never pulled a gun on anybody," Beatty said.

"What?" I sputtered. I felt an overwhelming urge to lunge at Beatty. I could almost taste the release that would provide.

"You're the only one who believes that bitch," Beatty said, still addressing Beck.

"Shut the fuck up!" said Alonzo Lopez, his voice strangled with rage. "If I see you around my house again, I'm going to *kill* you."

Beatty had the nerve to laugh. He was tempting fate. There were six of us surrounding him now, and all of us wanted to beat the shit out of him.

"I have one message for you people. Especially you." Beatty again singled out Beck, pointing a finger in his face. "Watch out."

With that Beatty swiveled on his cowboy boots, threw himself back into his SUV and roared away while the rest of us looked after him, huffing impotently.

It took over an hour for my blood pressure to return to normal. Even then, as I sat at my desk collecting my thoughts before the evening's strategy meeting, I felt like I had a fever. Of course, it was in the upper nineties outside, and humid as hell. The iced coffee I'd bought had already lost its ice. Only the pizzas we had ordered seemed immune to the oppressive heat, arriving in an unappetizing lukewarm state.

Still, we all gathered around the pies hungrily.

"So what are we going to do about Beatty?" Juan asked as he lifted a slice out of the box. "One of us is going to kill him if this keeps up."

"If he doesn't kill us first," said Malcolm.

"Beck's trying to nail him, but that may take awhile," I said, sipping my formerly iced coffee.

"I thought we were going to have a strategy meeting about the job actions," said Victor Pucciello. "Could we get started? My wife's feeling real crappy today. I got to get home." Victor, skinny and gray-faced, didn't look any too perky himself.

"Okay, let's start," I said. I glanced around the table at our assembly: the four suspended printers; Joe and two fellow lobster shift press operators, Dan Bledsoe and Diane Firestone; Silvia, Nita, and their fellow bindery worker Kevin McGarry; and Liz.

"I wonder where Al is," said Silvia. "You'd think he'd be sobered up by now."

"Has anyone heard from him?" I asked. Al's absence worried me. But then his presence always worried me too.

"I tried him," said Joe. "Nobody picked up."

I nodded. Maybe Al was sleeping off his hangover.

"So," I began. "It sounds like people are chomping at the bit to do job actions."

"People are dying to do what you guys did," Diane Firestone said, nodding toward Juan. "But we need a plan. I don't want us to get fired too." Firestone was a powerfully built woman with a voice to match. Her red hair was cut close to her skull, which emphasized the perfect smoothness of her pale skin.

"Your co-workers want to run the presses fast?" I asked.

Firestone and Bledsoe both nodded.

"Alonzo's got everybody on the lobster all riled up," said Juan, punching Alonzo lightly in the side.

Alonzo laughed.

"I was talking to Debbie Gustafson about doing a job action, and she said she'd want to know what the objective was," said Silvia. "What are we getting for the risk?"

Alonzo stared at Silvia. "I'll tell you what we're getting. A huge morale boost. A lot more support for the union. I mean, people see us doing something about the exact thing that's bugging them."

"You should've been in the bindery this afternoon," said Nita. "People had more fun at work today than they've had in years." Beside her, Kevin McGarry grinned.

"I know," said Juan, "but we can't afford to have more of us lose their jobs. Who knows if we'll ever even get them back." Beside him, Victor frowned.

"I think you've just got to be ready to face the music," said Alonzo. "I mean, how can you go around screwing stuff up and not risk getting fired?"

No one spoke for a moment, and then Diane Firestone said, "I want to do it anyway."

"Me too," said Bledsoe.

I looked at the group around the table. I wanted to hug them all. But I feared they were on a suicide mission. "Look," I said. "There's something called 'work-to-rule.' In a way, you guys already did it with your action on the Heidelberg."

"You're talking about following all the rules to the letter as a way of fucking everything up — right?" said Juan, grinning.

"Exactly," I said. "Technically, you're not breaking any rules. You're just not doing all the things you usually do that makes production go smoothly."

"Oh, we got a lot of stuff like that," said Alonzo.

"Oh, so do we, baby," said Nita.

"We bend everything to make it work," added Diane Firestone. "They'd be screwed if we didn't."

At this, the workers shared significant looks across the table and smiled at each other.

I'd seen it a hundred times before. In almost everyone lurks a little anti-authoritarian pixie just waiting to do mischief to the system.

"The thing is, you've got to be very organized and disciplined about it," I said. "We need to plan what we're going to do and how, so that we minimize the risk."

Around me, the workers nodded.

It took another hour to work out the details of that night's action: In a few hours, Diane Firestone and her crew would demonstrate just how much could go wrong with an aging sheet-fed press that was pushed a little too far.

After the meeting, Liz and Kevin left for another night out.

Nita and Juan and I squashed all the gummy pizza boxes into the garbage can and tossed the empty soda cans into the recycle bin. I was getting ready for my two-hour commute home when Juan stepped up to my desk.

"You want to have a quick drink with me?" he asked."Or — maybe just a nice seltzer?"

I looked at Juan. I wasn't sure if I was ready for either part of that equation: Juan or a drink.

Juan laughed. "Don't bowl me over with your response."

"I'm sorry. I'm — well, for one thing I haven't decided whether I should become a teetotaler or not."

Juan considered that for a moment. "Let's go to the Pretty Pony and decide there."

I laughed. "I have a pretty good idea what'll happen if I go to the Pretty Pony."

"Tonic? Ginger ale?"

"Wow. What a comedown. But if I had a real drink — "

"I'll definitely drive you home. I'd love to."

"You'd have to. My car's totaled. Plus I lost my license."

"I promise I'll be real nice to you," Juan said.

I looked at Juan, standing there smiling warmly at me, his hands resting just under his tooled belt. Don't be too nice, I thought.

The Pretty Pony was packed, but we managed to find adjacent chairs at the far end of the bar. I flagged the bartender, a balding man in his late fifties and a master at his craft. I thought his name was Lloyd, but I wasn't sure.

"Maybe I *should* have a ginger ale," I murmured, contemplating the wondrous array of bottles behind the bar.

"If you do, I will too," said Juan.

"That's sweet."

Lloyd came over and raised his eyebrows at me.

"Can I have a scotch on the rocks?"

Juan laughed. "Me too."

"But one is my new limit," I vowed.

Lloyd came back almost instantly with the drinks. He put two small square napkins down before us, then set the drinks on top. It all happened in the wink of an eye. He gave us a nod and a smile and was off to the other end of the bar.

Juan and I clinked our drinks together. I let the scotch sit in my mouth for a moment before I swallowed. It was so perfect – icy on my tongue, warm in my throat, and potent. Van Morrison was singing Brown-Eyed Girl on the jukebox. The bar was dim, with ceiling lights sending narrow rays of light into the black walls. The whole place was like a light sponge. I closed my eyes, inhaled the smoky air, and repeated "just one" to myself a few times.

"Some day we had today, huh?" said Juan as he set his glass down.

I smiled at him and nodded.

Juan regarded his drink and twisted it around on the napkin. "A year ago, if you'd asked me if Pantheon workers would do the kind of thing they did today, I would have said no way."

"Why not?"

Juan shrugged. "I don't know, people always seemed kind of passive to me. In the old days the Maloneys went pretty easy on us and nobody wanted to fight them over anything."

I nodded. "You start to disrespect people, it's amazing what they'll do."

Juan looked at me and his lips curved into a smile.

"What?"

"You're the reason, Ruth. It wasn't happening before."

I shook my head. "That's nice, Juan, but I disagree. You guys initiated that job action on your own, if you'll remember."

"It's because you've given us a feeling of being part of something big. *You* did that. Believe me, we didn't have this kind of feeling when Victoria was here."

I let go of my drink and sat back. I wasn't in the mood to talk about what Victoria had or hadn't done.

"I liked Victoria a lot, I really did," Juan added. "But she was just not as good at involving people as you are. She always gave you the feeling she was the expert, you know?"

"Yeah — whereas I would never give anyone that impression."

Juan laughed. He knocked his shoulder against mine gently and said, "I didn't mean it that way — "

"It's okay, I'm just teasing you." I took another sip of my drink and set it down, leaving my hand on the cold wet sides of the glass.

"Have you done a lot of campaigns like this?" Juan asked.

"A few. This is one of the bigger ones."

"Did you win the other ones?"

"Less than fifty percent."

Juan shook his head. "I guess that's just the way organizing is, right?"

I nodded. "Pretty much."

"Is it hard to keep going uphill like that?"

"Definitely."

"Have you ever been tempted to give up?"

I smiled. "Oh, yes." Like yesterday.

"Why? Because you don't win all the time?"

"Yeah. And frankly even when we win, we often lose."

"What do you mean?"

I took a breath. "I mean, the underdog's not doing very well these days. And I can't fool myself into thinking we're going to turn that around any time soon. And on top of that, we've got a lot of problems on our own side. Which I'm sure you've observed by now."

"Yeah," said Juan. He peered into his drink.

Well. It was one thing for me to stare dejectedly into my drink. But it was another thing when Juan did it.

"On the other hand," I said, straightening up on my stool, "I get to see people outdo themselves all the time. I see people risking everything to do the right thing."

"God, I hope we win," said Juan.

"Me too," I said.

"But even if we don't, this has been one of the best things that's ever happened to me."

I smiled and put my hand on Juan's shoulder. It was an instinctive move, an offhand show of affection. But the instant my palm made contact with that shoulder, a current went zinging through my body. I took my hand away quickly.

Juan gave me a long quiet look. He had rich brown eyes and his pupils were dilated. Then his eyes moved slowly down my body. Tingles followed his eyes all the way down.

I crossed one blue-jeaned leg over the other and looked down at my sandals, trying to regain my composure.

"So how did it go with John Beck this afternoon?" Juan asked.

"He called me 'sweetie' by accident and pissed off his girlfriend."

Juan laughed. "Sounds like you guys are still kind of entangled."

"I guess so. In a way."

"It's kind of like that with me and my ex-wife. We still like each other, and — "

"And every once in a while you sleep together?"

Juan nodded. "We don't even mean to do it. It just happens."

Behind Juan, someone was scraping stools around. Juan scooted his chair closer to mine to accommodate three men in suits who were talking loudly and lighting up cigars.

Now Juan's thigh was pressed hotly against mine. I was having trouble concentrating.

I inhaled and said in as light a tone as I could muster, "You got a regular girlfriend?"

Juan shook his head, a faint smile on his face. "I wish I did. How about you?"

I shook my head. "Not really."

"You've got your heart set on John Beck?"

I looked at Juan. "Kind of. But I shouldn't."

"Yeah," said Juan. He jostled my shoulder again lightly. "You okay?"

I nodded. Then Juan lifted up my chin with his fingers and turned my face toward him. He looked at me as he gently pushed back a coil of hair from my cheek.

I smiled at him and then he bent toward me and kissed me lightly on the lips. I dissolved. I pulled away and took a breath and looked down at my scotch. I'd only drunk a half a glass. Whatever judgment I was exercising, it was all mine, not the alcohol's.

Juan put his hand under my jaw again and drew me into a deep kiss that started out tender and became more and more insistent. It was no longer a kiss, it was some kind of merging. Juan's hands reached around my back and pulled hard. I came off the barstool and was suddenly pressed tightly against his body. And still we kissed.

After at least thirty seconds lost in ecstasy, some dim flicker of consciousness reentered my mind, some nagging awareness of place, and I pushed away from Juan and sat back down on the stool. I stared at him wide-eyed. He stared back at me. I laughed. He laughed. Then the bartender came over and said, "Wow."

I looked at the bartender and said, "Sorry about that."

"That's okay," he said.

"Is your name Lloyd?" I asked.

"Yes it is," he said.

"Good to meet you, Lloyd," I said, extending my hand for a shake. "I'm Ruth, and this — I pointed to a sheepish-looking Juan — is my friend Juan."

CHAPTER 28

I woke up at five the next morning to a noisy chittering argument between squirrels. I'd left my bedroom window open, and now sweet-smelling, sultry summer air filled my lungs. Cicadas sizzled somewhere nearby. I sat up and looked at the tangle I'd made of my sheets. It had been a largely sleepless night, and part of me regretted that I'd spent it alone.

Liz had still been out when I'd gotten home. I'd sat in bed for awhile worrying whether she'd had another run-in with Tim Beatty. But sometime after two, I'd heard the front door open and close, followed by the reassuring sounds of Liz washing up.

After that, I gloried in the memory of that kiss with Juan Acevedo. And then my mind moved on, inevitably, to John Beck. A few miles away, in Cobble Hill, Brooklyn, Beck was probably sleeping blissfully next to the beautiful Yvette. That hurt, but the pain was survivable. I expected Beck to sleep around. It was the love part that was killing me.

In the predawn hours, I'd begun wondering what had happened at Pantheon during the night. Had Diane Firestone's press gone haywire? Had she been fired?

I'm not one of those people who wake up after a night of dreams and musings with sparkling, fresh insights. No, when I survey what my semi-conscious brain has produced in the night, I find I've been wasting precious hours circling round a few dumb thoughts I should've dispensed with in seconds.

I quickly checked my mental status. There were six days left till the election. The work I had to do today was going to be scary and grueling. But damn it, I was ready. Even my little slide into the land of scotch the previous night hadn't changed my outlook.

A half hour later I presented myself at Sandy's door. It felt like years since our last morning jaunt.

Sandy opened the door dressed, like me, in shorts, t-shirt and sneakers. We set off down the hill, striding in perfect unison under the heavy summer canopy of sycamores.

"You've got news, don't you?" Sandy said.

I smiled. Sandy's nose for romantic intrigue was supernaturally powerful. "I don't know what you're talking about."

Sandy made a hissing sound to signal her disapproval. We walked a half a block further.

"I *know* there's something going on," Sandy tried again. "And it better not be with John Beck."

I glanced over at Sandy as we crossed the wide expanse of Fourth Avenue, still mostly devoid of cars at this hour.

"Actually, there *is* something going on. We've got job actions breaking out like wildfire."

"Ruth! You know that's not what I meant. Is there some new guy?"

"God, Sandy, don't you care about the organizing drive?"

"Of course I do. But I can't help you much with that. It's your love life I'm worried about."

"Okay, okay," I said finally. "No, I don't have a new guy."

"Somebody on the campaign, right?"

"It's not cool for me to sleep with people I'm doing a campaign with," I said.

Sandy elbowed me. "But you want to, don't you?"

I grinned, despite myself.

"I *knew* it!" said Sandy.

When I got back from the walk, Liz was waiting for me, all dressed and ready to go. She'd had only a few hours of sleep, but she still looked spunky in her little red denim mini and black cotton vest.

"So," I said, as we walked to the subway. "How'd it go with Kevin McGarry last night?"

"It was nice," Liz said mildly.

I glanced at her. "You don't sound all that enthusiastic."

Liz shrugged and flipped a braid over her shoulder. "He's nice, but he's like, a jock."

"Uh huh," I said.

"I mean, he's cute, but I keep thinking maybe we don't really have that much in common."

"I know what you mean," I said.

Liz glanced at me. "You never did like him."

"Hey. I didn't say that."

"You know who's really cute?" Liz asked, suddenly perky again.

"Juan Acevedo. You already told me."

"No, Malcolm Brown. Isn't he adorable?"

I smiled. "Uh huh, sure."

"Wasn't that cool what he did with the job action thing?"

"It was."

"Malcolm and I are going out on house visits together this morning."

"Good for you."

"Everything is so awesome!" Liz said.

I laughed. "What do you mean by everything?"

"I just didn't know there was this whole thing going on — people organizing and all that. I mean, I always knew you did that stuff but I didn't really get it until now. It's awesome!"

I glanced over at my niece. "Liz — "

"Stop! Stop!" Liz said, holding up her palm. "I know what you're going to say. About how fucked up the labor movement is and I shouldn't delude myself, blah, blah. I know all that. Just let me enjoy my little moment of naïve bliss before it gets spoiled, okay?"

I was speechless.

"Okay, Aunt Ruth?"

"Okay," I said finally.

I didn't get a report on what had happened on the lobster shift until nearly eleven a.m. Joe, my usual source of information about the shift, had gone straight from work that morning to Manhattan to meet with the detective investigating Victoria's murder. I felt guilty that I hadn't gone with him. But relieved.

When Joe did finally show up, he looked deflated.

"How about I get you a cup of coffee this time?" I said, leaping up from my desk.

"Now that would be nice." Joe groaned as he eased himself into a chair at the table.

I brought the coffee over and sat down next to him. "So what did the detective say?"

"He said he'd take my information into consideration." Joe scratched a spot just over his ear in an easy way and then took a sip of the coffee.

"Even after you showed him that porn shot?"

Joe nodded.

"Even after you told him what Schmidt's ex said?"

Joe shrugged. "Well, I never had any great hopes for the police anyway."

"I'm with you on that one."

We contemplated the failures of law enforcement for a moment before Joe turned to me and said, "Did you hear what happened last night?"

"What happened?"

"Nothing," said Joe, his eyes steady on mine.

"What do you mean? What about Diane Firestone's press? The work-to-rule?"

"See if you can figure this one out," said Joe. "One of Toro's guys was parked right next to Diane's press all night. Just sitting there on a pile of boxes watching. Diane decided not to risk it. So nothing happened."

"What do you think that guy was doing there?"

Joe shrugged. "I don't know, but everybody thought it was pretty strange. You realize we got lots of presses. This is just this one little sheet-fed machine. Why did they have that fellow stationed there all night?"

"I don't know," I said cautiously.

"Well, I just can't help thinking they knew what we were planning."

"But Joe, the only people at that meeting yesterday were — "

"You, me, Nita, Silvia, Kevin, Juan, Alonzo, Malcolm, Victor, Diane, and Dan," said Joe.

"And Liz," I added. "Sounds like you've been over that list a few times."

"I hate to think we've got some kind of spy on our side, Ruth."

"You know, there's probably some other reason that guy was hanging around. We're just not thinking of it at the moment."

"Mmm hmm." Joe looked skeptical.

"You know the scariest thing about spies? It's what the fear of them can do to you," I said. "I've seen whole organizing drives crash because people start suspecting each other. We can't afford that."

"I got ya," said Joe.

That afternoon, Joe and I went to visit a fence-sitter named
Joanne Healey, one of the four people who staffed Pantheon's
business department overnight. Joe thought she could swing her
three co-workers to the union, if only she could be convinced herself.

Healey lived in a third floor walk-up apartment on a quiet side
street near downtown Bloomson. Her apartment had been carved
out of an old Victorian that someone had attempted to modernize
with graceless vinyl siding. The entrance to the apartment was at the
back, up two flights of shaky covered stairs. We rang the doorbell
and waited in front of the metal door.

Healey opened up. She was a tall, stocky white woman in her
late twenties. She wore classic jeans and an oversized red t-shirt that
advertised pizza. Her fine brown hair was cut and curled in the
front, but hung straight and heavy in the back. I wondered if she had
to apply curlers to get the effect. I'd tried curlers once, when I was
eight, during a brief flight from my tomboy preoccupations. I'd
never tried again.

"Hey, Joe, come on in," she said, waving us inside.

"This is Ruth Reid, our organizer," said Joe. Healey turned her
eyes on me and smiled politely.

The old slanting floors of the Victorian had been covered with
pale green carpet, and the elaborate moldings that almost surely
covered the walls had been hidden by a layer of drywall. The place
smelled like cigarette smoke.

Healey had very little in the way of furniture. There were two
directors' chairs facing the TV, and Healey motioned for us to take
them. She disappeared into the kitchen and came back carrying a
chair in one hand and a pack of cigarettes in the other. Couches were
expensive — maybe she didn't like credit and hadn't saved up
enough money for one. Maybe she didn't spend any time here and
didn't care if she had a couch.

"You guys sure have been kicking up some shit," Healey said as
she sat down on the kitchen chair. "Mind if I smoke?" Joe and I
shook our heads. Healey pulled out a long slim menthol cigarette
and lit it. I watched with envy. If cigarettes weren't bad for you and
those around you, I'd have been a smokestack myself. She took in a
lungful of smoke, held it for a second as if it were pot, then let it all

out through her nose. I could almost feel the small rush of chemicals perking up her brain.

"The job actions, you mean?" Joe said.

Healey nodded. "You've got the bosses freaked out, I gotta say. But they sure got you back yesterday with that article, didn't they?" she said, turning to me.

"How have you been feeling about the union lately?" Joe asked. We had three more visits scheduled that day, and Joe wasn't wasting time on small talk.

Healey shrugged her shoulders. "Like I told you before, I kind of get why you guys on the floor would want a union. But I don't see why us office girls need one."

The self-description was jarring. Healey did not look like an "office girl."

"Why not?" I said. "How's the pay? How are the benefits? How are the working conditions?"

Healey took a drag on her cigarette and shrugged again. "Okay. Could be better. But we don't have a big fight with management. We just mind our own business. Especially us night owls. Nobody bugs us, we don't bug them."

"Didn't you used to work first shift?" asked Joe.

Healey nodded. "Hated it."

"Why?" I asked.

Healey laughed. "Gee, where do I start? You know that guy Miranda? The office manager?"

Joe nodded.

"I used to work for him. What a creep. He's a harasser."

"Sexual harassment?" I asked.

"Oh, yeah," said Healey. "Thinks he's one very handsome guy. Puts his hands on you, asks you out. Oh, he was so surprised when I told him to fuck off."

"What happened then?" I asked.

Healey shook her head. "I wanted to report him, but I really needed the job. So I transferred to this job on the lobster."

"He shouldn't be allowed to get away with that," I said.

Healey now looked uneasy at having opened up the topic. "I don't know. The thing is, I'm fine now." She tapped ash from her cigarette into the red plastic ashtray she held on her lap, then kept on tapping the cigarette nervously.

"I'm glad," I said, "but what about the next woman? Have you heard about any problems in that office since you left?"

Healey nodded slightly.

"The union should go after that guy," I said to Joe. He nodded.

"What are you going to do?" Healey asked, staring at me.

"When the union comes in, we'll collect all the information we've got on this guy and if he harasses again, we'll go after him."

Healey bit her lip and looked at me tensely. Her anger at the harasser and her timidity seemed to be at war inside her head.

"Why don't you come to the union office tonight?" I offered. "We can talk about it. And you can meet the other people on the organizing committee."

Healey winced, then stubbed out her cigarette. "I don't know," she said.

"So last time we talked you said Cindy was a little down on the union," said Joe. "How's she feeling now? And how about Elaine?" he asked, naming two of Healey's co-workers.

Healey shrugged. "They're kind of like me. We don't really see what a union's going to do for us."

I tried to tamp down my irritation. "Aren't there four of you? Who's the other worker?"

"Her name's Chris Allison. She's new on the shift. She's really quiet. I don't know what she thinks about the union." Healey drew out another cigarette and lit it.

"Was she working another shift before?" The name didn't ring a bell.

"Yeah. She was on first shift in the Human Resources Department."

"Oh really," I said. "When did she transfer?"

"Uh, it was just last week she started with us."

"Why did she change?"

Healey shifted in her chair and looked at me guardedly. My interest in her co-worker seemed to unsettle her. "I really don't know. Like I said, the woman hardly says anything."

"You don't happen to have her home number, do you?"

Healey looked at me like I had a screw loose. "Why would I?"

A few minutes later, we left Healey's apartment, having failed to move her out of the fence-sitter column. In the car, I asked Joe if he knew anything about Chris Allison.

"Never heard of her. But then they always keep those HR people kind of tucked away. "

I pressed my thumb into the Taurus's armrest. "I wonder if she might know something about those ghost employees."

Joe nodded slowly. "She might."

When we got back to the office later that day, I went riffling through our lists in search of Chris Allison's home number. I hadn't expected to find her name there, and I didn't. None of our lists included HR employees, and Allison's transfer had been very recent.

I grabbed the phone book and flipped it open to the As. No Chris Allison or C. Allison was listed for Bloomson or its two sister suburbs.

I sat down at my computer and typed Allison's name into a white pages search engine, narrowing the search down to people in New Jersey. There were five C. Allisons within a reasonable distance of the Pantheon plant.

I dialed all five and left voicemail messages for three of them. A fourth told me in her message that she was Carol Allison, so I declined to leave a message. The fifth C. Allison actually picked up the phone. It was a man. I apologized and hung up.

Maybe Beck would know how to find this woman's number. In the past I'd called Beck frequently and without hesitation. Now it was different. Our relationship seemed less sturdy, more fraught. And I didn't want to catch him alone with Yvette.

In the end, I decided to dump the job on Liz, who had just returned to the office after a house visit with Malcolm. Liz seemed to perk up at the challenge of finding Allison and promptly situated herself at the nearest computer.

About an hour later, she came trotting over to my desk.

"I found it," she said, plunking a piece of notepad paper down in front of me.

"How'd you get it?"

Liz just shrugged.

I looked at the number. It matched one of the C. Allisons I'd left a message for earlier. I punched in the number and left a second message.

Well, so much for that big lead. It appeared that Joanne Healey would stay a fence-sitter and those ghost employees would stay ghosts.

CHAPTER 29

"I want a pina colada," announced Nita suddenly, slapping her palm down on the table. "Who'll go to the Pony with me?"

It was past nine o'clock. My neck was killing me. So were my eyes, my head, and my back. I was pretty sure a scotch would fix all that. But I vowed it was going to be a seltzer night.

The Pretty Pony was, as usual, crowded, smoky and noisy. While Dolly Parton sang sweetly on the jukebox, the TV over the bar was blaring out a Yankees game. Unfortunately, the only available booth was closer to the TV.

I slid into the booth and rested my elbows on the surface of the thick wood table, slightly sticky with ancient spilled beer.

"Whoa! It's Silvia!" said Malcolm, as he squeezed in next to Liz at the end of the booth. "I thought you had to go home to be with your kids at night."

"Well, not this night," said Silvia. "The kids are already asleep anyway."

A waitress came by. It was booze all around, and one seltzer. This was killing me.

Across from me, Silvia was moving subtly to the music and smiling softly.

"We should dance," Malcolm said suddenly to Liz.

Liz smiled at Malcolm and raised her eyebrows in Silvia's direction.

Malcolm promptly turned to face Silvia. "Silvia, will you dance with me?"

Silvia looked startled. "Me? You should dance with Liz. Or Ruth or Nita or somebody. I'm too old."

"Are you kidding? Come on."

And then Silvia shrugged and slid out of the booth.

Nita squinted into the smoke as her sister and Malcolm began moving sinuously to the music, their bodies almost but not quite touching. "Oh. My. God," she said. "That girl hasn't been on a dance floor since high school."

"Pablo doesn't like to dance?" I asked.

Nita only snorted in reply.

I swirled my seltzer around a couple times. "You don't like him much, do you?"

"I can't stand him," said Nita. "I mean, has that man ever done a load of laundry in his life? I don't think so."

I nodded. The music ended then, breaking the spell the dancers had cast on the table. Nita got up to get drinks. Silvia and Malcolm sat back down. I stared into my deeply unsatisfying fizzy water.

"Hi," said a voice above me. I looked up, startled to see Juan standing beside our booth. I hadn't seen him since our stunning kiss the night before and the feel of his eyes on me now sped up my heart rate considerably.

"How'd you know where to find us?" asked Nita as she plunked down a fresh drink for herself and Silvia.

"You lushes?" said Juan. "Hey, when I saw the office was deserted, it wasn't hard to figure out."

At the word "lushes," everyone at the table turned to look at me, including an abashed-looking Juan.

"It's okay," I said. "I've never made any secret about being a lush."

Juan eased onto the bench next to me until our thighs were pressed together the same way they'd been the night before.

"How are you?" Juan whispered, in such an intimate tone that I blushed.

"Fine. How're you?"

"I feel great."

"Sorry about that thing last night."

Juan pulled back a few inches so he could look at me. "Sorry? Oh, no." His brown eyes pierced mine in a way that made it hard to breathe.

"I was being bad. But let's talk about it later," I said quickly.

"I like bad." Juan grinned.

When I looked up from this whispered conversation, my face surely the color of a tomato, I saw that Nita and Liz both had their eyes trained on Juan and me. Lip-reading, no doubt.

"So Juan," Silvia said briskly, taking mercy on us. "How did your house visits go?"

Juan shrugged. "Like hell. I just visited a guy who's gone totally cold on me. I think Schmidt used information about him from that damn file."

"I have a guy like that too," said Malcolm.

"You know, the company knows way too much," said Nita. "We've got Schmidt with the personal information, and now they seem to know about the work-to-rule campaign. What's going on here?"

Juan stared at Nita. "What do you mean?"

"You didn't hear? They couldn't do the job action last night because Toro sent a guy to watch Firestone's press all night."

"Are you saying somebody's leaking our plans to the company?" Juan asked, glancing at me.

"We don't know," said Silvia. "Do you have any other theory to explain it?"

"Hey," said Alonzo suddenly, in a tone that made everyone look up. "Look at the TV."

On the screen an anchorwoman was reporting the news. I couldn't figure out what was so interesting until I made out the image projected next to the anchorwoman. A man's face. It was Bernie Schmidt.

CHAPTER 30

By the time we had crowded around the TV, the anchor had passed the story on to an earnest, pale-faced correspondent who stood on a dark street under the hard white glare of the camera lights. He clutched the microphone tightly with one hand and gestured behind him with the other at a windowless, brick-fronted tavern on a barren street.

"Police say Bernard Schmidt's body was found earlier this evening in the parking lot of this bar on Hollis Avenue in Bloomson," the reporter was saying. "He had been shot twice in the chest. Workers at the bar, McFadden's Tavern, said they heard the shots at approximately nine-thirty p.m. and the police arrived immediately. Mr. Schmidt had been a security guard at the Pantheon Printing plant in Bloomson for the past eighteen years. A McFadden's Tavern employee told us that Schmidt was a regular at the bar and had spent a quiet evening drinking. Police say they have no suspects yet in the murder."

As the anchorwoman moved on to a story about childhood obesity, we still stood clustered by the TV. Finally, we stumbled back to the table and sat down in silence.

"What the hell happened there?" said Alonzo softly. The rest of us shook our heads. Liz looked at me from the end of the booth, her eyes wide and questioning.

Juan was staring down at the table. "You know the funny thing? How many times have I wished something bad would happen to Schmidt, that he would just disappear — "

"Yeah, and now that he has, it feels awful," finished Silvia.

I looked down at my seltzer, which wouldn't do a thing to dissolve the cold ball of anxiety that now sat heavily in my stomach.

"He did have a lot of enemies. I mean, the guy made new ones every day," said Alonzo.

"Yeah, and most of them were people at the plant. Like us," said Nita.

There was silence around the table, and finally Silvia said, "And Al."

I cleared my throat. My voice came out an octave higher than usual. "Did Al ever return that message Joe left last night?"

"I don't think so," said Nita.

"I don't like the timing of this," said Juan.

"But why now?" asked Silvia. "When's the last time he would have even seen Schmidt?"

"Look," said Alonzo. "Almost everybody hated Schmidt. He probably pissed off some guy in that bar he was in."

"But even if Al didn't do it, what are the police going to think?" asked Juan as he tapped the tines of a fork against the table. "The thing between Al and Schmidt is documented. I mean, that's why Al was fired. Everybody's heard him threatening Schmidt. It doesn't look good."

"You know what else I don't like?" said Nita. "In the back of my mind, I always sort of pictured Schmidt as the guy who, you know — "

"Killed Victoria?" I said.

Nita nodded, looking sick.

"Just 'cause somebody killed Schmidt, doesn't mean Schmidt didn't kill Victoria," said Alonzo.

Juan sat back from the table. "Or maybe nobody we know killed her. That's what the police have been saying all along. All this could be totally unrelated."

"Yeah," said Nita. "I don't think so."

I looked at my watch, suddenly aware that I was covered with sweat. The evaporation was giving me cold shivers. The hard beat of the Rolling Stones was pounding from the jukebox like a panic attack.

"I'm going to try Al right now," I said. Juan stood up so I could climb out of the booth. I stepped outside the bar into the relative quiet of the night.

Tina answered the phone before it had completed one ring. "Have you heard from Al?" she blurted as soon as I'd said hello. "I just called the union office but nobody answered. I'm getting really worried. I haven't seen him since yesterday morning."

I swallowed. This was not what I'd wanted to hear. "We're all at the Pony. We haven't seen Al since yesterday either. Are you going to call the police?"

"I was going to — but now I'm scared. And besides, he's done this before. I mean, stayed out all night."

"What do you mean you're scared?"

There was a pause. "You didn't just see the news, did you?" Tina asked, her voice faltering.

I inhaled. "Yeah, actually we just saw it here at the Pony."

"You saw about Bernie Schmidt?"

"Yeah."

There was a short pause before Tina asked, "What do you think happened to him?"

"I don't know, Tina," I said.

At four-thirty the next morning, I was churning under my sheet. I flipped my feather pillow over to the cooler side, just in case it would make a difference.

"God," I said to myself in the dark. Another sleepless night. I kept picturing Al shooting Schmidt. It was so easy to do. But was Al really capable of killing someone? And if he had killed Schmidt, had he also killed Victoria? What exactly had happened between Al and Victoria? I was sure the animosity had been intense. I didn't want to think about how Victoria would react to the news that Al had been talking to another union in the middle of an organizing drive.

Well, at least something had finally driven guilt over my DWI from my mind. It had been hours since I'd thought about it — a recent record.

I finally sat up in exasperation, snapping the sheets back. I got up and tread quietly down the hall. The door to Liz's room was open. She was lying on her stomach, her left arm draped over the side of the bed. I gently pulled the door closed and went downstairs. I padded into the kitchen and started the coffee.

As the coffee machine gurgled, I shuffled over to the front door and stepped outside. The sun was about to rise, at least outside the city. It would take another hour for the rays to rise above the buildings on my eastern horizon. Standing perfectly still, my feet on the cool stone, the intense humidity felt almost pleasant, like a blanket of moisture on my body. It was the knowledge of what was to come that made it seem oppressive, foreboding.

Liz and I arrived at Mr. Chicken at eight-thirty, and already it was in the nineties. As Liz raced up the steps, I lagged behind. It was as if the muscles had been sucked out of my body during the night. I couldn't figure out why some days my legs felt like fifty-pound bags of sand. Someone had propped the office door open with a phone book. For just a moment, I stood on the landing, pretending I was an outsider looking into the union office.

The office was even more disheveled than my house. Stacks of paper and files were piled high on every desk, riffling under the breeze from the rusty rotating fan on the windowsill, turning its head back and forth with slow deliberation. Items of limp clothing were strewn on chairs, contributing to the scent of sweat in the air. Later, of course, the smell of chicken fat would win out. A tumble of little white cartons from the local Chinese restaurant topped an already overstuffed garbage bin. Extension cords snaked across the floor, attached to fans, computer peripherals, and a toaster oven that had appeared in the office one day. Fat dust bunnies lurked under the desks, and the spider plant someone had put on the sill had died of thirst. Our desperation was showing.

Joe was on the phone. And the Heidelberg Four, as we'd come to call them, were huddled at the conference table. Liz settled herself in front of a computer and I went immediately to say hello to Mr. Coffee. I stuck my mug under the tap and pressed, causing a splutter of watery grounds to dribble into my cup. I groaned and dragged the coffee pot into the bathroom.

When I returned, Joe was waiting for me.

"Tina says Al finally made it home last night," he reported.

"Did he say where he'd been?"

"Tina says he's not talking."

"Shit. Maybe we should go see him — see if we can find out what happened."

"Not sure if that'd do much good right now. Tina said he's still drinking."

"Jesus. He's going to kill himself. I'd just feel so much better if I knew where he'd been."

Joe nodded. "Especially if it was anywhere but that tavern."

After slurping down half a cup of coffee, I was sufficiently alive to start making my calls for the day. I had over a hundred workers to call. But for some reason, everyone hung up on me. The first person I finally reached was a platemaker named Ernie.

"I can't believe you got the balls to even call," he said.

"What do you mean?"

"You didn't hear about Bernie Schmidt?"

"Yeah, I heard."

"Well, everybody thinks you did it."

"*Me?*" Gee, that was a new one.

"Well, the union. Or Al Zielinski."

"Oh," I said, nonplussed.

"Did he?"

"Did...?"

"Did Al kill Bernie Schmidt?"

"No! Why would you think that?"

My next fifteen conversations ran along similar lines. And then John Beck called.

"How are you feeling?" he asked over the familiar background buzz of the Star's newsroom.
"What do you mean?"

"Reid. Whiplash?"

"Oh." I tested out the status of my neck by rolling my head around a couple of times. "Much better. Is that why you called? If so, I'm touched." I leaned back in my chair and rubbed my neck. It had felt fine until Beck had asked about it.

"Actually, I'm calling about Bernie Schmidt. I saw the story in the Trumpet this morning. What the hell happened?"

"How many times am I going to have to answer that question today?" I whined. "How would I know what happened?"

"Who else is asking?"

"Everybody. At least half the workers think the union did it."

"The union? What, like you took a vote or something? Or Tommy ordered it?"

"When they say 'union,' they usually mean Al."

Beck was silent for a moment. "You think maybe they're on to something?"

"Jesus! They better not be. Listen. Can we talk about something else? How's the investigation going?" I got up from the chair and paced the few steps the phone cord allowed.

"I just got a federal investigator to confirm that the Queens Cappellinis are connected to that recycling company you guys told me about — Atlantic Environmental Services."

"What does that mean, Beck?"

"It means it looks like the Queens family is moving in on Pantheon."

I sat down on the edge of my desk as a feeling of hopelessness
stole over me. "Am I supposed to be happy about this? Because I'm
not. I mean, I'm glad you got your story, but what are we supposed
to do with this information?"

"I don't know, Reid. But when this story goes to press, things
are going to change, I can guarantee you."

"What? You think your story's going to chase the mob out of
town?"

"Could be. Or maybe a local prosecutor will pick it up."

"When are you planning to run this thing?"

"Not sure. I still need to pin down that ghost employee
question. I don't suppose you've been able to dig up anything on
that?"

"No. We found out that a woman named Chris Allison who
now works in the business office at night transferred out of HR a
week ago, and we thought she might know something. But she's not
returning our calls."

"How many messages did you leave?"

"Two."

"You obviously aren't a reporter."

"Did I ever claim to be? What would a reporter do?"

"Call and call and call."

"Look. I'll try her right now. If I reach her and she has anything
to say, I'll let you know. And Beck?"

"Uh huh?"

"You'll tell us before you run that mob story, right?"

"Absolutely."

"And you're not going to go chasing after Beatty without telling
me, right?"

"Uh," Beck grunted evasively.

After I hung up with Beck, I looked at my watch. As a night
shift worker, Allison might be sleeping at this hour. But since my
efforts to reach her later in the day had failed, maybe now was the
time.

"Hello?" After four rings a woman had picked up.

"Hi. This is Ruth Reid from the Pantheon organizing drive. Is
this Chris Allison?"

"How did you get my number?" Allison's voice was soft, but
the anxiety in it was unmistakable.

"It wasn't easy. But the reason I'm calling — we talked with your co-worker Joanne Healey the other day, and she mentioned — "

"Listen, I wish you luck with the organizing drive, but I really don't want to talk to you. Okay?"

"Look, Chris, I just have one quick question for you. Joanne told us you used to work in Human Resources, and — "

Then I heard the little click as Chris Allison became about the hundredth Pantheon worker to hang up on me so far that day.

It was a sweltering afternoon, and I now regretted the decision to walk to my appointment with a fence-sitting printer's assistant about a mile from the union office. The meeting had not gone well. The worker, who had seemed open to the union when I'd set up the visit the day before, had suddenly acquired cold feet. Although he wasn't saying it, I suspected he was spooked by the rumors about Al.

As I walked back to the office, my head was throbbing and waves of pain were radiating down my spine. The sun made boiling black pudding of the road tar on Bloomson Avenue. I could see heat waves radiating from the sidewalk in front of me. The soggy air wilted the young ailanthus trees that lined the avenue.

A half a block from the union office, I stopped and squinted. Was that a cherry top parked in front of Mr. Chicken?

I hurried forward, ignoring the rivulets of sweat rolling down my back and the screams of pain issuing from my spine. When I got to Mr. Chicken, I peered inside the fast food joint, hoping to see the cops. But I saw only neighborhood folks, half of whom I recognized.

Shit. I climbed the stairs to the office, thinking, What fresh hell is this?

CHAPTER 31

Two officers were sitting at the conference table with Joe. They all turned as I stepped in the door.

Joe introduced me to Detectives Branch and Wilson.

"We were just asking Mr. Dysart when he last saw Al Zielinski," said Branch, a handsome, plump African American woman in her mid-twenties.

I stared at Branch. "Why are you asking?"

Branch stared back. "We'd appreciate it if you'd just answer the question," she said, her voice low and clipped.

I glanced at Joe and then back at Branch. "We're within our rights not to."

Branch closed her mouth tightly and tensed her jaw. Beside her, Detective Wilson, a jowly middle-aged white guy with a sunburn, was not so restrained.

"You want us to take you to the station?" he barked. "Because that's what we're going to do if you don't answer our questions here."

Joe looked at me and raised his eyebrows. I knew what he was thinking. We had five days till the election, and it would be suicidal to spend one of them trapped in a police station. Personally I could think of any number of other forms of torture I would have preferred to another night in a cop shop.

Branch, sensing our ambivalence, tried again. "Let me just ask you this," she said. "What were you two doing last night?"

Joe gave me a quick look before offering, "We had a union meeting, and then we all went over to the Pretty Pony."

"The bar down the street?"

"Yep," said Joe.

"Was Mr. Zielinski with you?" Branch asked.

"No," Joe said softly.

"Wasn't Mr. Zielinski a leader of this union campaign?" asked Branch sharply, looking at me.

"He was one leader," I replied.

Branch frowned. "I understood that he was a top leader."

I tilted my head back and forth as if to say, "Sort of."

"So why wasn't he at this union meeting or at the bar afterwards?" Branch leaned forward, pressing her neat blue blouse against the table.

"I don't know. He doesn't always come to our meetings."

Both Branch and Wilson leaned back from the table and looked at each other, communicating something, I was sure.

"Mr. Dysart, we understand that there was a history of conflict between Mr. Schmidt and Mr. Zielinski," Branch said.

"Most workers didn't get along too well with Bernie Schmidt," said Joe.

"How had the two interacted recently? Had there been any arguments or fights?"

"They haven't been seeing each other all that much, ever since Al was fired," said Joe.

"Mr. Schmidt was opposed to the organizing drive, am I right, Ms. Reid?" Branch asked, turning her dispassionate brown eyes on me.

"Yes he was."

"Had Mr. Schmidt done anything in the last few days that might have precipitated a fight between himself and Mr. Zielinski?"

"Schmidt was always doing something that could precipitate a fight. But as far as I know, there was no particular situation with Al — "

"You have a bit of hostility to Mr. Schmidt yourself, don't you, Ms. Reid?"

"Maybe so, but like Al and the other organizers here, I don't view violence as a good way to deal with my opponents."

At this, the two officers looked at each other again. Then Wilson sat up straighter and asked Joe, "Do you have any reason to believe that the murder of Victoria Shales is in any way related to the murder of Bernie Schmidt?"

I drew in a sharp breath and looked at Joe, whose eyes had widened slightly at the question. "Well, no, I guess I don't," he said.

Branch's eyes drilled into mine. "Does it strike you as strange that two people so closely involved in this conflict have been murdered?"

"Uh, I guess so," I said lamely.

When the two officers left, Joe and I looked at each other.

"This doesn't look good," I said.

Joe shook his head.

"You think those officers have already questioned Al?"

"If they did, I sure hope Al was sober."

"That sounds like too much to hope for," I said. "I think we better find out what's going on with Al."

Joe nodded.

I picked up the phone and dialed the Zielinskis' number. Tina picked up immediately.

"Tina — " I began.

"Ruth. Have the police been asking you about Al?" Tina's voice was high and squeaky.

"They just left."

"Oh god, oh god," Tina whimpered.

"I take it they paid you a visit too?"

"It was horrible! Al was so rude I thought for sure they were just going to arrest him on the spot."

"Was he drunk?"

"He's been drunk for days."

"Did he tell them anything?"

"Nothing. He just said it was none of their business."

"Tina, do *you* know where Al was last night?"

"He won't talk to me about it." Tina suppressed a sob.

"Listen, Tina, you think Joe and I could stop by and talk to Al?"

Tina sniffled. "I don't know. I can't promise you he'll be very nice."

At a little after six, Joe and I pulled up in front of the Zielinskis' house. The transition from Joe's well air-conditioned car to the impossibly steamy outdoors felt intense and unnatural.

The family's black Ford Explorer was still sitting on the chalky concrete driveway. But as we approached, I noticed something new: the Explorer's left front fender was smashed in.

Tina opened the door before we'd rung the bell. She looked small and haggard but as tidy as before in her crisp checked shirt and jeans. She ushered us in, and we stepped into the chill again with relief. Tina led us through the kitchen, which was spotless and had the manufactured lemony smell of a household cleanser. As we approached the den, we could hear television chatter, something familiar. It was Daffy Duck. Five days from the election, and Al was spending the afternoon watching the Cartoon Channel.

The den was a dark curtained room taken up mostly with an orange, L-shaped sofa facing a big-screen TV. Al was slouched on one end of the couch. He glanced at us quickly, then turned his eyes lazily back to Looney Tunes. The room had the stale smell of the beer Al had clearly been drinking all afternoon. Three cans of Schlitz were assembled on the pressed wood table within easy reach.

"Ruth and Joe are here to see you, sweetie," said Tina. Then she turned to us. "Would you like anything to drink? I've got some iced tea already made." Joe and I both said no thanks. I wasn't in the mood to sit around and socialize. In fact, I was in the mood to leave as soon as possible.

Al made no move to turn off the silly television banter.

"You mind if I turn that off?" I asked.

Al looked up from the TV and scowled at me. "I'm watchin' it."

I glanced at Tina, who was leaning against the doorframe. She gave me an apologetic look.

"Look. Joe and I just stopped by to see how you were doing. And to talk to you about this Schmidt business," I said.

"I got nothing to say about it," growled Al.

Joe looked at me, then sat down next to Al on the sofa. "Here's the deal, buddy," he said. "People at the plant have got it in their heads that maybe you were the one who went after Schmidt. And we're starting to lose people."

Al's eyes rolled toward Joe. "What do you want *me* to do about it? You know, you can't have it both ways — shut me out of the campaign and then call me back in when you got a problem."

"Al," I said, irritated. "What happened last night? Where were you?"

Al turned to me, sneering. "You think I did it, don't you?"

"I didn't say that. But it sure as hell would help if we could tell people where you were last night."

"You know what?" Al said, his voice rising. "You pretended to be so different from Victoria, but you turned out to be the same thing — a bitch. The only difference between the two of you is that she was a whore and you're a whore with a drinking problem."

"Al!" Tina protested.

"We could use your help here, Al," I snapped. "In case you've forgotten, we've got a union election in a few days."

"You seem to be fucking things up just fine without me," Al muttered, his eyes returning to Daffy Duck.

Al was being even more infuriating than usual.

"I noticed your fender got smashed," I said, trying another tack. "What happened?" I glanced at Tina, who shrugged silently.

"Why the hell you asking?" Al bellowed. "Who are you, the police or something? They were already here."

"Al," said Joe softly. "What happened to the car?"

Al didn't say anything. Finally he muttered, "I don't know. I don't remember."

A look of understanding passed over Tina's face. "Al. You don't remember what happened last night, do you?" she said.

Al's belligerence evaporated. He turned to Tina and said, "I can't remember a thing."

I looked at Joe. He raised his eyebrows and shrugged. Well, this was bad news.

A few minutes later, we said goodbye to Al. He didn't bother to reciprocate.

"I'm really sorry about that," said Tina as we walked to the door.

I stopped in the foyer and faced Tina. "Has Al ever done this before — I mean, blacked out after a drinking binge?"

Tina nodded. "It happens a couple times a year. "

I nodded, thinking what a very bad moment Al had chosen to drink himself into oblivion. But then, I was hardly one to judge.

CHAPTER 32

My air conditioner chose that night to stalk off the job entirely. It was grinding on as always, but the air in my bedroom was stifling. At about two, I got up and walked over to the noisy machine. It blew its warm sticky breath on my hand. When I turned the machine off, it shuddered and gasped.

Only then did I hear the sound of Liz's voice drifting up the stairs.

"But we didn't *need* to talk about it," she was saying plaintively. "Neither of us ever said we were, like, a *thing*."

I got up and closed my bedroom door, then flopped back down onto my bed. My little brick rowhouse is over a hundred years old, and nothing in it is plumb or square. As a result, no inside door ever closes the way it's supposed to, especially when it's hot and humid.

"I don't have anything to hide — I *do* like Malcolm! What's wrong with that?" I heard Liz say.

I buried my head in the pillow. Liz and her tangled romances.

"So go ahead and date other people! Did I ever say you couldn't? God, Kevin, we only went out, like, three times!"

Exasperated, I sat up. If I had to have to hear this conversation, I might as well give it my full attention.

"I don't care if Ruth hears me!" Liz shrieked.

Oh. In that case, I thought, I'll just go downstairs and get a little snack.

Liz gave me an apologetic glance when she saw me step into the kitchen. I poured some wheat flakes into a bowl and carried it outside. I sat down on the porch swing and swayed gently back and forth as I munched my cereal.

The air was unbelievably moist, but it was a lot cooler than it was inside. Cool in that tentative, temporary way summer nights have. I felt the cold flagstone under my feet and observed, from my dark hideout under the trees, the occasional car sliding by. Well, Tim Beatty might still be out there prowling around, but Bernie Schmidt was gone forever. I pictured the desolate parking lot where Bernie

Schmidt had died. And a drunk Al Zielinski, crouching behind a car with a gun. It was awfully easy to conjure up that scene.

The front door opened, and Liz stepped out. She settled herself next to me on the swing and drew her knees up to her chest. "Did I wake you up?"

"Not really. The heat woke me."

"You need an air conditioner, Aunt Ruth. One that works." Liz rested her head on her knees. We watched a minivan with graffiti scrawled on its side roll down the street.

"Good point. Next time I have a few hundred extra dollars lying around, I'll get one."

"You don't make much money, do you?" Liz said, turning her head to peer at me.

"Nope."

"Do you wish you did?"

"I guess it depends on what I'd have to do to get the money." Like working for James Shawcross, I thought. I'd rather live in a sweatbox.

"Hmm." Liz took my hand. "Speaking of which, what *are* you going to do for a living, Aunt Ruth?"

I leaned my head back and looked up at the sycamore leaves. "I have no idea. I don't think I can work for a union again though."

"What do you mean? You *are* working for a union."

"But this is different. They hired me for just this organizing job. I'm not permanently under their thumb."

Liz, still leaning her head on her upraised knees, fussed with her chipped toenail polish. "Well, couldn't you keep doing that? Like, be a freelance troublemaker?"

I inhaled. The thought had occurred to me. It wouldn't be a very secure living. No health insurance, no vacation — but the idea of being my own boss was immensely appealing. "That's not a bad idea. It's between that or being a homeless wino. I haven't quite made up my mind."

"Hey. Maybe I'll go into business with you!" Liz suddenly raised her head up from her knees and looked at me.

I laughed. "You mean we'll be partners in the wino business?"

"Aunt Ruth! I mean I'll be, like, an assistant labor consultant." Liz raised her eyebrows and grinned.

"You don't really want to be a labor consultant. Do you?"

"Why not?"

"Oh. Well, you don't want me to go into all that."

"Actually, I don't," said Liz, resting her head on her knees again.

We were quiet for a moment. You could hear the grinding of a hundred air conditioners up and down the street.

"So it sounds like Kevin McGarry's kind of upset," I said after a moment.

"God, Aunt Ruth, he's so old-fashioned. He acts like I was cheating on him with Malcolm. But we never said it was, like, exclusive or something."

"Uh huh. So what are you going to do?"

Liz shrugged. "He'll get over it. I don't think he even likes me that much."

"Really?"

Liz didn't answer. And then her head popped up again. "But Malcolm — isn't he hot?"

It was six fifty-five in the morning, probably the coolest moment of the day, and drops of sweat were rolling down my back as I stood at the entrance to the Pantheon parking lot, my left arm hooked around several hundred purple flyers announcing the union election in four days.

"What time is it?" Liz asked from her position across the walkway from me.

"Five more minutes. See how much fun you'd have if you were in business with me?"

Liz was about to issue a smart-ass retort when a group of workers came plowing out the door.

"Union election on Saturday, union election on Saturday," I said over and over as Liz and I each peeled off leaflets for people to grab. The union had largely retreated from the parking lot because of Schmidt's harassment. I figured now was a good time to reclaim it. Besides, maybe I'd find Chris Allison in the crowd.

Most workers took the leaflets in silence and trudged on. A few gave us the finger or told us to go to hell, a few gave us a thumbs up or a smile. Five or six stopped to ask questions.

After a few minutes, Joanne Healey emerged from the building.

"What are you doing here?" she said as she stepped onto the grass beside me and pulled a pack of cigarettes from her bag.

I held out one of the flyers. Healey took it and glanced down at it unenthusiastically.

"By the way," I said. "I'm on the lookout for Chris Allison. If you see her, would you point her out to me?"

"She's out sick today. As per usual. That woman takes more sick days."

Healey whacked the bottom of the pack until the cigarettes emerged from the other end. She picked one out and lit it with a yellow plastic butane lighter, then sucked on it. "I got a question for you," she said as she blew the smoke upward.

"Shoot."

"Who murdered Bernie Schmidt?"

"I have no idea. Why do you ask?"

Healey glanced at me and then across at Liz, who was straining to hear the conversation. "Well, the company says Al Zielinski did it."

"They do?"

"Well, I don't know if that's their official line but the foreman last night, he said he thinks Al did it. He said the police think so too." Healey tapped the ash from her cigarette onto the ground and took another puff, looking at me through the rising smoke.

"There's no evidence for that charge. It's irresponsible for the foreman to be saying that. He's just using the situation to make the union look bad."

Healey looked doubtful. "Zielinski has a terrible temper and he hated Schmidt."

"But Joanne. That's not what this fight is about. We're talking about getting workers represented here. I'm sorry Schmidt was killed. But it doesn't have anything to do with this campaign."

"Okay, fine. All I know is, they make it sound like you're supporting a murderer if you vote for the union."

"And you're going to let that kind of intimidation determine your vote?"

"Maybe. Listen, I'm zonked. I'm heading home. Talk to you." Healey lifted her arm in a half-hearted farewell as she walked to her car.

Liz looked across at me again. "You know, this is really demoralizing. All these people telling us to fuck off. I feel like I'm some creepy salesperson. I mean, what makes us think we know what's good for these people?"

I shrugged. "We're here because most of the people in this shop said they wanted a union."

"But do we really know it'll be better if they get the union?"

"Probably it will be." I passed out flyers to another clump of workers. "You know," I said after they'd left, "maybe after you've worked a regular job you'll see why people want to organize."

"Gee, Aunt Ruth, I think I already have a clue. I mean, you get better wages and health benefits and stuff like that."

"Respect. That's the main thing," I said, thinking instantly of Joe. I hoped to god we won this election. I hoped if we did, we'd get a contract. I hoped if we got a contract, it would be a good one. I hoped the union wouldn't go completely to hell after the merger. I wasn't optimistic.

As I fretted, I kept my organizer's smile pasted on my face and handed out purple flyers to a couple dozen more lobster shift workers.

Then Joe appeared, looking rumpled, his pants smeared with ink. His head was down and he looked exhausted. He practically walked into me before he looked up.

"Hey. You should've told me you were coming out here. Would've met you on the stroke of seven," he said. Despite his effort to sound jaunty, Joe's eyes were puffy and bloodshot and the smile he gave me was weary.

"It was a last-minute thing." I put my hand on Joe's shoulder. "Joanne just told me that the foreman said Al murdered Schmidt. Did you hear that?"

Joe nodded. "Yeah, we've been fighting that one off all night. Just what we need. It's a big distraction."

"Are you worried about it?"

"A little."

"Besides that, how is it in there?"

Joe let out a sigh. "It's tense. We were going to try a little work-to-rule, but Toro's people were still camping out with us all night. We can't do a thing."

I squeezed Joe's shoulder and told him he should go home and get some sleep. He refused.

We spent the rest of the day sprinting. Liz went out on a series of house visits with Malcolm. Joe and I did the same. In between visits I called twenty-seven workers on our list of fence-sitters. Silvia, Nita and I spent two hours on the phone negotiating with a woman from the regional office of the National Labor Relations Board over who should be in the bargaining unit and thus eligible to vote in the union election. It was an exhausting process, made even more tiresome by Toro, whose positions were so extreme that even the NLRB official was getting testy with him.

One thing the day made clear: The progress we'd made — our heady job actions, the new energy of our enlarged organizing committee — was quickly being reversed by workers' suspicions about Al Zielinski. Al and the union were still so bound up in people's minds that it was as if the union itself was suspected of killing Schmidt. And as Joanne Healey had said, the company was taking full advantage of the situation. Meanwhile, Toro's people had effectively blocked our work-to-rule campaign and Beatty tailed any workers who had been seen talking with us.

The organizing campaign was like a car in an uncontrollable skid. I could see the landscape hurtling toward us, could tell that some horrible collision was in store, but I couldn't do anything to control the direction or the speed of the car.

CHAPTER 33

Maybe air conditioners die of stress and overwork just like we do, I mused as I slipped around in my sweaty seat on the New Jersey commuter train Liz and I took home that night. In the complete absence of air conditioning, someone had opened the windows to let in the swamp gas and airborne petroleum byproducts. Across from us, a young Asian woman held a white handkerchief over her face.

From there we transferred to a New York subway train, which could have doubled as a refrigerator car.

When we got home we both dropped our bags on the floor. Liz went upstairs to take a shower. I flopped down on the couch. About five minutes into a sweaty doze, the phone rang. I leapt up from the couch. Maybe someone was calling to tell me that Al had finally been arrested.

"Reid," said Beck in a raspy voice. I could hear traffic sounds in the background.

"Beck. Are you in your car?"

"Yeah. I'm just coming over the Verrazzano and I was wondering if you want to have a drink at the Rainbow."

I stood up straighter, suddenly perky. This was just like old times. I had the urge to ask "What about Yvette?" But I didn't want to do or say anything that would discourage Beck from seeing me.

"Sure!" I chirped.

"Ten minutes?"

"Perfect!"

I hung up the phone and trotted into the bathroom. I looked at my face in the mirror. Not encouraging. I had blue rings under my eyes. My hair was all afrizz. As I dabbed my face with makeup and fussed with my hair, I wondered at myself. No matter what Beck did, I always returned to him, like a masochistic homing pigeon. This man had just dumped me for a newer model. Why was I primping in front of a mirror for him at ten-thirty at night after a harrowing day of organizing?

And yet, I practically skipped down the dark streets to the Rainbow that night.

"Darlin," said Beck when I reached the stool where he sat. That was like old times too.

I blinked at the multi-colored Christmas lights that perpetually twinkled behind the booze bottles against the mirrored wall. So festive. The Rainbow was my favorite local bar, a comfy, dark, old-fashioned place that was a step above a dive. Best of all, you could get a scotch for two bucks less than in Manhattan. The thought of sitting here on this barstool in the Rainbow next to Beck after a long day and not having a scotch just felt impossible. Besides, my buddy Ernesto was bartending tonight, and he already had my scotch in hand when he came over to say hello.

Beck had stripped down to a tight white t-shirt that commanded my attention. I let my eyes move over Beck's round masses of shoulder muscle. Someone had put a country music tune on the jukebox and it went very well with Beck's t-shirt. Beck took my hand and looked at me, making my heart go all aflutter.

"Beck," I said in a choked voice. "Yvette."

The name was out before I could stop myself, and it had the very effect I had feared. Beck dropped my hand. "Never mind," he muttered.

"Sorry," I said softly.

We sat there in silence for a moment. I swished my drink around a few times. I raised the glass to my lips. The scotch was divine.

"How's the research going?" I asked after I'd given the scotch due appreciation.

Beck shrugged. "The question is, how's it going for you?"

"Horrible. Everybody thinks Al killed Schmidt, and it's going to do us in. And now it looks like the cops think so too." I told Beck about our encounter with Detectives Branch and Wilson the day before.

Beck looked at me sharply. "But what do *you* think? Have you talked to Al yet? "

"Yeah. He bit our heads off. And he told us he doesn't remember anything about that night."

Beck shook his head. "Not good. And the company's probably making hay with the whole thing."

"No kidding."

"The police aren't saying squat about Schmidt," said Beck.

"You did a story about the murder?"

"Just a couple grafs. I talked to the cops and I got a good comment from Joe. The Maloneys had no comment." Beck was looking down into his vodka tonic. What was he thinking? He seemed sad.

"You okay?"

Beck looked at me as if to say, No, I'm not okay, but I don't want to talk about it.

"So, you got anything new on the Cappellinis?" I asked.

Beck shook his head. "All I got is that evidence on the recycling business stuff. But I feel like there's some big piece of the puzzle missing. I guess there's no point asking you again about Chris Allison."

"I talked to her for a couple of seconds before she hung up on me. I wouldn't pin my hopes on her if I were you, Beck." I leaned back and looked down at my glass. It was empty. Down the bar, Ernesto arched his eyebrow at me playfully. I frowned and turned my glass over. Ernesto laughed and gave me a wink.

"You got something going with that guy?" Beck asked after Ernesto had come and gone.

"Of course. He's my neighborhood bartender, for god's sake."

Beck grunted dismissively but gave me a sideways glance to see if there was anything on my face that would give me away. I smiled.

I was finding it extremely difficult to keep my hands off John Beck. I decided it was time for me to go home.

When we stepped out of the bar onto the hot dark sidewalk, Beck grabbed me, covering my mouth with his. He kissed me hard and then pushed me against the Rainbow's brick outer wall, so that I was sandwiched between the cold hardness of brick and the hot firmness of John Beck. I felt like a desiccated plant in the middle of a drenching downpour. I ran my hands over his back. I was helpless.

I finally pushed Beck away a few inches and looked up at his face. And saw a little green stud glittering in his ear. Where had that come from?

"What about Yvette?" I said, trying to keep from huffing.

Beck suddenly looked dead sober. He squinted at me in a not very friendly way and removed his hands from my body.

"Forget about it," he mumbled. "Come on. I'll walk you home."

We walked the two blocks to my house without exchanging a word. When we got there, Beck waited on the sidewalk till I'd unlocked my door. Then he gave me a short, business-like wave, turned on his heel, and did his tough guy walk back to his car.

"We're losing," Silvia said to me as we bent over the conference table the following morning. We'd been sitting there for almost three hours, pouring over the numbers we'd gotten from our organizers in every department.

I looked at Silvia, her shoulders slumped, her reading glasses low on her nose. I hated to see her looking so defeated.

"We don't know that," I said. "We won't know until election day."

Silvia plunked a ballpoint pen down on her yellow pad, which was covered with names and numbers in her small, neat writing. "But Ruth, the tide is going the other way. Up till last week, we were gaining on them. Now look at it."

According to our best estimate, over 395 of Pantheon's 792 workers were now dead set against the union. And we knew of only 306 who were still firmly for it. Just a few days ago, we'd had 367 on the "firm" side. There was no escaping the bad news: We would lose unless somehow we could set off a huge new surge of support for the union.

I inhaled. "You think it's because of Al and Bernie Schmidt?"

Silvia nodded. "We've lost a ton of people over that. It's pretty understandable. I mean, we've had two murders here. People are spooked. Plus, Tim Beatty is still out there. He just threatened one of my contacts this morning, and now she's telling me she won't vote at all."

I looked over at Silvia, noticing that like me she had recently acquired a pair of bruised-looking semi-circles beneath her eyes.

I put my hand on Silvia's shoulder. "Listen. We're doing everything we can. And no matter what happens, you've been a fantastic organizer."

"I have?" Silvia raised her eyebrows and smiled. She looked ten years younger.

"Of course. You've really got the stuff. You're hard-working and smart, organized, persistent — "

"Okay, okay," Silvia poked my arm. "You cheered me up already."

"Hey. I'm not kidding about this," I said, looking at Silvia earnestly.

"You know — " Silvia began. She opened her mouth and then closed it. "Never mind."

"What?"

"Oh, I don't know." Silvia looked out the window for a moment. "It's just that I can almost believe you, I can almost feel what you're talking about. And it's the first time this has happened to me, where I felt really good at something — other than being a mom."

Silvia beamed at me. It made my heart ache. And what if we lost?

That evening, my little balloon of euphoria had long since burst. When the phone rang, I scowled at it. The phones that day had been supremely discouraging. If the numbers had looked bad this morning, they looked even worse now. Every hour took us closer to defeat.

The call was from Kevin McGarry, sounding wired. "Ruth? Can I talk to Liz?"

I looked around the room just in case Liz had arrived without my noticing. But only Silvia, Nita, Juan and I remained in the office.

"I don't see her, Kevin. Are you at work?"

"Yeah. You know where she is?"

I had a pretty good idea. The last time I'd seen Liz had been about two hours ago, when she'd gone downstairs with Malcolm Brown for what they had described as a breather.

"I'm not sure. You want me to tell her you called?"

I could hear Kevin breathing on the other end of the line. "Uh, I guess so. See ya."

I hung up the phone. "Has anybody seen Liz lately?"

"Not since she left with Malcolm," said Silvia. "Who was that?"

"Kevin McGarry," answered Nita.

I turned to Nita. "How did you know that?"

Nita smiled and shrugged. "Who else? He seems like the jealous type to me. And believe me, I ought to know." Nita gave her bra strap a little tug.

The mention of jealousy made me think of John Beck. I hadn't heard from the man all day. Probably that was because he was still dead-ending on his Cappellini investigation and had nothing to report. I rubbed my stinging eyes and wondered where he was. Maybe having dinner in Yvette's cute little apartment.

Liz and Malcolm soon reappeared in the office, breathless and laughing. Liz had taken off her sandals and the soles of her feet were black from running barefoot down the hot tar streets of Bloomson.

When I told her Kevin McGarry had called, Liz looked at me and blinked, as if the thought of a call from McGarry was sleep-inducing. "Oh. Okay," she muttered.

"Maybe you should call him," Malcolm prompted.

"He's at work," said Liz.

"You could just text him," said Malcolm.

Liz sank down into a vacant chair at the table. "Nah. He ought to be able to get through the day without talking to me, you know? The guy's kind of cloying!"

Nita and I glanced at each other. Maybe Nita was right — maybe McGarry was the jealous type. If so, Liz certainly wasn't doing anything to ease his pain.

I went back to staring at my notebook, my eyes glazing at the grim numbers I'd recorded that morning. What more could we possibly do to reverse our slide? We'd been calling, visiting, and leafleting like lunatics. We'd tried every conceivable kind of cajoling. It obviously wasn't enough. If we didn't try something radically different, we were headed toward sure defeat.

I looked around the office at the crew: Joe, Nita, Silvia, Juan, Malcolm, and Liz. I decided to call an emergency meeting.

We all looked so exhausted as we gathered around the conference table, I wondered if maybe the best thing would be to send everyone home. Personally, I wanted a scotch. Across from me, Juan leaned back in his chair, linked his hands behind his head and gave me a weary smile. Since our romantic interlude in the bar, I'd kept my distance from him, although I'd tried to be nice about it. I just couldn't afford a new and possibly intense entanglement in the closing days of the campaign. I wasn't sure I could afford it even after the campaign, given my confusing feelings about John Beck.

"Here's my question," I said once everyone had sat down. "What is the one thing we can do that will win us the most votes in the next two days?"

"That's an easy one," Nita said without hesitation.

"What?" I sat forward in my chair.

"Prove Al is innocent. That alone would get us a hundred votes back. I'm sure of it."

"Come on, Nita" said Silvia. "We're not murder investigators."

I had already sunk back in my chair. Silvia was right, it was probably pointless to even think about. We all sat in silence. If you could call it silence with the little fan wheezing away over by the window. A fly landed on the table and Silvia swatted at it impatiently.

"Okay, but let's just consider that for a minute," I said finally. "If Al didn't kill Schmidt, who else might have?"

Silvia blew air out her lips. "Almost anybody he ever met."

"Everybody hated him," said Malcolm.

"But no one as much as Al," added Nita.

"And the people he exposed with information from Victoria's file," said Silvia.

I looked over at Silvia. "That's what I was thinking. Who falls into that category?"

"Marie Couillard," said Silvia. "But she would never hurt anybody."

"Alan Bizzotti," said Nita. "He had a drug problem."

"Two of my contacts got hit with something from that file," said Malcolm, who had sat down next to Juan.

Juan was frowning down at the table. "I'm pretty sure Schmidt used something against two guys on my list — Bill Dreyfuss and Darien Tooley."

"Okay," I said. "So that's a start. Let's give all those people another call. See how they're feeling lately."

"You don't think someone's going to confess to murdering Schmidt just because we call them up, do you?" said Liz.

"Not really, but maybe we'll learn something," I said. "It can't hurt to try."

"Yeah," said Malcolm. "Maybe now that everybody knows the cops are onto Al, the guy who really killed Schmidt is getting a guilty conscience."

We all looked at Malcolm. It was a hell of a slender thread.

CHAPTER 34

The next morning, I finally reached John Beck. "I haven't heard from you in awhile. I was getting worried," I said.

"Don't be silly," said Beck, over the roar of traffic.

"You're driving," I said.

"Your powers of observation are amazing."

"Beck, are you by any chance trailing Tim Beatty? Because if you are, you're an idiot. The guy has a gun and I think he'd be happy to use it. Especially on you."

There was a little pause. "He hasn't spotted me," Beck said finally.

"Damn it, Beck!" What words would make Beck stop doing this dangerous thing? I could just see him in his little Miata, bearing down on that monstrous Expedition. I could just see the barrel of Beatty's gun, pointed at Beck's face.

"Reid. Calm down. I'll be careful. In fact I'm being so careful that I'm going to hang up. Because it's not safe to talk on the phone while you're driving, right?"

"John — "

"I'll call you later, babe. Okay?"

And then Beck hung up on me.

Joe, Juan, Alonzo, and I had been making and fielding calls like demons all morning. But for the past half hour, Juan had been mostly staring out the window, looking gloomy.

When I finished my call, I walked over to Juan's desk. "How you doing?"

"Okay."

"What's going on?"

Juan looked up at me. I could see the sleep deprivation on his face. He looked older, distinctly middle-aged. "You think you could spare a few minutes? I want to ask your opinion about something."

"Sure," I said, resisting the impulse to check my watch. Every minute from now until the last ballot dropped was critical.

"Can we walk around the block or something?"

"Okay."

The street was sizzling hot, and everyone on it seemed to be in a foul mood. Horns honked. Two guys were hanging out their car windows, pointing fingers at each other as they battled over a parking spot. Juan and I turned down a side street, our strides in sync.

"Okay, here's the thing," Juan said after a moment. "I called one of those guys I mentioned, Darien Tooley."

"Good. What happened?"

"Well, he kept asking me about whether Al was going to be arrested. And I just kept telling him I didn't know. But there was something — " Juan stopped, searching for the right word — "something desperate about the whole conversation."

I looked at Juan. "What's the background with Tooley?"

Juan took a deep breath. "He's been my contact since the drive started. He's a flyer, he's maybe in his forties — "

"Kind of old for a flyer isn't it? I thought those were really hard, low-paying jobs that the kids usually take."

"Yeah, Tooley's had some problems. Alcohol and drugs. He washed up at Pantheon a few years ago. He was probably lucky to get any job after that."

"Sad," I said.

"So I was hanging out with Tooley at the Pony a few weeks ago, trying to talk him into going for the union. And we both had a few beers and then out of the blue he made this confession."

"Confession about what?"

"He told me that one night awhile ago when he was doing a double shift, he got into the office when nobody was there and stole the petty cash — four hundred bucks."

"And he got away with it?"

"I guess. Anyway, after this conversation, I did something really stupid."

"Let me guess. You told Victoria about it."

Juan nodded. "I can't believe I did that. There was something about Victoria, the way she pressed you so hard for information, for inside stuff. Maybe I was just trying to impress her."

"Listen, Juan, you didn't commit a crime by telling Victoria."

"Anyway," Juan said, sighing, "a few days ago, Tooley suddenly got real cold to me. I had a feeling that Schmidt had used the info on him somehow, and Tooley traced it back to me."

"And now you're thinking maybe Tooley went after Schmidt?"

"I don't know," said Juan. "But I'll tell you this — the guy doesn't have a lot to lose."

I looked down at my sandaled feet and the remnants of my toenail polish. "So what do you want to do about it?"

"I think I want to go talk to the guy."

"You really think it's important enough to take time for that now?"

"It might be." Juan turned to face me, his brown eyes full on mine. Then, I did glance at my watch. And without knowing I was going to, I said, "I'll go with you."

Darien Tooley lived in a dank hovel of a house at the end of a dead-end street ten minutes from downtown Bloomson. Tooley's house was a gray shambles. It looked and smelled like it had been soaking up swamp water for years.

Juan knocked on the old screen door and waited. Through the screen, I could make out the worn carpet, the sloping floral patterned sofa set a few feet in front of the television, the cheap swag light hanging over the dining room table. The smell of cat piss wafted out to us.

"What is it?" a man's voice yelled from above. Juan and I looked up. A man was peering down at us from an upstairs window.

"Hey, Darien, it's me. And this is Ruth, our organizer."

"What do you want?"

"Look, could you just come down so we could talk for a minute?" Juan called.

Tooley disappeared from the window, and Juan and I looked at each other, wondering whether we had been dismissed or if Tooley was on his way down.

A minute later, Tooley pushed open the screen door and stepped out onto the concrete stoop with us, letting the door slap shut behind him. Tooley was a pale-faced, skinny guy with bad teeth and a sunburn. He wore a stretched out white undershirt, cutoffs, and a Mets cap that had seen better days. He needed a haircut.

"My kid's sick. Let's talk out here. What do you want? I already told you I'd vote for the union." Tooley's Jersey accent was powerful.

"Well, actually, I wanted to talk to you about Schmidt," said Juan.

Tooley looked down at his feet. "The fucking bastard," he muttered.

"You know, we never talked about it, but I was worried that some of the things you told me that night at the Pony kind of came back to haunt you," Juan said.

"Why in the hell did you tell people about that? I couldn't believe you did that!" Tooley exclaimed suddenly, his eyes flashing at Juan.

"I told our organizer, Victoria. And as soon as I did it, I knew I shouldn't have. I'm sorry," Juan said.

Tooley scowled. "Yeah, I heard all about that. I know you guys think Schmidt stole that fucking file."

As Tooley spoke, my eye caught motion above his head. I glanced up and saw a figure standing next to the upstairs window.

"Did Schmidt ever use that information in any way?" Juan asked gently.

"God damn it!" Tooley exploded. "Why are you coming here and asking me about this shit?"

"Because of Al," Juan said simply. "Because we need to know what really happened."

"Jesus, don't tell me about Al." I could hear the anguish in Tooley's voice.

"What did Schmidt do?" Juan persisted.

Tooley suddenly grabbed Juan's shirt and pulled him closer. "You know what he did? He told my fucking kid. He told my *kid!* The one person on the whole planet who didn't think I was a fucking loser idiot."

Tooley sank down until he was sitting on the porch step and held his head in his hands.

I glanced up to the window again, and at that moment a child's voice, thin and high, called out, "Tell them, Daddy."

Tooley looked up and choked out a laugh. "My kid thinks I should confess. He thinks somehow everybody'll understand and I won't have to go to jail."

Juan and I looked at each other. I could hardly believe my ears.

Just then the front door opened, and a small boy, maybe eight years old, emerged, his face wet with tears. Without a sound he climbed onto his father's lap and put his thin arms around Tooley's neck. "Tell them, Daddy, tell them, Daddy, tell them Daddy," he chanted, between sobs.

Then Tooley, his arms wrapped tightly around the boy, said softly, "I will, Jody."

CHAPTER 35

At an emergency meeting that afternoon, we agreed that we had to reach every worker to tell them the news of Al's innocence and remind them to vote. At the end of the first shift, over a dozen volunteers came to the office to make calls. The noise they created was deafening. They all seemed to be talking at high volume while moving chairs and equipment around.

I decided to call Tommy from the relative quiet of the stair landing.

"Tommy, we need a lawyer." I said, my voice echoing down the stairwell.

"What for?"

"For the guy who killed Schmidt."

"Don't tell me you're talking about Al Zielinski."

"No, the guy's name is Darien Tooley." Then I told Tommy about the conversation with Tooley. I told him how Schmidt had intercepted Jody Tooley on his way home from school and taunted him about his father's theft. About how that same evening, Darien Tooley had found Schmidt at one of the bars he frequented and waited for him in the parking lot, stooping behind his car with a rifle in his hand. Tooley had said he'd only wanted to scare Schmidt, but when Schmidt saw Tooley's rifle, he had pulled out the pistol he always carried. In response, Tooley had fired.

"Jesus Christ, Ruthie, and you want the union to defend this guy?"

I tightened my grip on the phone. "Look, Tommy, none of this would have happened if it hadn't been for the organizing drive – Juan getting the information, Victoria recording it, Schmidt stealing it. And besides," I added, "I promised we'd help Tooley if he went to the cops."

"Ruthie, why in the hell did you do that?"

"To get Al off the hook."

"Oh, Christ!"

"Please Tommy? Could we get Ulrich to talk to Tooley today? I told him we could." Ulrich was the union staff attorney, a man with an appetite for going after the bad guys.

"Jeez, Ruthie, Ulrich isn't a criminal lawyer."

"I know, but he's smart and I figure he could point Tooley in the right direction, you know?"

Tommy issued a few more exclamations before finally agreeing to ask for Ulrich's help.

After I hung up with Tommy, I sat mutely on the step for a minute.

Then, for the third time, I called Beck's cell, and for the third time I left a message. I'd already told Beck the news about Tooley, I'd already begged him to stop trailing Beatty. All I could do was repeat myself. I beeped off, then filled my lungs with air and braced myself to go back into the office.

"Ruth?" Silvia nudged my shoulder.

"Huh?" I'd managed to fall asleep sitting up. My hand was still resting on the phone in anticipation of my next call. I sat up and squinted in the direction of Silvia's voice. The light was blinding.

"You should go home and get some rest, Ruth. I'll drive you."

I rubbed my eyes and looked around the office, now empty except for Silvia and me. "You know where Liz is?"

"She said to tell you Malcolm would drive her home. She said don't wait up." Silvia smiled.

"Thanks, Silvia. If you could drive me to the train station, I'll take it from there."

By the time we emerged onto the sidewalk, I was fully alert. Nervous, in fact. Instinctively I scanned the street for the white Expedition. It was nowhere in sight.

"I heard he was tailing Alonzo today," Silvia said.

We walked down the avenue a half a block and turned onto the side street till we reached Silvia's car. We climbed in.

"What an incredible day," said Silvia as she pulled the car out on the street.

"Yeah," I said.

"I'm so relieved it wasn't Al."

"Yeah, me too." I just wished I could get that picture of Tooley and his kid out of my mind.

Silvia sighed. "I hardly remember what my kids look like."

I glanced at Silvia. "How're they doing?"

"They're a little tense these days." Silvia's eyes were focused on the dark road ahead.

"Over you being gone so much?"

"Over the bad vibes they've been picking up between Pablo and me."

"How bad?"

"Put it this way. I'm starting to think I may be a single mom soon."

I twisted to face Silvia. "You know, you won't always be working so much. If we win, the union might take some of your evenings, but nothing like this."

"No, it's not just that. It's just – this whole experience has brought out a lot of other problems. I'm so happy lately – I've found this new thing, something I really care about and that I'm good at." Silvia glanced at me and smiled. "And Pablo doesn't like that very much. Lately when I come home I've got a thousand things I want to tell Pablo about what we've been doing. And he doesn't want to hear it. He just wants to complain about how I didn't get dinner on the table again. It's like we have nothing to share with each other anymore."

I watched Silvia as she made a turn. "Have you been able to talk to Pablo about it?"

But Silvia didn't answer. She was staring with wide eyes into the rear view mirror. I looked out the back window, but saw only indistinguishable headlights.

"What?" I asked.

"I think I just saw that damn car come out of a side street."

"There are lots of big white cars around," I said. Thank god Liz was riding home with Malcolm tonight, I thought.

"I'm going to pull over. Maybe he'll just pass us by." Silvia steered the Ford to a bus stop area and we waited tensely as two dark cars went by, followed by a white SUV.

"That's him," Silvia whispered.

"Silvia," I said urgently. "Could you just wait here for a second?"

"Okay," said Silvia, sounding perplexed.

I jumped out of the car and stood by the side of the road, squinting at the two cars now coming down the road. Sure enough, the second of the two cars was a red Miata. I stepped further into the street and waved.

The Miata pulled over and came to a sudden stop a few feet from me. Beck half climbed out of his car and yelled across its low roof to me. "What the hell are you doing?"

"Trying to flag you down. Just a minute."

I turned to Silvia. "Silvia, I'm going to go with John Beck. He'll give me a ride home."

"Are you sure?" Silvia looked up at me through the open window, her face full of doubt.

"Yeah. Thanks, Silvia. I'll see you first thing tomorrow morning."

With that I turned and leapt into Beck's car before he had a chance to object.

"Carry on," I said the instant my butt was in the seat. I motioned forward.

"But — "

"Better hurry up or we'll lose him." I grabbed the shoulder belt and snapped it into place.

CHAPTER 36

"We lost him," Beck said five minutes later, his voice low and accusatory.

"Be patient. Maybe we should go back to Main Street and park somewhere until he comes by."

Beck glanced at me. "What makes you think he will?"

I shrugged. "You have to go down Main to get anywhere in Bloomson."

"What makes you think he wants to go somewhere in Bloomson? This guy has taken me all over central Jersey today."

"Did you learn anything?"

Beck shrugged. "The guy really likes Burger King. Other than that, he was trying to rattle the people Alonzo Lopez made house visits to."

Beck tucked the car into a vacant spot along Main Street and then turned to me. "So what the hell are you doing here?" Beck was wearing jeans and a work shirt. I could smell his sweat. It didn't smell acrid or unpleasant, it just smelled like Beck.

"I want to get Beatty," I said. "I want to nail down this mob thing as much as you do."

"What good is it having two of us in danger?"

"Aha! So you admit it's dangerous!"

"Ruth, don't be silly — "

"Beck — here he comes!" I interrupted, pointing at the road.

The Expedition was speeding down Main in the opposite direction. Beck let one beat go by, then did a quick u-ey. Beatty was now two cars in front of us. We drove in silence, Beck's jaw tensed, his hands tightly encircling the wheel.

A few blocks later, Beatty sped through an intersection as the light turned red, leaving us stranded on the other side. Beck let out a parade of expletives while I bit my lip and muttered as we waited for the light to change. When it did, Beck gunned the engine and the Miata roared.

The Expedition hadn't gone far. It was stopped several blocks ahead at another red light. We came to a stop, still two cars behind. Beck's car was now standing directly under the bright glare of a streetlight.

"You know, this car of yours is cute and everything," I said as we idled. "But have you ever considered getting something a little less flashy?"

Beck glanced at me. "Shut up. Aren't you the one with the lime-green Neon?"

"Not anymore."

Beatty pulled through the intersection before the light changed. By the time our turn came, we had a green. Ahead, Beatty swerved onto the ramp that led to Route 297 heading south. Apparently the guy never signaled and showed only occasional compliance with traffic rules in general. Either that, or Beatty had spotted Beck's Miata and was trying to lose us. Or maybe he just wanted to make sure we were following him before he whipped out his gun again.

Beck took his foot off the gas as we exited, making our tail a little less obvious. But when we got onto Route 297, we saw that the Expedition and the Miata were the only two cars on the road for a half mile. The distance between us was spreading.

"Jesus. You're going seventy. What do you think he's doing?"

Beck shrugged. "Ninety?" The Miata lurched forward and my head snapped back. I cried out involuntarily.

"Oh jeez, I'm sorry. You okay?" Beck asked.

"Oh yeah. Just a little reminder of that night," I said as I rubbed my neck. I wouldn't have this damn pain if it hadn't been for that asshole, I thought as I stared ahead at Beatty's taillights. Who was this man, and why was he scaring the hell out of me and the other organizers? Screwing up the drive and robbing people of their rights? And how dare he threaten my *niece*? I pictured pulling Beatty out of his stupid SUV, wrapping my hot hands around his neck and squeezing until he was dead. I shuddered with a combination of horror and pleasure at the thought.

Okay, I was going off the deep end. I willed myself to take some deep breaths. I wasn't going to murder Beatty. But at least tonight I wasn't going to run away from him. Tonight, for once, we were the hunters and Beatty was the prey.

About three miles later, Beatty took an exit to a suburb called Sheltonville. Beck followed suit. The exit ramp curved, and the

Expedition soon moved out of view. By the time we got to a stop sign where we had a choice of heading either east or west, I saw no big white car in either direction.

"Shit," said Beck. "Preference?"

"You choose."

Beck turned right. Three blocks on, we still hadn't seen the Expedition.

"Maybe we should go back the other way," said Beck.

"Let's go a few more blocks."

Two blocks on, I spotted Beatty's familiar taillights heading down the road to our left. "Beck!" I said, pointing out my window at the retreating SUV.

Beck made the turn suddenly and the car let out a squeal. Up ahead, we saw the Expedition pull over to the side of the road.

"Oh shit," said Beck. "Maybe he spotted us."

"Or heard us."

"What should we do?"

"Let's pull over right here and see what he does."

Beck pulled over and brought the car to a rapid halt, then looked at me. "Why would he stop here?"

"Maybe he lives here. Or maybe he wants to go make life miserable for somebody on this block."

Beck cut the lights but kept the engine running. I was clutching the armrest so tightly that my muscles ached.

"What do you think he's doing in there?" I asked after a moment. Beatty's car was still idling.

"Don't know."

I looked around. We were on a quiet, ordinary-looking residential street for people who were neither rich nor poor. The houses were older two-story numbers in reasonable condition. I figured the subdivision had been built in the 1920s — enough time for some maples and tulip poplars edging the street to grow to majestic heights.

Beck turned off the engine and we listened. A dog was barking somewhere. And then the Expedition's lights went off. A few seconds later, a car door slammed.

"Is that him?" I asked.

"Yeah, I see him. He's going up the walk."

"Oh. I see him now. You should have brought binoculars."

Beck glanced at me irritably.

"Did he go in?" I asked.

"Looks like it."

"Let's go take a look," I said, opening the Miata's door.

Without another word, we crossed to the opposite sidewalk and approached Beatty's car. I could hear Beck breathing beside me. The Expedition was dark and empty. It was parked in front of an unremarkable white, green-shuttered house. A dull yellow glow emanated from behind the curtains in a downstairs room.

Wordlessly Beck grabbed my sleeve and pulled me off the sidewalk to a spot behind a clump of juniper bushes. We both crouched down and waited, our eyes on the downstairs window. As we watched, the front curtain parted and someone peered out. Then the curtain fell closed again. Now it was my breath I was hearing.

After five minutes that felt like a half hour, the downstairs light went off. Seconds later, an upstairs light flicked on.

I glanced at Beck. He raised his eyebrows. It seemed Beatty was retiring for the night. We watched for a few more minutes, then Beck tugged on my sleeve again and we emerged from the bushes and walked rapidly back to the Miata.

The sound of our doors slamming seemed deafening after all that silence. I was hyperventilating and my legs were shaking.

"What do we do now?" I asked after my breathing had returned to normal.

"I know what I'd do, but now that you're here, I can't," said Beck grumpily.

I turned to face Beck. "Look. Will you lose the attitude? What do you want to do? Camp out here for the night? Fine. Like I said, I want to get this guy as much as you do. At least." I glared at Beck.

He rolled his eyes. "Don't be ridiculous. You've got one more day till the election. You can't afford to spend the night sitting in a car waiting for this asshole to do something."

"Let me be the judge of that. I don't sleep anyway. I might as well not sleep here."

Beck still looked irritated, but less so. He sighed, seeming to accept the inevitability of my presence. "Well, I guess while we're stuck here I could show you this book I found." He reached into the back seat and grasped a battered paperback, then flipped on the dome light.

"Check this out," he said, handing me the book. "It's got a whole chapter in there on the Cappellinis. And pictures. Look at the middle section there."

I found the plates and began paging through them.

"Wait. Stop. There they are." Beck tapped his index finger on the open page, which contained a black-and-white photo of a group of five unsmiling men in suits.

"The Cappellini brothers?"

"That's them. In the early days."

I held the book up close to my face and studied it. "Which is the one who disappeared?"

"It's Lawrence, the one on the far left."

The men in the picture all closely resembled each other, except Lawrence, who looked pale and sickly next to his brawny brothers. And the odd thing was, he also looked faintly familiar. I stared at the photo.

"I feel like I recognize that guy," I said.

"Huh?"

"Doesn't he look kind of familiar?" I asked, pointing to the face of Lawrence Cappellini.

"Umm, not really."

"Oh well," I said, flipping to the chapter on the Cappellinis. "Did you learn anything new in here?"

"A little. Some more details about the family split."

"No mention of Tim Beatty, I guess?" I ventured.

"Nah, nothing like that," said Beck. He leaned back in his seat.

When I looked up from the book a few minutes later, Beck was glancing at his cell phone, which was in a holder between the seats.

"You want to call your girlfriend? Be my guest. I'll even get out of the car so you can have some privacy," I said, beginning to tug on the latch.

"No, no," Beck said, touching my arm. "It's okay. I'll be just a second."

He picked up the cell and pushed two buttons, then pressed the thing tightly to his ear.

"Oh, hi hon," he said brightly after a moment. "Listen, it looks like I'm not going to make it home tonight. I finally got this guy's tail and I'm just going to sit tight. Okay?"

I looked out the window, as if I'd seen something of deep interest out there among the bland suburban houses.

"Uh huh, I know I said that," Beck said after a moment. "Hon, I'm really sorry, but you know how long I've been trying to nail this guy." Silence as Beck listened. Now I wished I had gone outside. It felt like the air pressure in the car was rising. As if a second atmosphere was pressing down on us.

"I don't know. I'll just see you in the office sometime tomorrow." Beck's leg started bouncing up and down.

"Of course I'm alone!" he said sharply, glancing at me. "How the hell should I know where she is? Probably out getting drunk somewhere — " Beck said, then put his hand over his mouth.

I stared at Beck. He looked at me, embarrassed.

"What? Look, hon, you're breaking up here. I'll call you at the Star first thing, okay? We'll talk."

Beck beeped off. There was a moment of quiet in the car. I had the urge to fling myself out the door and run down the street, run for miles until I was lost and exhausted.

"I'm sorry, Reid," Beck said, resting his hand on my thigh. I stared down at it. I loved that hand. So foolish.

"So you think I'm a lush too. Don't feel bad. Everybody does."

"Reid — "

"I wonder why Yvette was asking about me."

Beck inhaled and sat heavily back in his seat. "She's obsessed. She thinks — I don't know, that we have something going on that I'm not even aware of."

I laughed. "Not aware of? What, am I casting spells on you or something?"

Beck looked embarrassed. "Yeah. I think that's what she thinks. She thinks I'm in love with you and just don't know it."

"Oh." My breath caught in my throat. "Pretty silly, huh?"

Beck looked over at me pleadingly. "I don't know, Reid. You think we can change the subject?"

I nodded and plucked my cell phone from my bag. I texted Liz that I'd see her in the office in the morning. I knew I'd pay a price. Liz would conclude I had gone home with somebody and she'd be poking her elbow into my side all day.

"Reid," Beck said beside me. He was pointing toward Beatty's house. The upstairs light was off. The Expedition was still parked in front.

I looked at Beck and nodded.

"You try and sleep," Beck said. "I'll keep watch."

Just minutes before, Beck had hurt my feelings. Now I wished he would kiss me. But he didn't. He just sat up in his seat and squinted into the night.

So I pulled the recliner lever, easing the seat down till it was almost flat. I closed my burning eyes and crossed my arms on my chest. And then, against all expectation, I fell soundly asleep.

"Reid! Reid!" I was being jostled awake. My throat hurt. And my back was killing me. I opened my eyes and felt a surge of panic. Where the hell was I?

John Beck peered into my face. "Ruth! I think he's leaving — we're out of here."

"Oh, jeez. Are we still here?" I groaned. I found the lever and brought my seat up so quickly that it knocked the breath out of me.

Beck laughed. "You're really out of it, aren't you?"

I looked at him irritably. "My throat hurts."

He smiled. "I'm not surprised. You were snoring all night."

"I was? I couldn't have been. I don't snore."

Beck let out a belly laugh. He didn't even bother with a verbal retort.

"Where is he? I don't see him," I said, peering down the street. Everything was foggy and dim. I looked at my watch. It was just after six a.m.

"Here he comes with the garbage cans," said Beck.

"Weird. Even thugs take out the garbage." I rubbed my eyes. Now that Beatty had taken his cap off, I could see that his most prominent feature was his enormous pale brow, made larger by a receding hairline. He was a tall man with a tendency to lope.

"If this guy works for the Queens Cappellinis, how come he's got this boring house in New Jersey?" I asked.

Beck shrugged. "Maybe it's not his. Maybe he's just borrowing it for this campaign."

"Beck. He's getting in the car."

"I see him." Beck let a moment go by after the Expedition pulled out, then followed.

I yawned. "I need a cup of coffee. Big time."

"Hey. At least you got some sleep."

"You're right. In fact, this is the best night's sleep I've had since I started this campaign."

"I must put you at ease," said Beck lightly.

I looked down at my wrinkled shirt. Well, not at ease, exactly, I thought. But at home, maybe. I glanced over at Beck. Our eyes met for a moment. I looked away. So why are you with Yvette? I thought. And yet somehow, I couldn't believe Beck would ever be completely available, not to me anyway. There was some fundamental essence of Beck, something that made him always seem just out of reach.

I shook my head and wondered: If Beck were completely *in* reach, would it cool my desire for him? The idea of a totally available John Beck wasn't as appealing as it ought to be. I sat back in my seat. If that's really the way I felt, then I had an affliction, a mental illness.

"I have to pee," I announced.

Beck frowned. "You're just a little bundle of needs, aren't you?"

"I appreciate the sympathy."

"Look, we can't stop right now. Let's just see where he's going. As soon as he stops, we'll figure something out, okay?"

"Okay." Ahead, the Expedition turned left onto a major road. I blinked. "Aren't you following kind of close?"

"Just let me do the driving," said Beck tensely.

We went on for four blocks, then Beatty made another turn, then another, and suddenly we were in the parking lot of a Dunkin Donuts.

Bathroom! Coffee! I thought. But I knew that would have to wait.

"Let's just watch for a minute," Beck said. "Then we'll find a bathroom."

Beck had backed the Miata into a spot so that we were facing the restaurant's plate glass windows. I could see Beatty standing in line in front of the counter behind a large white woman with a toddler on her hip.

Beatty got his order – a bag of something and a large coffee — and romped over to a table. There were plenty of empty tables, but Beatty chose instead one that was already occupied by another man.

I snapped to attention. "Who's that?"

"Don't know." Beck was leaning forward, his forearms resting on the steering wheel as he peered into the restaurant.

The man did not even look up to greet Beatty, but kept his head down, as if intent on his food. Beatty sat down in the chair across from him.

"That guy," I said. "Doesn't he look familiar to you?" Suddenly I was having trouble catching my breath.

"Yep," said Beck softly.

"Well — " I swallowed. "Who do you think it is?"

Beck looked over at me. "I think it's Kevin McGarry."

CHAPTER 37

I sat as if paralyzed, staring into the Dunkin Donuts at Beatty and the man who was beyond a doubt was Kevin McGarry. The two men weren't doing much — eating crullers and talking in a subdued way.

"I think you've finally found your spy," Beck said after a moment.

"Beck, I should have known. McGarry! Of course he knew all about the work-to-rule campaign. He helped plan it. And who else could have known about my drinking and my thing with you?"

"And McGarry told Beatty. Who told Toro. Who apparently told Shawcross. Quite a little whisper campaign."

"He used Liz." I stared into the restaurant, where McGarry was wiping his mouth with a napkin.

"Big time," said Beck.

"What a bastard! I wonder what he's saying right now. Probably telling Beatty who to terrorize next."

"Hold on, hold on," Beck said abruptly. "I think they're putting down the tip." Beatty had leaned back in his seat to retrieve his wallet and was now dropping a bill onto the table.

"Listen," said Beck in a tense staccato. "I don't want to lose Beatty now. We need to keep trailing him."

I stared at Beck. "No way! You think I'm going to let McGarry out of here without confronting his ass?"

"It's not safe! What if Beatty pulls his gun? Would you at least wait till Beatty's gone to go after McGarry?"

"What if McGarry leaves first?" I said, my hand on the door handle.

"Then you'll just have to come with me," said Beck.

I gave a groan of consent, slung on my backpack and climbed out of the Miata. I found a spot on the nearby curb where I was tucked between two cars but still had a clear view of the restaurant's entrance. I just hoped neither car was McGarry's.

Beatty and McGarry walked through the doors, first the loping Beatty, and then McGarry, looking furtive. Without a word, Beatty turned toward his Expedition, McGarry toward a dented Ford F-150.

Fortunately, Beatty was the first to pull his vehicle out of the lot. About thirty seconds after the Expedition roared away, Beck's Miata sped out after it.

Once the two noisy vehicles had exited the lot I could hear that McGarry was struggling with his ignition. The truck's motor turned over but wouldn't quite catch.

I strode over to the truck and pulled open McGarry's door. I was staring him in the face before he even registered who I was. He flushed suddenly when he did.

"Ruth! Hey!" he said. Even if I hadn't just seen him chatting with Beatty his exclamation would have seemed false.

"Why in the hell are you talking to Tim Beatty?" I thundered.

"What?"

I stepped closer to McGarry and stuck my face into his. "I said, why in the hell were you just talking to that thug Tim Beatty?"

"Oh, god, well, we've been friends since grade school. It has nothing to do with — "

"Bullshit! You're the spy! You've been telling Beatty about our plans and using Liz to get information about my personal life. You fucking bastard!" My fury was overflowing. I wanted to kick McGarry. Or throw something at him.

"Wait, wait," McGarry said, his voice shaking. "I wasn't using Liz. I care about Liz! I was protecting her!"

"*Protecting* her? Give me a fucking break!"

"No, believe me, Ruth. If I hadn't — I mean, I convinced them that using her to get to you — well, that it was better to use Liz as a source of information — " McGarry sputtered.

I stared at McGarry. "Are you saying that the criminals you work for wanted to kidnap Liz to force me off this campaign?"

McGarry swallowed and nodded.

"And you persuaded them to use her as a source instead."

McGarry nodded again.

"So we should be grateful to you for spying on us."

"I know it sounds weird. But it's true, I swear to god! When I started out I was just doing a job for this guy I knew. I figured some people were going to be for the union and other people were going to be against it and I was just working for one side. I mean, who cares? It was only later I figured out how connected these people were, you know?"

"You're saying you didn't know the Cappellinis were involved?"

McGarry shook his head. "See, I knew Tim Beatty from way back. And I knew he was a hood and stuff. But he offered me some pretty good money, he said just to keep an eye on the organizing drive. And I did, but then I really started to believe in the whole union thing. And in Liz. I swear to god!"

Tears were suddenly coursing down McGarry's cheeks. He glanced around the parking lot self-consciously.

McGarry's tears did little to soften my anger. "You stabbed us in the back — Joe and Silvia and Nita — and especially Liz. You screwed up everything we tried to do. Because of you, Toro's people knew our every move in advance. And Beatty knew just who to intimidate."

"I never talked to Toro or anybody else but Tim, I swear."

"Oh, that's nice. The only person you told is the guy who tried to blow my head off on the highway a few days ago."

"He'd never kill anyone. He's just trying to scare people."

A car backfired somewhere nearby. The sound made McGarry jump and look around with frightened eyes. Only when a second explosion sounded did I realize what I was hearing: gunshots. From just down the road. And suddenly all I could think of was John Beck.

CHAPTER 38

I scanned the road for Beck's car. I saw nothing resembling the Miata.

Without a thought of McGarry, I turned and ran down the wide unoccupied sidewalk toward the gunshots. I glanced back and saw McGarry's truck tearing out of the parking lot, heading in the opposite direction.

I sprinted past fast food restaurants and auto repair shops, past a florist, an RV sales lot, past a bus depot, the air singeing my lungs.

Suddenly I saw the Miata. It was parked on the oil-stained pavement of an abandoned gas station. I raced up to the car and came to a sudden stop, my heart pounding impossibly hard, my entire body quaking. I peered inside. Empty. And Beatty's Expedition was nowhere in sight.

And then I heard an unearthly, rasping sound that seemed to come from nowhere. Was it just my imagination, or had I heard my name in that rasp?

But where was Beck? I circled around the Miata, breathing hard.

And there, lying flat on his back by the far rear wheel, was John Beck. "Reid," he whispered again. The panic on his face was contagious. Something terrifying was happening here.

"Beck!" I cried, kneeling down. And then I saw the spreading red stain on the right side of Beck's shirt. I stared at it, paralyzed. A sucking sound was coming out of Beck somewhere.

Beck saw the terror in my eyes and it seemed to add to his own. "I can't breathe!" he whispered, his eyes staring at me pleadingly.

I tore open Beck's shirt.

"Oh, jeez," I blurted. There was a small red hole in Beck's chest. Blood was bubbling out of it, leaving a trace of froth on the skin surrounding the wound. The sound it made was horrifying. The sound of Beck's breath being taken away.

"It's okay, John, it's okay," I said, trying to keep the tremble out of my voice. From what I could see it was anything but okay. For several seconds I knelt there, quaking. Beck was going to suffocate. I pawed frantically through my bag till I found my cell phone. I could hardly see and my fingers were shaking so badly I struggled to align them with the buttons. When the operator asked me where I was I drew a complete blank.

"Look at the street signs!" she commanded.

I leapt up and raced toward the intersection. One of the signs was missing. "Samson Boulevard and — " I stuttered into the phone. I could just barely make out the street sign a block away. "One block from Poplar!" I yelled.

"We'll be right there," the woman said, clicking off. I looked back at Beck.

His breathing was jagged. And that horrible sucking sound went on and on.

"I'm scared," Beck whispered.

I managed to summon my senses enough to reply, "It's going to be okay, Beck. The ambulance will be here in a minute. You're going to be fine."

"I think I'm going to pass out," Beck said weakly.

"Just hold on," I said. I wiped my face, which was wet with tears.

By the time the firefighters arrived, Beck was unconscious and his lips were turning blue. I was gripping his hand, kneeling there with tears and makeup streaming down my face.

Five gigantic men in rubbery olive-colored suits surrounded us on the pavement. One of them knelt down and examined Beck. I backed away.

"Bullet got him in the lung. Hear that?" the firefighter said. "Gimme that aluminum foil stuff," he commanded the member of his crew with the first aid case.

The crewmember ripped open a white plastic tube and pulled out a roll of foil. The firefighter tending to Beck unrolled the foil and held it over Beck's chest. He waited till Beck exhaled then gently placed the foil over the bullet hole, quickly sealing it with tape. The sucking sound immediately stopped.

"Lung should refill now," the firefighter said, looking at me with a smile.

The feeling of relief that flooded through me was so intense, it made me dizzy. "Thank you so much. Thank you so much," I blubbered.

"Hey, it's our job," the man said, patting me on the shoulder. "You okay?"

I nodded, then stepped back as an ambulance pulled up. Two EMTs, one male, one female, leapt out and bent over Beck. There was a quick exchange of medical jargon and codes I didn't understand.

And then they lifted Beck onto a stretcher and whisked him into the ambulance. I had an impulse to leap in after them, but then I took in the sight of Beck's car. If I left it here now, it might be a skeleton by tomorrow morning. I flung open the driver's door and sat down in the seat. The keys were still in the ignition. I started the engine and followed the ambulance out onto the street.

An hour and a half later, I was sitting in a stifling green-upholstered waiting room at Sisters of Mercy Hospital in Burgoyne, New Jersey. I hadn't seen Beck since he was hauled into the ambulance, but I'd gotten two reports. The first was that the bullet had been removed, that it had punctured Beck's lung but had apparently hit no other major organ or artery. The second was that Beck was in the recovery room and I could visit him in fifteen minutes. That had been 40 minutes ago. The nurse at the desk had assured me repeatedly that the staff would let me know when I could see Beck.

My eyes settled on my new comrades, the three people I'd been sharing this small waiting room with — a middle-aged couple who were extremely worried about their thirteen-year-old daughter's abdominal surgery and an elderly woman whose husband was getting a cancerous growth removed. We were all in the same boat: Scared, vulnerable, and verging on panic. And worst of all, completely helpless. Every few minutes one of us would trudge over to the poor nurse on duty and ask for news. It was all we could do.

I leaned back on the vinyl sofa and closed my eyes. I'd already read every article in the year-old issue of Good Housekeeping and I'd looked at hundreds of photos of half-starved women in the thick, battered, and coverless issue of Vogue.

It was just after eight in the morning but it felt like the middle of the night to me. The last day before the union election and here I was at the Sisters of Mercy Hospital. I wondered who was in the office right now. I'd left a message reporting what had happened. I had also left messages for Beck's wife Beth and for Yvette at The Star. I figured one or the other of them would be arriving in the hospital soon. It wasn't something I was looking forward to.

"Ms. Reid?"

I looked up to see the same Filipina woman who had delivered the earlier news about Beck's status, standing in the hallway that led from the waiting room.

"Yes?"

"You can visit your brother now. But only for a few minutes."

I jumped up and followed the woman down the hall.

Beck had already been moved from ICU to a room nearby. It was spare but clean. Beck was lying flat, looking very pale, but no longer blue-lipped. He smiled faintly when he saw me. At least he could tell who I was. His eyes had a stoned look that told me not to expect too much from him this morning.

"Reid," he whispered. "You should have told me we were related."

"Beck," I said. I sat down in the chair next to the bed and squeezed his hand.

Beck looked at me with soft eyes and said nothing.

"How do you feel?"

"Breathing kind of hurts."

I nodded. "The good news is, they say you're going to be fine. They might let you go home tomorrow."

"Good. Work to do."

"Beck," I said. "Don't be ridiculous. You can hardly breathe. I'm sure walking is going to be excruciating. I think maybe you should take a little break from work."

"I'm getting really close."

I nodded and squeezed Beck's hand tighter.

"I hate these drugs," Beck drawled. "Don't want to sleep."

But sleep was definitely in Beck's immediate future. His eyes were drooping as he spoke.

Beck closed his eyes with such relief that I knew it was time for me to leave. Except that he had hold of my hand again and didn't seem to want to let go. I bent over and kissed Beck's forehead before pulling my hand away.

And in that tender moment, the door burst open and Yvette marched in, followed by Beth.

I heard the little intake of breath as Yvette took in the scene. She had stopped cold in the middle of the floor and was staring at me, her mouth in a tight frown. Her hand was resting on her smart red leather bag. Her hair was pulled back in a glossy ponytail. Her perfume, which smelled of fresh laundry, drifted through the room.

"How — how is he doing?" she stuttered, as her eyes moved from my hand in Beck's to Beck's pasty and swollen face.

As if on cue, Beck opened his eyes. His look was foggy at first, then sharpened quickly when he saw who was in the room. Beth, Yvette and Ruth. What a combination.

"Let me just see," said Beth briskly, moving past Yvette to a spot across the bed from me. She stood there for a moment, stiffly upright, in her well tailored navy pantsuit. Beth was a handsome woman who seemed to embrace her status as a middle-aged professional. She matter-of-factly examined the dressings on Beck's chest. Then she peered into his face.

"How are you?" she asked.

"The doctors say I'll be fine," Beck rasped. He looked haplessly from Beth's face to Yvette's. Then he rolled his eyes over to me. I gave him an ironic smile. Beck turned his face back to Beth, as if prepared to swallow a bitter pill.

"You've got quite a harem here," said Beth.

Yvette's face contorted into a look I could not quite decipher — anger, consternation, embarrassment? I let out a little snort of a laugh.

Beth and Yvette both swiveled their heads in my direction and snarled. The last time I'd felt such a powerful and unacceptable urge to burst into peels of laughter was sitting in the silent pews next to Aunt Penny at the McCracken Presbyterian Church when I was thirteen.

"What's so funny?" Yvette hissed. "The man has been shot."

"I'm sorry," I muttered.

"Do you mind if I talk to John for a moment? If you could possibly break away?" Yvette said, glaring at me.

"You certainly have a sense of entitlement about my husband," said Beth coolly.

Yvette froze. Her fingers were pressed so hard into her purse that they were turning white.

"Well," she said, clearing her throat, "Everyone has the right to be loved."

That was a show-stopper. Beth brought her brows together. "Are you referring to yourself?"

"No, actually, I was referring to your husband."

Whoa. That Yvette was tougher than I'd thought. Beside me, Beck swallowed and shifted in the bed. He looked like a torture victim.

I gave Beck's hand one last squeeze and prepared to vacate my spot before Yvette hit me with something.

"Alas, I must be going," I said. "I'll just leave you two gals to, uh, look after my friend here."

"Wait," Beck whispered, grabbing my hand again. "Listen."

I stopped and leaned forward so that my ear was close to Beck's mouth.

"It wasn't Beatty," he whispered.

I stood up suddenly. "Hold on," I said, releasing Beck's hand. "You're telling me Beatty wasn't the one who shot you?"

Yvette looked from me to Beck and back again.

Beck rolled his head from side to side on the pillow.

I swallowed. "Are you sure? I mean, what makes you so sure?"

"Gun wasn't drawn. The shot came from across the street."

"*What?*" I said, more loudly than I had intended.

Beck just looked at me, his eyebrows raised.

"Well, who did it then?"

"Don't know. McGarry?"

I shook my head. "McGarry was with me when we heard the shots. Then he took off in the other direction."

Beck's hand climbed up to my sleeve and tugged on it. "Be careful, Reid. You hear me?"

I nodded slowly and stood upright again. Yvette and Beth were both staring at me as if I had been the one with the shocking new information.

"Okay, Beck, so I'll keep you posted, okay? Don't worry," I said, backing away from the bed and letting Yvette slip into my spot.

"So, I'll be seeing you guys," I said breezily to Yvette and Beth. But hopefully not for a really long time, I added to myself as I slipped out the door.

I went back to the waiting room to retrieve my bag and my cell. I had three voice messages. One was from Liz, from about an hour before.

"Hey!" she chirped. I just wanted you to know I won't be in the office till later this morning. Kevin called all upset and really wanted to talk. So I thought, Oh god — might as well get it over with, right? Like you keep telling me. So anyway, he's meeting me at the train station. And, umm, so I'll see you later!"

A screaming alarm went off in my head. How could I have let this happen? How could I have let McGarry go and not warned my niece about him?

I thrust the phone in my bag and pulled out Beck's keys as I went flying down the hallway.

CHAPTER 39

As soon as I settled into the Miata, I pulled out my cell again. I needed to check the other messages in case Liz had called again. But the messages were from Silvia and Joe, both wanting to know which hospital Beck was in and how he'd been injured, apparently information I'd omitted in the frenzied message I'd left on the office machine earlier. I called the office and Joe picked up.

"Joe," I said, my voice quivering. "Beck's in the Sisters of Mercy Hospital in Burgoyne. And it looks like he's going to be okay — "

"Who shot him? Was it Beatty?" Joe asked.

"Beck says it wasn't. He said the shot came from across the street."

"But — " Joe began.

"Listen, Joe, I can't talk now. I've got to find Liz. You haven't seen her in the office this morning, have you? Or Kevin McGarry?"

"Nope, no sign of them here."

"Okay, listen. Maybe you can pass this on to the other people on the committee. This morning, Beck and I trailed Beatty to a meeting at the Dunkin Donuts. And the person he was meeting with — it was Kevin McGarry."

There was silence on the line.

"Are you saying Kevin is the one who — " Joe seemed unable to form the word.

"Yeah. He's the spy. I confronted him and he admitted it. But I let him get away. And now I'm scared he's with Liz — "

"Oh lord."

"So Joe, if you see or hear from Liz, call me, okay?"

"Ruth — " Joe began. But I didn't have time. I beeped off.

I dropped the phone and took off, driving erratically down the unfamiliar streets in Beck's unfamiliar car as I glanced down at the map I'd found in Beck's glove compartment. I'd paid no attention to where I was going when I'd followed the ambulance to the hospital, and I didn't have a clue how to get back to Bloomson.

My hands were shaking badly and I couldn't seem to catch my breath. I just hoped to god my bad driving wouldn't attract the cops, because I had no license and I was out on bail.

I kept picturing Kevin McGarry and Liz together, and the image made me nauseous with fear. McGarry was hustling a terrified Liz into his pickup and speeding away to some deserted place. Then, with Liz quivering beside him, he would call me from his cell phone to tell me he'd kill her if I told anyone about him. Or if I didn't drop the Pantheon campaign. Or if I didn't stop John Beck from publishing another story.

After a few wrong turns, I found myself on the road to Bloomson. I didn't see the sign for the Broadway Diner until it was almost too late. I stepped on the brakes, inciting a cacophony of honks from the cars around me. I swerved into the lot and tumbled out of the car. I stood there in the doorway of the diner, panting and scanning the room. Liz wasn't here.

"Shit!" I ran back out again.

Where else, where else? My mind went immediately to the Pretty Pony. But it was only ten in the morning. Nobody went to a bar in the morning. It was probably closed anyway.

On the other hand, I thought as I sat in the Miata, I had no other bright ideas. I started up the car and headed to the bar.

The Pony looked closed when I passed by. But wait. Wasn't that a light I saw? I put the car in the reverse, causing more horns to honk. Yes. It was a light.

I pulled into the first spot I saw, hurtled out of the car, and ran to the bar. I pulled open the door and was assaulted by the familiar beery smell of dives like the Pony, so jarring at this time of day. Inside the darkness was so complete I hesitated to take a step. After a few seconds, my eyes began to adjust and I could make out the empty stools lining the bar.

I strode to the back of the bar, checking the booths.

And there, in the last booth, were Kevin McGarry and my niece.

I brought my hand to my chest. My heart was beating so hard it felt like it was about to pop out of my body.

"Liz!" I called as I raced toward the booth.

"Aunt Ruth!" Liz called back.

I stood breathless over the table, trying to gauge the situation. McGarry was in tears. Liz did not look terrified. I let out a huge store of air I must have been holding since I left the hospital.

"Are you okay, Aunt Ruth?" Liz asked. "Why don't you sit down? You look like you're going to faint or something."

I sat down next to Liz.

"I think you're the only person I know who would have looked for me in a bar at this hour," said Liz.

"What's happening here?" I asked.

"Kevin told me everything. How he spied and told that Beatty guy everything he found out about you. And how sorry he is."

I glanced over at McGarry, who looked extremely uncomfortable sitting across a table from me.

"Don't tell me you're going to forgive this guy," I said to Liz.

"Are you kidding? I just got done telling him what an ass he is." Liz looked over at McGarry.

"But what am I supposed to do?" McGarry wailed. "I really am sorry. I don't want to spy for Tim anymore. But he's going to be expecting information from me. If I don't give it to him – "

"What?" I said. "You want us to help you figure out what to do to save your ass, after what you've done?" I looked over at my niece. "Are you ready to go? Because I'm not going to leave this bar without you."

"Yep," said Liz.

I slid out of the booth and Liz followed. As we walked down the sidewalk to Beck's car, I had to concentrate to keep my knees from buckling. We had been incredibly lucky. Beck would survive. And Liz was safe. Now if we could all just stay that way through the election.

Back in the office, the sight of Joe's face was enough to bring tears to my eyes. I walked straight across the room and hugged him. Joe held me gently, saying nothing.

Then I sat down with everyone in the office at the time — Joe, Juan, Malcolm, Alonzo Lopez, Liz, and Silvia — and gave a full report of all that had happened from the moment Silvia and I had left the office the night before.

"Sweet Jesus, who would have thought Kevin would do such a thing?" said Joe.

I watched my fingertips trace the surface of the fake woodgrain table. "It is unbelievable," I said. "But even so, I should have figured it out. I mean, this guy immediately snuggles up to Liz — "

"Thanks, Aunt Ruth," snapped Liz. "I'm sure there was no real attraction there."

"Well, it sounds like he really did fall for you in the end," said Silvia.

"Yeah, but he's a bastard anyway," Liz said, grabbing one of the blueberry muffins Joe had brought in.

"I should have figured it out too," said Silvia. "You realize McGarry only started working at Pantheon about three weeks before the drive started? He was knocking down the doors to join the committee. But it never felt like he was working very hard to organize people."

"I'm just glad both Liz and John Beck are okay," said Juan.

"They've pumped Beck full of painkillers," I said. "I hate to think how he's going to feel when they wear off."

"Maybe it was the drugs talking when he told you that weird story about the shot coming from across the street," said Malcolm.

"I hope you're right," said Alonzo. "I mean, Schmidt's dead. Who else goes around shooting people? Besides Darien Tooley?"

We sat silently for a moment.

"You know what?" I said finally. "It's horrible about Kevin, and it's awful what happened to Beck. But there's only a few hours left till the election. We've got to do a major blitz. And I think we need to let people know about McGarry."

Alonzo tilted his head. "Wouldn't that be kind of sending a mixed message? People won't know whether to trust us or not."

"I don't see that we have a choice. It would be irresponsible for us not to warn people that he's a spy."

"I agree," said Silvia. "We may take a hit for it. But I think we've got to be honest and let people make up their own minds whether to trust us."

"Maybe we can turn it to our advantage," said Liz. "You know, like 'fight the spies and the thugs – vote union!'"

The workers smiled at my niece.

"Sounds like a plan," said Alonzo.

It was another soggy scorcher of a day, and the heat of the two dozen people packed into the office, all of us verging on hysteria, seemed to raise the temperature inside another ten degrees. For the first time in days, I couldn't smell chicken fat. It had been overwhelmed by the smell of our sweat.

I spent a solid twelve hours with my ear pressed to the phone. Every five or six calls, I'd go rotate myself in front of the fan or douse myself with water from the bathroom sink. I'd always hated selling things, but that's what I was doing, in essence, every minute of that day. After making sure people had heard the news about Al, I tried mightily to turn the focus back to what we viewed as the best arguments for unionizing: more respect on the job, an end to the speedup, fairer hiring and promotions and challenging discrimination — as well as better pay and benefits. I saved the report about Kevin for last, hoping that the real issues would provide a better context for the news. Even so, as Alonzo had predicted, some people were spooked that a member of the organizing committee had been a spy.

Our calls were interrupted by a visit from the police, who were investigating the shooting of John Beck. I told them everything I knew about Beatty, including our evidence that he was connected to the mob, and everything I had seen that morning. But their questions seemed pro forma, and I worried that chasing down Beatty didn't rank too high on their list of priorities, given that Beck wasn't mortally wounded. Beck had told them his thesis that Beatty wasn't the shooter. Did I have any suspicions about who it might have been?, they asked. No, I surely didn't.

I called the hospital twice. Both times a weary-sounding nurse told me that Beck was "resting comfortably," whatever that meant. I wondered what the fallout was from the miserable collision of Beck's three women in the hospital room.

Late that afternoon, Al appeared in the office for the first time since his drinking binge, looking sweaty and bloated. And shaken. His cocky belligerence was gone. For now, anyway.

Al relieved Malcolm Brown, who had lost his voice after seven hours of phoning. I walked over to Al and said hello.

"Listen," Al said, looking at his feet. "I'm sorry I was such a bastard when you and Joe stopped by the other day. I'd been drinking too much and, you know, I was feeling pretty out of luck that day."

"I know, Al," I said, resting my hand on Al's huge shoulder. His shirt was warm and damp with sweat. "You know who you're going to call?"

Al nodded. "I know I got a lot of enemies, but I still got a few friends, people I might turn at the last minute here."

"Sounds good," I said.

I went back to my desk and watched Al as he made his first call. I felt guilty now that I had suspected Al of Schmidt's murder — not to mention Victoria's.

As far as I could tell, we were no closer to knowing who had murdered Victoria. And had the same person shot Beck?

I sent Liz home at seven-thirty that evening. She had gotten very little sleep in the past few nights, and the exhaustion on her face was starting to make me feel like an evil aunt.

At nine forty-five, I got a phone call.

"What on earth have you been doing to this girl?"

"Sandy."

"Ah, so you recognize my voice."

"Look, I miss you too. But the vote is tomorrow. After that, I'll reacquaint you with all my annoying qualities, I promise."

"Do you realize that your niece has aged five years since the last time I saw her? Do you realize how *dehydrated* she was?"

I laughed.

"There's nothing funny about dehydration," said Sandy earnestly.

"God, no," I said "At least I know she's in good hands now."

"I came over as soon as I saw the lights on. Which I noticed they never were last night."

"Talk about nosy neighbors. My god!"

"Anything to report?" Sandy's voice turned up suggestively.

"What are you talking about?"

"Come on, you little minx."

"Minx," I said. "I can't even remember the last time I was a minx."

Only around midnight did the crowd in the office thin out. It was too late to call anyone. I'd already gone through my list of known night owls.

"It's gotten cooler in here – you notice?" Nita said drowsily. She was standing in front of the fan, looking out the window.

"What do you think our count is?" Silvia asked me.

I shrugged. "Beats me."

"But what's your gut feeling?" Silvia said. She was sitting at the big table, her head resting on her arms.

"My gut feeling is, it's damn close," I said. Each word was a struggle to form, my words sounded slurred. And it wasn't booze — the scotch bottle was still sitting quietly in the drawer.

Silvia looked so restful with her head on her arms, I decided to give it a try myself. Once I'd put my head down, I felt like I'd swallowed half a bottle of sleeping pills.

CHAPTER 40

Consciousness returned slowly. Soft voices murmured around me, weaving into my dreams. It took me a while to realize the voices were in the real world and that they were talking about me.

"Poor baby. She's hardly slept a wink in the last two weeks."

"I felt bad leaving her here last night, but she was sleeping so soundly. And snoring — oh my god!"

"You think she'd want us to wake her up now?"

My head was resting heavily on my arms, so heavily that my right arm had gone to sleep. I opened an eyelid, detected blindingly bright light overhead, and shut it again. I'd been drooling on my arm. Lovely. I raised my head and wiped my arm in what I hoped was a smooth, unrevealing gesture.

Joe, Silvia, and Nita were standing around me in a protective huddle.

"Morning, sweetie," Silvia said gently.

"Sorry we woke you up," said Nita.

"Want some coffee?" said Joe. I smiled and nodded in Joe's direction, still squinting against the light.

Silvia put her hand on my shoulder and rubbed it back and forth. "It's our big day."

I nodded. Words eluded me. I reached out my hand – the one that was still working — and grasped the mug Joe passed me. One hot pungent sip and I was halfway restored. I blinked a few times and looked around.

The blinding light came from the fluorescents overhead. Outside, it looked as though the sun had barely risen.

"What time is it?" I asked. My voice came out as a croak.

Silvia glanced at her sleek silver watch. "Five-thirty. In the morning," she added for clarity.

"It's so dark outside." I took another sip of coffee and flexed my right arm, which responded with a burst of pins and needles. Despite my groggy state, I had just had my second night of real sleep, and I realized that I actually felt pretty rested.

"Yeah, it's weird out there," said Nita. "It looks like it's going to pour."

"Great," I said. "It better not keep anybody from coming out to vote."

"They'll come if I have to carry them on my back," said Nita.

"Want some breakfast?" asked Joe. "We got bagels over here."

Bagels. They'd been in my dreams too. Great piles of warm toasted bagels. Five bags of them sat invitingly on the long table, giving off a yeasty aroma. Juan and Malcolm were beginning to unpack them and pile them onto paper plates along with little plastic tubs of butter, cream cheese, and jelly.

I rubbed my eyes. "Sounds great. Let me just wash up." I got up with a groan and made my way to the bathroom, precious coffee mug in one hand, my bag in the other.

On the stair landing, I stopped, stunned. A few steps down, a familiar face looked up at me.

"Ruthie!"

"Tommy!" I exclaimed, falling into Tommy's arms. His embrace was warm and all enveloping.

"How's your boyfriend doing?" Tommy asked when we'd pulled away from each other.

"Tommy. Since when do you believe Renee Natavsky's gossip?"

"He still in the hospital?" Tommy asked, ignoring my protest.

"I don't know. I haven't talked to him yet this morning."

"Did Ulrich give you a call?"

I nodded. "Yeah, last night. He said he's going to call a couple of criminal defense lawyers he knows and try to get them to take Tooley's case. And he's meeting with Tooley himself this afternoon."

Tommy nodded. "Good," he said, peering into my face. "By the way, Ruthie, you look like hell. What did you do — sleep in the office?"

"Thanks, Tommy. You look like hell yourself, but I had enough tact not to mention it."

Tommy laughed as I stepped into the bathroom, slamming the door behind me.

I splashed some cool water on my face, then regarded myself in the mirror over the sink.

"My god," I muttered. My eyes were marshmallows. In fact, my whole face looked swollen. From the perfect crease on my lower right cheek, I gathered I'd had my face pressed against a stack of paper for the past five hours. Very attractive.

My hair was a wild nest of tangles and curls. It looked like I'd spent the night being chased through a blackberry patch.

I looked down at my clothes. My cotton blend buttoned shirt never looked exactly crisp, since I refused to iron. But at the moment it wasn't remotely presentable, a mass of creases and rumples. However, my black knit skirt was as tidy as ever. This was the advantage of fabrics made from toxic chemical processes.

After brushing my teeth with the travel toothbrush and toothpaste I found in my bag, I had a painful session with my hairbrush. Then I rummaged around in my backpack and produced a makeup bag. As I maneuvered around my face with eyeliner, lipstick, and mascara, I was alarmed to see that my hand was shaking. I ruled out DTs and Parkinson's. I must have been more anxious than I'd thought. I blotted my shirt with wet paper towels, trying to flatten out the wrinkles.

Despite all my efforts, my face was still bloated and creased. However, I considered my appearance to be vastly improved, and I emerged from the bathroom feeling almost decent, if you didn't count the wet shirt.

I was astonished to find the office suddenly crowded. Had all these people arrived while I was repairing myself in the bathroom, or had I been too catatonic to notice them before?

I went back to my desk and called the hospital. They put me right through to Beck's room. When he answered, he sounded alert. Wired, even. Fine, fine, he was doing fine, he assured me impatiently. But he'd gotten no word on when he would be released.

"How did it go with Yvette and Beth yesterday after I left?" I asked.

Beck groaned. "Well, I was pretty out of it, as you might have noticed. But I'll say this. Yvette was not very comfortable with the proceedings."

"I bet."

"I'm not sure Yvette's exactly ready to deal with, uh — "

"How complicated your life is?" I offered.

"Yeah, you could put it that way. And it's not really fair for me to ask her to, uh — "

"Deal with your complicated life?" I tried again.

"Yeah, actually that is what I was going to say. But I hope you don't get into the habit of completing my sentences, because — "

"Because it's irritating?"

Beck laughed. "So anyway, I've had a lot of time to think, lying here. And the upshot is, I think I better find another place to crash for awhile."

I found myself leaning flat against the wall. "You're kidding. You mean, you're going to move out of Yvette's apartment?"

"Yeah. I haven't told Yvette yet. But I have a feeling she won't be that sorry about it. I think this whole thing — we moved too fast. I pushed too hard, moving right in like that."

I was flummoxed. "Well, are you moving back in with Beth?"

Beck laughed weakly. "Uh, no. *That* move was long overdue. Anyway, at least I've got a place for tonight. I took a room at the Sheraton off the interstate. Experience tells me it's going to be a late night."

"Beck! You're not covering the election today, if that's what you're thinking."

"We'll see," Beck said.

"Beck!"

"Which reminds me. You know what happened to my car?"

"Yeah. I took it. It's parked down on Ninth. I figured somebody would strip it if I left it where it was."

"Good. If you'd be its guardian for a little while longer, I'd appreciate it. I don't think I'm up to driving just yet."

"Okay," I said. Not that I was such a great guardian, being licenseless.

"You know, I never heard what happened. Why were you parked in that gas station?"

"Well, I saw Beatty pull over there, so I pulled in next to him. And he was just getting out of his car to bully me when this shot came from across the street."

"Are you *sure* it wasn't Beatty?"

"Reid, I'm sure. I'm a reporter, remember?"

At six a.m., an hour before voting would begin, we pushed our assortment of chairs into a circle. There were almost twenty of us, too many to fit around the table. We collected our bagels and coffees and found seats. As I was about to ask everyone to introduce themselves to Tommy, a sharp crack of thunder sounded nearby, dimming the lights momentarily. The building shuddered in the thunderbolt's aftermath.

After the introductions, we confirmed our plan for the day. Voting would take place in Pantheon's cafeteria. One crew, including Al, would stay in the office making reminder calls and arranging transportation to the plant for anyone who needed it. Another, led by Alonzo Lopez, would be stationed at the plant gate, where they would urge workers to vote. Some of our organizers were on their usual seven to three shift, where they would also remind co-workers to vote. Joe, Silvia, and Nita had been certified as election observers for the union — to be matched by three observers assigned by Pantheon — also, by law, rank-and-file workers. I would move around as needed.

At six-forty-five, we all set out for our cars – the more cars today, the better to transport workers to the voting site. I carried a stack of paper and supplies to Silvia's car a block from the union office. I set the stuff on top of the trunk, then watched as Silvia made her way up the sidewalk. There was another roll of thunder, more distant now. I looked up at the sky, a dim gray-green color I associated with hail. The wind whipped my hair around.

When we arrived at Pantheon, we saw that the National Labor Relations Board officials who were overseeing the election had already put up signs directing us to the side entrance that workers would use to get to the voting station.

I pulled open the door with my free arm and held it for Joe, Silvia, and Tommy. More NLRB signs pointed us down a set of wide cement stairs and into the brightly-lit cafeteria. I looked around at the bare beige walls and inhaled the room's warm, sticky air. Why did cafeterias always smell like boiled cabbage?

The NLRB workers had used mobile dividers to section off a quarter of the cafeteria for voting. They had moved two long formica tables on either side of the door. This was where arriving voters' names would be checked against the official Excelsior list. Despite arduous discussions between us, the NLRB, and Toro over who was eligible to vote, we still didn't agree. I expected ballots would be challenged by both sides.

A woman in a somber-looking pantsuit, her flat brown hair pulled back into a painfully tight ponytail, was reaching over one of the tables, taping a piece of paper to it that said "A to J." When she stood back up, she smiled at us. Her badge said "NLRB Agent Genevieve Appel." We introduced ourselves to Appel and then to agent Michael Kristoff at the other table, a tired looking man with a mop of curly gray hair.

Kristoff handed Joe, Silvia, and Nita their observer badges and a set of instructions. Then he directed Silvia and Joe to sit at his table and Nita to sit at Appel's. He pointed me toward a dozen metal folding chairs that had been lined up along the wall, far from the table with the three sanctified cardboard boxes where workers would drop their ballots.

My chair was blessedly cold. I looked at my watch. The polls would open in ten minutes, just in time for the lobster shift workers to vote before going home.

I skimmed over the instructions Kristoff had handed me. They specified that there could be no conversation during voting. And we weren't allowed to write down who had come in to vote. We were prepared for this. Joe, Silvia, and Nita would have a good grip on who was missing, especially from the lobster and first shifts. They would relay the information to me, and I and other organizers would call pro-union people who hadn't showed up.

I looked up as F.H. Toro stalked through the gym doors, followed by a young woman and a young man, both white, both in business suits. How sad that Sam and Oscar would choose proxies to represent them at an important time like this.

When the first few night shift workers arrived to vote, I was sitting bolt upright in my chair, my sweaty hands clenched. Of the clump of five first arrivals, I was pretty sure that three of them were pro-union. I ran my palms over my skirt and tried to breathe normally.

Another half a dozen workers came through the door, including one guy who gave me the finger as he approached the table. Kristoff frowned and shook his head sharply at the man.

A half hour later, the tension and the need to stay relatively immobile and expressionless were killing me. If I didn't take a break soon, I'd have to stand up and scream. I got up and walked quietly to the door.

As soon as I left the cafeteria, I let in a huge gulp of air and felt instantly better. But as I stepped out into the parking lot, I found a hellish world. Above me, dark low-hanging clouds were being roiled into strange shapes by a wailing tropical wind.

Late that morning, things were not looking good for the union. We'd thought most lobster shift workers would have voted by now, but less than half had showed up. Even worse, we estimated that about fifty-five percent of those who had cast their ballots had voted no. Every organizer had taken a list of lobster shift workers' names to call.

Liz and I had been leaning against the wall of the plant making phone calls for the past hour. Almost everyone we'd called had promised up and down that they would cast their ballot by the time polls closed at eleven-thirty p.m.

"Aunt Ruth, this sucks!" Liz exclaimed. "We're going to lose!"

I wiped the back of my hand across my forehead, which was slick with sweat. "You never know until the votes are counted. And even then you usually don't know."

Liz looked at me with alarm. "What do you mean?"

I sighed. "Look. Let's just cross that bridge when we get to it, okay?"

"Another stupid cliché," Liz said irritably. "I've decided you labor people are mentally unstable."

I smiled. "That has the ring of truth. What do you mean?"

Liz pretended to wring the sweat out of her shirt. "I mean, busting ass, hardly sleeping, going totally nuts for weeks, and all so we can get, like, *flattened!* It's like, you're all masochists!"

I laughed. "Let's go suffer over there," I said, pointing to a picnic table on the grassy strip along the parking lot. We sat on top of the table and looked out over the crowded parking lot and the expanse of tall grasses beyond, thrashing violently in the wind. Thunder boomed again.

A newish blue Toyota pulled into the lot. I looked at my watch. Maybe this was someone returning from an early lunch hour.

The woman who emerged from the car looked slightly familiar. As she rummaged around in her trunk, I tried to remember where I'd seen her before. She was white, in her thirties, attractive in a mild, conventional way, and wearing a shapeless pastel-toned sleeveless dress. Her streaky shoulder-length hair had a fried look, as if it had seen too much dye in its lifetime.

She finally slammed the trunk, stood up straight and peered around the parking lot with big anxious-looking eyes. Then she spotted me and her eyes got even wider. Well, it appeared she could identify me even if I couldn't identify her. To my surprise, she began walking in our direction, her sandals scuffling slightly on the pavement. I still couldn't place her. I was almost sure she wasn't one of the twenty-six people I'd just called.

"Hi. You looking for the Pantheon union vote?" I asked in the cheeriest voice I could muster.

"You're Ruth Reid, aren't you?" the woman asked hoarsely. I knew that voice.

"Yes. Who are you?"

"I'm Chris Allison."

CHAPTER 41

I stood there with my mouth agape for a second before I regained my composure. Here, at last, was the former HR staffer I'd been pursuing for days. And why, after pushing me away, was she now standing before me, looking like she had something to say?

"I'm glad to meet you," I said, extending my hand, which, despite the unbearable heat, was icy. "And this is Liz Reid," I said.

"I've actually seen you before," Chris Allison said to me as she shook Liz's hand.

"I thought so. But when?"

"It was when you first came to Pantheon. You were talking to Larry Lemke in the hallway. I was sitting behind him in the office."

Now I remembered. Chris Allison had been the mousy woman I'd glimpsed after that first explosive meeting with management.

"And now you work in the business office on lobster shift with Joanne Healey," I supplied.

"Yes."

"Are you planning to vote today?"

Allison nodded. "I'm voting yes."

I smiled. Allison smiled too, faintly, but when she brought her hand up to push back the hair that had blown in her face, I saw that it was shaking.

"I guess I told you why I kept pestering you. We thought you might know something about these ghost employees we found in the shipping department."

"Well, I think I'm ready to talk to you now, if you've got a minute."

"Absolutely," I said, patting a spot on the table next to me. "Have a seat."

Allison glanced at Liz and smiled nervously. "I hope you don't mind, but I'd like to talk in private."

"That's okay," said Liz.

"There's a trail that goes around the swamp," said Chris. "Would you mind if we walked a little ways?"

"Sure," I said, giving Liz an apologetic look. Liz made a sweeping gesture with her hand that said, Just go.

Allison led me along the edge of the parking lot till we reached a gravel path that meandered away into the tall grass. Beside it a marker read "Pantheon Nature Trail, 1.25 miles." This was the trail that the Maloney brothers created to deflect criticism from environmentalists.

"Mind if I smoke?" asked Allison when we were a few steps down the path.

"Not at all."

Allison opened the flat black canvas bag that hung from her shoulder and extracted a pack of long skinny cigarettes. She slapped a cigarette out of the pack and put it in her mouth, then leaned forward, using my body to shield her lighter from the wind. She drew delicately on the stick till it was lit, then pulled away from me again. We began a slow stroll down the pathway, our shoes crunching on the fine gravel.

"The ghost employees, or whatever you call them — they started that five years ago, right after we moved to the new plant. I knew there was something wrong about it, but I was too scared to mention it to anybody. Then this winter, they suddenly switched all the names. And I decided to ask Larry about it — Larry Lemke. He said it was an accounting problem and he'd deal with it. So I just shut up about it. You know, they didn't include those people in that Excelsior list they gave you."

I turned and stared at Allison. "Were you the one who sent us that list?"

Allison smiled nervously and nodded. "One day, I found the list right in the middle of Larry's desk, and I looked to see if those extra employees were on it. And they were. So, I — I thought maybe the union could use that information."

I tilted my head. "What made you want to do that?"

"Well, I don't like this underhanded stuff going on at Pantheon. But I also kind of had an interest in getting back at Larry."

I nodded. "Why is that?"

"Well," Allison began slowly. "It's kind of hard for me to talk about. But my co-worker Joanne Healey — she told me you'd had a conversation with her about, about — "

"About sexual harassment?" I ventured.

"Yes," said Allison said quickly, as if relieved to have the words out.

My mind went back to the conversation with Healey. She had been harassed by her former supervisor, which had prompted her move to the lobster shift. I'd promised that if the union came in, we'd go after sexual harassers. I looked over at Allison, but she was watching her feet. Around us, the oat-colored grass was whipping in the wind, creating a lonely whistling sound.

"Well, I'm probably going to lose my job for telling you this, but I had the same experience as Joanne before I transferred to the night shift."

I stopped walking. "You're not talking about Larry Lemke, are you?"

Allison nodded. And then she blurted, "He's a real bastard!"

"What happened?"

We resumed walking. Allison took a drag off the cigarette. "He made me feel like being with him was some kind of requirement of the job," she said, all in one breath.

"Being with him?"

She nodded, meeting my eyes only briefly.

"Did you — did you go along?" I asked, searching for the least offensive words.

Allison nodded and then gestured toward a wrought-iron bench that rested on a concrete pad by the side of the path. We sat down.

"And then after a couple of months, he dropped me like — I don't know — like a piece of garbage."

"What happened then?"

"He — he took up with someone else. And that's what I decided I needed to tell you — "

Allison's voice trailed off.

"What did you want to tell me, Chris?"

Allison looked squarely into mine for the first time since I'd met her. They were big, moist, and gray.

"It was Victoria Shales."

"*What?*"

"Oh, god," said Allison. She glanced around as if expecting to see someone emerging from the tall grass.

"Are you saying that Victoria had an affair with Larry Lemke?" As my mouth formed the words, the absurdity of the charge struck me. The glamorous union organizer Victoria Shales with a creepy bureaucrat like Lemke?

"I know it's hard to believe," Allison said. "I could hardly believe it myself. At first I didn't think there was anything going on. But she came around a lot and she called him all the time. She was trying to get something out of him, I could tell."

I nodded. That part sounded highly plausible.

"And Larry — he's such a gladhander. He always wants everyone to like him. And he's a real womanizer too. I learned that the hard way."

"What do you think Victoria was trying to get out of him?"

Allison shook her head. "I don't know. But he's been at the company forever, so he knows a lot. And he's been on the outs with the Maloneys recently and he's very upset about it. So he had a reason to talk. And Victoria – well, I hate to say this, but she was like a shark that smells blood in the water. She was all over him."

I nodded. "Then what happened?"

"Well, the first thing that happened was, he dumped me. Just like that." Allison made a soundless snap with her fingers. "And he seemed obsessed with Victoria. He always wanted to know what she was doing and where she was."

"What made you think they were having an affair?"

But Chris Allison was no longer looking at me. She was looking past me to the stretch of path we had just traveled. Her eyes were wide and frightened.

"Oh my god," she gurgled, gripping my arm. I twisted around to see what Allison was looking at. There, standing perfectly still about twenty feet down the path, was Larry Lemke.

CHAPTER 42

Chris Allison's hand tightened on my arm as Lemke took several more steps toward us, an unreadable expression on his face. He looked uncharacteristically sloppy. His pale blue oxford shirt was untucked and blew loosely around him.

"Ruth, you can't believe a thing this woman says, I hope you realize that," Lemke said. He continued to walk slowly toward us, his feet crunching on the gravel. Instinctively, I gripped Chris Allison's hand and stood up, pulling her up with me. Lemke had attempted a tone of reasonableness, but I could hear the hard edge of something else underneath. "She's just jealous, she's emotionally unstable — "

Sweat was rolling down Lemke's face. Huge drops of rain were beginning to dot the path, creating dark gray circles of moisture on the pale gravel. "I'm not proud of it, but I'll confess that Ms. Allison and I had a relationship for a short time. And when I called it off, she went crazy. But I decided not to fire her. I'm not that kind of guy — "

As Lemke spoke, something about his pasty face was bothering me. It reminded me of someone else. Someone whose face I had been studying very recently.

"You're Lawrence Cappellini, aren't you?" I blurted out.

Lemke froze in mid-sentence, his mouth open, staring at me. Allison stared at me too. Then Lemke quickly reassembled his face. And when he spoke, his voice had a strange evenness.

"No, I *was* Lawrence Cappellini. I left that family. I wasn't interested in organized crime. And I'm not ashamed of that. I have nothing to hide."

"Then why did you take a new name?" I said.

Lemke shrugged. "I didn't break any laws."

"You — were *you* the one who got the Maloneys that big loan five years ago?"

"I don't know what you're talking about." Lemke's words came out in a jerky staccato.

"That's when he became director of human resources," said Chris Allison.

"But then the Jersey branch of the family was busted and the loan came due," I said, the pieces coming together as I spoke. "And now your brothers from New York are moving in. No wonder you're on the outs!"

Lemke looked agitated now. "This is pure speculation, it's crap!" he cried.

"And — and when you realized John Beck was about to uncover you, you shot him."

Lemke said nothing.

Suddenly, understanding flooded my brain. "Victoria was on to you too, wasn't she?

At the mention of Victoria's name, Lemke's whole body seemed to sag. "Don't talk to me about Victoria. You don't know anything about Victoria and me."

"What do you mean, Victoria and you?"

Lemke looked frantic. "She was crazy about me — "

"No, " said Allison. "She was pretending to be crazy about you. She just wanted to get information out of you."

"That's not true! She loved me!" said Lemke.

"And once she got what she needed, she rejected you," I said. "And then you killed her."

Lemke stared at me for a second. And then I saw his hand move under his billowing shirt and into the waistband of his pants. A spike of panic ran through me and involuntarily I leapt backward, almost falling over the bench behind me. Chris Allison screamed and fell into a crouch. Lemke had a gun.

"Wait, Larry, wait, what are you doing?" I said, my voice high and taut.

Lemke stretched out his arm and pointed the gun straight into my face. I could see the end of the barrel, and I could see that it was shaking in Lemke's hand. All the blood suddenly left my head and my vision became a dark tunnel. My knees wobbled beneath me. I struggled to hold onto my senses and to think of some action, some way of escaping.

And then, for no apparent reason, Lemke turned the gun away from me and bent it slowly toward himself. The relief I'd begun to feel evaporated, replaced by horror. "No!" I screamed.

At that instant, the gun tumbled almost silently onto the gravel, and Lemke ran past us down the path further into the swamp, his shirt flapping. And then I found myself sitting on the bench with Chris Allison sobbing in my arms.

CHAPTER 43

Only after midnight did we finally learn the outcome of the union election. It had been a very long night, preceded by a very long day. I had reluctantly spent part of the afternoon at the police station, telling the cops about our encounter with Lemke. By late afternoon, Lemke had been found, wandering around in the swamp in the drenching rain. According to an officer Beck interviewed, Lemke had confessed to the murder of Victoria Shales. He also confessed to shooting Beck with the same pistol, which police had recovered from the trail.

I'd spent most of the late afternoon and early evening at the union office amid laptops and piles of paper, empty paper cups that had once contained some terrifically bad coffee from Mr. Chicken, and a couple of half-closed pizza boxes each with a few congealed broccoli-topped slices somebody had ordered but nobody wanted.

We'd gone over the names and numbers so many times that our heads swam. Occasionally, some new piece of information — like the outstanding pro-union turnout among the press operators — would propel us to near euphoria. Other moments — as when Toro twice convinced the NLRB officials to discount bungled ballots of people who had meant to vote for the union — we veered toward despair. In the end, we were simply unable to predict the outcome of the election.

The storm that had been threatening all day had finally come and gone, delivering lightning, thunder, hail, and pelting rain. The sweltering heat of the past week was broken. By evening, the rain became intermittent. And then a few first shift-workers, huddling under umbrellas, appeared in the Pantheon parking lot. By seven, the rain finally stopped altogether. Clumps of workers began arriving then, and by nine, a solid crowd had assembled in the parking lot. The workers were not boisterous, emitting only the low droning buzz of a hundred soft conversations. Everyone stayed respectfully away from the area Kristoff had designated for late arriving voters.

At eleven-thirty, the polls closed and the officials allowed our core organizing committee members to enter the cafeteria to observe the counting. At twelve-forty a.m., we were still leaning against the walls, waiting. I held Liz's hand in my left and Silvia's in my right, watching as Appel and Kristoff methodically counted the votes for the third time. They had not disclosed the results of the first two countings, and we were hoping the third count would finally satisfy the officials.

At last, Appel raised her head up from the table and announced, "I am ready to read the vote totals. Anyone who wants to listen is welcome to come in. If they're quiet about it."

Nita and I looked at each other and then moved rapidly to the door.

"They're about to announce the vote," Nita called out to the crowd. "And they said we can come in and listen. But we have to be really quiet."

Nita stood on one side of the door that led to the cafeteria stairs and I stood on the other, both of us pantomiming energetically, waving people in and pressing our fingers to our lips to urge silence. Finally we turned around and wove our way through the crowd back into the cafeteria, now packed with fidgety but strangely quiet people.

As we approached the table where our team was waiting, Nita and I were clenching each other's hands tightly. My body was shaking as if I'd just emerged from a pool of ice water. Liz came up behind me and clasped my shoulders.

Across the room, Sam and Oscar Maloney had finally joined Toro and his team. Sam looked older than when I'd seen him last, and he had a tentative look about him, as if something had knocked the wind out of his sails. I wondered how the news of Lemke's arrest and confession had affected him. Even the cocky Oscar was looking deflated.

Genevieve Appel stood up from her table and cleared her throat.

"The count is as follows," she said, her voice booming across the cafeteria. "Voting for the union, we count 339." Silvia looked at me, horrified. The number was significantly lower than what we'd expected. I pressed my jaws together.

"Voting against the union, we count 318." Now Silvia's eyes widened with surprised delight. But I held up a finger to warn her from drawing any conclusions. The election now depended on how many ballots would be successfully challenged by Pantheon.

"Challenges, we count eight by the union, and nine by the employer."

We all looked at one another in bewilderment. I grabbed Nita's pen and clipboard. I was so rattled I had to write the numbers down to achieve the simple math: If Pantheon won every one of its challenges, and we won none of ours, we'd have 330 unchallenged pro-union votes – and the anti-union vote would total 326.

I raised my head up from the clipboard on which I had scribbled these numbers.

"We won," I said into the utter silence.

And suddenly the gymnasium exploded with sound. The first person I turned to was Joe. He smiled at me with watery eyes. And I thought: dignity.

CHAPTER 44

The hugs and high fives went on for over a half hour. At some point when I was between embraces, Sam Maloney appeared before me. He had a small, ironic smile on his face, and I wondered if it felt strange for him to be on the other side as the Pantheon workers celebrated so joyously. I felt sure Sam had more in common with printers like Juan or Joe than he did with the suits from Toro's entourage.

I didn't know what else to do, so I extended my hand, which Sam shook without hesitation.

"Congratulations," he said. "That certainly took balls, what you did."

"Thank you. And what do you think'll happen now?"

Sam shrugged "Doesn't that depend on you people?"

"Well, I can tell you that we'll be looking to get a decent first contract as quickly as possible. And full reinstatement of everyone fired or suspended during the drive. Do you plan on resisting that the way you have everything else?"

"I'm tired of resisting, as you call it. But I'll tell you this – if you people get too greedy, we'll go out of business, and then nobody'll have a job."

"How about Toro? Are you keeping him on?"

Sam's eyes flashed. "I don't mind telling you now that in my opinion Toro ruined everything. I told Oscar that after this election, it's either him or me."

"I take it you heard about Larry Lemke — "

Sam nodded and looked down at the floor.

"You realize that his whole story — the Cappellinis and the loan, and all that — it'll be out in the papers soon."

Sam gave me a disgusted look. "Larry Lemke spent his whole life trying to run away from that family, and now everyone's going to smear it in his face."

I tilted my head and peered at Sam. "I don't get it. Getting that loan from his New Jersey cousins was hardly running away."

"That was a one-shot deal. He did it as a favor for us."

"Is that why you kept Lemke on even after the loan went bad and his brothers moved in? I can't believe they didn't pressure you to get rid of him."

Sam looked up at me suddenly. "Why should I tell you any of that?"

Three hours later, it was almost closing time at the Metropolis Bar in Bloomson, New Jersey. The Metropolis was not as cozy and familiar as the Pony, but it had the advantage of being the latest-closing bar in Bloomson. And I'd even managed to hold to my one-drink limit.

About eight members of the Pantheon Organizing Committee and friends were still seated at the clustered tables at the back of the bar, still rowdy, although tending now to tilt in our seats. Nita was leaning against me, her smooth brown arm resting hotly against mine.

"I still can't believe it," Nita said.

"Is everything going to change now?" asked Silvia.

"Of course everything is going to change!" Nita exclaimed.

"What will it be like? I've never worked at a union shop," said Silvia.

I looked around the table to see who might volunteer a response. Joe was sitting upright, arms crossed on his chest, but his eyes were closed — perhaps having a peaceful little snooze. Malcolm was concentrating on sketching something on his napkin. Almost everyone else, including Nita, Al, Juan, Alonzo, and Liz, was looking at me and waiting for a response.

I inhaled and sat up a little straighter. "Well, the first thing is to try to get a first contract — a decent one — and it's got to get everyone's job back. To do that we've got to try to win over the people who voted no today. Or else they'll just keep driving at that wedge."

"You think the Maloneys will keep after us like that?" asked Juan. His eyes trailed down to my neckline. I shivered.

"I don't know," I said. "Sam told me just now he's tired of fighting. But Oscar may be a different story." I stopped. I kept using the words "we" and "us," but I doubted if the union would keep me on to fight for the first contract. I realized that I missed these workers already. And I was worried for them.

When I looked up, everyone was still looking at me, so I continued. "And, uh, after that, a lot depends on you. I mean, a lot of people think the union is this outside service that comes in and does something for you, but if that's what you're thinking, you'll be very disappointed. I always think of it as a tool – like a vehicle, maybe — that you can drive. But you've got to learn how to drive and figure out where you want to go. Know what I mean?"

"Not really, hon," said Silvia. Everyone laughed.

"I just mean the union is what you make of it. And it can be a bit of a struggle. Because the union, you know, has some problems. There are internal fights, problem personalities, bureaucratic bullshit — "

"Tell me about it," said Al. I was unaccustomed to this new Al, who sat alertly in his chair, drinking club soda. I wondered if Tina had given Al an ultimatum. Or maybe Al was moving on his own steam.

"And now, with this union merger," I went on, "we really don't know what the new union will be like. You've got to fight on that level too — try and make the union what you want it to be. If Tommy McNamara keeps his job, you'll have a least one good ally there."

Malcolm looked up from his drawing, which I saw now was a remarkably accurate caricature of Larry Lemke in a fedora, smoking a cigar and carrying a machine gun. "Man, you make it sound like we just *lost*."

I laughed. I realized I was already entering my customary post-battle let-down. I hated the way I had to leave people like this when my job was over. "You know what?" I said, trying to sound perky. "You guys are going to build a powerful union now. I can just tell."

Malcolm wasn't convinced by my revised attitude. "Are we going to have to fight the mob too?" he asked.

"I sure as hell hope not," said a voice behind me.

I wheeled around and there was John Beck.

"What the hell are you doing here?" I said.

"Hey. Good to see you too," said Beck. Despite the attempt at breeziness, Beck's voice was strained and he looked dangerously pale.

"Jesus, sit down," I said, pulling a chair over from a nearby table.

Beck sat, then fidgeted in his seat trying to get comfortable. But it seemed no position was going to make the pain in his chest go away.

"Are you okay, John?" asked Silvia.

"Yeah, I just wish I could have been there for the vote count."

"Us too," said Joe. "But you should be resting, guy. Not sitting here in a bar with us."

Beck shifted again in his seat. "Well, I wanted you guys to know that I've got almost everything I need for a story about the New York Cappellinis. And if the paper'll let me, I intend to keep following it. If we're lucky, the exposure will make the Cappellinis go away — if the feds don't get them first."

Joe tilted his head. "It sounds like the Maloneys have been depending on the Cappellinis for a long time. Won't they have trouble paying off that loan and doing without the other help they've been getting? It seems like it was that financial situation that set off this whole thing — the layoffs, the speedup, Toro — "

"I don't know how the company will survive financially," Beck replied. "But I've done enough stories about the mob to know you'd be better off without them."

"Toro and Tim Beatty and his friend Kevin McGarry – they were all working with the New York Cappellinis, right?" Nita asked.

"Right," said Beck. "When the New York family moved in, they forced the Maloneys to hire Toro to squeeze out the money Pantheon owed on the loan," said Beck. "And later, they pressured the Maloneys to hire Beatty and McGarry to keep the union out. I guess they didn't want a union siphoning money and control away from their operation."

"And Sam Maloney pretty much confirmed just now that Larry Lemke was the one who got the loan from the New Jersey Cappellinis," I added.

"Jesus. A mobster as head of HR," said Juan.

"Kind of," I said. "Actually Sam told me Lemke really had tried to run away from the whole Cappellini family. But I guess the chance to get that loan was too big an opportunity to pass up. And right after that Lemke got his big promotion to head of HR."

Silvia nodded. "Lemke's a climber if I ever saw one."

"Chris Allison said he just wants everyone to like him. She called him a gladhander," I said.

"And those ghost employees," said Liz. "The Cappellinis got the Maloneys to put those people on the payroll as a way to pay back the loan?"

"Apparently," I said. "From what Chris Allison told me, it sounds like the practice started with the New Jersey family and later the Queens family put in their own people."

Beck nodded. "And that's clean money, too. Salaries. "

"How about the employee list?" Nita asked. "Ruth told us that Chris Allison mailed it back to us. But who stole it in the first place? Was it Schmidt, like we thought?"

I shrugged. "If I had to guess, I'd say it was Lemke. He either gave it to Victoria or she stole it from him. And he stole it back. And he was smart — he gave that file of personal information to Schmidt knowing Schmidt would use it — "

"Which would deflect suspicion onto Schmidt," finished Silvia. "Plus, he left that porn shot, which is exactly the kind of thing Schmidt would do. That *is* smart."

"So Schmidt had nothing to do with the Cappellinis?" Joe asked.

"I think he was just an anti-social bully," I said.

"I'm floored about Lemke and Victoria," said Nita. "I always thought that was a strange relationship they had, but — "

I turned to face Nita. "You knew they had a relationship?"

"No, not that kind. But it was weird the way she was always talking to him and being so secretive about it. I still don't get it."

"I guess we don't know the real story," I said. "But I can imagine Victoria doing whatever she thought she had to do to get information out of Lemke — especially if she thought the information was critical in winning the election."

"She probably wanted to find out about the mob because she thought if they stopped intimidating us, we could win," said Juan.

"Yeah," I said. "And it looks like she was planning to go public with everything she knew about the mob on the day she died."

"Is that why Lemke killed her?" Nita asked.

"I just got an account of Lemke's statement to the cops," said Beck. "He said that he went to Victoria's to persuade her not to go public with the information. But then they got into an argument and she called him 'slime,' and he shot her. Then he took some jewelry to make it look like a robbery."

"Wow," said Malcolm.

We were quiet for a moment.

"It's hard to believe that Victoria had all that stuff up her sleeve, and she didn't say a thing about it to us," said Juan.

I shook my head. For some people, the end justifies the means. But the end Victoria got was not the one she'd expected.

Liz draped her arm over my shoulder on a joint excursion to the women's room.

"So what are you going to do now?" I asked.

"I knew you were going to ask me that. You're desperate to get me out of the house, aren't you?" Liz said, smiling.

"Of course not," I said. Not desperate. Looking forward to, maybe.

Liz laughed. "That's okay, Aunt Ruth, I know you're the independent type. I like that about you."

I smiled, trying to resist the temptation to press the issue of plans. Exhausted as I was, I was still a noodge. Almost as bad as Sandy.

"Well, I know this. I'm not going back to live with my parents," Liz said firmly. "I'm thinking about going to one of those labor colleges."

I stopped in front of the women's room door and stared at Liz. "Really? You think your folks would spring for that?"

Liz laughed. "I don't think so. But I don't really want their money anyway. I was thinking I could work my way through. Malcolm thinks I might be able to get a part-time job at Pantheon."

"Huh," I said. "A union job." It was a sweet idea. But I still couldn't quite picture my pampered niece working in a bindery and taking classes on the history of collective bargaining.

"Closing time, folks." The bartender, a wiry young man with a shoulder-to-fingertip tattoo, had been patiently ferrying our drinks for hours. He'd been a good soldier, but now he looked very eager for us to go.

I looked over at Liz, who was leaning sleepily against Malcolm's shoulder, her eyes barely open. She smiled at me contentedly. She'd already told me she would be heading home with Malcolm that night.

"You're not going all the way back to Brooklyn tonight, are you, Ruth?" Liz said.

I looked at Beck.

"Why don't you get a room at the Sheraton tonight? That way you can take care of me," Beck said, giving me a funny look. I couldn't quite decide what it meant. Was it simple need? Or was there something else there?

Juan looked at Beck and then at me.

I gave Juan a sad smile. "That's probably a good idea," I said. Juan nodded slightly in acceptance.

I was shoulder-to-shoulder with Beck as we all filed toward the door. "No need for another room, actually," he muttered in my ear.

"Beck. You have got to get some rest."

"I'll rest. Eventually." Beck wrapped his hot hand tightly around my upper hip, pressing his fingers firmly into my flesh. I felt my body zing to attention. Just like old times.

CHAPTER 45

"What a monumental idiot," Sandy said beside me.

"No shit," I said.

Above us and about twenty feet away, on a stage mounted on the back of a flatbed truck, James Shawcross was roaring into the microphone, as he did at every Labor Day parade. Behind us, stretching down Manhattan's Seventh Avenue a half-mile or so, a crowd of perhaps fifty thousand — it shrank every year — was not paying the slightest attention. People were talking about sports or computers or their recent shopping triumphs, all shouting to be heard over the annoying noise of Shawcross. Nearby, a group of about thirty carpenters, completely tanked and still boldly guzzling their beers, were chanting something bawdy.

"I saw that man of yours," Sandy said.

I turned and looked at her. "John Beck?"

Sandy nodded. "He was just over there, talking to some woman."

I laughed. "Yeah, I bet."

"I don't know what's wrong with you. You're a masochist."

"True."

"Did he ever apologize to you for going off with that little reporter?"

"Why should he?"

Sandy only rolled her eyes. "Probably he'll go back to his wife again now that he's had his little flight of freedom."

"I don't think so. The guy enjoys being single. And so do I. No problem there, right?"

Sandy sucked in her cheeks, exasperated. "Don't save yourself for that man," she said.

I laughed. "Are you kidding?" The truth was, I was still hooked on Beck. But ever since Yvette, I felt I'd been let off some invisible leash. I liked to think I was free to love someone else, if the chance

. In the past couple of weeks, Juan and I had had a couple of nice dates.

"Well, you can have my men if you want them. I'm done with m." Sandy gave me her brilliant smile and took a long swig of her ᴏttled water.

I laughed. "Uh huh. I believe that."

In front of us, Shawcross was still talking.

"And I am proud to announce, this Labor Day, that the labor movement has achieved a magnificent victory, at the Pantheon Printing Plant in Bloomson, New Jersey," Shawcross intoned. "A thousand workers have joined our ranks!" Shawcross punched out each word, accentuating them with his upraised fist.

"Make that seven hundred and ninety-two," I said.

"He makes it sound like he did it," said Sandy.

"Yeah, that's the kind of thing he does."

"And it was in New Jersey. And it was weeks ago," added Liz, who was standing behind me, her arm draped over Malcolm's shoulder.

"So what? Now's his chance," I said.

"They ought to put you up there, Aunt Ruth."

"No way. They ought to have Joe and Silvia — they had a lot more on the line than I did. And besides, people ought to be introduced to the new leaders of Local 1107."

Joe, on my other side, laughed. "I don't do public speaking."

"I do. I'll go up there right now," Silvia said.

"Yeah, go up there," said Nita, jostling her sister from behind. "Tell him you want to say something on behalf of the people who actually did the organizing."

But when we looked back up at the stage, we saw that Shawcross had finally stopped talking, and an organizer was instructing the crowd about the march route.

Silvia shrugged and smiled at me.

"Next Labor Day, maybe you'll replace Shawcross altogether," I said, nudging Silvia's shoulder.

"Dream on," said Silvia.

16256258R00171

Made in the USA
Lexington, KY
14 July 2012